When the Dead Speak

Sheila Bugler grew up in a small town in the west of Ireland. After studying Psychology at University College Galway (now called NUI Galway) she left Ireland and worked as an EFL teacher, travelling to Italy, Spain, Germany, Holland and Argentina. She is the author of a series of crime novels featuring DI Ellen Kelly. The novels are set in South East London, an area she knows and loves. She now lives in Eastbourne, on the beautiful East Sussex coast. Eastbourne is the location for her series of crime novels featuring investigative journalist Dee Doran. When she's not writing, Sheila does corporate writing and storytelling, she runs creative writing courses, is a tutor for the Writers Bureau and is a mentor on the WoMentoring programme. She reviews crime fiction for crimesquad.com and she is a regular guest on BBC Radio Sussex. She is married with two children.

Also by Sheila Bugler

An Eastbourne Murder Mystery

I Could Be You
When the Dead Speak

SHEILA BUGLER

WHEN
THE
DEAD
SPEAK

CANELO CRIME

First published in the the United Kingdom in 2020 by Canelo

This edition published in the United Kingdom in 2020 by Canelo

Canelo Digital Publishing Limited
31 Helen Road
Oxford OX2 0DF
United Kingdom

A CIP catalogue record for this book is available from the British Library.

Print ISBN 978 1 78863 965 1
Ebook ISBN 978 1 78863 964 4

Look for more great books at www.canelo.co

Printed and bound in Great Britain by Clays Ltd, Elcograf S.p.A.

To Sean, Luke and Ruby — lockdown with you guys has been a gift

Prologue

I dream about her. Each night when I fall asleep she's there, waiting for me. Laid out on the church altar, like an offering. She would have looked beautiful, even in death. An angel. I wonder if Vicar Rawlings thought she was beautiful when he found her. Or if the horror of it all came too fast and he didn't have time for thoughts of beauty and angels.

Of course, I never saw her body, but that hasn't stopped me imagining it and dreaming about it. The details of the dream merging with my own memories of that night until I cannot untangle it all. I dream that I'm running through the streets, searching for my son, but he's nowhere to be found. Then I see the church and I know: that's where I'll find him.

The doors are closed. But when I push one of them, it creaks open and I step inside, ignoring the voice in my head telling me to turn around and run far away from this place. My son is lost and I have to find him.

It's cool inside the church. Cool and peaceful. My heart, racing so fast moments earlier, slows down. The door shuts behind me with a gentle click and I am alone. Outside, daylight has broken. Sunshine streams through the stained-glass windows. Something is dancing in the air. Shades of amber and copper, captured in the light. When I put my hand out, some of it lands softly on my palm. The texture reminds me of the barbs of a feather, but this thing in my hand is no feather.

I let the strands fall, watching them drift down to the stone ground. A gust of wind blows through the church, stirring it all up again. The pieces whip through the air, brushing against my face and clogging the inside of my nose and throat when I try to breathe.

Hair. Lots of it. All around me now, covering the floor of the church like a carpet of gold confetti, sticking to my skin.

I open my eyes and I see her. She's lying on the altar. Her eyes are closed and her hands are folded neatly across her stomach. She's captured in the sunlight, tinted the same colours as the glass. Shades of red and yellow and green dotted across her body.

I move closer, until I'm standing over her, so close I can see the scatter of freckles across her nose, and the gaping red gash across her white neck. And her hair, her beautiful hair, is gone. Hacked away from her head and scattered around the church. It's tragic. A beautiful young woman with her whole life ahead of her, killed in such a brutal manner. The fear and the pain and the horror of her final minutes are beyond imagination.

And yet… In my dreams, as I stand over her and breathe in the smell of her death, I don't feel sad or angry about what's happened. The only thing I feel is relief. Because now she's dead, she cannot cause any more trouble for my family.

One

Dee Doran was having a good morning. She'd experienced a moment of pure joy when she'd woken up and realised she wasn't alone. Ed Mitchell had spent the night. It wasn't the first time he'd stayed over. In fact, it was becoming something of a habit. Ed was becoming something of a habit. Which wasn't a situation she'd ever have envisaged when she first met him seven months ago.

They'd spent the last hour lying in bed, curled against each other, looking out Dee's bedroom window, watching the shifting colours of the light moving across the sky and sea and beach.

'It's so beautiful here,' Ed said, his breath warm and comforting against Dee's neck. Dee didn't say anything. Ed already knew how she felt about this place. The house, on a deserted stretch of beach on the eastern edge of Eastbourne town, was her childhood home. Dee had moved back here from London after the break-up of her marriage to nurse her widowed mother through the last few, painful months of her incurable cancer. Now, she couldn't imagine ever living anywhere else.

Dee's father, an architect, had designed the house when Dee was a child. She'd spent most of her teenage years yearning to get as far away from Eastbourne as she could.

It was only when she moved back a few years ago that she started to appreciate just how special it was.

'You should move in.'

The words were out of her mouth before she could stop them. She tensed, waiting for Ed's excuses. Unsure whether she'd even meant it. They'd only been dating for five months. They were still getting to know each other. Things were pretty good at the moment, so why change that? They both enjoyed the independence of living alone, not having to do something just because the other one wanted to. They didn't even like the same TV programmes. There were so many reasons why it was a bad idea. The only excuse Dee had for mentioning it was the sense of security she'd felt lying beside him. That weird feeling that, just for once, life was exactly as it should be. Why she had to wreck it by saying something so stupid was beyond her.

'Really?'

There was a softness in his voice that made her turn around so she was looking at him. He smiled and – God help her and forgive her but she couldn't help it – she smiled back.

A piece of her hair had fallen across her cheek. Ed brushed it back, his hand lingering on her face.

'Dee Doran,' he said. 'Did you just say you'd like us to live together?'

There was a lump in Dee's throat that made it impossible to answer. She swallowed, thought of the many different ways she could apologise for saying something she didn't mean to say. Opted instead for something simpler:

'Yes.'

'In that case…' But before he could finish his sentence, his mobile phone started to ring. He groaned, rolled onto his back and groped for his phone on the bedside table.

'It's Rachel,' he said, frowning, when he looked at the screen. 'Why's she calling on my day off?'

Rachel Lewis, Ed's colleague. They worked together as senior detectives with East Sussex Police. If Rachel was calling Ed on his day off, it could only mean bad news.

'You'd better call her back,' Dee said.

'Nah.' Ed pressed a button and the phone stopped ringing. 'I'm sure it can wait.'

He put the phone down and turned back to Dee.

'Now then,' he said, wrapping his arms around her. 'Where were we?'

Dee started to speak but her words were lost as the ringing started again.

'It's okay,' Dee said. 'She wouldn't be calling if it wasn't urgent. We both know that.'

While Ed took the call, Dee slipped out of bed and went into the bathroom. Through the closed door, she could hear the low rumble of his voice. The phone call went on long enough for her to know this was the end of their day together. Which meant the conversation about moving in together would have to wait. Part relieved, part disappointed, Dee reached into the shower and turned the water on.

—

Forty minutes later, Dee was in the passenger seat of Ed's car as he drove west along the seafront.

'I'm sure it's nothing to worry about,' Dee said.

5

'You're probably right,' Ed said. 'Although it's difficult not to worry when Rachel wouldn't tell me why she needs me there.'

'Tell me again what she said?' Dee asked.

'A body has been found,' Ed said. 'In St Mary's church. I thought she'd forgotten I was on leave today, but she hadn't. She said this was important, and I'd understand when I saw the crime scene.'

'Not the victim,' Dee mused. 'But the crime scene. A funny way to put it, don't you think?'

Ed didn't reply, but Dee knew he was worried. Rachel was more than capable of dealing with the initial stages of an investigation. Which meant there was something unusual about this case. Something she wasn't willing to tell Ed over the phone.

Dee had already called her cousin, Louise, to check she and her family were okay. But Louise hadn't picked up. As Louise was a journalist and editor of the local newspaper, the chances were that she was already at the scene. And even though Dee tried to tell herself she didn't need to worry, she was relieved when Ed finally pulled up outside the church in Old Town and she saw her cousin's blond head among the group of people clustered behind the black and yellow police tape blocking the entrance to the church.

'I have no idea how long this will take,' Ed said. 'What do you want to do?'

'I'll catch up with Lou first,' Dee said. 'And maybe I'll have a coffee in the Lamb. After that, if you're still not ready I'll head home.'

Ed leaned over and kissed her.

6

'I haven't forgotten our conversation this morning,' he said. 'Why don't I come over later and we can continue where we left off?'

'That would be lovely.' Dee patted his knee and smiled. 'Right then, detective, see you later.'

They got out of the car. Dee watched as Ed approached the uniformed policewoman standing at the entrance to the churchyard.

'Any idea who she is?'

Louise's voice at her shoulder made Dee jump. She hadn't seen her cousin move away from the crowd and come over to where she was standing.

'Not a clue,' Dee said.

She looked at Ed, still chatting comfortably with the policewoman instead of getting his skates on and going inside the church to view the victim. 'Apart from Rachel, I don't know any of Ed's colleagues.'

'Not *her*,' Louise said, waving her finger in the direction of Ed and his companion. 'The victim.'

'How do you know it's a woman?' Dee said.

'Everyone knows it's a woman,' Louise said.

Everyone except Ed, Dee thought.

'Although that's about all we know,' Louise continued. 'Ed didn't say anything else, did he?'

'Nothing.' Dee decided not to tell Louise that – by rights – Ed shouldn't even be here. 'God Lou, your lips are blue. How long have you been standing out here? And where's your coat?'

It was a chilly day. Yesterday's clouds had disappeared but there was no warmth to the early March sunshine and a wind was whipping in over the downs, bringing icy temperatures with it.

'I came straight from the gym,' Louise said. 'Left my coat in the locker by mistake.'

'Well you can't stay out here any longer,' Dee said, hooking her arm with Louise's. 'I'm taking you to the Lamb and buying you a hot drink.'

'I need to stay out here,' Louise said. 'Sooner or later, someone's going to come out and tell us something.'

'There's no good them telling you anything if you're so cold your ears have stopped working,' Dee said.

It didn't take much to persuade Louise to leave the freezing outdoors for the cosy warmth of Eastbourne's oldest pub. The two women settled by the open fire, warming their hands on the flames while Natalie, the landlady, served up a pot of coffee and a plate of bacon sandwiches.

'You look like you need feeding up,' Natalie informed Louise. She smiled across at Dee. 'And I've never known you to say no to a bacon butty, my love.' She nodded at the window that looked across to the church. 'Heard the vicar found her when he opened up this morning. Poor bloke's in a right state, apparently. I made some sandwiches earlier for the coppers they've got standing outside. One of them told me it's definitely murder. No doubt about it, he said.'

'Do they have any idea who she is?' Dee asked.

'Suppose we'll find out soon enough,' Natalie said. 'Difficult to imagine, isn't it? Some poor family will have woken up this morning not knowing the tragedy that's about to hit them.'

Dee thought of Trevor and Billy. Two men she'd loved – one her ex-husband, the other a dear friend – who had both died in the past year. Once again, she felt the overwhelming sense of disbelief that two people could suddenly cease to exist. Despite his faults, which were many, her ex-husband had always seemed full of life. There were times, even now, when that desperate longing for something impossible – to see him one final time – almost broke her. At some point over the next few days, everyone who had known and loved the dead woman inside the church was going to know exactly what that felt like. The thought was so sad that, for a moment, Dee wished the dead woman was a person without friends or loved ones. Someone whose passing wouldn't trigger a wave of grief that would affect so many people.

–

Ed had seen the body the moment he'd pushed open the heavy wooden door and stepped inside. Impossible to miss it, really. Laid out on the altar like some sort of sick offering. He'd been too far away to make out any of the detail, or even if the victim was male or female. Normally, he'd have asked Rachel. But something about the way she'd looked at him when he first arrived – a question in her face that he didn't have the answer to – prevented him from doing that.

He was aware of Rachel walking beside him as they made their way up the aisle towards the altar, their footsteps loud on the stone floor. Walking side by side through the church, like two people following an ancient religious tradition. He was more than halfway along the aisle before he was able to see her properly. Her, because there was no doubt the body lying on its back on the altar was that of a woman. Something was scattered on the ground near the altar. Confetti, he thought at first. Although he'd never seen confetti this colour.

9

He stopped walking. Not confetti. Something else.

'You okay, Ed?' Rachel's voice sounded far away, although she was right beside him.

'I don't understand,' he said.

'You see why I needed you to be here?'

Ed didn't answer. He couldn't stop looking at the dead girl, at the chunks of her hair, scattered across the ground. Trying to find the crucial piece of information he knew he was missing. Flashes of memory rushed towards him. His childhood, his grandmother. The dark secret at the heart of his family that he'd learned it was better never to speak about. Something only a handful of people outside his family knew about. Two of them here in the church. One standing beside him; the other lying dead on the altar.

'Her name's Lauren Shaw.'

The words came out of his mouth, but he had no control over what he was saying. Because even though he knew the victim's name, he knew she couldn't be lying here like this. That had happened to another woman. A woman called Mary Palmer, who'd had curly auburn hair, blue eyes and a smattering of freckles across her nose. Just like Lauren.

Sixty years ago, Mary Palmer's throat had been cut open, her auburn hair had been hacked short. And when the killer was finished doing those things, he'd laid Mary Palmer's body on the altar of this church. Exactly the way Lauren Shaw's body was laid out today.

Two

Details of the body in the church trickled through on social media and news websites all afternoon. By early evening, Dee had read everything she could about the murder and was no closer to understanding why Rachel had needed Ed to see the scene for himself.

At six thirty this morning, the vicar of St Mary the Virgin had discovered the body of a young woman when he'd unlocked the church. According to rumours on social media, the victim was a twenty-three-year-old local woman called Lauren Shaw. The police hadn't confirmed this yet. Dee knew, from her years working as an investigative journalist in London, that formal identifications didn't happen this quickly. There was no information on how the killer had managed to get the body inside the locked church, or whether the vicar – or anyone else – was a suspect at this stage in the investigation.

Several times throughout the day, Dee had tried to call Ed. Each time, she'd got his voicemail. She hadn't bothered leaving a message, knowing he'd call when he could. But she couldn't shake off the nagging anxiety that had been with her since he'd got the phone call this morning.

A photo of the dead girl accompanied the stories about her murder. She was a stunner – a mass of copper-coloured hair and the sort of wide, bright smile that would light up any space. It was too terrible to think she'd never smile again.

Dee thought of Ed, walking into the church and seeing the dead girl's body. It must have been awful.

She was about to try calling him again when her doorbell rang.

'Finally,' she muttered, hurrying to let him in.

Except instead of Ed, Dee's visitor was Eliza Macko, a young Polish woman Dee had met two weeks earlier.

'I want to talk about Joana,' Eliza said.

Joana was Eliza's friend. Another young Polish woman, who had disappeared five weeks ago. Believing the police weren't doing enough to find her friend, Eliza had approached the *Eastbourne Recorder*, where Louise worked as editor. The paper had written a story, appealing for anyone with information about Joana to contact them. But the story didn't prompt any responses, and Louise had put Eliza in touch with Dee.

'Ten years ago,' Louise explained to Dee, 'we might have been able to do more. But today, with all the cutbacks? Not a chance. You could help her, though. Do a bit of digging, see if you can find anything. You're an investigative journalist. Investigating is what you do best.'

Dee didn't point out that this wasn't exactly accurate. She'd barely worked when she first moved back to Eastbourne. Admittedly, that had changed recently. A story she'd written about a murder that had happened outside her house had attracted a lot of attention. Since then, though, she'd only written one other piece – a personal account of living with her ex-husband, a chronic alcoholic.

Financially, she didn't need to work. Her house in London had sold recently for a ridiculously large sum of money. Living in the house that had once belonged to her parents meant she had no mortgage to pay. All of which led her to decide that, rather take jobs she didn't want to, she'd wait until she found a story she wanted to write about. It was starting to look as she'd found it.

At 7 p.m. on Saturday 8 February, Joana Helinski left the flat she shared with Eliza and Eliza's boyfriend Marcel, to meet someone at the Aldrington Hotel on Eastbourne's seafront. And she hadn't been seen since. Dee had spoken with the staff at the hotel and none of them remembered seeing Joana that evening. She had, quite simply, disappeared.

When Dee had asked Ed why the police weren't doing more to find the missing girl, he'd explained that it was common for young men and women from Eastern Europe to move around from place to place. They did it to avoid being caught by the authorities. In the absence of any evidence of wrongdoing, the police would assume Joana had simply moved on to somewhere else.

But Eliza was convinced Joana wouldn't leave Eastbourne without telling her, and Dee believed her. So she'd continued to try to find the missing girl. She did this partly because she wanted answers for Eliza, and partly because she'd become increasingly interested in the situation facing so many foreign nationals working in Eastbourne and the rest of the country. Young men and women like Joana and Eliza, all working for low wages on zero-hours contracts, vulnerable to corrupt business owners able to force their staff to work in conditions no one should ever have to work in.

The more she learned, the more convinced Dee became that these people were her story. She'd already pitched an outline idea to several broadsheets. Yesterday, an editor at the *Guardian* had got in touch asking if she'd consider a series of stories, rather than a single article.

'Come inside,' Dee said. 'Would you like a drink? I've got coffee, tea, water or wine.'

'I don't want a drink,' Eliza said, following Dee into the sitting room. 'You've seen the news this evening?'

'What news?' Dee sat down, gesturing for Eliza to do the same.

'The dead girl in the church. Lauren. She worked at the Aldrington Hotel.'

'How do you know where she worked?' Dee asked. There'd been no mention of the Aldrington in anything she'd read about the murder.

'Facebook,' Eliza said. 'There's a group for people in Eastbourne who are looking for work in hotels and restaurants. Someone posted about the girl this evening, saying Lauren was her friend and everyone at the hotel is devastated.'

'Show me.'

Eliza took a phone out of her jacket pocket, tapped the screen a few times and passed the phone to Dee. The Facebook group was called 'hospitality workers Eastbourne'. There were already several posts about Lauren, people expressing their shock and sadness.

'See?' Eliza pointed at a photo someone had posted. It showed two girls, standing outside the Aldrington Hotel. The girls had their arms draped around each other as they posed for the camera. Dee recognised one of the girls instantly. Lauren Shaw with her auburn curls and her freckled face.

Beneath the photo someone had typed, 'No words my gorgeous friend. #Aldringtongirlsforever #Tooyoung-toosoon.'

'Okay,' she said. 'Lauren worked at the Aldrington. So what?'

'So, maybe Lauren was killed because she knew something about Joana's disappearance.'

'Is there any way you can make this photo bigger?' Dee's reading glasses were four years old. Getting her eyes tested was on the long list of the things she would get around to doing one day soon.

'Like this.' Eliza leaned across the marble and moved her index finger and thumb across the screen.

'That girl with Lauren,' Dee said. 'I know her. She's the receptionist at the Aldrington.'

'You showed her Joana's photo?'

'Yes,' Dee said. 'She didn't recognise her.'

'What about Lauren?'

'I didn't see Lauren when I was at the hotel,' Dee said. 'She mustn't have been working that day. Besides, Eliza, just because Lauren worked at the hotel, it doesn't mean she knew Joana.'

Eliza slapped her hand on the arm of her chair. 'Bullshit. Joana was meeting someone at the Aldrington the night she disappeared. Lauren Shaw worked at the Aldrington, and now Lauren is dead. We need to speak to Lauren's friends and ask them what Lauren knew about Joana.'

'It's a bit of a stretch,' Dee said. 'But you're right. It's worth checking out.'

'You'll go back to the hotel?'

'Yes,' Dee said. 'But if I find anything that proves they knew each other, you'll need to tell the police.'

Eliza shrugged. 'Police don't listen to me. You know that, Dee.'

'This is different.'

The words were out before she could take them back. She stopped speaking, but it was already too late. Eliza stood up.

'Different because Lauren is English,' she said. 'That's what you mean, isn't it?'

Dee tried to protest but Eliza held her hand up, stopping any more stupid words coming from Dee's mouth.

'Thank you, Dee. It is good to know what you really think.'

'I didn't mean it like that,' Dee said. Pointlessly, because Eliza had already stormed out of the room. Dee ran after her, arriving at the front door just in time to see Eliza climbing into the passenger seat of a white van that had seen better days.

'Eliza!'

The engine growled into life and the van sped off, leaving Dee with nothing but a mouthful of diesel fumes and a head full of unanswered questions.

—

Ed took his phone out to call Dee, then changed his mind. There was so much to tell her, but he had no idea how to start. He was in his car, parked outside a house in the village of East Dean. The downstairs lights in the house were on, which meant the woman who lived there hadn't gone to bed yet. Which meant he had no excuse.

He would have to talk to her tonight. He drummed the steering wheel with the tips of his fingers, trying to think through what he would say. Trying to find a way of saying it that would allow him to stay on the case. But no matter how the conversation played out in his mind, it always ended the same way – with Ed being told he couldn't be part of this investigation.

Because he knew the victim.

The image of Lauren's body was burned onto his mind. The gaping black slash across the pale skin of her throat. The auburn curls, on the ground and lifting gently into the air every time a breeze drifted through the cold, lonely church.

A sudden burst of noise as it started to rain, water battering against the car, pounding through the silence of the East Sussex night. Ed took the key out of the ignition, got out of the car and ran through the deluge to the detached cottage on an empty stretch of downland between East Dean and Birling Gap. The house belonged to his boss, DCI Sharon Spalding. He'd only been here a handful of times before. On those occasions, it was because he'd been invited. Tonight, he was here because he needed to tell her something she wouldn't want to hear.

He rang the doorbell and waited, sheltering from the rain under the insubstantial front porch. When the door opened, he was too close and he jumped back, out into the rain.

'What the hell?' Sharon said, peering out at him. 'Christ Almighty, Ed. You look like a drowned rat. Come inside before you die of exposure. Or drowning. Or whatever ailment afflicts the snowflakes these days. Not that

I'm calling you a snowflake, you understand. You're too old for that.'

Sharon continued talking as Ed followed her into the house, closing the front door behind them.

'Take your shoes off,' she said over her shoulder as she marched to the kitchen at the back of the house. 'I got that carpet laid last month. The last thing it needs is your mucky footprints marking it. I'm having wine. I can pour you a glass or you can make yourself a cup of something. It's up to you.'

'A small glass of wine would be good,' Ed said.

'Very small.' Sharon poured some of the red wine into a glass, which she shoved towards him across the farmhouse table that took up too much space in the generously proportioned kitchen. 'Drink driving laws being what they are.'

She smiled at him, while giving herself a generous top-up.

'To what do I owe this dubious pleasure? I assume it's not a social visit?'

'I can't lead the investigation into the church murder,' Ed said.

Sharon crossed her arms over her substantial chest and studied Ed, waiting for him to go on.

'I know the victim,' Ed said.

'In what context?' Sharon's voice was low and controlled, but only an idiot would miss the icy undertone to her question. And Ed Mitchell was no idiot.

'In a context that means there's no way I can be involved in the investigation,' Ed said. 'I can't have anything to do with it.'

Sharon reached for her glass, took a long, slow sip of her wine.

'Okay.' She put the glass back down and nodded at Ed.

'Start at the beginning. Don't leave anything out, including why you've waited the best part of a day to tell me this. Because hell will freeze over before some jumped-up defence solicitor accuses me or my team of mishandling this investigation.'

Three

According to Eastbourne Tourism's website, the town was the sunniest in the UK. A claim that was difficult to believe on days like today, when the heavy rain meant Dee could barely see through the windscreen as she drove into town along the seafront.

The radio was tuned in to More FM, the town's local radio station. When the news came on, Lauren's murder was the main story. The chirpy female reporter gave an update on the reaction of Lauren's friends and family ('devastated') and announced that the dead girl's boyfriend, Kyle French, was helping police with their inquiries. Dee knew that most murder victims were killed by people they knew. Kyle would be one of the prime suspects until he could prove his innocence. If he could prove his innocence.

Because of the rain, there was more traffic around than usual. Which meant fewer parking spaces than usual in a town that never seemed to have enough of them, even during the winter months when tourist numbers dwindled.

Dee found a space on the seafront, less than a minute's walk from the Aldrington Hotel. But less than a minute was plenty of time to get drenched. By the time she stepped into the welcoming warmth of the hotel lobby, she was soaked through.

She peeled her jacket off, cursing her own mix of stupidity and optimism that meant she hadn't bothered looking for an umbrella before leaving the house. Running her hand through her hair, shaking off the worst of the water, she approached the reception desk, fixing her face into what she hoped was an open and friendly smile.

Until last week, Dee hadn't stepped foot inside the Aldrington since she was a teenager. Back then, the place was less hotel and more crumbling B&B, with a dodgy reputation and a lax attitude towards alcohol licensing laws that meant its bar was a magnet for teenagers not old enough to get served anywhere else. Dee had lots of happy memories from those times, along with a host of fuzzy memories and more than one blank where chunks of a night had been forgotten for ever.

A decade ago, a local builder had bought the hotel and spent a small fortune refurbishing the Aldrington to its original, pre-teenage-drinking-years glory. Today, it was a luxury boutique hotel packed full of original Victorian features, with sweeping views of the English Channel and the South Downs.

Dee recognised the young woman working behind the reception desk. She had spoken to her when she was here before, asking about Joana. The girl clearly remembered Dee too and, just as clearly, wasn't pleased to see her back so quickly.

'No one's seen her,' she said. 'I told you I'd call if anyone recognised her. But so far, no one has. I'm sorry, but I really don't think the girl you're looking for worked here.'

'Good afternoon to you too,' Dee said. 'Jaime, isn't it? I never said Joana worked here. I said she was meant to be meeting someone here the night she disappeared.'

'Sorry,' Jaime said. 'I didn't mean to be rude. We're a bit all over the place today.'

'Lauren?' Dee said.

Jaime's eyes filled with tears. Using her hand to brush them away, she nodded her head.

'She was my friend. I can't believe it's happened. I mean, this is Lauren we're talking about. Who would...? How could someone hurt her like that?'

'Are you sure you should be working?' Dee wondered whether it would be okay to walk around the reception desk and give the girl a hug. She knew what it felt like when someone close to you was killed – the feelings of grief and rage and disbelief that could completely over-whelm you.

'Derek said it was okay,' Jaime said. 'He told me I didn't need to be here but I said it was better working than sitting at home by myself all day. And this is where I feel closest to her. We started working here at the same time, you know? When Derek took on Lauren, he told her there was another vacancy going and asked if she knew anyone. Of course, she thought of me right away. We're... we *were* best friends since for ever.'

The tears started falling in earnest now. Too many for Jaime to wipe away with her hands or the sleeves of her crisp white shirt.

'Here.' Dee reached into her bag, pulled out a packet of paper tissues and handed it to the girl. Jaime took the tissues and mumbled something that could have been thank you. She pressed two tissues to her eyes but now she'd started crying, it was like she couldn't stop.

Deciding a hug was definitely in order, Dee walked around the desk and wrapped an arm around her shoulders.

'I'm sorry,' Jaime wailed, burying her face into Dee's shoulder. Ironically, the one area of her clothes that had been protected by her jacket and wasn't already soaked through.

'It's okay,' Dee whispered. 'Just let it out. You'll feel better in a minute.'

When a minute turned into five and the queue of people standing the other side of the desk grew longer and longer, Dee started to wonder if the girl would ever stop crying.

'Can't you find someone to help you?' a tall woman with cropped grey hair demanded, staring at Dee down a nose that was too long and too narrow.

'I don't work here,' Dee said. 'But if you could just wait a moment, I'm sure someone will be with you. As I'm sure you can see, she's very upset.'

She had been intermittently scanning the lobby, trying to catch the attention of one of the uniformed men standing at the hotel entrance. One of them had eventually noticed her and, when he'd seen the state of Jaime, he'd rushed off somewhere. Dee assumed he'd gone to find the manager, but he'd been gone so long she was starting to wonder if she'd assumed wrongly.

Eventually, she saw the man coming back. Walking alongside him was a tall, broad, middle-aged man with cropped blond hair that looked dyed, and the unmistakable air of authority about him. As he crossed the lobby, he clicked his fingers in the air and three of the men Dee had taken so long to get to notice her jumped to attention immediately.

Within minutes one of them had led Jaime away, and the other two were dealing with the queue of impatient guests. Which left the man in charge free to deal with Dee.

'Derek French.' He held out his hand. 'You were very kind to poor Jaime, I appreciate it. Can I treat you to a complimentary drink in our bar?'

Dee remembered the news she'd listened to on the drive over. Lauren's boyfriend was called Kyle French. She wondered if the two men were related. Deciding not to ask him just yet, she shook his outstretched hand and introduced herself.

'The journalist?' Derek said. 'I assumed you were one of our guests. My mistake. Well Dee, the offer of a drink still stands if you'd like one?'

'A coffee would be lovely,' Dee said. 'Thank you.'

'We'll go to my office,' Derek said. 'It's a little more private. This way.'

She followed him across the lobby to the lifts, getting into the first one that arrived. Inside, the lift was all chrome and mirrors and low lighting. As it ascended, Derek made small talk with an American couple who'd got into the lift at the same time. Dee was impressed with the way he seemed to already know so much about the couple – their names, where they were from and even, impressively, the names and ages of their three children.

The couple – Sherri and Shaun – travelled with them all the way to the top floor. When the doors opened Derek put his hand out, gesturing for the Americans to go in front of him. He stepped out next, holding the lift doors open for Dee. He led her along the corridor, more low lighting and tasteful decor, to a door accessed by a keypad. He entered a code and the door swung open.

'This hotel's been a labour of love,' he told Dee as they walked. 'I bought it ten years ago. Invested everything I had into it.'

'You've done a beautiful job,' Dee said. 'I remember coming here as a teenager. It was very different back then.'

'It was a dive,' Derek said. 'Now, I'm proud to say, it's one of the UK's most successful hotels. Ah, here we are.'

He stopped outside a room at the end of the corridor and pushed open the door.

'My office.' He stood back to let Dee go into the room ahead of him.

'Wow,' Dee said, walking into the room. 'You kept the best space for yourself.'

Situated at the corner of the building, the room had views across the Channel and, to the right, the start of the South Downs. Even on a wet day like this, it was a spectacular sight. A polished black desk and matching chair took up one corner of the room. There was a slim-line MacBook Air on the desk, and nothing else. In the opposite corner, there were two black leather couches with a glass coffee table in between them. The walls were painted white and hung with several pieces of modern art by an artist Dee didn't recognise.

'How do you take your coffee?' Derek asked, switching on a complicated coffee machine plugged into the wall behind his desk.

'Black, no sugar,' Dee said. 'Thanks.'

As the room filled with the smell of freshly brewed coffee, Dee wandered to the window and looked down on the seafront. Despite the weather, there were lots of people out and about. Mostly tourists, she guessed, taking advantage of some of the cheap hotel deals that kept the town busy even out of season.

'Coffee's ready,' Derek said after a few minutes. 'We can sit here,' he gestured to the leather couches, 'while we drink it.'

'How did you know I was a journalist?' Dee asked when they were both sitting down. 'I've barely written anything in years. Even at the height of my career I was hardly a household name.'

'Eastbourne's a small place,' Derek said. 'I read the piece you wrote last year about your husband. Very moving. If you don't mind me saying so.'

'Thank you,' Dee said, wondering if she'd misjudged him. On first appearances, everything about Derek French screamed flash bastard. The hair that was a shade too blond, the tan a shade too orange, and the three-piece suit more than a little OTT. He'd struck Dee as the sort of man more comfortable reading the sports sections of a tabloid than an in-depth piece on the devastating ways alcohol addiction can ruin a life.

'My old man was a drinker,' Derek said. 'What you wrote resonated with me. Although I have to admit, I'm not quite sure why you're here today. Lauren's death is tragic and we're all bloody devastated, but if you think I'm going to speak to you about it for some story you're writing, you can think again.'

'I'm not here because of Lauren.'

'No?' Derek leaned forward, and stared at her intently.

'I'm writing a piece about Polish workers in the UK,' Dee said. 'I'm particularly interested in a young woman called Joana Helinski. She was due to meet someone here at your hotel on Saturday the eighth of February. She hasn't been seen since.'

As she spoke about Joana, Dee's guilt resurfaced. She'd called Eliza several times this morning, but all her calls went straight to voicemail. Dee had left a message, apologising – again – and asking Eliza to call back. So far, Eliza hadn't called, and Dee didn't blame her.

Derek dropped eye contact so he could take a sip of his coffee. When he looked back up, he was frowning.

'You say the eighth of February?' he said. 'That's over a month ago, Dee. Is there any reason I'm only hearing about this now? If someone went missing here in my hotel, then I shouldn't be the last person to know about it. Have the police been notified?'

'They're not doing much to find her,' Dee said. 'Apparently it's quite common for Polish nationals to move around a lot. They think the most likely explanation is that Joana's simply moved on somewhere else.'

'And you? What do you think, Dee?'

'I don't know,' Dee said. 'Her friends say there's no way Joana would leave Eastbourne without letting them know. I came here last week and showed a photo of Joana to some of your staff. It never occurred to me to speak to you as well. I'm sorry.'

'Doesn't matter.' Derek dismissed her apology with a wave of his hand. 'I'm guessing none of them told me because they didn't think there was anything in it. I'm assuming none of them recognised her?'

'No,' Dee admitted. 'Although Eliza – that's Joana's friend – she came to see me yesterday and she thinks Joana and Lauren knew each other. So, of course…'

Derek shifted in his chair and drank some more of his coffee.

'I'm not very comfortable with this conversation, Dee. If you think there's some connection between your missing girl and Lauren, shouldn't you be talking to the police instead of interrogating me?'

'I didn't realise I was interrogating you.' Dee took out her phone, opened the photo she had on there of Joana and slid the phone across the desk. 'This is Joana. Do you remember ever seeing her hanging around the hotel?'

Derek looked at the photo for a full five seconds before shaking his head. When he looked back up, his expression was neutral, not giving anything away.

'Never seen her before in my life. You're barking up the wrong tree with this, Dee. I know my hotel and I know my clientele. If something bad happened to that girl, it didn't happen in my hotel. And I hope you're not insinuating I hire illegal workers? All my staff are on the books, I can assure you. Now then, I'm afraid I've got a conference call in just under five minutes. If I walk you back as far as the lift, are you okay making your way back from there? Unless, of course, you have any other questions you'd like to ask me?'

Dee did have another question, but it could wait. She could easily find the information she wanted elsewhere. She thanked him for his time, and left. Something about the encounter hadn't felt right. He'd been charming enough, but there was something odd about the conversation that she couldn't put her finger on. Maybe it was way he'd kept repeating her name when he spoke to her. Filing this as something to think about later, Dee took the lift back down to the ground floor.

On her way out of the hotel, she noticed that Jaime was back at the reception desk. She was checking in a group of Italians; Dee waited until they'd all been dealt with before approaching the girl.

'Just wanted to make sure you're okay?' Dee said.

'I'm fine,' Jaime said. 'Well, not fine exactly. But I'm not going to start crying again. Thank you, by the way.'

'It's okay,' Dee said. 'Actually, Jaime, can I ask you something?'

'Sure,' Jaime said.

'Derek French,' Dee said. 'Is he related to Lauren's boyfriend, by any chance?'

'Related?' Jaime gave Dee a watery smile. 'Kyle's his son. Why?'

'No reason,' Dee said, although she thought it was odd that Derek hadn't mentioned his son's relationship to the dead girl. Something else to think about later.

She had crossed the lobby and was trying to build up the courage to step outside into the rain when she felt a tap on her shoulder. Turning around, she saw Jaime standing behind her.

'The girl you were asking about,' Jaime said. 'She's Polish?'

'That's right,' Dee said. 'Why?'

'It might not be anything,' Jaime said. 'But there's a bar in town, it's really popular with a lot of the Eastern Europeans. The Anchor in Seaside. You know it?'

Dee nodded. She knew the Anchor. She'd already been there and asked about Joana, but hadn't found anyone who could tell her where the girl might have gone.

'I don't drink,' Jaime said. 'So I don't go out to bars that much. But I know some of the other staff here, they're friends with a lot of the people who drink in that pub. I'll show them the photo of Joana if you like?'

'That would be brilliant,' Dee said. 'Thanks so much.'

She doubted it would make any difference. It didn't seem likely that Joana and Lauren's paths had ever crossed, but it was worth a shot. And at least she'd be able to tell Eliza that she tried.

'Lauren loved that place,' Jaime said.

'The Anchor?' Dee said.

'She used to go there at least once a week,' Jaime said. 'It was her favourite bar in town.'

'You think it's possible she knew Joana?' Dee asked.

Jaime frowned.

'I guess. I mean, she was friends with lots of the people who went there. Well, not friends exactly. More sort of acquaintances, I suppose.'

'Make sure you show them that photo,' Dee said. 'Thanks so much, Jaime.'

She pushed her way through the revolving door and ran into the pouring rain. It was starting to sound like Eliza had been right. Joana and Lauren knew each other. Dee wasn't sure yet what that meant, but she was going to find out.

From the diary of Emma Reed

22 March 1960

I'm ashamed of how I feel in the dreams. It's not something I'd ever admit apart from here, within the pages of my diary. Despite the trouble she caused, I never wished her any harm. Naturally, I hoped Graham's infatuation with her would pass. And yes, I would have liked her to have behaved a little more sensibly. She led him on. I don't think she did it maliciously, but it's the truth nonetheless. She was young, and young people think differently. Particularly this generation, untouched by war and tragedy. They haven't had to grow up the way we did. In some ways, they're still children; children with adult bodies and adult needs and desires. It's a dangerous combination.

I think she was fond of Graham in her own way. But it was never more than friendship, and he couldn't see that. A girl like that was destined to be with a successful man, not someone like my son.

Her murder has rocked our community. There are times I wonder if we'll ever find a way to move past it. Because it's not just the murder, which is terrible in its own right. There's the aftermath too. That brings another form of horror. The suspicion and the rumours. The whispered conversations in shops and on the street, that seem to stop abruptly as soon as I appear. The sly, side-eyed gazes; the sheer endlessness of it all. I know what people are saying, and I know my son did not kill her. Graham might not be the best or the brightest, but he's not a murderer.

I confess, it crossed my mind. At the very beginning, when I heard she had been murdered, I wondered if he could have done it. In my defence, he'd been gone all night and I was already half out of my mind with worry, wondering where he was and what trouble he'd found himself in this time. The fear grew inside me as each minute passed. I knew something bad had happened. How could I not, after the terrible argument that had taken place in our house earlier that same evening?

I didn't write about it then. It was too painful and my mind was too distracted with worry to sit down and write. But I want to write about it now. I started this diary as a record of my life. Proof that I was more than just a mother and a wife. I was a woman, too, with my own mind and my own opinions.

So, the night of the murder...

Graham had gone to the pub in the early afternoon and he was late home for supper. I'd suggested that we wait a few minutes, but James wouldn't hear of it.

'This is my house and we eat when I say so,' he said. It's always 'his house', despite the fact it was my parents' money that paid for it.

James, Nicola and I had been at the table for about ten minutes when I heard the fumble of Graham's key in the front door. My spirits sank. Until that moment I'd hoped he might come back sober. But as I listened to him trying to fit his key into the lock, I knew. James knew too. His body stiffened, his mouth turned down and his frown deepened until his face looked as if it might split in two.

He blames me for Graham. Naturally. My husband has many shortcomings but when it comes to blaming other people, he excels. According to James, it's a mother's job to teach her child how to behave. I've tried telling him that both parents have a role to play in raising a child, but he refuses to listen. There was a time, when we first got married, I believed our opinions were of equal value. Experience has shown me how foolish I was to ever think such a thing. Opinions in a marriage are like every other part of the union – the wife's feelings, thoughts and desires are of no relevance whatsoever.

It was like watching a disaster unfold in slow motion. It reminded me of those awful days during the war when families were waiting to hear the fate of their sons or husbands and you knew that one day soon they would receive the news that would shatter their lives for ever.

Nicola and I sat between them, silent and scared, as they shouted across the table at each other. I wanted to do something but I was frozen, incapable of moving or speaking or thinking. It was only when Nicola started to cry, sobbing silently in her seat, fat tears rolling down her lovely face, that I sprang into action. I jumped up, told them both to stop it, please, please stop it.

My words had an effect. They fell quiet, and the silence was such a relief. I sat down, my whole body shaking. It should have ended there. It would have ended too, if James had stayed quiet. But he had to have the last word.

'Look at what you've done to your mother and your sister,' he said, his voice low and cold and icy with anger. 'You ought to be ashamed of yourself. I never thought I'd live to see the day when a child of mine behaved the way you do.'

I swear that I felt those words shoot across the table and enter my son's heart, wounding him. He pushed his chair back, stood up and reached across the table for the teapot. He swung his arm back and, with a roar that sent shivers of fear through my body, he hurled the teapot across the room, aiming for James's head.

I want to pretend it never happened, but if I look up from my diary now I can see the brown stain on the wall where the teapot crashed and broke. My mother's teapot. One of the few things I had left that belonged to her.

I'm not sure if James ducked his head in time or if Graham's aim was off. Either way, the teapot didn't hit its mark. Which is how I've ended up with a stain on the wall – but that's infinitely better than my husband ending up in hospital. Or my son ending up in prison.

I'd never seen that side of Graham before. Yes, he could be difficult, but he'd never exploded like that. It chills me to think of it. He stormed out immediately after the incident, and didn't come home until the following morning. I know because I stayed up all night, sitting here in the kitchen, unable to write my diary, waiting. Several times, I went outside and walked up and down the street, as if the simple act of looking for him might make him suddenly appear. But it made no difference and, in the end, I gave up searching and stayed inside. Eventually, when I'd almost given up hope, he staggered in and went straight up to bed. He still has no idea I was sitting up, waiting for him.

Ten hours he was gone. Ten hours of his time unaccounted for. And at some point, during those ten hours, she was murdered. I haven't told a soul, not even James, that Graham didn't come home that night. I know what people will think if they find out. They're already thinking it, and if they know he wasn't at home, their suspicions will rapidly turn into misplaced certainty.

So it's my job to make sure no one finds out. I know my son. He can be volatile and he loses his temper too easily. He has problems interacting with people and he gets things wrong a lot of the time.

But he's not a killer.

Four

Dee pulled up outside the row of Victorian terraced houses on Motcombe Road. When she took the key out of the ignition, she noticed the slight tremor in her hand. She was nervous. She'd called Ed's mobile and, when she got his voicemail, she'd tried his work number. One of his colleagues answered the phone and told Dee that Ed wasn't at work today. Dee knew he was meant to be on leave this week, but she'd assumed his leave would have been cancelled. She thought he'd be leading the murder investigation.

When he opened the door, he looked surprised to see her.

'It's Friday,' he said. 'I thought you'd be with Ella and Tom.'

Most Friday evenings, Dee and her neighbours got together to eat pizza and catch up.

'They couldn't make it,' Dee said. 'We're doing break-fast tomorrow instead. Sorry for coming over without calling first. I wanted to check you're okay.'

'You didn't need to.' Ed smiled, clearly making an effort. 'But I'm glad you did. Come in out of the rain.'

Dee held up the shopping bag she was carrying. 'I brought wine and some food from Waitrose. Thought we could have dinner together?'

'Good idea.' He pulled her towards him and kissed her. His breath smelled of beer. Which was unusual, because he wasn't the sort of person to sit and drink alone.

'You okay?' she asked.

'Better for seeing you,' he said. 'Come on, let's go through to the kitchen. Place is a bit of a mess, I'm afraid. If I'd known you were coming over I'd have tidied up.'

Ed's definition of mess wasn't the same as Dee's. Apart from an unwashed plate and mug in the sink, she thought his kitchen looked pretty tidy.

'Sorry,' he said, putting the mug and plate into the dishwasher.

'Leave those.' Dee took the bottle of wine out of the bag. 'Sit down and have a drink with me.'

He crossed the kitchen and put his hands on her shoulders. 'I'm glad you're here, Dee. But I have to warn you, I'm in a really shitty mood right now… not sure I'm not fit company for anyone.'

'This case?' Dee guessed. 'I've been following it on the news. Sounds awful.'

'It is awful. In fact, do you mind if we speak about something else?'

'Of course.' Dee nodded at the bottle of wine. 'Open that, would you?'

Ed did as he was told, opening the wine and pouring two glasses.

'I'm completely wiped,' he said, handing one of the glasses to Dee. 'I've spent most of last night and all of today thinking about nothing else. I'd really like to stop for a bit. Tell me about your day. What have you been up to?'

It wasn't like him to shut her out. His openness was one of the things that had drawn her to him. Then again, she'd never seen him looking lost like this. Clearly, there were things about this case that the police hadn't made public yet. Besides, Dee had come here to make him feel better, not worse. So she changed the subject, telling him about her visit to the hotel and her encounter with Derek French.

'Do you know him?' she asked when she'd finished. 'I'm trying to work out whether I liked him or not, but I can't make my mind up.'

'That's not like you,' Ed said. 'Although I can't say I'm surprised. He's a slippery bloke. Married for years, but he's got a reputation for being a bit of a womaniser.'

'Does his wife know?' Dee asked, thinking of her ex-husband, Billy. He'd had one affair and that was the final straw in a marriage that was already in trouble. She wouldn't be able to stand living with a man who repeatedly cheated on her.

'I suspect she turns a blind eye,' Ed said. 'She's very conservative. I doubt she'd ever agree to a divorce. She told me once that marriage is a sacred union that should never be broken.'

'But she doesn't have a problem with her husband breaking it by sleeping with other women?'

'Who knows?' Ed threw his hands up. 'She's an odd woman.'

'How do you know them?'

'Rugby club,' Ed said. 'I coached their son for a few years.'

'Kyle?'

Ed nodded. 'It was a while ago now. Before he decided girls and surfing were more fun than playing rugby.'

'And who can blame him for that?' Dee said. 'What's he like?'

'A decent kid.'

'Is that what's getting to you?' Dee asked.

'What do you mean?'

He sounded defensive and she knew she should stop. But she wanted to know what was bothering him.

'If you know Kyle, I imagine it must be difficult having to interview him?'

Ed drained his glass and refilled it. When he offered to do the same for Dee, she shook her head. She'd barely touched the wine in her glass.

'You're right. None of this has been easy,' he said. 'And I know I sound like a grumpy git this evening. It's been a tough couple of days, that's all.'

'Well, that's why I'm here.' Dee leaned forward and kissed his cheek. 'Why don't you go into the sitting room and put some music on? Drink your wine and relax. I'll get the food ready and we can eat on the sofa in front of the TV when it's done. After that, you can crawl into bed and get a decent night's sleep.'

Ed started to protest but Dee put a finger on his lips, silencing him. 'For once in your stupid life, Ed Mitchell, would you please let someone do something for you instead of the other way around? You've done so much for me over the last few months. You've been there for me when I've needed you, you've taken care of me and cooked me beautiful dinners and taken me out for some lovely meals. Won't you please, for the love of fucking God, let me do this one thing for you?'

The corners of his lips twitched.

'For the love of fucking God? Is that something you learned in that Catholic school you went to?'

'Don't get sassy,' Dee said. 'Or I may change my mind and you'll be making your own dinner.'

Thirty minutes later, the pots had been washed and the dishwasher emptied, and the food was almost ready. Pouring herself a glass of wine, Dee pushed open the sitting room door. Spanish classical guitar music played through Ed's Sonos sound system. Beautiful, haunting music he had introduced Dee to several months earlier. Although the beauty of the music was currently lost on the person who'd put it on, and almost impossible to hear over the steady drone of his snores.

He was sitting on the sofa, his head thrown back, mouth wide open, eyes wide shut. The glass of wine, barely touched, was on the ground by his feet. Dee crept into the room, kissed the top of his head and took the glass into the kitchen. Before leaving, she switched the oven off, went upstairs, took the duvet off his bed and draped it over him. He didn't stir once.

She thought about staying, but decided what Ed needed more than anything was a night of uninterrupted sleep. After emptying both wine glasses down the sink and rinsing them out, she let herself out of the house.

On the drive home she tried to ignore the gnawing anxiety in her gut, telling herself there was nothing to worry about. Ed hadn't been himself this evening, but what had she expected? Investigating a murder, especially when one of the suspects was someone he knew, must be awful. No wonder he'd been so reluctant to talk about it. But no matter how hard she tried to convince herself there was nothing to worry about, she didn't quite succeed.

Something wasn't right, and if Ed refused to tell her what that was, then how could she help him?

–

Four hours later, Ed woke with a sharp pain in his neck, a dry throat and the vague sense he'd done something he shouldn't have. Gradually, his eyes adjusted to the dark and he realised he'd fallen asleep on the sofa. Normally when he woke up like this he was cold. Tonight, he was almost too warm. Looking down, he realised he was lying underneath his duvet. He tried to work out how that could have happened – and then he remembered.

Dee! With a rush of shame, he threw back the duvet and went into the kitchen. No Dee in here, although it was clear she'd cooked, tidied and cleaned before she left. He was mortified. Falling asleep while Dee cooked his dinner and cleaned his kitchen was the worst sort of behaviour. She deserved better than this and he wouldn't blame her if she was angry as hell with him. He picked up his phone to call her, but when he saw the time – fourteen minutes past midnight – he thought better of it. Waking her up wasn't going to make this situation any better.

He had a new text message from Dee. The guilt intensified as he read it:

> You looked too cute to wake up. Sleep tight and call me in the morning. Xxx

'Cute,' he muttered, turning on the tap and filling a glass. 'Cute.' It wasn't a word usually used to describe him, but Ed reckoned he could get used to it. Especially when it was Dee doing the describing. She was pretty cute herself, come to think of it. Although 'cute' was woefully inadequate for describing a woman with more heart and guts and personality than anyone he'd ever known.

He started to reply, then changed his mind. Anything he told her now would add to the deceit. If he'd known she was coming over this evening, maybe he'd have been better prepared. Instead, he'd been evasive and defensive and right now she was probably wondering what the hell was going on. Except he didn't know what else to do. There was already so much he hadn't told her. And by being a total idiot this evening, now there was a whole lot more she didn't know. He shook his head, disgusted with himself. He hadn't even told her he wasn't part of the murder investigation.

A quarter past midnight and he was wide awake. He should go to bed, but there wasn't a cat's chance in hell he'd be able to sleep. So what now? Before he could make a plan, his phone pinged with an incoming text. Not from Dee, but the other woman in his life, Rachel Lewis.

You still awake by any chance?

He started to type back, then changed his mind and called her.

'Hey,' he said. 'How's it going?'

'Shitty,' she said. 'It's a bloody horrible case, Ed. Her poor parents... you know she was an only child?'

'Yeah,' Ed said. 'I know.'

He thought of the many times he'd willed something bad to happen to Nigel Shaw. Now it had, there was no pleasure in it. Whatever vague 'bad' thing he'd wished on the man, it hadn't ever been something like this.

'Sorry to get in touch so late,' Rachel said. 'I wanted to call earlier but it's been so busy.'

'It's fine,' Ed said. 'Can I help with anything?'

'Not really,' Rachel said. 'I just wanted to let you know there's going to be something in the papers tomorrow about Lauren's relationship with Mary.'

'This soon?' Ed asked. He'd been expecting it, of course. From the moment he'd recognised the body, he'd known it would come out. He hadn't expected it to happen this soon, that was all.

'A journalist at the *Mail* got hold of it,' Rachel said. 'Sharon's decided to go public with the information. It's not ideal. People are going to make all sorts of assumptions and that's going to complicate the investigation. But we don't have a choice. I'm sorry, Ed.'

'How much do they know?' he asked.

'They know that the two women were related,' Rachel said. 'And they know how Mary was killed. I'm sure they'll focus on the similarities between the two murders. I don't think anyone's made the connection with you. Not yet.'

Ed breathed out a sigh of relief. 'That's something, I suppose.'

'It's only a matter of time before someone works it out. You know that, don't you?'

'Yeah,' he said. 'Thanks for letting me know, Rachel. I appreciate it.'

After hanging up, Ed went into his kitchen. Without turning the light on he went across to the window. From here, he had a clear view of the spire of St Mary the Virgin. At night, lit up like this, it was beautiful. He looked out at the church, thinking of the two women whose bodies had been found there.

A large chunk of Ed's teenage years had been spent researching Mary's murder, doing everything he could to prove Graham Reed didn't kill her. But he'd never found a single thing to back up that belief and, over time, he'd given up. Like everyone else in his family, Ed pushed all the circumstances surrounding Mary's murder to the back of his mind, and did everything he could to forget all about it.

Apart from one drunken night five years earlier when he'd told Rachel, he never mentioned it and rarely thought about it. Until Lauren Shaw had burst into his life a few months earlier and the memories had come rushing back. Now Lauren was dead. And no matter how hard he tried, Ed couldn't help thinking that if he'd acted differently, she'd still be alive.

Five

Saturday morning, Dee was up early to cook breakfast for her neighbours, Ella and Tom and their son, Jake. She'd hoped Ed might join them, but he'd sent her a text earlier telling her he was going to Norfolk first thing this morning to visit his sister. She'd tried calling him back, but she'd got his voicemail and hadn't bothered leaving a message. Now, she was more worried than ever. The text confirmed there was something going on with him. Why else would he run off to Norfolk in the middle of a serious investigation? Unless Ed's sister was, somehow, part of the investigation. But that didn't make any sense.

Deciding not to spend the morning tormenting herself over Ed, Dee put some music on and set about preparing a full English. She'd just finished setting the table and was making a second pot of coffee when she heard footsteps on the shingle beach outside her house. She slid open the back doors that led onto the decking, smiling so wide her face ached. These three people, along with Louise's family and Ed, were the most important people in her life.

'Jake!'

When she called his name, he let go of his mum's hand and ran forward.

'We got kossants and muffins,' throwing himself at Dee.

'Kossants.' Dee laughed. 'My favourite.'

She lifted him off the ground and carried him into the house, letting his incessant chatter soothe her. It was no secret to anyone – including Ed – that no one could ever compete with Jake for Dee's affections. The three-year-old boy was, quite simply, the centre of her universe. She loved him as much as if he was her own child (or grandchild, Ed liked to correct her, a little too frequently for Dee's liking).

Jake and his parents lived in an extended mobile home a few yards along the beach from Dee's house. The mobile home belonged to Dee – Tom and Ella rented it from her. It was too small for the three of them, but they were saving money for a mortgage. Dee wanted to give them the plot of land that the mobile home stood on. That way, they could knock the place down and build their own, permanent home on the site. It was in her interests to do this – she loved having them as neighbours and couldn't bear to think about them leaving one day. The problem was, Tom and Ella were both too proud to accept Dee's repeated offers to give them the land. Which meant a significant proportion of Dee's time was spent trying to think of other ways to persuade them to stay. She'd almost lost Ella and Jake once before. She'd do anything to make sure that never happened again.

'Where's Ed?' Jake demanded, as the four of them sat around the table.

'He's gone to visit his sister,' Dee said. 'But he asked me to say hello to you.'

Jake seemed pleased with her answer, and tucked into his plate of scrambled eggs.

'I thought he'd be working on the investigation into that poor girl in the church,' Tom said.

'I think it's proving quite stressful,' Dee said. 'He just needs a break for a few hours.'

In truth, she had no idea whether Ed would be away for just today or longer than that, but there was no point telling this to Tom and Ella.

She was saved from having to explain anything else, because Jake wanted to know who the woman in the church was and they had to change the subject.

'Breakfast is great,' Tom said, after a moment. 'Just what I need after the week I've had.'

'How's work going?' Dee asked.

'Busy,' Tom said. 'Which is good, on the one hand. But I hate all the travel, you know? I miss Ella and Jake so much when I'm away.'

'We miss you too,' Ella said.

Tom threw his arm around her shoulder, pulling her close.

'It's a shame most of the work I do is based in Ireland,' he said to Dee. 'I sometimes think we should up sticks and move back altogether. My folks would love having us a bit closer.'

'It's not going to happen,' Ella said. 'Don't look so worried, Dee. If we moved to Ireland, there's no way we could afford to live in Dublin, which is where most of Tom's work is based.' She looked at Tom. 'So we still wouldn't see you during the weeks. Besides, where would we ever find a house right on the beach like we have here? The most we could hope for in Ireland is some horrible new-build on a soulless estate in the middle of nowhere. We'd both hate that.'

Dee should have felt more relieved, but she couldn't shake off the feeling it was only a matter of time before

Tom got his way. And who could blame him? He'd given up his old life to move to Eastbourne when he discovered Ella was living here with his son, who he'd never known about. Sooner or later, he was going to want to go back to the country he still called 'home'.

The last thing Dee should do was stand in the way of Jake spending more time with his grandparents. Except, every time she thought of them leaving, she couldn't imagine how she would cope if it were ever to become a reality.

After breakfast, Tom and Ella insisted on tidying up, giving Dee a chance to catch up with Jake. They put their coats on and went onto the beach, where they spent the next twenty minutes playing 'chase the waves'. It was a game Dee had played with her own mother, and she loved that she was able to play it now with Jake. It involved standing on the edge of the water and seeing how long you could stay without getting wet, before running back as the waves washed in over the shingle.

Midway through playing, Louise called.

'One moment,' Dee told Jake. 'I need to take this.'

'Have you spoken to Ed?' Louise said.

'Good morning to you too,' Dee said. 'What do you mean, have I spoken to Ed?'

'Has he told you how Lauren was killed?' Louise asked.

'Of course not,' Dee said. 'What do you take him for?'

'He's not part of the investigation,' Louise said. 'Did you know that?'

'Sorry?'

'He hasn't told you?'

'Oh that,' Dee said, when she was able to speak. 'Yes, he did mention something about it.' God damn the man, she thought. What the hell was going on with him?

'I don't think there's anything dodgy about it,' Louise said. 'I mean, I don't know, but I didn't get that impression.'

'What are you talking about?' Dee said.

'I spoke to their press officer yesterday,' Louise said. 'Naturally, we're covering the murder in this week's paper. I always cross-check my facts with the police. People get very upset if you get even the slightest detail wrong. Anyway, they've got this new woman handling the press office. Thank God, because the last one was bloody useless. According to Melanie, that's the press officer, Rachel Lewis is leading the investigation, not Ed.'

'So what?' Dee said.

'He didn't tell you why?'

'Louise, I've barely spoken to him since the murder. He's been busy.'

'Strange,' Louise said. 'Well, I'm sure he'll tell you when you see him. In the meantime, check the *Recorder's* home page and call me when you're done.'

Then, before Dee could ask her what the hell she meant by that, Louise had hung up. Putting her phone back in the pocket of her jeans, Dee decided the *Recorder's* home page could wait and she turned her attention back to Jake.

They stayed outside until Tom and Ella came to join them on the beach.

'We need to head back,' Ella said. 'Tom's got some work to do, and I promised Jake I'd take him to the cinema. Why don't you come with us?'

'I've got work to do,' Dee said. She could barely wait for them to go so she could get online and read the latest news about the murder.

She hugged each of them and said goodbye before going onto the deck and watching them walk back across the beach, the crunch of footsteps on the shingle loud in the silence of the crisp spring morning. When she could no longer see or hear them, she stayed where she was, looking out at the vast expanse of sky and ocean and thinking about the many ways her life was good right now.

Two years ago, if you'd told Dee she'd still be living in Eastbourne and actually enjoying it, she would have told you where to get off. Right before slugging down a large glass of wine and refilling it to the brim. Wine and loneliness had been her sole companions after the death of her parents and the break-up of her marriage.

She'd fallen into a depression so dark and deep it seemed impossible to imagine she'd ever find the strength to crawl her way out of it. But somehow, she'd managed it. Thanks in no small part to little Jake.

When Dee first got to know Ella and Jake, Ella had been living under an assumed identity. She was running away from a haunted past but, as she'd discovered, the past has a way of catching up with you.

A lot had changed since then, including Ella and Tom getting back together. Over the last few months, Dee and her neighbours had settled into a way of being together that suited all of them. They saw each other regularly, without living in each other's pockets. Dee babysat Jake any chance she got, they met up most Friday nights and, at least once a week, she and Ella would get together for

49

a walk or a coffee or a glass of wine. Somehow, Dee had lulled herself into believing things might carry on this way indefinitely. But Tom's throwaway comment earlier had got her worried. She didn't want to lose them, but she couldn't see a way of making sure that didn't happen.

She went inside, made some coffee and sat by the window while she opened her laptop and found the home page for the *Eastbourne Recorder's* website. Louise was right. Once Dee had read the story – several times to make sure she'd got all the details correct – her mind was buzzing.

The first part of the story gave the shocking details of how Lauren had been killed. As Dee started to read it, she wondered why the police had released this information so quickly. It was only when she reached the next part of the story that it made sense. There was no way of keeping something like this hidden.

Lauren Shaw's body had been found on the altar of St Mary the Virgin church. There was still no detail on how the killer had got inside the church, but plenty of information on the damage done to poor Lauren. Her throat had been cut open and, bizarrely, the killer had cut off all her hair. This in itself was shocking enough. But what came next was the bit that Dee couldn't get her head around. Because the article went on to talk about another murder that had happened in Eastbourne sixty years earlier.

The victim was a young woman called Mary Palmer. According to the *Recorder*, and every other news site Dee visited, Mary Palmer had been eighteen years old at the time of her murder. On 5 March 1960, Mary's body was discovered on the altar in the church of St Mary the Virgin. The same church where Lauren's body had been found yesterday morning. The similarities didn't stop there. Like Lauren, Mary Palmer had long auburn hair and a smattering of freckles across her nose. Dee could just make out the freckles in the grainy black and white image accompanying the story. Mary's throat had been cut open and all her auburn hair had been cut off.

But the thing that stood out about this story, over and above everything else, was this: Lauren Shaw and Mary Palmer were related. Lauren's father and Mary Palmer were first cousins.

'What the heck?' Dee said when she called Louise back.

'Ed hasn't mentioned this?' Louise said.

'I've barely seen him,' Dee said. 'He's been so busy.'

'Busy doing what?' Louise said. 'Why isn't he part of the investigation? Did he know Lauren?'

Dee's stomach churned. For a moment, she thought she was about to throw up. She looked at Lauren Shaw's photo on her laptop. The girl was undeniably beautiful. A few days ago, Dee would have said her relationship with Ed was rock solid. Now, she was starting to doubt what they had together. Could she have got him that wrong?

Then she got a grip. Ed Mitchell was straight as die. It was one of the reasons she'd let down her guard and fallen in love with him. Because, unlike her alcoholic ex, Ed was someone she could trust. Yes, there was something he wasn't telling her. But it certainly wasn't that he'd been having an affair with a girl young enough to be his daughter.

'It can't be the same killer,' Louise said, jumping from subject to subject the way she always did when she was fired up by something. 'Mary's killer died soon after she did.'

'It looks as if whoever killed Lauren deliberately recreated Mary's murder,' Dee said. 'Maybe it's… I don't know, some kind of warning?'

'To the family? That's possible, I guess. I was hoping to go and see them today but there's not a chance of that happening now. They'll be inundated by journalists trying to talk to them.'

Dee looked at the images of the two dead girls on her computer screen. The physical similarities were obvious, despite the poor quality of Mary's photo.

'I've got to go,' Louise said. 'Martin's just come back from golf. He'll be looking for something to eat.'

'Have fun,' Dee said. 'Oh, and Lou?'

'Don't,' Louise said. 'I know he's more than capable of getting his own food, but I like doing it for him, okay?'

'I guess so.'

Dee said goodbye and hung up. There were things she needed to do. Like try to speak to Ed and ask him what the hell was going on. But she didn't move, transfixed by the images of the two women. Both dead, killed by a monster. No. Dee shook her head. Not one monster. Two.

From the diary of Emma Reed

11 April 1960

There's a sick feeling that never leaves me these days. Fear. It sits in the pit of my stomach, burning like acid. It's with me when I fall asleep at night, and it's there when I wake up each morning. Fear for my family, for what will happen to all of us if this campaign of hate against my son continues.

James has stopped playing golf. There's no point, he says, if you can't find anyone who'll play with you. Golf is more than a game for him. It's a way of meeting people, making connections and ensuring he has all the contacts he needs to further his career. He's spoken about moving to a different part of the country, making a fresh start. But we can't consider something like that with this terrible cloud of suspicion hanging over all of us.

Earlier this week, Nicola came home from school in tears. The other girls have been ignoring her. When she tries to join in their conversations, they taunt her, telling her terrible things about her brother. Lies they've heard from their parents that they repeat, in their ignorant way, in the brutal world of the playground. Teenagers can be so cruel. I tried speaking to the headmaster but he made it clear that, while Nicola was living under the same roof as a 'suspected murderer', there wasn't anything he could do. The man is an incompetent fool.

The weather is warm and humid, much as it was this time last year when we attended the Palmers' garden party. Such a beautiful afternoon. I was so thrilled we'd been invited, knowing how important it was for James to be seen there. And yes, I confess to feeling a little smug too, knowing others hadn't been so lucky. Anyone who'd got on the wrong side of Annabelle, for example. As George's sister, Annabelle is a powerful ally and a dangerous enemy. A spinster, she's lived with George ever since his own wife passed away. Now that her poor niece is dead, she is likely to inherit all of George's fortune one day. Which will further strengthen her position within our community.

But why am I writing about this now? In the hall, the grandfather clock continues its relentless tick-ticking. A constant reminder of the minutes and hours that have passed while I've sat here, waiting for Graham to come home. Another night of worrying and waiting.

I shouldn't have let him go out. It's not safe for him at the moment. People are angry about Mary. They want someone to pay for the crime and, increasingly, Graham is becoming the target of all this anger and desire for retribution. Each time I leave the house, it's there. The hostility in people's faces, the whispered conversations that stop when I draw close. Worst of all are those who greet me with fake smiles, pretending they haven't been gossiping about me moments earlier. Hypocrites the lot of them.

Graham has already been questioned by the police, and released without charge. You'd think that would be enough to stop the gossips but if anything, it's made things worse. People think that James's friendship with the chief constable is the only reason Graham isn't already behind bars.

The grandfather clock chimes five times. Through the curtains, fingers of grey morning light are trickling into the room. Twenty minutes ago, I heard footsteps outside. I ran to the front door, my heart filled with hope, relief already flooding every part of me as

I imagined opening the door and taking my son into my arms. Prepared to hold him tight and never let him go again.

But it wasn't Graham. It was Richard Partridge and two of his friends. Despite the early hour, the men's spirits were high. They seemed animated, arms over each other's shoulders, wide smiles on their faces as they wound their way along the street. I stepped back inside the house and shut the door before they could see me. But the sound of their laughter, loud and careless, chased after me. Taunting me.

James and Nicola are asleep upstairs. I don't know how James will react if he gets up and Graham still hasn't come home. He'll be angry, I expect, and he'll want to blame someone, so that will be me. He's angry all the time these days. As if it's my fault that people are gossiping about us and no one wants to play golf with him. I've tried talking to him about it, but he'd rather be angry than talk.

I need to stop writing. I thought it would help, but putting it all down like this has made everything worse. The fear spreads through me until I can taste it, sour metal coating the inside of my mouth. It's got a substance to it that makes it every bit as real as my heart and my lungs and my kidneys. And like those vital organs, I can't rip it out or pretend it's not there.

Four words are pounding repeatedly inside my head:

Something bad has happened.

Six

Ed sat in the kitchen of his sister's house, nursing a cup of instant coffee.

'Want a top-up?' Nessa asked, nodding at the empty cup.

'Not unless you've got any proper coffee hiding in those cupboards,' Ed said.

'Sorry,' Nessa said. 'Since Javi and I gave up caffeine we've stopped buying real coffee. I keep a jar of instant for visitors but, truthfully, most of our friends don't drink it, either. That jar's probably been there for years.'

Which explained why it tasted so dreadful. Along with caffeine, Nessa and her partner had given up most foods and drinks Ed considered essential to a happy life, including all alcohol, meat and dairy products. Not for the first time, he was grateful he'd found a partner who enjoyed the finer things in life every bit as much as he did.

'So,' Nessa said. 'If you don't want coffee and you've run out of small talk, do you want to talk about why you're here? Not that it's not lovely to see you. The kids are so excited you're here. But I know my big brother.'

'Maybe I just wanted to see you,' he said.

'And maybe those pigs in my back yard will fly one day,' Nessa said.

'Have you decided what you're going to do with them yet?' Ed asked. 'I'm not sure what you're meant to do with pigs if you're not planning to eat them.'

'That's disgusting.' Nessa leaned across the table and whacked his arm. 'They're lovely, intelligent animals. We're keeping them as pets. Cielo and River adore them.'

Ed arranged his face in a smile and kept his mouth shut. The thought of his beloved nephews frolicking around in Ness's overgrown garden with two pigs wasn't something he wanted to dwell on. The only problem was, now the image was in his head he couldn't get rid of it.

'Gloucester Old Spots are known for their gentle nature,' Nessa continued. 'If you ever bothered spending time with them you'd see just how adorable they are. And I promise, you'd never want to eat bacon again.'

'It would take more than two cute pigs to make me give up bacon,' Ed said.

Nessa rolled her eyes.

'So?' She took a sip of her mint tea and looked at Ed, waiting. He took a deep breath, unsure where to begin. Part of him didn't want to tell her. It was so nice just being here, spending time with her. He always forgot, when he was away from her, how relaxed she made him feel.

It hadn't always been like this. When she was younger, Nessa had been wild, unmanageable. As a teenager, she'd got into all sorts of trouble. Drugs, bad boyfriends, a few visits to A&E to have her stomach pumped. Ed had always been the steady, sensible sibling while his sister ran wild.

For a long time, their lives had diverged. Ed became a detective; Nessa moved to Spain, working as a hostess in dodgy nightclubs and going out with a string of successively dodgier boyfriends. Then, when her father and brother had almost given up on her, she completely turned her life around. She moved back to the UK with her Spanish boyfriend and trained as a Reiki healer. Within a few years, Nessa was earning more money with her healing than Ed could ever hope to earn as a detective.

Ness and Javier moved to Norfolk, bought this rambling old house on the coast and started a family together. To date, this family included two children, the two pigs, four cats and a sloppy St Bernard. The animals had all come from the animal rescue charity where Javier worked. In Spain he'd had a job as an investment banker, but he'd given up all of that to start a new life in the UK with Ness. An act of spontaneity and faith that Ed had never been able to match in his own life.

'You know why I'm here,' he said.

Nessa sighed. 'Yes I do. You want to talk about Lauren. But what if I tell you I don't want to talk about it?'

'How can you not want to talk about this?' Ed asked.

'Because it won't make any difference,' Nessa said. 'We know what happened, and we know the terrible damage it caused. I don't want to dwell on that. I just want to get on with my life, Ed. Don't you want to do that too?'

'There's something you don't know,' Ed said.

But Nessa put her hand up, stopping him.

'No.' She shook her head. 'No way, Ed. Please don't do this.'

'Do what?' Ed asked.

'Dig it all up again,' Nessa said. 'It's history. Bad history. Can't you leave it alone?'

She was getting angry. She wasn't the only one.

'Leave it alone?' Ed said. 'How am I expected to do that? Lauren's murder was a message. You can't expect me to ignore that.'

'I don't believe this,' Nessa whispered.

'Ness.' Ed reached across the table and squeezed his sister's hand. 'There's something else. I knew Lauren. That's what I want to talk to you about.'

Nessa pulled her hand away. For a long time, she didn't speak.

'I'm sorry,' she said eventually. 'I don't want anything to do with it. I don't want to know how you knew Lauren, or why. Everything that happened, it messed us up, and I'm sick to death of being messed up.'

'Are we messed up?' Ed asked.

'You're not,' Nessa said. 'Although for a long time I thought your inability to commit to a long-term relationship might be connected to our childhood. But since you've met Dee I'm not so sure about that.'

'I just never met the right person,' Ed said.

'Until now?'

A series of images played through his head. Walking on the beach with Dee. Watching her as she moved around her kitchen, preparing one of her chaotic dinners that never seemed to follow any recipe but, somehow, always ended up tasting delicious. Being in bed with her; sex with her. The odd feeling he'd had ever since he'd got to know her, that something monumental had changed in his life.

'Until now,' he agreed. Although even as he said it, he felt a pang of guilt. Because he hadn't been honest with Dee, and he knew how important honesty was to her. He didn't want to think about how she'd react when she found out he'd been keeping secrets from her.

Nessa smiled. 'You've changed since you've been with her. You're more relaxed these days. Happier.'

'What about you?' Ed said. 'You're one of the least messed-up people I know. How can you say our child-hood affected the way your life's turned out?'

'I wasn't always like this, though,' Nessa said. 'You know that.'

'You were young,' Ed said. 'Nothing unusual about experimenting with different lifestyles while you try to work out what sort of person you really are.'

Nessa shook her head, frowning.

'It was more than that,' she said. 'And you know it.'

'I thought you'd want to know,' Ed said. 'That's all.'

'Well I don't. The past is the past, Ed. And that's how I want to keep it. Of course, it's terrible what's happened to that poor girl, but I'm telling you now, you're not to try to involve me in this. Okay?'

'Nessa, you don't understand. The press already know half the story. What will we do when they work out the rest of it?'

'We don't do anything. I don't give a damn what the papers say, and neither should you. Within a week it will have blown over and everyone will have moved on to the next big story. I've worked so hard to put all that behind me. I hope you can find a way to leave it too. You've got a good thing going with Dee. That's what you should be focusing on now. This obsession of yours, it's not healthy. Let it go. It's the right thing to do, believe me.'

Seven

Eliza had finally returned Dee's calls. They'd agreed to meet that afternoon at Seasons, Dee's favourite place in the Harbour. The Harbour – Sovereign Harbour to give it its full name – was a fifteen-minute walk from Dee's house. She walked fast, bundled up in her winter coat, but she was windswept and freezing by the time she arrived.

Eliza wasn't there yet, so Dee ordered coffees for both of them and took a seat by the window. The waitress had just set the coffees on the table when Dee saw Eliza hurrying along the path.

'It is so cold,' Eliza said, keeping her denim jacket wrapped around her as she sat down opposite Dee.

'You're underdressed,' Dee said. 'You need a thick coat and a scarf for this weather.'

'Coats cost money.' Eliza shivered. 'Thank you for the coffee, by the way.'

She wrapped her hands around the mug and held it against her. Dee wondered how she could offer to buy the girl a winter coat without offending her.

'I'm really sorry,' Dee said.

Eliza smiled. 'This weather is your fault?'

'Not for the weather,' Dee said. 'For the other day, when you came to my house.'

'You already apologised for that,' Eliza said. 'It's okay, really. I know you didn't mean it the way it sounded. I'm just so worried, Dee. The longer Joana is missing, the more worried I become. Each morning I wake up and it's with me. The feeling that something really bad has happened to her. You know, I spoke to her grandmother the other day. She hasn't heard anything. Not since Joana disappeared.'

'How is Jakub doing?' Dee asked, referring to Joana's four-year-old son.

'He's missing his mom,' Eliza said. 'He's used to hearing from her five or six times a week. She phoned or Skyped with him whenever she could. This is how I know she's in trouble. She loves her boy. The only reason she would stop calling him is if she wasn't able to. So, Dee. What did you want to see me about?'

'I went back to the hotel,' Dee said. 'And you're right. I think Lauren and Joana might have known each other. Apparently Lauren was a regular at the Anchor. You know the pub?'

'I know it. Although I've never been. I don't like pubs. But Joana, she loves them.' Eliza smiled. 'She's a real extrovert, you know? Always out and about, meeting people and making new friends. So this proves I'm right, doesn't it? If Lauren knew Joana, then maybe someone killed her because she knew what happened to her.'

'I'm not sure about that,' Dee said. 'And unless we can prove they knew each other, I don't think there's much point speaking to the police. They won't be interested.'

'They don't care,' Eliza said. 'They are doing nothing, and they will continue to do nothing, because she is Polish and what do they care about someone like us?'

'It's not that they don't care,' Dee said. 'But with no evidence of any wrongdoing, there's very little they can do. Joana's an adult. You can't blame the police for assuming she's simply moved on. And you told me yourself, you had a row a few days before she disappeared.'

'We were best friends,' Eliza said. 'No row in the world would make her leave like that.'

'Have you been following the news stories about Lauren's murder?' Dee asked.

'Of course.' Eliza frowned. 'But I haven't seen anything about Joana. Why?'

'You know Lauren's body was laid out to replicate another murder?' Dee said.

'So what?'

'Isn't it more likely,' Dee said, 'that Lauren's murder had something to do with the earlier murder?'

Eliza shook her head. 'Of course not. Mary's murder happened a long time ago. Whoever killed her is most likely dead.'

'*Is* dead, according to the papers,' Dee said.

'Well that proves it, then. There is no connection.'

'How can you be so sure?' Dee asked.

'Because it's obvious,' Eliza said. 'Lauren's killer made it look like Mary's murder to distract people. That's all this is, Dee. It's a distraction.'

'Maybe,' Dee conceded. 'I've spoken with quite a few people at the hotel now. No one remembers seeing her that night. Do you think it's possible she never made it as far as the Aldrington?'

'Where else could she have gone?'

'I don't know,' Dee admitted. 'But I think it's worth looking into, don't you?'

'I guess.' Eliza took a sip of her coffee. 'But why would she lie to me? She was so excited, convinced that this time it would be different. This man, whoever he was, he was really into her apparently. He was going to help her find a proper job and she wouldn't have to work as a cleaner any more. I knew it was bullshit but she wouldn't listen to me. She wanted to believe it so badly.'

Eliza's eyes filled with tears. She wiped them away before she continued.

'It makes me so angry. This bastard, he told her exactly what she wanted to hear just so she'd meet him and let him have sex with her. It was all a lie.'

'I'm so sorry,' Dee said.

Eliza smiled. 'Always with the sorry. It's not your fault. It's men with power who think they can use that power to get a pretty girl to have sex with them. It's disgusting.'

Dee agreed. She felt a rush of anger, thinking about the way certain men preyed on young women like Joana, whose desire for work and money made them vulnerable.

'All she wanted was a better life for her son,' Eliza said. 'And so what if she liked rich men? Who can blame her for that? Normally, she was so careful. I mean, she liked to date men who had money, but she never took their lies seriously. This time, she seemed to really believe what he told her.'

'And you've no idea who he was?'

'I wish so many times I'd asked her more about him,' Eliza said. 'But I was angry, so I didn't ask the questions I should have.'

'I can't help thinking it's strange,' Dee said, choosing her words carefully. 'If I was living in a foreign country and I was going to meet some guy in a bar, I'd make pretty sure my friend knew exactly who he was and where I'd be.'

'Not if you knew the friend would disapprove,' Eliza said.

'And you disapproved because you thought the man was lying to her?'

'Not just that,' Eliza said. 'I didn't like what she was doing. Letting men pay her to have sex with her. She was worth more than that.'

'So when you told me before that Joana liked to date rich men,' Dee said. 'You didn't mean just dating, did you?'

'I thought you'd judge her if I told you everything. I'm sorry. I should have told you before.'

'You should have told the police, too,' Dee said. 'This is important information. If Joana was... well, if she was being paid for sex, she was potentially putting herself in a lot of danger.'

'You think it will make any difference if I tell the police?' Eliza said.

'I'd hope so.' Dee tried to think through the implications of what she now knew about Joana. 'If she was meeting men, who set these meetings up for her? Was she working alone or with someone else?'

'You mean like a pimp?' Eliza scowled. 'It wasn't like that. They were dates. The men she went out with, she met them in clubs or bars or on the beach. All the usual places people meet. She's not a prostitute, if that's what you're thinking.'

'What would you call it then?' Dee asked.

'A young girl having a bit of fun,' Eliza said.

'So why did you get angry with her?'

Eliza's shoulders slumped.

'I was worried she wasn't being careful enough,' she said. 'Some of the men she went out with, she knew nothing about them. I kept telling her it wasn't safe. And I was right, wasn't I?'

Dee reached across the table, took hold of one of Eliza's hands and squeezed it.

'I'm glad you told me,' she said.

'You think it will help?' Eliza asked.

'I hope so,' Dee said.

–

After leaving Eliza, Dee walked through the marina towards the beach and the path back to her house. She hadn't gone far when Ed called her.

'Hey,' she said. 'How's Norfolk?'

'Windy,' he said. 'But good to see Nessa and the kids. Forgot how fond I am of the little buggers. How have you been?'

Dee stopped walking and leaned against the railing that separated the path from the water, gazing over the collection of luxury yachts moored here. Sovereign Harbour was a vast development on the east side of town, half a mile from Dee's house. The marina consisted of four separate harbours, a retail park and a dizzying number of houses and apartment blocks. It had transformed the landscape of Dee's childhood and, for a long time, she'd hated it. Recently, partly thanks to Ed, her feelings had changed. They came here a lot, eating in one of the restaurants or wandering along the paths looking at the yachts and imagining what it would be like to own one of them.

'I didn't know you'd been planning to visit them today,' she said.

'It was a bit of an impulsive thing,' he said. 'I woke up this morning and suddenly realised I missed them. You don't mind, do you?'

'Of course not.'

It was true. He could visit his sister whenever he wanted. But not telling her his real reasons for doing so, that was a different matter.

'How about you?' he said. 'What have you been up to?'

She wanted to ask him what the hell was going on, why he hadn't bothered to tell her he'd been taken off the investigation. But it wasn't a conversation to have over the phone. So instead, she told him about the meeting she'd just had with Eliza.

'What do you think?' she asked, when she'd finished.

'I think that's your story,' Ed said. 'Young girls coming to the UK to make some money, ending up having to work as prostitutes.'

'The way Eliza tells it,' Dee said, dragging her mind back from daydreams to the conversation, 'it was Joana's choice. She didn't have to do it.'

'If these girls were protected by UK employment law,' Ed said, 'they wouldn't have to take crappy jobs that didn't pay them properly. The situation for Eastern European workers in this country is appalling. I'm surprised more journalists aren't writing about it.'

'Maybe you're right,' Dee said. 'But if I focus on that, how's it going to get me any closer to finding out what happened to Joana?'

'You said she was meeting men in hotel bars,' Ed said. 'Start there. Visit the hotels along the seafront – just the high-end places. Don't bother with the budget ones. Show Joana's photo around and see if anyone recognises her.'

'I've already done that at the Aldrington,' Dee said. 'With zero success.'

'You only have Eliza's word that's where she was going that night. Joana could have lied about where she was really going.'

'You're right.' Dee's mind raced ahead, the story already coming together. Young women forced to sell their bodies for sex, and nobody giving a damn about it. Because the young men and women who came to this country in their thousands to do the shitty jobs that British people didn't want to do were invisible. They had no workers' rights, no rights to anything.

They carried on speaking, talking about inconsequential things and making plans for what they'd do when Ed came back from Norfolk. It was good to hear his voice, and she should have felt happy. But the conversation didn't feel right. There was so much he wasn't telling her. And Dee didn't like that one little bit.

From the diary of Emma Reed

14 April 1960

He is dead. There. I've said, so it must be real. Although it feels anything but. He is dead. Three words. One for each day that has passed since I lost him. I cannot live in a world like this. How is any mother meant to endure such pain?

They killed him.

Three more words.

They killed my son. Those sick and evil men. I say men because a killing like this isn't the work of women. Although as sure as summer turns to autumn, women also played their part in Graham's death. The whispering and the gossiping and the half-truths that are passed around in the grocer's and the butcher's and inside the houses where women gather to drink tea and chatter, chatter, chatter because they don't work and they are bored, bored, bored so they spend their idle hours troublemaking through the stories they tell each other.

I hate all of them.

How can I continue living in this town, knowing what was done to my son and knowing justice will never be served? Because they think it has already been served, don't they? Those stupid, evil men and women who have destroyed my life for no reason other than ignorance.

See this! The front page of today's Recorder:

It's a lie, but they don't care. Lies sell newspapers. 'Found dead' is a euphemism. They chased him through the streets, and they cornered him by the stone wall that surrounds Manor Gardens. They attacked him with cricket bats and metal bars and beat his head and body and face until there was nothing left to identify him except the shoes on his feet and the navy blue trousers I'd bought him last month.

I thought I understood the pain of loss. Those of us who lived through the war are accustomed to losing loved ones. But there is nothing on this earth that can prepare a mother for losing a child. There is a rage building inside me. An anger so deep and terrifying I don't know what to do with it. I need to get out of this house. I need to walk up onto the downs and scream until my throat is raw and my face and body burn from it. I want to lift a cricket bat and swing it high in the air and bring it down on the bodies of those men who hurt my baby.

Women are called the weaker sex. It's only men who truly believe this. Every woman who has ever given birth, who has endured the messy, dirty, violent business of forcing a child from her body, knows that she has a strength that men could never imagine.

He is dead. I have to live a different sort of life now. Until three days ago, we were a family of four. A square. Now, we have to learn to be a triangle. I don't know how we'll do that. But I know this. I will not rest until I find the people who took him from me. I want them to pay for what they did. I want to look them in the eye and tell them they made a mistake. They killed my son to punish him for a crime he didn't commit. I want them to know this truth, and then I want to kill them with my own hands and watch them as they die.

Eight

The bar at the Aldrington Hotel bore no resemblance to the shabby room where Dee had wasted too many hours as a teenager. Like the rest of the hotel, it had been restored to its original Victorian glory. Packed full of atmosphere and original features, with a curved mahogany bar in the centre, stained-glass windows and plush red seating, the room was a delight.

'Wow.' Ella stopped in the doorway and took her time looking around the room. 'Tom is so bringing me here for my birthday. Why on earth haven't we been here before?'

'It's too expensive. Come on. Let's grab some drinks and find somewhere to sit down.'

They were halfway across the room when they were intercepted by one of the most beautiful men Dee had ever seen in her life.

'Please, ladies.' He graced them with a smile that turned Dee's knees to water. 'Take a seat and one of our team will be with you right away to take your order. In this bar, it's table service only.'

'He is divine,' Ella whispered as they sat down at a table by the window.

'He's certainly easy on the eye, isn't he? Here.' Dee picked up the cocktail menu and handed it to Ella. 'Choose something lovely to drink. My treat.'

Another, equally beautiful, man took their drinks orders. Minutes later, the drinks were delivered to the table alongside a bill that made the air disappear from Dee's lungs when she read it.

'Hang on,' she said as the man was about to leave. She fished Joana's photo out of her bag and showed it to him.

'Do you recognise this girl?'

The smile slid off the man's face.

'Sorry?' he said.

'It's a simple question, Lewis,' Dee said, reading the man's name from the silver badge on his waistcoat. 'Have you ever seen this girl before?'

'Who wants to know?' Lewis said.

'Me,' Dee said.

'Are you the police or something?' Lewis asked.

'A concerned friend,' Dee said. 'This girl's been missing for five weeks. The last time she was seen she was on her way here to this hotel.'

'Oh, okay.' Lewis nodded. 'Well then, I'm sorry. No. I don't know who she is.'

'Any chance you could take this photo and show it to some of your colleagues?' Dee shoved the photo into his hand before he had a chance to refuse. 'My phone number and email address are on the back. If anyone recognises her, tell them to get in touch.'

'Sure.' Lewis nodded and moved away before Dee could ask him anything else.

'You think he'll do anything with the photo?' she asked Ella.

'I doubt it.' Ella frowned. 'He looked scared, didn't he? Like he couldn't wait to get away from you.'

'Why?' Dee wondered.

'Maybe the staff have been warned not to speak to any journalists,' Ella said.

Maybe, Dee thought. Or maybe Lewis was lying.

'This cosmopolitan is divine,' Ella said.

'At fifteen quid, it better be,' Dee said.

'So, this is where Joana came the night she disappeared?'

'According to her friends,' Dee said. 'The problem is, none of the staff I've spoken to so far remember seeing her.'

Earlier, Dee had taken Ed's advice and visited some of the seafront hotels with Joana's photo. In two of them, staff members recognised Joana. In both cases, she'd been seen drinking in the hotel bar. She'd been a regular in the bars of both hotels, and hadn't hidden the fact she'd been there to pick up men.

'But if she was doing it regularly,' the barman in the second hotel told Dee, 'then the Aldrington's your best bet. That's where girls in this town go to find their sugar daddies.'

So Dee had come here tonight with Ella. And judging by the waiter's reaction just then, she'd made the right decision. Clearly, the photo of Joana hadn't been circulated as widely as she'd hoped.

'If she was here to meet men,' Ella said, 'she came to the right place. Have you noticed how many single men are in here tonight?' She frowned. 'You said Joana worked as a cleaner? How did she afford to drink somewhere like this on a cleaner's salary?'

'I think the idea was to get someone else to pay for her cocktails,' Dee said.

'And what did she offer them in return?' Ella asked.

'What do you think?' Dee said.

'It looks to me as if most of the women here tonight are on the prowl,' Ella said. 'I'm guessing coming here and picking up a guy with money is the closest they'll ever get to real money.'

Dee scanned the bar, watching the lovely young people gliding around the room, openly eyeing each other up.

'How do you know they aren't all successful working women who are paying their own way?' she said.

'I'm sure that's true for some of them,' Ella said. 'But so far I've seen three different men order a cocktail and have it delivered to one of the women sitting at the bar. I know I sound cynical, and I'm sure there are women who've come here with their friends because it's beautiful and they can afford to drink cocktails at fifteen pounds a pop. But that wasn't true for Joana, was it?'

'No,' Dee agreed. 'She came here to meet men with money.'

'Well good for her,' Ella said. 'If men are stupid enough to buy expensive drinks just so a pretty girl will talk to them, that's their problem.'

'And what if they think buying a drink gets the pretty girl to do more than just talk?' Dee asked.

'I guess it's up to the girl,' Ella said. 'I'm not saying I agree with it, Dee. But girls like Joana, earning crap money doing crap jobs, what other choice do they have?'

'Right.' Dee made a decision. 'I'm not going to rely on that muppet Lewis to help us.' She took another photo from her bag. 'I'm going to have a chat with some of the customers, see if anyone remembers seeing our girl in here before.'

'Leave a photo with me too,' Ella said. 'If anyone tries to chat me up, I can ask them about her as well.'

Half an hour later, Dee had spoken to several people who recognised Joana's face. They all confirmed she'd been a regular, although none of them could recall seeing her the night she disappeared. But at least Dee now had the proof she needed that Joana had been telling Eliza the truth about where she was going that night.

Dee was on her way back to Ella when she saw Derek French coming towards her, weaving his way through the tables.

'Dee Doran,' he said. 'A pleasure, I'm sure. Although, from what I've been told, this isn't a social visit? I wish you'd told me you were coming. I've already shown your girl's photo to my staff. They tell me she did drink in our bar from time to time, although not the night she disappeared apparently. I was going to call you tomorrow. You could have saved yourself a trip.'

He was bluffing. His voice just a little too loud, his smile a little too forced; and the grip on Dee's arm when he tried to lead her out of the bar was more than a little too tight.

'I need to get back to my friend,' Dee said, pulling her arm free. 'She's over there.'

When Derek looked over at Ella, his smile grew wider and he strode across the room.

'Derek French.' He held out his hand. 'Proprietor, manager and general dogsbody. I don't think I've had the pleasure?'

'Ella.' She shook the outstretched hand. 'I'm a friend of Dee's.'

'Your first time here?' Derek asked. Then, before Ella could answer, he launched into a detailed description of what the hotel had been like when he'd first bought it, and the work that had gone into renovating it.

'It's beautiful,' Ella said, when he paused for breath.

'Very kind of you to say so,' Derek said. 'I hope you'll do us the pleasure of visiting again. Although,' he looked at Dee, 'I'm afraid I must ask you to go through me if you plan to interrogate my customers again. People come here to relax and have a nice time, not to face the Spanish bloody Inquisition.'

'It was hardly an interrogation,' Dee said. 'Actually, Derek, I'm curious. When you say people come here to have a good time, what exactly do you mean?'

His face hardened and she knew he'd understood.

'It's a bar,' he said. 'Bars are where people come to let their hair down at the end of a long day.'

'Is that all Joana was doing when she came here?' Dee asked. 'Because there's something I don't understand. How did a girl like that, on a cleaner's wages, afford to drink in a bar like this?'

Derek shrugged.

'You'll have to ask her that question yourself. Whoops, I forgot. You can't do that, can you? She's done a runner. You know what I think, Dee? I think there are a lot of girls who use their looks to get them what they want in life. My guess is that's exactly what your little foreign friend has done. She's found herself a rich boyfriend to look after her and she's done a bunk with him. You're wasting your time trying to find her. It's not easy finding someone who doesn't want to be found, you know.'

Dee exchanged glances with Ella. It wasn't easy, but they both knew it was possible. Ella had spent three years of her life hiding from her past, although in the end it had caught up with her. The past had a way of doing that. Dee fervently hoped that whatever dark secrets were hidden in Derek French's past, they would catch up with him one day soon. Because there was one thing she was certain about: he was a man with dark secrets.

—

'That hotel is incredible,' Ella said, when they left a few minutes later. 'Shame I can't say the same about the owner.'

'He knows what happened to her,' Dee said.

'How can you be sure?' Ella asked. 'I mean, he definitely came across as a bit of a sleaze, but sleazy men are everywhere. Not all of them make women disappear into thin air. If that was the case, there'd be no women left anywhere.'

As they hurried along the seafront to Dee's car, Dee noticed Louise climbing out of the driver's seat of her red SUV, parked across the road.

'Here.' She thrust the car key into Ella's hand. 'You get into the car. I'll be with you in a sec.'

She ran across the road, shouting for Louise to hold up a second.

'Oh hello,' Louise said, turning around. 'What are you doing here?'

'I told you I was going out,' Dee said. In fact, she'd sent a text to Louise earlier, asking if she was free that evening. Louise had told Dee she was working. 'I thought you were working. You look pretty fancy for work.'

'I've got a thing on at the Cavendish,' Louise said. 'Some boring Chamber of Commerce dinner. Actually, Dee, I'm running late. I'd better get going.'

She air-kissed Dee's cheeks and tottered off on heels that looked far too ridiculous for a night as cold and damp as this one. Dee ran back across the road and got into her car. As she drove off, she caught a final glimpse of Louise in the rear-view mirror. She slowed down, keeping her eyes on Louise, watching as she walked straight past the entrance to the Cavendish Hotel and up the steps and through the ornate doors that led into the lobby of the Aldrington.

For a split second, Dee had an image of her cousin sitting at the bar eyeing the men in the room, deciding which one she was going to pick up tonight. But common sense pushed the image away a moment later. Dee knew her cousin as well as she knew anyone. And there was no way respectable, uptight Louise was going into the hotel to pick up a stranger. The idea was so ridiculous, Dee started to laugh.

Nine

Sunday morning, Dee woke early and went for a walk along the beach. She'd had a text last night from Ed, telling her he was back in Eastbourne and asking if she fancied meeting up later. So far, she hadn't replied. She didn't know how she felt about seeing him. To distract herself from thinking about Ed, she called Louise.

'I'm rushing to the gym,' Louise said. 'You okay?'

'Just phoning to say hi,' Dee said. 'Wondered if you fancied meeting for a coffee or a drink later in the week?'

'I'd love to,' Louise said. 'But can I let you know when would be best? This week is pretty manic.'

'Of course,' Dee said.

'Great. I'll send you a text later today. Catch you later!'

'One more thing,' Dee said. 'How was last night?'

'Last night?'

'The Chamber of Commerce event,' Dee said. In her mind, she was watching Louise again, walking past the Cavendish and up the steps to the Aldrington Hotel.

'Oh that.' Louise sounded relieved. 'It was boring. You know what these events are like. Lots of people there all wanting to tell you about their business and how wonderful it is and why I should write about them and how I could be doing my job better. It wasn't my idea of a night out, to be honest. I was running late so I managed to slip in just before the meal, but it still dragged on.'

Dee didn't say anything, because being honest was not what Louise was doing right now.

'How about you?' Louise said. 'What were you doing when I met you last night?'

'Having a drink with a friend,' Dee said.

'Anyone I know?'

'No,' Dee said. Which was ridiculous, because of course Louise knew Ella. But if Louise was going to lie, then so was she. She said goodbye and hung up, feeling more despondent than ever. What was it with the people she was closest to? First Ed, now Louise. Unless neither of them were hiding things and the problem was her, not them. She had a tendency to overthink things, something that had been a bone of contention with her ex-husband.

When she arrived back at the house, she saw Ed's car parked outside. She'd given him a key a couple of weeks ago. At the time, it had made sense. She wanted him to feel he could come and go as he pleased. Now, she regretted that. She was angry that he hadn't told her he wasn't part of the murder investigation. Angry, and embarrassed that she'd had to hear about it from Louise. It made it look as if she and Ed weren't open with each other, and until this week, Dee would have said openness and honesty lay at the heart of their relationship.

The smell of coffee and bacon that hit her as soon as she opened the front door went some way towards improving her mood. The warm hug and the soft kiss that greeted her when she went into the kitchen helped too.

'I wanted to make up for the last few days,' Ed said, pouring freshly brewed coffee into a mug and passing it to Dee.

'You've had a lot to deal with,' Dee said. 'You don't have to make up for anything.'

'I think I do,' Ed said. 'So if you don't mind, would you kindly take a seat and let me serve you a bacon butty with as much coffee as you want?'

'Why not as much bacon butty as I want?' Dee asked.

'That too,' Ed said, smiling. 'Obviously. Pass the ketchup, would you?'

'Brown sauce for me,' Dee said, sliding the bottle of Heinz across the worktop.

'Duh.'

'Sorry.' Dee took a sip of her coffee. 'Oh my God, this is good. Hurry up with the food, would you? I've already walked ten thousand steps today. I'm starving.'

They ate in a silence that would have been comfortable if Dee hadn't sent her mind into overdrive trying to work out how to ask him about the investigation. In the end, all her worrying was for nothing because Ed broached it himself as soon as he'd finished his second sandwich.

'There's something I need to talk to you about.'

'Well you've got a captive audience.' Dee gestured at the pieces of bacon still left. 'I'm not moving from here until all of that is eaten.'

'About two minutes then,' Ed said. 'I'd better be quick.'

'Smart-arse.' Dee took another two pieces of bacon, laid them on a slice of white bread and covered the whole lot with brown sauce.

'I'm not going to be part of the investigation into Lauren Shaw's murder,' Ed said.

'Any reason for that?' Dee took a bite of her sandwich, waited for him to say something else.

'I knew her,' Ed said after a moment. 'Not very well, but clearly any personal involvement means a potential conflict of interest so...' He shrugged. 'I'm off the case.'

'Maybe you could take a few days off?' Dee suggested. 'We could take that trip to Venice you've been talking about.'

'I think Sharon has other plans,' Ed said. 'There's some fraud case she wants me to get involved with. We'll still get to Venice one day, I promise.'

'How did you know her?' Dee asked.

'Barely at all,' Ed said. 'Her family and mine, there's a bit of uncomfortable history there.'

'What sort of history?' Dee thought of the days and nights they'd spent together over the last six months, sharing so much of their past with each other. Foolishly, part of her had thought she knew all the important information there was to know about Ed's life.

'It's nothing, really,' Ed said. 'I have a tricky relationship with Nigel – Lauren's father. We've never really seen eye to eye. And I know Maxine, of course.'

'Maxine?'

'Lauren's mum.' Ed frowned. 'I've told you about her before, remember?'

Vaguely, Dee remembered Ed mentioning a girlfriend called Maxine.

'I thought that was years ago,' she said.

'It was. But I still know her. Anyway, Sharon and I agreed it was better for me not to be involved.'

Dee took another bite of her sandwich while she thought about this. His explanation sounded plausible, so why did she have the feeling he wasn't being entirely honest with her?

'You sure that's all there is to it?' she said.

'What do you mean?'

'I mean, you said you sort of knew Lauren,' Dee said. 'Then a moment later you said you didn't really know her, but you didn't get on with her father. And then you said you can't work on the case because you used to go out with her mother. So, which is it?'

'Does it matter?' Ed asked.

'It matters to me.'

'Why?'

'Because I have trust issues,' Dee said. 'And I'm sorry if you find that difficult to deal with, but it's the truth.'

'When have I ever given you the impression you can't trust me?' Ed said.

'How about now?' Dee said. 'There's something you're not telling me, and I want to know what that is.'

Ed pushed his chair back and stood up. 'You can want all you like, Dee. But believe it or not, I don't have to tell you about every aspect of my life if I don't feel ready for that. If you can't handle that, if you can't cope with an adult relationship where two people trust each other enough to let them work through some things by themselves, then maybe I'm not the right person for you.'

'You were the one who came here this morning,' Dee said. Her voice was calm but she could feel a red-hot rage burning inside her. 'You didn't have to do that if you didn't want to talk to me. You didn't even have to tell me you'd been taken off the stupid case if you didn't want to. But you were the one who brought it up, and you can't blame me for wanting to know why you're not being straight with me.'

Ed put his two hands flat on the table and leaned forward until his face was close to hers.

'I have never not been straight with you,' he said. 'But no matter what I do, no matter how hard I try to prove to you that I'm not the same as your scumbag ex-husband, it's never going to be enough, is it? Because you've already decided that all men are lying bastards and it seems there's nothing I can do to change that.'

'Don't you ever speak about Billy like that again.'

Ed stepped back and Dee waited for him to say something else.

He shook his head.

'Why does everything with you have to be so bloody difficult? Why do you have to challenge everything and question everything? It makes me feel like I'm on trial the whole time, you know that?'

Dee couldn't think of a single response that wouldn't make this stupid row worse than it already was. So she said nothing. Not even when Ed grabbed his jacket and stormed out, slamming the front door so hard as he left that the whole house seemed to vibrate.

Ten

Three hours later, Ed stood outside his house, waiting for his heartbeat to slow to something approaching normal. He'd got into his running gear as soon as he'd got home from Dee's and gone for a long run – across the downs as far as Beachy Head and back again. At some point while he'd been running, the irrational anger that had made him act like such a massive arse subsided. Replaced by shame. He'd replayed the conversation over and over in his head, trying to find some rational explanation for the way he'd reacted. But each time, he reached the same sorry conclusion: he had behaved like a complete and utter idiot. No wonder Dee had got so angry.

He put his key into the lock and opened the door. He was going to shower and drive over there right away and beg Dee to forgive him. Then he would tell her the real reason he'd been taken off the case. And he'd try to explain why he hadn't felt able to simply tell her the truth the first time around. He just hoped she'd accept 'because I'm an idiot' as an adequate explanation.

He'd left his phone behind when he'd gone for his run. Picking it up from the table in the hall, he saw that Dee had called while he was out. He called her back, his mood lifting at the prospect of getting past this ridiculous argument. The call went straight to voicemail, so he left a message telling her he was sorry and asking her to call him back.

After drinking some water, he went upstairs to shower and get changed. He had just finished dressing when his mobile started to ring. He answered it without checking the caller ID.

'Dee? Thank goodness you called back. I'm so, so sorry for earlier.'

'Ed?'

A woman's voice, but not Dee.

'It's Karen,' the woman said. 'Karen French?'

Derek's wife and Kyle's mother. Ed knew Karen from the rugby club. Clearly, she'd kept his number stored in her phone even after he'd stopped coaching her son.

'Hey, Karen.' Ed sat on the side of the bed.

'They told me you'd been taken off the investigation,' Karen said. 'Is that right?'

'Yes it is. Listen, Karen, I'm so sorry about Lauren. You all must be devastated.'

'Utterly heartbroken,' Karen said. 'That poor child. I've prayed for her soul each night since we heard the terrible news.'

'And Kyle? How's he doing?'

'How do you think?' Karen said. 'His girlfriend's been murdered and your colleagues think he killed her.'

'I'm sure that's not true.' Ed was starting to regret answering his phone. His interactions with Kyle's mother had always been tricky. While she claimed to be a devout Christian, Karen was more than happy to be derogatory about the other players on the team, particularly if she thought they were getting better treatment than her son. She could be charming when she wanted to be, but she could also be demanding and difficult when she wasn't getting her own way.

'Well I'm sure it is,' Karen said. 'That's why I'm calling. I need you to speak up for Kyle. You know him, Ed. You were his rugby coach for five years. Can't you tell Rachel Lewis that Kyle would never do something like that?'

He'd been a good kid, Ed remembered. Unlike a lot of the young rugby jocks, Kyle was a real softie. The sort of bloke you couldn't imagine ever hurting anyone. Although experience had taught Ed that even good people were capable of murder when pushed too far.

'I've already told Rachel I think Kyle's a good kid,' Ed said. 'But she has a job to do, and that means investigating everyone who knew Lauren.'

'If you're not part of the investigation,' Karen said, 'couldn't you do some detective work on the side?'

'What do you mean?'

'Ask around, see what you can dig up. Everyone knows what really happened. Nigel killed her, and now he's bullied Maxine into covering up for him.'

Ed's body stiffened as he was assailed with a series of memories from his childhood, incidents he'd done his best to forget.

'Why would you say that?'

'Lauren and Nigel weren't even on speaking terms at the end,' Karen said. 'A few weeks before she was killed, they had a terrible row. She moved out. Came to live with us. Which wasn't ideal, as I'm sure you can imagine. I didn't approve, of course. But Kyle is an adult now and Derek says I have to let him live his life the way he wants to. Anyway, my point is that everyone knows Lauren and Nigel argued, but no one's going around saying he killed her. Instead, they're so focused on poor Kyle they're ignoring everything else. You need to tell Rachel to look at his alibi a bit more closely. He claims he was with Maxine the night Lauren was killed, but he's lying.'

Ed needed to get his thoughts in order; make sure he didn't let his hatred of Nigel Shaw get in the way of the right thing to do.

'I can't do that,' he said. 'I'm sorry, Karen.'

'So you won't help.' Karen's voice was flat, devoid of all emotion. If Ed had felt bad after his row with Dee, he felt a whole lot worse now.

'I would if I could,' he said.

'Sure you would,' Karen said. 'Thanks for nothing, Ed.'

She hung up before he had a chance to say anything else. Ed put the phone down and buried his face in his hands. Once again, his mind flashed back to last week. The email from Lauren telling him she needed to see him. The email he'd ignored, because he was trying to do the right thing.

—

Dee knew she'd lied. Louise spent the rest of the morning running over their conversation, wondering what she'd let slip. She couldn't think of a single thing. And yet, somehow, Dee had guessed she wasn't telling the truth.

'Everything okay?'

Martin's voice made her jump. He'd come into the kitchen without her realising.

'Fine,' she said, struggling to keep the irritation out of her voice. Knowing it was her fault, not his, that he was annoying her. Everything he did these days seemed to annoy her. But she couldn't tell him that without telling him the reasons why. So she kept quiet instead. Letting her frustration fester until, if she wasn't careful, she would simply snap one day and tell him everything. And there was no way she could do that.

'Kids are asking if they can go to the park for a bit,' Martin said. 'I thought we could take them together. Maybe stop off somewhere for a drink afterwards?'

The neediness in his voice made her want to scream. All these years, when he'd spent more time away from his family than with them, why now did he suddenly want to have all this time together?

'I've got work to do,' she said. 'And I haven't even started on the dinner yet. Why don't you take them and I'll see if I can finish up here as quickly as possible. Maybe I can come and join you for that drink after that?'

'Okay.' Martin nodded. 'Sure.'

He turned to go, then paused. She tensed, waiting for the inevitable question.

'You sure everything's okay with us?'

'Absolutely.' She forced herself to smile, even though all she wanted to do was scream. 'I'm just tired, Martin. Work and the kids, you know what it's like.'

'I know it's not easy when I'm away,' he said. 'And I'm sorry you've had to carry so much by yourself. But I'm trying my best to change, Lou. I really am.'

'I know.' She kept the smile fixed onto her face, but stepped out of the way when he leaned forward to kiss her.

'Right then.' He nodded. 'I'll tell the kids to get their shoes on. I'll call you when we're done in the park and see how you're getting on.'

'Great.'

She wondered if he knew she wouldn't meet him later. He wasn't stupid, Martin. He knew something wasn't right between them. She'd done her best to protect him. But it wasn't easy protecting someone when every moment you were with them they drove you crazy.

The worst of it was, she could see how hard he was trying. He was right. It hadn't been easy all those years when his job as a pilot meant he spent more time away from his family than with them. Although she could hardly blame him for that. She'd known what she was getting into when she'd married him. But juggling a full-time job and taking care of two children had been harder than she could ever have anticipated. Over the years, it had ground her down, but she'd never found a way to tell him how hard she was finding it. She'd always felt the need to prove, not just to Martin but to everyone else too, how capable she was. When all the time, deep down, she hadn't been capable at all. She'd been falling apart.

And now, just when she should be reaping the rewards of all those endlessly difficult years, she'd done something so catastrophically stupid she risked losing all of it – the nice house, the loving husband and her children.

She stood alone in the kitchen, listening to the familiar noise of her family as they bundled themselves into coats and shoes and hats for their excursion to the park. She was about to run out and tell them to wait, that she'd changed her mind, when she felt her phone buzzing with a text message. She knew she should leave it. But she didn't. She couldn't. It was too late to go back and change what she'd started. And even if she was able to, she wasn't sure that was what she wanted. Forgetting all about her husband

and children, she took her phone out of her pocket and read the text, her fingers already tapping a reply as the front door slammed shut.

Eleven

When she eventually calmed down, Dee felt bad about the way she'd reacted earlier. She called Ed to apologise, but he didn't answer. Instead, she got an electronic recording telling her to leave a message. As there was no way she was apologising to a robot, she hung up without saying anything. She'd tried, at least. Sooner or later, he'd see that she'd tried to call him. And then it was up to him whether or not he wanted to call her back.

To distract herself from thinking about him all afternoon, she decided to work. The story that had started out as an investigation into a missing woman had turned into something else. Something darker and more complicated. Dee sat on her living room floor, a piece of A3 paper laid out in front of her. It was how she liked to work. Writing down all the different pieces of the story and trying to find the connections.

She worked in the way she'd done since she started as an investigative journalist twenty-five years ago. Putting each piece of information onto the page, and using lines to indicate a connection – a dotted line for a possible link between two things or people, an unbroken line where there was a definite link, and no line if there was no connection.

She started with the things she knew, writing 'Aldrington Hotel' in the middle of the page. From this, she drew a straight line to Joana's name. Over the line, Dee wrote the date Joana had last been seen. Working quickly, she added more names, until the page contained as much information as Dee could remember about Joana's disappearance, and Lauren's murder.

When she was finished, she sat back and looked at it all. There was nothing on the paper she didn't know already, but seeing it laid out like this helped clarify her thinking. She'd been right to start with the hotel. There were too many lines connecting it to the other information on the page. Something had happened there. And because of that, one girl was missing and another was dead. What was it? The answer wasn't there on the paper in front of her. It was hidden behind those connecting lines somewhere. Dee couldn't see it yet, but she would find it.

By the time she'd finished, the sky had grown dark outside and it had started to rain. She'd left her phone charging in her bedroom. When she went to get it, she saw a missed call from Ed and a voicemail alert. When she'd finished listening to his message, she stood by the bed, looking out the window at the dark night, listening to the steady rhythm of the rain beating against the house, wondering whether or not to call him back. In the end, he got there first.

'Hey,' she said, putting the phone to her ear. 'I'm glad you called.'

'I'm sorry,' he said. 'I shouldn't have got so defensive. You had every right to be angry with me.'

'No,' Dee said. 'I overreacted, and I shouldn't have done that. I'm sorry.'

'We're both sorry then. Any chance we could put this behind us?'

'Of course,' Dee said, wondering if she meant it. 'Actually, there's something I wanted to ask you.'

'Anything.'

She smiled. 'Don't say that until you know what it is. I've been going back over Joana's disappearance. I want to dig a bit deeper into how she and Lauren knew each other.'

'I thought we'd already spoken about this.'

'Not really,' Dee said. 'You told me the two things weren't connected. But you can't know that for certain.'

'But you've seen the news.' Ed sounded frustrated. 'It's clear that whoever killed Lauren was sending some sort of message about Mary Palmer's murder.'

'Is it?' Dee frowned.

'Yes. Besides, it's not your job to start investigating Lauren's murder.'

'Because I'm only a journalist?'

'I didn't mean it like that.' Ed sighed. 'If you want to look into it, then go ahead. I just think you'll be wasting your time, that's all.'

And thank you so much for that vote of confidence, Dee thought. She wanted to tell him his attitude was patronising, but she didn't. The last thing she wanted was another row. Besides, she needed his help, and she was more likely to get that if she stayed on his good side.

'You're probably right,' she said, adopting a tone she hoped was conciliatory. No easy task, given the mood he'd put her in. 'But if I did look into it, would you help me?'

'How?'

Dee noted sourly that he'd gone from offering her 'anything' a moment ago to sounding as if he didn't want to help at all.

'I'd like to speak with Kyle,' she said. 'And I was wondering – as you already know him, would you possibly put in a good word for me?'

'I'm sorry, Dee. I would have done – really I would. But I've just had a falling-out with his mother. I'm pretty sure any recommendation from me would make things worse.'

'You're not just saying that?' The words were out before she could stop them.

'What's that supposed to mean?'

'Nothing,' she said.

'It didn't sound like nothing. Do you really think I'd lie to you just to avoid putting in a good word on your behalf?'

'No. I don't think that. I'm frustrated, Ed, that's all. A young woman is missing and, from what I can see, hardly anyone seems to care. Now I've got something that might help me find out what happened to her—'

'Okay,' Ed interrupted. 'You're right. I genuinely don't believe looking into Lauren's murder will help you find out what's happened to Joana, but I understand why you feel you have to do it.'

'You do?'

'Yes, actually. You care a lot about people, and I've seen how much Joana's disappearance is getting to you. I can understand why you're desperate to prove the two things are connected. Even though it's obvious they're not.'

'Not to me. And for your information, I'm not desperate. I'm simply doing my job.'

'I just think your passion for what you do means you lose focus sometimes.'

'You do?'

'Just a little. I mean, look at it logically for a minute.'

Dee bit down hard on her lip to stop herself screaming that looking logically at Joana's disappearance was *exactly* what she'd been doing.

'Every bit of evidence so far,' Ed said, 'points to a clear link between Lauren's murder and what happened to Mary Palmer. Which means you're wasting your time trying to find some other reason for why she was killed. That's the problem with journalism. When you're a detective, you go where the evidence takes you. Nowhere else. But journalism lacks that strict discipline, which means it's easier to get distracted by information that's not directly relevant to the story you're writing.'

'Well then,' Dee said. 'Thanks for that. Goodness, what would I do without you? My little woman's brain could never have worked that out all by myself. I'm really sorry I've wasted your time talking about this. Clearly, that was a mistake.'

Ed started to say something but she didn't hear. She'd already hung up. And when he called back a moment later, she switched her phone off so she wouldn't have to listen to another second of his patronising attempts to mansplain her job and her motivations.

Twelve

Karen French was nothing like Dee had imagined. Unlike her husband, who was flashy to the point of trashy, everything about Karen's appearance seemed designed to make her as invisible as possible. Wiry grey hair, cut short; a brown cardigan over a cream blouse; a knee-length woollen skirt, also brown, and a pair of brown, sensible brogues on her feet. The only items of jewellery she wore were a silver chain necklace with a crucifix pendant and a gold wedding ring.

She didn't seem pleased when Dee introduced herself.

'My husband's told me all about you,' Karen said. 'You've been asking questions at the hotel. Upsetting his staff, from what I hear.'

'I've done my best not to upset anyone,' Dee said. 'But a young woman is missing, and I seem to be the only person trying to find her.'

'Well I don't know anything about that,' Karen said. 'And if you think I'm letting a journalist into my house to start interrogating my family, you can think again. Hang on, was this Ed's idea?'

'Ed?'

'You are his girlfriend, aren't you?'

'How do you know that?' Dee asked.

'I make it my business to know what's going on.' Karen frowned. 'Dee. What sort of name is that?'

'My full name is Delilah.' Dee was starting to dislike the woman a lot.

'Book of Judges,' Karen said. 'It means *faithless one*, did you know that?'

'I went to a Catholic school,' Dee said. 'So yes, I'm more than familiar with the story of Samson and Delilah.'

She didn't bother pointing out that her father had actually named her after the doomed woman in the 1968 Tom Jones classic, rather than a character from the Bible.

'I know I asked Ed if he could help,' Karen said. 'But I didn't expect him to send you. We've had more than enough trouble from your lot these last few days.'

'Ed's told me what a great kid Kyle is,' Dee said, seeing her chance and grabbing it. She hadn't known that Karen had asked Ed to help her. Another thing he'd forgotten to tell her. 'I'd love to help prove he didn't kill Lauren. If you'll let me? I know that's what Ed would want too.'

In fact, the opposite was true. If Ed knew Dee was offering to try to prove Kyle's innocence he'd have a fit. But right now, Dee didn't care what he thought. She'd woken up this morning every bit as angry with him as she'd been the previous evening. If he didn't like what she was doing, that was his problem.

'I'm not sure,' Karen said, but Dee sensed she was wavering.

'What's the harm?' Dee asked. 'We both know Kyle is innocent, right?'

'So what do you suggest?'

'Let me speak to him,' Dee said. 'Once I've done that, I can think about how best I can help.'

'Why?' Karen said.

'Why what?'

'What do you get out of helping him? Because you can't write about this, you know. I'm not letting you into my house if that's why you're here.'

'If Kyle is innocent,' Dee said, 'then helping him is the right thing to do.'

'Call me cynical,' Karen said. 'But I don't believe someone like you would be willing to help someone just because it's *the right thing to do*.' She used her index fingers to make speech marks as she said this.

'Maybe it's better if I leave then.'

Dee turned to go, but Karen called her back.

'Wait,' she said. 'This isn't easy for me. My family is everything, you see. And right now, the police are threatening to rip us apart and I can't stand it. I simply cannot endure what's happening to us.'

'It must be very difficult,' Dee said. Although she couldn't help thinking of Lauren's family. However bad this was for Karen, it was nothing compared to what Lauren's mother must be going through right now.

'It's a living nightmare,' Karen said. 'I truly don't know what we've done to deserve this. I do wish Ed had sent someone else, but you're here now. You can speak to Kyle on one condition.'

'What's that?'

'I don't want you asking him about that girl who's missing.'

'Even if I believe her disappearance might help prove Kyle's innocence?'

'It won't,' Karen said. 'We all know who killed Lauren and why. And that's got nothing to do with that other girl.'

'What do you mean?'

'Her father did it,' Karen said. 'I know it. The police know it, and your friend Ed certainly knows it. But Nigel's an influential man and the police are too scared to do the right thing and arrest him.'

All of this was news to Dee and she felt another surge of anger at Ed for keeping this from her as well.

'You might as well come in,' Karen said. 'But remember, you speak to him about Lauren and nothing else, understood?'

Dee opened her mouth to answer but Karen was already speaking again.

'I'll take you into the kitchen. You can wait there while I go and get him.'

Dee followed Karen down a wide corridor into a big, modern kitchen with doors leading onto the garden. It should have been a light, airy space but the black fixtures and fittings made the room seem gloomy despite the sunshine.

'I'll be back in a minute,' Karen said, leaving Dee alone.

True to her word, a few minutes later Dee heard the murmur of voices in the hallway.

'Just remember what I told you,' Karen whispered before she opened the door and ushered her son into the kitchen.

'This is Kyle,' she said.

He was a handsome boy. Or he would be, if grief hadn't washed all the colour from his skin and left him hunched up as if he didn't have the strength to support his own body. He was tall, like his mother, with his father's sandy-coloured hair and blue eyes.

'And this,' Karen said to her son, 'is Ed's friend. She's going to help prove you didn't kill Lauren.' Then, before Dee could explain that wasn't exactly true, Karen asked if she wanted coffee.

'Coffee would be lovely,' Dee said. 'Kyle? It's good to meet you. I'm so sorry about Lauren. Is there somewhere we could go and chat?'

'What's wrong with the kitchen?' Karen asked.

'I'd like to talk to Kyle by myself,' Dee said. 'If that's okay with you, Kyle?'

She didn't want to talk to him here, with his mother beside them listening to every word the boy told her.

'Yeah,' he said. 'Sure.' And then, when his mother started to protest, 'It's okay, Mum. I don't need you with me every second of the day making sure I'm okay. Let me talk to Dee by myself.'

'Just be careful,' Karen said. 'She's a journalist. We both know what they're like.'

'I'm sorry about my mum,' Kyle said as they left the kitchen. 'She can be a bit funny when she's upset, that's all.'

Funny was one way of describing it, Dee thought. Downright rude was another.

'We can talk in the den,' Kyle said. 'It's just down here.'

He led her into a large room at the side of the house that was clearly his space. Unlike the rest of the house, this room was bright and light and full of colour and mess. Posters of rugby teams on the wall. Brightly coloured cushions, sofas and several beanbags scattered across the floor.

'My ex-husband was murdered last year,' Dee said, when they were both sitting down. 'I don't think you ever really get over something like that. But time does help, Kyle. I promise.'

'She wasn't my ex,' Kyle said. 'Everyone keeps telling me time is a great healer. But I know in here,' he punched his chest, 'I'll never stop loving her and I'll never stop grieving.'

Dee wanted to tell him both those things were true but also that he'd find a way to move on with his life. That one day, he would fall in love again, maybe even marry and have kids of his own. But she didn't say anything because she knew that, when you are in the grip of a great grief, those sorts of sentiments are meaningless.

'What was she like?' she said instead.

'Beautiful,' Kyle said. 'Clever, funny. Not perfect, of course, because no one's perfect. But better than perfect, in a way. More interesting, if that makes sense.'

Dee smiled. 'I've always thought perfect people are the most boring sort of people.'

Kyle nodded and looked as if he was about say something, but Karen came into the room before he could speak. She was carrying a tray with two mugs on it and a plate of chocolate biscuits.

'Coffee,' she said brightly. 'And some biscuits in case anyone's hungry.'

She placed the tray on the coffee table and handed a cup to Dee.

'Is everything all right?' she asked.

'Fine,' Dee said. 'Thank you.'

'Kyle? Would you like me to stay?'

'I'm okay,' Kyle said. 'Really, Mum. Stop worrying. I'll come and find you when we're finished, okay?'

She looked like she was going to refuse, but instead she sighed and said: 'At least I know I've tried. Don't forget to tell her about Nigel. She needs to understand what he's like.'

And then, before Dee or Kyle could respond, Karen left the room.

'Do you really think you can help find out who killed her?' Kyle asked.

'I'm not sure,' Dee said honestly. 'But I'd like to try, at least.'

'You promise you're not going to write about this?'

'Cross my heart.'

'I keep thinking my phone's going to ring,' Kyle said. 'Or someone's going to call around to the house telling me this is all some terrible mistake.' His voice wobbled. 'But then I realise that's never going to happen. She's actually… dead.'

He stopped speaking and Dee could see he was struggling not to cry. She had to fight down the urge to cross the room and wrap her arms around him.

'Tell me about the last time you saw her,' she said.

'We had a row,' he said. 'That's why the police keep questioning me. We argued and lots of people saw us. The police seem to think that because we rowed, that was enough for me to do *that* to her.'

He looked at Dee, as if she might be able to explain the unexplainable to him.

'What did you row about?' Dee asked.

'She'd changed,' Kyle said. 'A few months ago, she decided she was going to write about Mary Palmer's murder. You know Mary was her dad's cousin?'

Dee nodded and Kyle continued speaking.

'They didn't know each other. Obviously. Lauren wasn't even born when Mary was killed. But I suppose if you grow up knowing about something like that, it affects you. Lauren wanted to be a journalist. Like you. She'd tried writing a few pieces but didn't have much luck. She started thinking about what else she could do, and she came up with the idea to write about Mary. She was really excited about it, at first. And I was happy for her, because I knew how much it meant to her. But one day it all changed. She'd gone to her grandmother's house to look through her things. Research, she said. And she found something. I don't know what, because she wouldn't tell me. But after that, she stopped talking about Mary's murder. Any time I asked, she changed the subject. And then, that night, I asked her about it again, and she lost it. I mean, she went mental. We had this huge row and she stormed off. That was the last time I saw her.'

He broke off, unable to hold off the crying any longer.

'I didn't kill her,' he sobbed. 'I swear to you, I would never have hurt her. I loved her. I loved her so much and now she's gone I'll never be able to tell her how much she meant to me.'

This time, Dee did cross over and sit beside him. She held him while he cried, letting him sob until there were no tears left. His pain was so raw it was all she could do not to cry herself.

'Sorry,' he mumbled after a while. 'It's all I do these days. I sit here in this house crying and thinking of her. It's like a really bad nightmare, except it's worse than the worst nightmare because I know I'll never wake up.'

'You've no idea what she found?'

'She wouldn't tell me,' Kyle said. 'But whatever it was, it caused friction with her dad. They'd always been really close and suddenly – bam. She refused to have anything to do with him. I wanted to help, but how can you help someone if they won't talk to you?'

'Do you think Lauren's dad killed her?' Dee asked.

'Maybe,' Kyle said. 'It's what my mum thinks. I mean, part of me can't imagine him hurting her like that. But I can't imagine anyone doing that. Yet someone did, didn't they?'

He trailed off and Dee didn't push him any further. She'd wanted to show him a photo of Joana and ask if he recognised her, but she was worried his mother would come back in and catch her in the act. She would have to find another time to ask him about Joana.

Kyle looked exhausted and ready to burst into tears again. Dee promised she'd do some digging around, took his phone number and asked if it was okay to call him again in a few days' time.

As she was getting into her car, she glanced back at the house and saw Karen standing at one of the upstairs windows, watching her. She was still watching as Dee drove away, a dark shadow in the rear-view mirror, fading to grey and then disappearing entirely as Dee turned out of the long driveway onto the road.

From the diary of Emma Reed

24 April 1960

Yesterday, we buried him. Today, I want to write about him. This diary is for him now. One day, someone will read what's written here and they will know. My son was innocent. He was a victim, just like poor Mary. There's an evil in this town. It festers beneath the surface and it's not immediately apparent. But once you've seen it, you can't unsee it.

Graham Reed, my son. Born 2 February 1942. A war baby. It was a difficult birth, worse than anything I could have imagined. Later, as he got older and we realised there was something wrong with him, I wondered if the birth had damaged his brain in some way. I wanted to ask someone, but there was no one I could speak to because James would never admit there was a problem.

He was a lovely baby, cherubic almost, with his rosy red cheeks and big brown eyes. We thought he was perfect. It was only after he started school that we realised there was a problem. They were little things, at first. He was behind with his learning. His teachers said it was insolence, that he could learn if he put his mind to it. After all, it wasn't as if Graham came from one of those families whose parents are barely able to read and write. We are educated people and there was an expectation that our son would excel in his academic life.

But he didn't excel, not in anything. He didn't make friends easily. The other children teased him and there were too many days when poor Graham would come home in tears because of some incident that had taken place. Nine times out of ten, when I'd sit him down and try to find out what had caused him to be so upset, Richard Partridge's name would get a mention. Richard and, sometimes, his brother David.

David wasn't a bad boy, but he was too easily led by his older, nastier brother. I suspect he still is. Too often when Richard stared teasing Graham, David joined in. I tried to tell Graham he needed to stand up for himself, but he didn't seem to know how. I should have spoken to someone about it, but I never did. I was reluctant, I think, to be open about my son's weakness. I regret that now, along with so much else.

Graham was a handsome boy, and a handsome young man. As he grew older, I would notice the way girls looked at him. In those moments, I was proud to be his mother. I should have been proud all the time, but I was too shallow to see that the things I thought were important – our standing in the community, our desire to live vicariously through our children's successes – counted for nothing.

If Graham had been a girl, no one would have cared that he wasn't clever. A pretty girl can go a long way on her looks alone. But being handsome isn't enough for a man. Men have to be clever as well, because they have to get an education and a good job so they can support a wife and a family. There are plenty of women who would be more than capable of supporting a family if they were allowed to get an education and a good job. But that's not the way society works. We thought it would change after the war. We were foolish.

Graham got through school, but his options after that were limited. Even if you come from a good family, no university's going to take a man who can barely read and write. I worried for him, but I held on to the hope that things would come right for him eventually. He had his whole life ahead of him and I was confident that, with time, he'd find his path.

I should have stopped worrying. I should have been content to simply let him be. Why wasn't it all right for him to live with us and let us take care of him the way he needed and deserved? Why did I, his mother, who should have protected him and kept him safe, feel the need to keep pushing and pushing?

Because I was jealous. There. I've said it. I was jealous of other parents, who had 'normal' children who led 'normal' lives and didn't cause their parents endless problems and worry. Dinner parties were the worst. The men puffed up with their self-importance, and the women preening and twittering like birds. Inevitably, the conversation would turn to our children, all of them vying to prove how brilliant and successful their offspring were. As if their children's successes in life were proof of their own brilliance.

I hated all of it, but James insisted, and I had no choice but to go along with what he wanted. At least now, I won't have to pretend. No one will be inviting us to dinner parties any time soon. We are pariahs.

People say my son is a murderer, but these people are ignorant and small-minded and they don't know what they are talking about. He wasn't clever, but that doesn't make him a killer. A person can be stupid and good, just as they can be clever and evil.

An evil person killed poor Mary. And evil people killed my son. I will not rest until those people are found, and made to pay for what they've done.

Thirteen

Ed sat in the canteen with Rachel, drinking bad coffee and trying not to think about Dee. He still didn't understand why she'd got so angry yesterday. Trying to prove that Lauren's murder had something to do with the missing girl was a complete waste of time. Sooner or later, Dee would work that out too. In the meantime, all he could do was wait until she'd calmed down and was ready to speak to him.

'Are you actually listening to a word I'm saying?' Rachel's voice dragged Ed back to the canteen and the dreadful coffee.

'Sorry,' he said. 'I was miles away.'

'I could see that,' Rachel said. 'What's got you so distracted?'

He told her about the row with Dee, expecting her to understand. Instead, when he'd finished her lips were twitching and she looked suspiciously like she was trying not to laugh.

'You think it's funny?' he said.

'Telling Dee she was wasting her time and her job lacked discipline?' Rachel grinned. 'I'm not surprised she wasn't too happy about that.'

'I was only telling her the truth,' Ed protested. 'It would be worse if I lied, wouldn't it?'

'There are different ways of telling the truth.' Rachel shook her head. 'Why do men find it so hard to understand that?'

He had no idea what she was trying to tell him, and no inclination to talk about it any further, either. If Rachel couldn't see things from his perspective, what was the point?

'How's the investigation going?' he asked, getting to the real reason he'd come in early and asked her to go for a coffee with him.

'Not very well,' Rachel said. 'The only possible suspects we've got are Kyle and Nigel. Both are reported to have argued with Lauren, which serves as potential motive. They both have alibis – Nigel's wife and Kyle's mother – but we don't know if they're telling the truth or lying to protect their loved ones.'

'Nigel's a bully. I wouldn't put it past him to make Maxine lie for him.'

'You know I can't talk about that.' Rachel looked at her watch. 'I've already said more than I should have. I need to go. I've a busy day ahead of me.'

'You're still investigating possible links with Mary Palmer?'

Rachel put her cup down, so hard the table vibrated.

'I am not going to have this conversation,' she said. 'You knew the victim. And, as for Nigel, it's no secret to anyone who's been working on this case that you and he can't stand each other.' Her face softened a little. 'I know how weird this feels, Ed. It's weird for me too. We're used to being a team. You know if there was any way I could work with you on this, I'd jump at it. Instead, I'm stuck with Barry bloody twatface O'Connor. Who, by the way, has become unbearable since we've started working together. He's so bloody ambitious I don't feel we're really working as a team. Not the way you and I do, anyway.'

'You could always bounce ideas off me,' Ed said. 'In a completely unofficial manner, of course.'

'I could,' Rachel said. 'But I won't, so let's change the subject. How's your case going?'

Ed shrugged. He'd been given a fraud case to look into but, so far, the work wasn't exactly challenging.

'It's sad,' he said.

'How so?'

'The suspect's a single mother with a severely disabled child,' Ed said. 'She's worked as an accountant with the same firm for the last fifteen years. During this time, she's siphoned off the best part of three-quarters of a million pounds.'

'Wow.' Rachel frowned. 'I don't get what's sad about it, though?'

'She took all the money to care for her son,' Ed said. 'At least, that's what she's claimed, and I think she's telling the truth.'

'I can see that's sad,' Rachel said. 'But it's not your problem, is it? Your job is to build a case for the CPS.'

'I know,' Ed said. 'I've got more than enough evidence to do that. But it doesn't stop me feeling sorry for her. She'll be prosecuted, and if she's convicted she's looking at up to five years inside. Her son's never been cared for by anyone else, and there aren't any other relatives. He'll be taken into care.'

'And that there's your problem, Ed Mitchell,' Rachel said. 'You're a big softy at heart. Oh Jesus, look who's just walked in.'

Barry O'Connor, Rachel's interim partner, had come into the canteen and was making a beeline for their table. He was a tall, broad man and his footsteps echoed loudly against the tiled floor and concrete walls of the canteen.

'Boss is looking for us,' he told Rachel, ignoring Ed. 'I've been trying to call. Where's your phone?' He was breathing heavily, as if he'd been running.

'On silent,' Rachel said. 'But I told you I was going for a coffee. I'm not sure what the problem is.'

'It's the boss,' Barry said. 'She wants to see us. Pronto.'

Rachel rolled her eyes at Ed as she stood up.

'Let's try to catch up in a few days,' she said. 'You can tell me more about your case.'

Ed watched them leave, trying to ignore the unpleasant feeling of being left out of something important. Barry strode ahead of Rachel, not even bothering to hold the door open as he pushed through it in front of her. Rachel was right. Barry O'Connor really was a Grade A idiot.

At least office politics was something he didn't need to worry about over the next few weeks. He sighed. Speaking to Rachel had been a waste of time. He should have known she wouldn't open up to him about the case. She didn't understand. No one did.

Fourteen

On Monday, Louise called Dee and asked if she fancied a night out. They arranged to meet at seven o'clock at the Lamb. It was a clear evening and Dee decided to walk. A decision she regretted by the time she finally arrived at the pub, almost half an hour late. Breathless from walking too fast for the last half-mile, she plonked down on the seat opposite Louise and breathed a sigh of relief.

'Sorry,' she said, when she was able to speak. 'I didn't realise it would take me so long.'

'You walked?' Louise said. 'It's freezing out. And it must be – what? – five miles from your house to here?'

'Five and a half,' Dee said. 'Even you can't say I don't deserve a large glass of wine after that.'

She leaned over, lifted the bottle of Sauvignon Blanc Louise had already ordered and poured a generous measure into the empty glass in front of her. She took a long sip and smiled. 'Now you're talking.'

'I assume we're eating,' Louise said. 'I've got some menus but I was waiting for you before ordering.'

'Good girl.' Dee scanned one of the menus, stopping when her eyes landed on steak and chips. Exactly what the doctor ordered for a chilly night like this.

They ordered their food and relaxed into easy conversation about everything and nothing.

'So,' Dee said, after she'd poured them both a second glass of wine. 'How are things?'

'Fine,' Louise said.

'You sure?'

'Yes, I'm sure.' Louise frowned. 'Why wouldn't I be?'

'When I met you last week on the seafront,' Dee said. 'You weren't going to the Cavendish for a Chamber of Commerce event, were you?'

'What makes you think that?'

'I saw you,' Dee said. 'You walked right past the Cavendish and went into the Aldrington instead.'

'Ah.' Louise flushed. 'Okay, you caught me. I was actually meeting someone for dinner.'

'Why couldn't you simply tell me that?'

'It was about a job,' Louise said. 'I didn't want to jinx it.'

'You were pretty dressed up for a job interview.'

'It wasn't an interview. Not really. I met this woman at a networking event recently. She owns a PR company in Brighton. We got talking and she said she might have some work for me. So I met her for dinner, but nothing's come of it. Which is why I'm telling you now.'

'Is everything okay?' Dee asked. 'I thought you loved your job. I didn't know you were thinking of leaving.'

Their food arrived then, served by one of the regular young men working behind the bar. Dee watched Louise making small talk as he laid out the food, asking about his university course and telling him she was hoping to catch up with his mother soon. Dee marvelled at the way Louise was able to switch her public personality on and off so effortlessly. It was one of the things that made her so good at her job. As editor of the local newspaper,

Louise knew everyone and everything there was to know in Eastbourne.

'Father died last year,' Louise whispered to Dee as the waiter walked away. 'Suicide. It was a big scandal at the time. He owned a business, but lost all his money on the horses. The wife's become a friend. I check in with her every now and then, just to make sure she's okay.'

'You were about to tell me why you're looking for a new job,' Dee reminded her.

'I shouldn't have said anything.'

To Dee's horror, Louise's eyes filled with tears.

Dee put down the forkful of steak she was lifting towards her mouth.

'Lou? What's going on? Please. Whatever it is, you can talk to me.'

'It's nothing.' Louise dabbed her eyes with her napkin. 'Sorry. I'm just stressed at the moment. Everything seems to be getting to me these days.'

Dee wanted to tell Louise, like she'd told her hundreds of times already, that she couldn't juggle two children and a full-time job and keep a household running to the standard she did with no help whatsoever from her husband. But every time Dee tried to speak to Louise about Martin, it ended up in an argument.

'What can I do?' she said instead.

'Ignore me.' Louise smiled, but it looked forced. 'I'm tired and grumpy and probably pre-menopausal. I wanted a night out with my cousin this evening, that's all. And it will be good for Martin to spend time alone with the kids. They miss him when he's away and if I'm always around when he's at home, then they never get any quality time with him.'

Dee knew Louise well enough to know that, whatever her reasons for wanting to meet tonight, giving Martin a chance to spend 'quality time' with his children wasn't one of them. But she decided not to push it. Whatever was on her cousin's mind, she would find out later.

'Have you thought about seeing a doctor?' Dee asked.

'For stress?' Louise frowned. 'I'm not that bad. It's just… there are some days when I wonder if I've made the right choices in my life. Does that ever happen to you?'

'All the time. But in my case that's probably justified.'

Dee reached across the table and took one of Louise's hands in hers.

'Something's worrying you. And I don't think it's your job, is it?' Her stomach contracted as she thought of something. 'Oh God. It's Martin, isn't it? What's he done?'

'Why do you always blame Martin when something's wrong?' Louise pulled her hand away. 'It's not Martin. It's work, like I said. They've made more cuts and it's difficult to picture myself still doing this job in a few more years. It's becoming more and more web-based, and most of the content these days is a cut and paste job that anyone could do. If I lose this job, then who am I, Dee?'

'You're still *you*,' Dee said. 'One of the cleverest and most capable and all-round best people I've ever met. If this job ended tomorrow, you'd find something else. I know you would.'

Louise ran her fingers through her blond bob, puffing up the layers at the back. 'Why is being an adult so difficult?'

'It's not all bad,' Dee said, thinking about her own life. Despite the ongoing issues between herself and Ed, she felt she'd reached a good place – she was old enough to know what she wanted and how to get it; young enough to still enjoy it. All in all, the first year of her fifties was turning out to be far better than the ten years that had preceded it.

'Maybe.' Louise reached for the wine bottle and refilled both their glasses. Another sign something wasn't right. Unlike Dee, Louise had always been able to exert an iron control over the amount of alcohol she drank. Dee had rarely seen her cousin drink more than two glasses of wine on a night out. This evening, she was already on her third glass.

'How are you getting on trying to find Joana?' Louise asked.

'I'm not having much luck, to be honest. I keep think I'm making progress and then I hit another brick wall. I've been trying to find a link between Lauren's murder and Joana's disappearance. But I can't find anything.'

'Isn't that a bit of a reach?'

'Maybe,' Dee admitted. 'But there are so many coincidences. Joana and Lauren knew each other. Lauren worked at the Aldrington, which is where Joana was going the night she disappeared. And there's something decidedly dodgy about Derek French, who just happens to run the hotel where one girl who worked there was murdered, and another girl disappeared from.'

'Derek's not dodgy,' Louise said.

'I didn't realise you knew him.'

'I don't. Not really. I mean, I've met him a few times, that's all.'

'So how can you be so sure there's nothing dodgy about him?' Dee asked.

'How can you be so sure there is?'

'Gut instinct,' Dee said. 'Plus I've met his wife, and there's something seriously off about her too.'

'Well everyone knows their marriage is a sham,' Louise said. 'He works all the time earning money so she can spend it. At least, that's what I've heard. But really, Dee, isn't their marriage their own private business?'

'Unless he killed his son's girlfriend,' Dee said. 'Then it's everyone's business.'

'Oh my God.' Louise looked horrified. 'The poor man's son has just lost his girlfriend in the most horrible way and you're making jokes about it?'

Dee opened her mouth to tell Louise to take a chill pill, but Louise held her hand up and continued speaking.

'Besides, for your information, he's got an alibi for the night Lauren was killed. Because of course the police have already questioned the entire family. Because they're doing their job properly. Derek was with his brother all night. He couldn't have killed Lauren.'

'I didn't know it meant that much to you.'

'I'm just sick of all the gossip,' Louise said. And, because she was clearly upset, Dee didn't have the heart to point out that this was probably the first and last time in Louise's life she would make that statement.

'I wish you'd tell me what's really going on with you,' Dee said.

'It's nothing,' Louise said. 'Really, Dee. Just let it drop, would you?'

But Dee noticed the way her cheeks flushed and knew she was right. Louise was hiding something from her. An image drifted into her head – ridiculous and impossible but, hard as she tried, she couldn't completely ignore it:

her cousin with a pair of scissors in her hand, chopping chunks of auburn hair from Lauren Shaw's body as she lay lifeless on the altar.

Fifteen

The sound of her phone ringing woke her up. Dee opened her eyes, confused. She'd gone to bed later than usual, and felt as if she'd only been asleep a few minutes. It was still dark outside. Without getting up, she reached out for her phone on the small table by her bed. She saw the time on the screen when she picked it up. Three thirty in the morning. Caller ID unknown. She sat up, suddenly wide awake. Images of the people she loved lying injured filled her mind.

'Hello?'

Silence.

'Who is it?' she said. 'Who's calling?'

She heard something then. Breathing.

'Hello?'

More breathing. Louder this time.

Disgusted, she hung up and switched off her phone. Even though she knew it was nothing more than a prank call, some sad loser with no life dialling numbers at random, she still felt shaken. She lay in bed, her mind in overdrive, jumping from subject to subject. Louise, Ed, Joana, Lauren. Louise. The more Dee tried to calm her brain, the more other thoughts crowded in. Until she knew if she lay there a moment longer, letting her head fill up, she'd go mad.

She got dressed, went into the kitchen and made a pot of coffee, which she carried onto the deck. It was freezing outside, but she'd rather stick out the cold than be cooped up inside with only her thoughts for company.

Before going to bed last night, she'd started reading a book she'd downloaded to her Kindle. The self-published book, *An Old Town Murder: the unsolved death of Mary Palmer*, was written by a local historian called Philip Flint.

As the sky gradually changed colour and the sun started creeping up beyond the horizon, Dee read the rest of the book. It was surprisingly well-written and the author had clearly done his research. By the time she'd finished, Dee had a real feeling for many of the key people involved in Mary's tragic story. She also had a compelling need to know more about the victim and the circumstances surrounding her death.

Mary Palmer was the daughter of a prominent East-bourne family who'd been residents of the town since the eighteenth century. Her ancestors had played a key role in the development of the town during the nineteenth century and the family were living in comfortable pros-perity in Meads, the leafy, affluent suburb on the western edge of town, when Mary was murdered. Her mother had died soon after Mary was born, and she'd been raised by her father and his sister, Annabelle Palmer.

The most interesting thing, for Dee, was the author's assertion that Graham Reed, the man widely assumed to be Mary's murderer, was innocent. In Flint's opinion, there was never any evidence that Graham had killed Mary. Unfortunately, Graham was killed before he had a chance to prove his innocence. Which, according to Philip Flint, meant that Mary's murderer was never caught.

The book included some quotes and interviews from news reports after Mary's death. Lots of people ready to confirm that Graham had been 'obsessed' with the dead woman. One – unnamed – neighbour of the Reed family was quoted as saying: 'It's no secret to anyone who lives here that he's a strange one. I've always told my children to keep their distance. Because you never know with people like that, do you?'

The extracts didn't make it clear what the neighbour meant by 'people like that', but Dee could guess. Outsiders, eccentrics, people who found it harder to fit into conventional society than those around them. It was depressing to think that as far back as the Sixties, there were journalists willing to focus on this sort of small-minded bigotry instead of doing their jobs properly and trying to find the truth.

At the end of the book, there was a link to the author's blog full of quirky facts about Eastbourne's history. The blog also had an option to contact Flint through the site.

By now, the sky had shifted through several shades of colour and settled on a dull grey. The sun had risen and was there somewhere, hidden behind the thick blanket of clouds. Dee stuck it out as long as she could, but when the rain started she was finally driven back inside.

She got her phone from the bedroom, switched it on and sent an email to Philip Flint, introducing herself and asking him to get in touch. There was a text from Ed, asking how she'd slept. They'd spoken yesterday evening and sort of made up. Sort of, because although he'd apologised, Dee didn't think he really believed he'd done anything wrong. He'd asked to see her tonight, but she'd told him she planned to work through the evening. Not true, but she wasn't about to let him think she was a walkover. She agreed to meet him tomorrow evening instead, telling him he could come over when he'd finished work.

There was a text from Ella as well, asking Dee to call her when she was awake.

'I would have popped over,' Ella said, when Dee phoned her back. 'But it's bucketing down and I can't find an umbrella.'

'Want me to come to yours?'

'There's no need,' Ella said. 'I wanted to ask a favour. Is there any chance you could babysit tomorrow evening? Tom's going away for work – a last-minute thing. I'd planned a night out with the girls. It's Judy's birthday and she's had such a tough time recently with the divorce and everything, I'd really like to be there if I can.'

'It should be fine,' Dee said. 'Ed's coming over. Any chance Jake could come here? It might be a bit easier.'

'I don't want to mess up your plans,' Ella said. 'I can always say no to the girls. I know Judy will understand.'

The girls. A group of women Dee had never met. Ella knew them from Jake's playgroup and seemed to be spending more and more time with them. Dee was glad she'd started making new friends, but a small part of her missed the way things had been. When it had been just Dee and Ella and Jake. Before Tom and Ed and *the girls.* Before she'd found out Ella had been lying to her all the time she'd known her.

'Don't be ridiculous,' Dee said. 'Tell you what. Let him spend the night. He loves his sleepovers here, doesn't he?

And that way, you can stay out as late as you want and drink as much as you want without having to worry.'

'That would be great,' Ella said. 'Thanks, Dee. You're the best.'

After hanging up, Dee tried not to dwell on how her relationship with Ella and Jake was changing. The previous year, when Ella was living under an assumed identity, she and Jake had disappeared suddenly and Dee thought she might never see them again. When she did finally find them, she resolved to do everything she could to keep them in her life this time.

That was almost seven months ago. A lot had changed since then. Ella had spent a brief period in prison, waiting to hear if she would be charged for killing a man in self-defence many years earlier. During that time, Tom – Jake's dad – had moved in to look after his son. When the CPS decided it was in no one's interest to prosecute Ella, she was allowed to come home. Since then, Dee and her neighbours had settled into a way of being together that suited all of them.

But Dee's relationship with Ella had changed. They weren't as close as they'd used to be. Dee had tried, but it wasn't easy to be close to someone who'd lied like that. She understood why Ella hadn't been honest about who she was, but the deceit lay between them and Dee, at least, was unable to get past it.

Now, the same thing was happening with Ed. He hadn't been straight with her, and she was struggling to forgive him. During the row, he'd accused her of making everything difficult. He was probably right, but Dee didn't know how to change who she was. Worse, she didn't see why she should have to. Was it really so bad to expect people to be upfront and honest? She didn't think so. And if other people felt differently that was their problem, not hers.

Sixteen

Dee spent Wednesday morning working. Following a long conversation with the editor at the *Guardian*, she'd now been commissioned to write a series of stories about the growing number of foreign nationals coming across the Channel – legally and otherwise – to live and work in the UK.

She was tired, and found it harder than normal to concentrate. She'd had two more prank phone calls. One yesterday afternoon, and another just before she went to bed. Each time, it was the same. No caller ID and, when she answered, nothing except the sound of someone breathing into the phone. She'd gone online earlier and ordered a whistle, due to arrive tomorrow. If he called again, she'd do her best to deafen the creep.

By the time the afternoon came around, she needed a change of scene. She decided to pay Kyle another visit. Despite what his mother had said, Dee wanted to ask if he could shed any light on how well Joana and Lauren knew each other.

She sent him a text asking if he was free to meet up. An hour later, when he hadn't replied to her text, she decided to drive across to his house instead. But when she arrived, Karen told her Kyle wasn't at home.

'He goes to the beach in the afternoons,' she said. 'It's the only time he gets out of the house these days. If Derek and I had our way, he'd be back at work, but he insists he's not ready for that. Maybe I can tell him you called around and ask him to give you a ring when he's back?'

'Don't worry,' Dee said. 'If you tell me which part of the beach he's on, I'll go there now.'

'Oh, I wouldn't have a clue,' Karen said. 'Sorry.'

Dee thanked her and turned to go, but Karen called her back.

'I wanted to apologise,' Karen said.

'For what?'

'For how I behaved the last time you were here,' Karen said. 'I wasn't very polite to you. I'm sorry.'

'It's okay,' Dee said. 'You're worried about your son, I understand that.'

'We've been under so much pressure,' Karen said. 'You don't have children, of course, so you couldn't possibly understand what it's been like for us.'

'It must be difficult,' Dee said, wondering why women with children always assumed women who didn't have them were incapable of understanding what it was like to love a child.

'It's so hard, knowing who really killed her and not being able to do anything about it.'

'How can you be so sure it was Nigel?' Dee asked. 'It's a big accusation to make without any proof.'

'A woman's intuition,' Karen said. 'You haven't met him yet, I can tell. I would have thought speaking to Lauren's parents would be a key part of your investigation.'

Dee didn't bother pointing out that she wasn't carrying out an investigation and, even if she was, harassing Lauren's grieving parents wouldn't be high on her list of things to do.

'How did you and Lauren get on?' she asked.

'Well enough,' Karen said. 'Considering.'

'Considering what?'

'That my son was besotted with her, and I knew she didn't feel the same way about him. Oh, don't get me wrong. She loved Kyle. In her own way. But the thing about Lauren, the thing no one will tell you because everyone hates to speak ill of the dead, is that the person Lauren loved most of all was Lauren.'

'You're right,' Dee said. 'No one else has said that about her. How about your husband? What did he think of her?'

'I'm surprised you haven't asked him yourself,' Karen said. 'All that time you're spending at the hotel. What can I tell you? Regardless of Lauren's faults, we're both devastated. She was the closest thing we'll ever get to a daughter of our own. And she was kind, when she wanted to be. Quite often, you know, she'd come to church with me and help with the flowers.'

'The flowers?'

'I look after the floral arrangements at St Mary the Virgin,' Karen said.

'Could that be why the killer chose that church, do you think?' Dee said.

'Because he knew she used to go there sometimes?' Karen frowned. 'The police have already asked about that. And I'll tell you the same thing I told them. Nigel's an atheist. He hated that Lauren was helping me. He used to tease her about it, apparently.'

'So you're saying he killed her and left her body in the church because he hated her helping out there?'

'It makes sense,' Karen said. 'I had a key, you see. So I could go in whenever it suited me to do the flowers. The last time I was there, Lauren came with me. When we were finished, I gathered up the old flowers and took them out to my car. I dispose of them with my own garden waste each week. I gave my key to Lauren and asked her to lock up. Later, I forgot to ask her for it back.'

'And you think her father used the same key to get her body inside the church.'

'That's exactly what I think.'

'But why go to all that trouble?' Dee wondered. 'If he killed her, why take her to the church afterwards and lay her body out like that?'

'Well, you'd have to ask him that,' Karen said. 'Obviously. Derek and I have already told all this to the police. Now, we simply have to trust them to do their jobs properly.'

'How do you think Derek's bearing up?' Dee said. 'It can't be easy for you, if he's at work all the time and you're left to deal with Kyle.'

'It's different for men. They can compartmentalise. Mothers can't do that. Besides, his work is what gives us all of this.' Karen gestured to the house behind her. 'He offered to stay at home but I told him there was no point. He's no use to me when he's here. I'd rather he keeps the business going while I take care of everything else. Now if you don't mind, I need to go. It's choir practice this evening. I don't want to be late.'

Dee said goodbye and left quickly. She didn't like Karen French. For a practising Christian, she'd shown a remarkable lack of empathy for the dead girl and her grieving family.

Instead of getting back into her car, she walked to the beach near the house. It didn't take long to find Kyle. He was sitting alone near the Martello tower, throwing stones into the dark grey sea.

'Hey Kyle.' Dee scrambled over the shingle and sat down beside him. 'How're you doing?'

He picked up another stone and flung it into the water.

'The police have kept away the last few days,' he said. 'Which is good, but no one will tell me what's happening. I called over to see Lauren's parents the other day and her dad went mental. Screamed at me like I was some sort of animal. It was awful.'

'He's grieving,' Dee said. 'People don't always behave well under those circumstances.'

'My mum says he's a nutcase and I should keep well away.' Kyle glanced at Dee, as if gauging her reaction. 'Maybe she's right. But I can't help feeling sorry for him. After he stopped screaming at me, he burst into tears and he couldn't stop crying. It was horrible to see him like that.

'Mum says he killed Lauren because of the row they had. But I argue with my dad all the time – it doesn't mean he's going to kill me.'

This was news to Dee. Neither Karen nor Derek had given any indication that Kyle and his father didn't get on.

'What do you argue with him about?'

'Everything.' Kyle shrugged. 'He thinks I'm not ambitious enough, I don't have enough drive. He wants me to be more like him. He doesn't understand being like him is the very last thing I'd ever want.'

Dee thought of her own interactions with Derek French and didn't blame Kyle for not wanting to turn out like that. She felt a new respect, and pity, for the boy.

'How did Lauren and your father get on?' she asked.

'How do you think?' Kyle said. 'You've seen pictures of Lauren, right?'

Stones were digging uncomfortably into Dee's bum. She shifted, trying to get more comfortable, as she thought about how to ask her next question.

'You mean he found her attractive?'

'He finds any woman with a pulse attractive. Sorry. Maybe that's not fair. We had a row earlier and I'm still angry with him. Don't get me wrong, he'd never have… you know… with Lauren. He wouldn't do that. Besides, there's no way she would have even if he'd wanted to.'

Dee didn't have Kyle's faith in his father. She made a note to go back to the Aldrington and see what Derek had to say about his feelings for Lauren.

'The last time I spoke to you,' she said, 'you told me Lauren had started to write something about Mary Palmer's murder. Did she ever show you what she'd written?'

Kyle shook his head. 'She was super-secretive about it. And like I told you, she changed her mind anyway. But it's the reason she was killed, right? It has to be. Lauren found out something about Mary's murder. That's why I think Mum could be right about Nigel.'

'But Mary's murder was sixty years ago,' Dee said.

Kyle shrugged. 'There's this group on Facebook, Lauren joined it a while back. A true crime group. Lots of people there have all sorts of theories about who killed

Mary. If the killer's still alive, and he found out what Lauren was up to, isn't that reason enough to kill her?'

'Except we know Nigel couldn't have killed Mary. He wasn't even born when she was killed. If Mary's killer is still alive, he'd be in his eighties. I'm not sure someone that old would be strong enough to subdue a strong young woman like Lauren.'

'He could have had help,' Kyle said.

'That's possible,' Dee said. 'On this Facebook group, who do people think the real killer is?'

'Everyone has a different theory,' Kyle said. 'You should take a look. You have to join the group first, but they don't seem too fussy about who they let in.'

'I'll do that,' Dee said. 'Thanks. Are you a member then?'

He shook his head.

'Lauren showed it to me a few times. But now she's gone, I'm too scared to try to join. I don't want to see what people are saying about her. Or me.'

'I can understand that,' Dee said. Then, changing the subject, 'Kyle, can I ask you about something else?' She took the photo of Joana from her bag and showed it to him. 'Do you recognise this girl?'

He looked at the photo for a long time before he spoke.

'Joana. She used to drink at the Anchor pub on Seaside.'

'Used to?' Dee asked.

'Haven't seen her for a while,' Kyle said. 'Why are you asking about her?'

Patches of red had appeared on his cheeks, and when he handed the photo back to Dee, his hand was shaking.

'Joana's disappeared,' Dee said. 'Her friends and family don't know where she is. But I thought you would have already known about this. I've asked the staff at the hotel to circulate her photo.'

He shook his head, like he didn't know what she was talking about.

'One of Joana's friends,' Dee continued, 'thinks that Joana's disappearance and Lauren's murder are connected.'

'Oh.' Kyle looked relieved. 'I see. I don't think there's any chance of that.'

'Why not?' Dee asked.

'Because they barely knew each other,' Kyle said. 'I mean, they'd chatted to each other in the pub a few times, yeah. But apart from that, I don't think they had anything to do with each other.'

'You sure about that?' Dee asked.

'Absolutely positive,' Kyle said.

'Your mother didn't want me asking you about Joana,' Dee said. 'Do you have any idea why she wouldn't want me to talk to you about her?'

'She probably didn't want you upsetting me,' Kyle said, after a moment. 'I mean, it's not very nice, is it? Saying her disappearance has something to do with what happened to Lauren.'

'I guess not.' Dee stood up. 'Well thanks for looking, anyway.'

She offered to drive him home but he said he'd rather stay on the beach. He used to come down here in the evenings with Lauren to watch the sunset, and that's what he planned to do this evening. Sit here until the sun had set beneath the horizon, alone with nothing but the memories of his dead girlfriend to keep him company.

Louise sat in her car on Motcombe Road, watching the entrance to Ed's house. She knew he was inside. She'd seen him go in there fifteen minutes earlier. Since then, she'd been sitting here in her car, wondering how she was going to tell him what she'd discovered earlier today. Detective Inspector Ed Mitchell, with his cleaner-than-clean reputation, had a secret. Louise couldn't understand how he'd kept it to himself until now. Especially in Eastbourne, where no one's business was a private matter for long.

No matter how fond she was of her cousin's boyfriend, Louise knew she had no choice: this was a story she had to print. So far, none of the journalists from the national papers who'd swooped down on the town since Lauren's murder had picked this up. It was Louise's responsibility to make sure the first any of them would hear of it was when it was the front-page story in this week's *Recorder*.

Her phone buzzed with an incoming text. She swiped the screen, smiling when she read the message, and tapped a quick reply. When she was done, she put the phone back in her bag and got out of her car. She'd already sat here for long enough. It was time to get this over and done with.

She walked up the short path to his front door, rang the bell and waited. Thirty seconds later, Ed opened the door.

'Louise!' He smiled and pulled the door open wider, telling her to come inside out of the cold. 'This is a surprise. What can I do for you?'

'I need to speak to you about something,' Louise said, swallowing down the lump at the back of her throat. His genuine pleasure at seeing her had triggered an unexpected pang of guilt that made her question if she was doing the right thing.

'Is Dee okay? Only I've just tried to call her and it went straight to voicemail. The signal can be a bit patchy where she lives. I've told her she should get a landline but you know what she's like. Never one to do what anyone else tells her—'

'Dee's fine,' Louise interrupted. 'Well, I assume she's fine. I haven't actually seen her or spoken to her today. She's not the reason I'm here.' She paused, took a deep breath and continued before she had a chance to change her mind.

'I want to speak to you about Lauren Shaw. I know why you're not working on the case. We're running the story this week. I'm here to ask if you'd like to give your side of the story.'

From the diary of Emma Reed

6 May 1960

Mary's funeral took place today. The long delay between her death and funeral must have been difficult for George. She was buried at St John's, where her father worships. People came from all over the country, so I've heard, to pay their respects to the dead girl and her family. Last night, James said we should go too. People will talk, he said, if we stay at home and don't do what is proper. I told him people are already talking, and he could go if he wanted to, but he'd be going alone.

In the end, he decided not to go. I knew he wouldn't. He can't face people ignoring him, whispering behind his back. He'd rather hide himself away. I couldn't bear to be in the house with him, watching his miserable face and knowing that his misery is for himself rather than our son. So I left him alone and walked across town to Mary's funeral. Like everyone else, I was drawn to that church as inevitably and irresistibly as a moth is drawn to a light burning in the dark.

I stayed on the other side of the road, on the corner of Staveley Road and St John's Road, hunkered down behind someone's garden wall, hiding as best I could. Unlike everyone else in attendance that beautiful, sunny morning, I did not go to be seen. I went to see.

I watched the slow procession of people dressed in black, their faces hidden beneath their hats or veils. As they disappeared inside the church, more people followed. They kept coming, long after the church was full, spreading out across the grounds like a black blanket.

They made a lot of noise for people attending a funeral. The sound of their chatter carried across to me. They didn't care, I realised. This was a day out, an adventure, a chance to say, 'I was there when they buried her.' A young girl has been murdered, her poor family ripped apart by this terrible tragedy, and all these people turned up, dressed in their best clothes, behaving as if this was a party they were attending, not a funeral.

It felt like an age before the funeral cortège arrived. Four black horses, each one with a white stripe down the front of its face, pulling the black carriage. And poor George walking behind it, his face bent into his chest, his body heaving with sobs. His grief was like a mirror of my own. It was unbearable. My own sobs caught in my throat and I had to push my hand into my mouth to stop me crying out.

He wasn't alone, at least. His sister, Annabelle, was by his side. Holding her head high, no sign of grief or sadness on that woman's face. A terrible thought occurred to me – she'll have no problem finding a husband now. Because with Mary dead, Annabelle will inherit all of George's money.

As the cortège passed through the crowd into the church, I saw Richard Partridge. He was part of a group of young men and women huddled together outside the church. I scanned the group, searching for David, but there was no sign of him, which was odd because usually those brothers are inseparable.

My back had grown tired of being crouched down. I stood up, realising no one was going to be looking across the road. They were all too focused on what was happening inside the church.

But Richard must have felt me watching them, because he nudged one of his friends and they both turned to look at me. I stared back, not caring what they thought of me. *Without taking his eyes off me, Richard leaned in and whispered something in his friend's ear. The two men burst out laughing, and the sound triggered a memory.*

I'd heard that laughter before. The night Graham was killed. They walked past my house – Richard and his friends. Their footsteps loud and fast and full of vigour; their laughter mocking me as I waited for my son to come home.

And in that moment, I knew. They killed him.

They think they've got away with it. But I know, and I will make it my life's work to make them pay for what they've done.

Seventeen

Ella dropped Jake over at six thirty. Dee spent the next half-hour building a Lego train track with him. When she'd had enough, she suggested they go down to the beach and look for foxes. After she'd helped him put his shoes on and wrapped him up in his coat and scarf, they walked over the shingle to the sea. Jake chattered the whole time, telling Dee about his trains and Spider-Man and his friend Max who had a big house.

The clouds had cleared and a full moon hung low and bright, reflected in the still surface of the dark sea. In the moonlight, Dee could see the silhouettes of five foxes, walking towards them along the edge of the water.

'Shh.' Dee bent down and whispered in Jake's ear. 'Hold my hand, Jake. If you stay still, the foxes will come right up to us. They won't hurt you, I promise.'

Jake nodded and held on tight to Dee's hand. The foxes took their time, sniffing and exploring as the gradually came closer. One of them saw the humans on the beach and stopped. The other foxes stopped too, all five of them staring at Jake and Dee.

'Baby,' Jake whispered, a rapt expression on his little face. The foxes started moving again, the smaller one running around Jake and Dee several times before chasing after the adult foxes, who had already moved past on their slow journey along the beach.

Dee had no idea where the foxes lived during the day. She never saw them in daylight hours, but at night they roamed the beach freely. As a girl, her father had taken her out to see them and it had been years before she'd grown out of the thrill of standing here in the dark, letting them get so close you could touch them. She loved that she was able to give Jake the same experience.

She hadn't taken her phone out with her. When she got back to the house, she saw she had two new voicemails. One was from Louise, asking her to call when she got a chance. Making sure Jake was happy playing with his trains, Dee listened to the other message as she was putting the fish pie in the oven.

'Hello, Mrs Doran.' A man's voice; frail, as if he was elderly. 'This is Philip Flint. You asked me to get in touch.'

He gave a phone number and told Dee he'd be happy to talk to her any time before ten thirty this evening. Dee checked the time. Seven fifteen. Ed would be here at seven thirty, which meant she just had time to call Philip back first.

'Jake,' she said. 'Ed's coming over in a few minutes. Let's get you into your pyjamas and then you can stay up late as a special treat. How does that sound?'

As expected, Jake was delighted with this news. Dee helped him into his pyjamas, then settled him in front of the TV while she returned Philip Flint's call.

She moved further away from the TV, peering out the windows onto the road that ran behind the house, impatiently waiting for Ed's car to appear.

'Eastbourne 324455,' a man's voice said as the call connected.

'Is this Mr Flint?' Dee asked. She knew it was; she recognised the polite well-spoken tone.

'That is correct, yes.'

'Mr Flint, this is Dee Doran. You left me a message earlier?'

'I did,' he replied. 'You asked me to get in touch, so that's precisely what I did. Unfortunately I got your recorded answering service. I almost didn't leave a message. I hate those machines.'

'Well I'm very grateful you did,' Dee said. 'And I'm sorry about the machine.'

'You're not the first person who's contacted me about the book,' Philip Flint said. 'I've been very popular recently.'

'I'm sure,' Dee said. 'Lots of people must be interested in any possible connections between the two murders.'

'A few journalists have been in touch too,' Philip said. 'I haven't spoken to most of them. You're only the second, in fact. I decided to make an exception.'

'That's very kind,' Dee said. 'Can I ask why?'

'I remembered the piece you wrote last year about the woman who was killed in the hit and run. Katie Hope, I think her name was? It was very moving. The story stayed with me, as did the name of the journalist who wrote it. When I received your email earlier today, I was intrigued.'

'That's very kind,' Dee said, warming to him immediately. A bit of full-on flattery had that effect. 'Is it all right if I call you Philip?'

'Absolutely, my dear. In your email, you asked about Graham Reed, the boy convicted of Mary's murder. What did you want to know about him?'

'Reading your book,' Dee said, 'it struck me that people were too quick to assume Graham was the killer. Why do you think that is?'

'Poor Graham was a bit of an oddball, really. These days, we'd probably say he was somewhere on the spectrum, but that wasn't something people would have been aware of in those days. So he was simply labelled as being different. In my experience, people don't like difference. I'm on the spectrum myself, you see, although this is something I've only come to realise late in life. This means I feel a certain empathy for poor Graham. He was an outsider, struggled to fit in, that sort of thing. But being an outsider doesn't make someone a murderer, does it?'

'It certainly doesn't,' Dee said.

'That poor young woman came to see me, you know,' Philip said.

'Who?'

'Lauren Shaw. She was asking about Graham, just like you are. I sincerely hope that doesn't mean you're about to meet the same fate as she did. She was a determined young thing. A bit too pushy for my liking, but maybe that's how young people are today. I must confess I was surprised to learn she was Annabelle's granddaughter. She never mentioned the family connection, you see.'

It took a moment for Dee to place the name. Then she remembered. Annabelle Palmer – Mary's aunt.

Outside, lights appeared at the end of the road. No one ever came out this way at night unless they were visiting Dee or Ella's houses. The car had to be Ed's.

'Graham's mother spent her life trying to seek justice for him,' Philip said. 'But she never succeeded. And I must say, Dee, after all my extensive research, I never found anything conclusive to prove my theory that Graham didn't kill Mary. Which means I can't prove he was innocent.'

'But you still believe he didn't do it?'

'There was some speculation that Graham was in love with Mary,' Philip said. 'But she was, by all accounts, a beautiful young woman, so that's hardly surprising. If all the men who liked pretty young girls killed them, there wouldn't be any pretty girls left in the world, would there?'

'I suppose not.' Dee smiled. The more he spoke, the more she liked him.

'It doesn't seem as if the other members of Graham's family shared his mother's determination,' Philip said.

'What do you mean?'

'The impact on the rest of his family was catastrophic,' Philip said. 'His mother, Emma, took her own life eventually. Threw herself off Beachy Head, like so many other poor souls before and since. I think she simply lost hope of ever clearing her son's name.'

'What about the others?' Dee said. 'His father, brothers and sisters?'

The car drew closer, stopping beside her house. She went and opened the front door, waving to Ed as he got out of the car and took his bag from the boot.

'Graham's father died of a heart attack shortly after his wife's suicide,' Philip said. 'He had one sister, Nicola. She married and had two children. They're both adults now. I contacted them when I was writing the book, but neither of them wanted to speak to me.'

'And Nicola?'

'Poor woman died a few years after her mother,' Philip said. 'Cancer, I believe.'

'How sad,' Dee said.

As Ed came closer, Dee could see how tired he looked. Suddenly, her frustration towards him disappeared and all she wanted to do was wrap her arms around him and hold him tight.

'Indeed,' Philip said. 'I'm sure her children want to keep themselves as far away as possible from this renewed interest in Mary's death. Although it's not going to be easy for them. Especially Nicola's son, I would have thought.'

'Why's that?' Dee said.

She smiled at Ed and gestured for him to go inside. He leaned forward and kissed her cheek, sending a shiver of electricity through her body.

'Nicola married a man called Henry Mitchell,' Philip said. 'They had two children – a boy and a girl.'

Dee closed the front door and walked back to the sitting room. Jake had dragged Ed to the Lego train set and was issuing instructions on what needed to be done. Ed must have sensed her eyes on him, because he looked up at her and smiled. She turned away from him without smiling back.

'What year was the son born?' she asked.

'Edward Mitchell was born in September 1967,' Edward said. 'Which would make him, what? Fifty-three now. You can find him easily enough if you wanted to try talking to him. He's local as well. A detective with the East Sussex force. Would you like me to see if I can find his contact details?'

Dee looked out the window, at the moon, bright and white in the endless black sky, its perfect reflection shining back at itself from the flat, black sea.

'It's okay,' she said. 'I think I know how to find him.'

She hung up.

Jake was pushing a plastic train around the track, making loud chugging sounds. Ed had another train and was pushing it in the opposite direction, orchestrating a collision between the two trains.

Dee couldn't bear it. She turned away, walked back down the corridor, pulled open the front door and stepped outside. She closed her eyes and lifted her face to the cool night air and tried not to think of the trauma in Ed's family that she'd known nothing about. He'd carried this pain the whole time she'd known him and she'd never once picked up on it.

She'd thought he was her soulmate. Now, she realised she barely knew him. And this new knowledge frightened her. For the first time since they'd got together, she didn't know what to do.

Eighteen

'I wish you'd told me,' Dee said.

'Would it have made any difference?' Ed asked.

'I don't know,' Dee said.

She'd always thought of Ed as remarkably grounded. Far more grounded than Dee herself. Yet all the time she'd been thinking she was the person with 'issues', poor Ed had had to deal with so much more. And he'd had to do it alone, because Dee had been too caught up with her own problems to think about what he might have been going through.

'You don't mind that I know now?' she asked.

She'd considered keeping quiet and not saying anything. But she couldn't do that. She'd waited until Jake was in bed, and then she'd told Ed they needed to talk. She'd opened a bottle of wine, poured them both a glass, sat beside him on the sofa and told him what she'd found out. When she'd finished, he took her hand and told her he was sorry.

'I've wanted to tell you for so long,' he said now. 'Then Lauren was killed and it became even more important to tell you, but it was harder too, because I hadn't said anything before and I knew you'd be upset that I hadn't felt able to talk to you about it.'

He was right. She was upset that he hadn't talked to her. And she couldn't help wondering whether he'd ever have told her if she hadn't found out.

'Ironically, I was planning to tell you this evening,' he said. 'Except you got there first. Louise came to see me earlier. It's the front-page story in tomorrow's *Recorder*.'

Dee remembered the message on her phone from Louise. If she'd returned the call, she would have heard all this from Louise first. She didn't want to think about how she'd feel if that had happened.

'Graham Reed was your uncle,' she said. 'And he was accused of killing Mary Palmer, Nigel Shaw's cousin. That's why you're not part of the investigation?'

'More or less, yeah.'

'More or less? You mean there's another reason?'

He had he grace to look embarrassed. She would remember that later, when she tried to rationalise his behaviour.

'Lauren came to see me,' he said.

'Excuse me?'

'I didn't tell you because, well, because I wasn't ready to talk about Graham. She was writing about Mary's murder and she wanted to ask me some questions. I told her I wasn't interested, and thought that was the end of it.'

'When was this?'

'A few months ago.'

A few months ago, and he'd said nothing. Not one word. Worse, she hadn't picked up that anything was wrong.

'What do you mean you thought that was the end of it?'

'I didn't hear from her again. And then, a week before she was killed, she sent me an email. She said she needed to

147

see me. Told me it was important. I assumed she wanted to ask more questions, and I never replied to the email. I'm such a bloody idiot.'

And a bloody liar, Dee thought. She took a sip of wine, but it tasted sour and she put the glass down again.

'Ed,' she said, when she was able to speak. 'This is a lot for me to take in. Do you think you could start at the beginning and tell me everything that's been going on?'

'I've just told you,' he said. 'Haven't I?'

'Not really. You've told me Graham was your uncle. And you knew Lauren. But you haven't told me what it was like for you, growing up with all of this. Or what happened after your grandmother died. Or why you've never had any help dealing with all of this. Because, clearly, it's had a profound effect on you and I really think it would do you good to talk to someone about it all.'

'I don't need to talk to someone,' he said. 'I've got you, haven't I? But you're right. You deserve to know more than I've told you. I'm sorry.' He took a gulp of wine. 'Okay. I haven't spoken to you about this before because it wasn't something we ever spoke about in my family. Well, my gran spoke about it – all the time – but everyone else preferred not to. My mother, especially. I was close to my nan, and I was very sad when she died. My parents tried to shield me from what had happened, and they did that by never talking about any of it. Nessa and I learned quickly that Graham's death and Nan's suicide were strictly off-limits.'

'And now?'

'I don't know, Dee.' Ed ran his hands through what was left of his hair. 'Over the years, I've tried to put it behind me, but I've never really been able to let it go. Then this happened. I'm not coping very well, to tell you the truth.'

'You have been a bit of a grumpy git.'

He smiled.

'I know. Sorry.'

'It must have been hard for your mum,' Dee said. 'Growing up knowing everyone thought her brother was a murderer.'

'Graham's death affected her a lot,' Ed said. 'She was depressed for most of my childhood, although that was something else we didn't speak about. I know she hated me spending time with Nan, but she never tried to stop me from seeing her. In some ways, I was closer to my grandmother than I was to my own mother.'

'What was she like?' Dee asked.

'Nan? Eccentric. And very opinionated. Thought she was cleverer and better than other people. She had a sharp tongue and was very judgemental. But all of that just made me laugh when I was a kid. She drank far too much – something my mother thoroughly disapproved of. Kept a bottle of gin under the sink that she used to put in her tea.

'She loved telling me about Graham. Used to say I looked just like him. She told me he'd been killed by bad men, but she knew who they were and she was going to make them pay for what they'd done. I believed her, Dee. I was only a kid, and I loved her.'

'Do you remember when she died?'

'God yes. My mother couldn't face telling me and Nessa the truth. She told us that Gran had been killed in a car accident. It wasn't the cleverest thing she'd ever done, but she was trying to protect us. Back then, in the days before the internet, it was easier to think you could get away with keeping a secret like that.'

'But it didn't work,' Dee said.

Ed shook his head, but didn't expand. He didn't have to. There were too many ways he could have discovered the truth. All it took was one careless conversation. A story like that would spread through the community. Dee tried to recall if she'd ever heard any rumours when she was growing up. It was quite possible she had, but back then Ed Mitchell was so far off her radar she wouldn't have retained that information for too long.

'For a while, I became obsessed with Mary's murder,' Ed said. 'I had this idea that I needed to finish what Nan had started. I spent days in the library, reading all the archived news stories. Desperate to find anything that would prove my uncle wasn't a murderer. But I never found a single thing. After a while, I stopped trying. Life got in the way, I suppose. My mum died, Nessa went off the rails and that sort of took over everything else for a bit. I stopped thinking about Mary and Graham and started focusing on trying to save my sister. Then Nessa sorted herself out, I became a detective and life moved on. But I always felt guilty for giving up.'

Neither of them spoke for a moment. Dee drank some of her wine and wondered what it would be like to grow up in a family full of secrets that no one ever spoke about.

'So what happens now?' she asked.

'I want to know the truth,' Ed said. 'It's all I can think about. I feel like I'm that kid again, trying to clear my uncle's name and make my grandmother proud of me. I've barely thought of anything else since Lauren's murder. I know I did the right thing taking myself off the investigation, but it doesn't mean I'm going to sit back and do nothing. I need to find out who killed her. I owe it to Lauren, and my own family, to find out what really happened.'

'Shouldn't you leave it to Rachel and her team?' Dee said.

'I can't do that,' Ed said. 'You'd do the same thing in my position. Don't pretend you wouldn't.'

'Okay,' Dee said, after a moment. 'You're right, I probably would do the same thing.'

His face cleared. He reached out and pulled her into his arms.

'Have I ever told you what an amazing woman you are?' he said.

'Not often enough,' Dee replied.

She rested her head on his chest while she thought about how she could help him.

'Has Rachel spoken to you about the investigation?' she asked.

'She refuses to do that,' Ed said. 'I've tried speaking to her but she shut me down right away.'

'I may know something that could help,' Dee said. 'I went to see Kyle. Don't say anything, I know you didn't think that was a good idea.'

'How you do your job is none of my business,' Ed said. 'I should have kept my mouth shut.'

'Glad we both agree on that,' Dee said. 'Anyway, Kyle told me that Lauren found something at her grandmother's house that made her change her mind about the story she was writing about Mary.'

Ed pulled back and looked her.

'You mean Annabelle's house – Nigel's mother?'

'I think so.'

'What did she find?'

'I'm not sure.' Dee tried to remember Kyle's exact words. 'But whatever it was, it caused a huge row between Lauren and her father.'

'That's why she got in touch!' Ed extricated himself from Dee and jumped up, pacing back and forth as he spoke. 'She wanted to tell me what she'd found. Why didn't I do the right thing and agree to meet her? She could still be alive, you know.'

'Ed.' Dee spoke sharply and it worked. He stopped pacing and stared at her.

'Can you please sit back down?' She reached for the bottle of wine and refilled their glasses. 'Have a drink and calm the fuck down. Please.'

'Such an eloquent way with words,' Ed said, doing as he was told. 'What else did Kyle say?'

'Nothing. Lauren wouldn't tell him what she found.'

'But it caused a row between her and Nigel. Jesus.' Ed put his head in his hands. 'She worked it out. Somehow, Lauren uncovered the truth about Mary's murder. You know what this means, don't you? It means she was about to prove that Graham didn't kill Mary. But now she's dead and her father's doing all he can to cover it up. Why? I need to speak to Rachel. Make sure she knows about this.' He looked around the room. 'Where's my damn phone?'

'Listen to me.' Dee put her hand on his arm. 'I know this is all very personal for you. But you're making some pretty big assumptions based on very little information.'

'I must have left it in the car,' Ed continued, not seeming to notice that she'd spoken. 'I'm going outside now to call Rachel.'

The wine Dee had drunk sloshed inside her stomach, refusing to settle. This wasn't the rational, reasonable Ed she'd fallen for. This man was someone else. Someone who was starting to scare her.

'It's late,' she said. 'Rachel will be asleep, and we should be too. She'll have already interviewed all of Lauren's family. I'm sure if Lauren found something, Rachel already knows about it. And if she doesn't, you can tell her. But wait until the morning, okay? Get some sleep and tomorrow we can decide – together – what to do next.'

She thought he was going to refuse. But after a moment's hesitation he nodded his head and said 'Okay.' She hoped that might be the end of it. That a good night's sleep would calm him down and give him a sense of perspective.

But when she woke up the following morning, the space beside her in the bed was empty. She went into the kitchen, but he wasn't in there either, and he wasn't outside on the deck where he sat some mornings if he woke up before her. She walked around to the front of the house, and saw an empty space where he'd parked his car last night.

Ed was gone.

Nineteen

The sensible thing was to do nothing. Steer clear of the investigation and trust Rachel to do her job. But Ed couldn't do that. His uncle, his grandmother and now Lauren. They haunted his dreams and chased him during his waking hours. The sense of responsibility weighed him down. He owed it to these people to uncover the truth.

Rachel would say that was her job. But Rachel didn't have a family who'd been destroyed by Mary Palmer's murder. She couldn't understand what it was like to spend your whole life wanting to rewrite your family's past, and suddenly be given the opportunity to do just that.

So he'd made his decision. While Dee was still sleeping, he'd got up and driven across town to Meads. Nigel and Maxine Shaw lived on Baslow Road, one of Eastbourne's most sought-after, and expensive, streets, leafy and hilly with large detached Victorian mansions and far-reaching views to the sea and the South Downs. As much as Ed liked to scoff at Meads, and the majority of its blue-rinse, right-leaning residents, he could see the appeal of living somewhere like this.

He'd driven past the house countless times since Lauren's murder. Until a few days ago, there had been a group of reporters hanging around the entrance. Men and women, with cameras and microphones and recording equipment, all crowded around the entrance gates to the house.

Today, the street was quiet. A sad sign of how quickly the media moved on from one tragedy to the next. Ed didn't know what today's big story was, and he didn't want to know. It would involve some other poor family's life being ripped to pieces by a media that didn't give one damn about the people involved.

He parked on the street outside the house and walked through the open gates, across the gravelled driveway, past a silver Lexus and a red Mazda, up the flight of stone steps that led to the green front door.

He rang the doorbell. While he waited, his mind slipped back to the week after his grandmother's funeral. Ed was twelve years old, and still struggling to deal with the grief of losing her so suddenly and unexpectedly. She'd been a constant presence in his life, and he'd never imagined a time when she wouldn't be there for him. He'd been walking home at the end of his first day back at school. Walking slowly because he couldn't face going home and seeing his mother. Her grief and loss too much for her twelve-year-old son to bear.

He hadn't even seen them until it was too late. Nigel Shaw and two of his loyal sidekicks. Nigel was the ringleader, of course. He'd had it in for Ed for as far back as Ed could remember.

'Here he is,' Nigel crowed, shoving Ed against the wall of the building he was trying to walk past. 'Little granny's boy has lost his granny. Boo hoo, Eddie boy. How does it feel knowing she didn't love you enough to stick around?'

The rage came from nowhere. A burning, blinding, scalding thing that rose up inside him and demanded he do something. He went for Nigel, roaring so hard his throat hurt for days afterwards. Punching and kicking, shoving Nigel to the ground and throwing himself on top of him. Relishing the crunching sound the bones in his hand made as they connected with Nigel's face. But there were three of them and only one of him. He'd barely started on Nigel when the other two pulled him off. They all laid into him after that, punching and kicking and jeering and laughing. He curled into a ball, pulled his hands over his head. An instinctive move that protected his face, but couldn't protect his stomach and kidneys and back and groin. Pain rained upon pain and part of him welcomed it while another part knew he would die if it went on for much longer. And then, just as suddenly as it had started, it stopped. He heard a sound and realised it was coming from him – a low groaning that turned into a sob.

Someone grabbed his hair and pulled his head up, the pain making him scream even though the last thing he wanted was to let them know how badly they'd hurt him. And then Nigel's face appeared, pushing itself so close to Ed's he could smell the sweat on Nigel's body and the stink of onion on his breath.

'What's it like, Eddie?' Nigel hissed. 'Knowing Granny hates you so much she had to kill herself to get away with you.'

Nigel let go and Ed's head fell, his face smashing into the ground. His face exploded in pain and his mouth filled with the taste of metal. Nigel's words, repeating over and over in his head like some nightmare melody. Trying to make sense of the incomprehensible.

It was the first time anyone had told Ed the truth about how she'd died. His parents and extended family of aunts and uncles had all rigidly stuck to the same story: that his grandmother had been involved in a tragic car accident.

When Ed told his mother he knew the truth, she'd broken down, sobbed and said she was sorry for lying. Told Ed she'd been trying to protect him, and begged him to forgive her. It took time, but eventually he forgave his mother, who had, after all, had his best interests at heart. But he'd never forgiven Nigel Shaw for what he'd done that day.

The front door opened, and Ed was face to face with his old enemy. The last time he'd seen Nigel was at the golf club about a month earlier. Then, Nigel had been red-faced and jovial. Surrounded by a group of his cronies, all of them speaking in that loud, braying manner so common in men like that. Men who'd grown up priv-ileged and secure, unquestioningly accepting of their elite place in the world.

Today, there was no trace of that bluff bravado. Nigel was more like a ghost than a real person. His skin was pale with a yellow tinge to it; bloodshot eyes and the rank stink of stale booze and unwashed body.

'What do you want?' he said.

'To offer my condolences,' Ed said.

'Well I don't want your pity,' Nigel said. 'So you can piss off back to whatever rock you crawled out from under.'

He started to close the door, but Ed pushed himself into the gap so that Nigel had no choice but to step back and let Ed into his house.

'If you don't leave I'll call one of your colleagues,' Nigel said. 'You've got no right to be here. You're not part of the investigation. I made sure of that. I told your superiors I wanted someone competent dealing with it.'

'It was my choice not to be part of the investigation,' Ed said. 'There's a clear conflict of interest.'

'That's right,' Nigel said. 'Your uncle, the murdering bastard.'

'Not because of Graham,' Ed said. 'The conflict is Lauren.'

'What do you mean?'

'She sent me an email, Nigel. The week before she was killed.'

'So bloody what?'

'She was looking into Mary's murder, wasn't she?'

A flash of pain across Nigel's face, so sharp and real that Ed felt a twinge of sympathy.

'I'm sorry,' he said. 'This must be so terrible for you both.'

'How would you know what it's like for us?' Nigel said. 'No one in the world can imagine what we're going through right now.'

He should go. He should thank Nigel for his time, turn around and leave the man to mourn in peace.

'I think the two things are connected,' he said instead. 'I think whatever Lauren found out about Mary's murder, someone didn't want that information to get out and that's why she was killed.'

'Listen to yourself,' Nigel said. 'Still obsessed with trying to save your family's reputation. It's pathetic. You're pathetic.' He stepped forward. 'My daughter is dead. She has been murdered and it's got nothing to do with your uncle or your family.'

'How can you be so sure?'

'I don't have to explain myself to you,' Nigel said. 'Your uncle killed Mary. That's a fact, whether you like it or not. My daughter is dead. That's another fact. And you're using this tragedy – my tragedy – to try to salvage your own family's reputation. You're disgusting, Ed Mitchell.'

He pushed the door shut, forcing Ed to step back before it slammed into him. He stared at the green wood, half-tempted to ring the doorbell again, and keep ringing until Nigel opened the door again. But there was no point. Nigel wasn't going to suddenly change his mind and speak to Ed.

Which meant Ed would have to find another way of getting the information. Because if Lauren had found something that proved Graham Reed's innocence, Ed would find it. One way, or another.

–

Dee was tidying up after breakfast when Ella arrived to collect Jake.

'Excuse the mess,' Dee said. 'We made pancakes and things got a bit out of hand.'

'He likes to try to flip them,' Ella said. 'Sorry. I should have warned you.'

'It's not a problem,' Dee said. 'Quite the opposite, in fact. We had fun. How about you? Good night?'

'The best,' Ella said, beaming. 'Wine, dinner, dancing and lots of laughs. God, it was so good to get out and let my hair down for once. Thank you so much, Dee!'

'Any time,' Dee said. 'You know that.'

'I know.' Ella bent to kiss Jake, who was watching TV and had barely acknowledged her arrival. 'Did you miss me, darling?'

'We made pancakes, Mummy,' Jake said. 'Look!' He pointed to the ceiling, where a half-cooked pancake was stuck solid.

'How will you get it down?' Ella asked Dee.

'Hopefully it will come down by itself,' Dee said. 'If not, that's what ladders are for.'

'Let me get it down now for you,' Ella said. 'Where do you keep your ladder?'

'Don't be silly,' Dee said. 'Come on. Sit down and have a coffee. You can tell me all about last night.'

Ella shook her head.

'I'd love to,' she said. 'But I've got a tonne of house-work that I've been putting off for days. Tom's home this evening, but he goes away again tomorrow morning.'

'How long will he be away for this time?' Dee asked.

'Just two nights,' Ella said. 'Then he's home with us for two whole weeks. I can't wait.'

'I bet you can't,' Dee said. She frowned, thinking of something. 'Does that mean Tom won't be here Friday?'

'Afraid not,' Ella said. 'But don't worry. Some of the girls are coming around with their kids. They're all staying for a sleepover. It should be fun.' She must have noticed the disappointment on Dee's face, because she stopped speaking. 'Oh Dee, I'm sorry. In all the rushing around, it didn't occur to me to let you know.'

'Don't worry about it,' Dee said, waving her hand in the air, trying to give the impression she didn't mind in the slightest. Friday nights were one of the highlights of her week, and this was the second one in a row that Ella had cancelled.

'I thought you'd be relieved,' Ella said. 'You can spend your Friday night with Ed for a change. Instead of taking care of all of us.'

'You're right.' Dee smiled. 'It'll be nice to do something different.'

'You sure?' Ella said.

'Positive,' Dee said. 'Now then, let's find Jake and you can get home and face into that housework.'

She helped Ella gather up Jake's belongings and said goodbye to them both, holding Jake for a little longer than normal when he ran to give her a hug. As she watched them leave, she couldn't shake off the feeling that they were slipping away from her. She didn't like it. She'd let her guard down with Jake and Ella, allowed them to become important to her. Even though she must have known – hadn't she? – that life moved on and the closeness they'd once shared wouldn't last for ever.

Maybe it was for the best. After all, it wasn't as if Ella and Jake were family. Ella had every right to widen her circle of friends. And of course she'd want to spend time with women closer to her own age. After everything she'd been through, Ella deserved some happiness and a chance to live a normal life. Dee would have to put her own feelings to one side and encourage Ella to spend as much time with her new friends as possible. Whether it was what Dee wanted, or not.

From the diary of Emma Reed

22 March 1961

I have him. Finally. Months of trying to find something that will prove what I know, and now it's happened. It didn't take me long to work what he'd done. Once I realised he'd killed Graham, I started to question the reasons for it. Because if anyone knows what sort of man my son was, it's Richard Partridge. He spent enough years of his life tormenting poor Graham and working out what made him tick. Richard always knew Graham couldn't have killed Mary. Because it was Richard who killed her, wasn't it?

I've already laid out my reasoning many times here in this diary. I'm going to do it once more now, because I want to make sure I have my story straight when I go back to see Chief Constable Brown tomorrow morning.

The signs had been there all along. In the months leading up to her death, Richard was always by her side. He wasn't the only one, of course. There were a group of young men who constantly vied for her attention. My son was one of them.

But Richard is different. He is arrogant and dangerous and a poor loser. Ever since he was a little boy, he hasn't liked losing. I remember the temper tantrums, fits of pure rage, he would go into whenever he lost at a game. He's still that same little boy, who's grown up to be a dangerous, violent man.

He wanted her, and Richard was used to getting the girls he wanted. But Richard's family aren't wealthy, and Mary Palmer had ambitions. She would never have settled for a man with no higher education, no prospect of a proper job and no ambition. No matter how important Richard likes to think he is, the truth is this: he's a nobody from a family of nobodies.

The problem is, I haven't been able to prove it. I've spoken with so many people, but everyone treats me as if I'm a madwoman. James has told me he will no longer tolerate my 'obsession'. Two people have been murdered — one of them is his son, his own flesh and blood. Yet James would rather we didn't talk about it. Last night, he told me I was drinking too much. This, from a man who used to spend more time at the 'nineteenth hole' at the weekends than he ever did with his own family.

The police have made it clear they don't want to get involved. The chief constable's words still smart each time I remember them.

'Go home and try to move on with your life. You're wasting your time and mine, Mrs Reed.'

Speaking to me as if I was some foolish little woman with no brain or sense. It's been clear all along that he thinks I'm making the whole thing up. He'll regret that tomorrow when he hears what I've got to tell him.

Because I've seen Richard's fiancée. He's living in London now, but he brought her home this weekend to meet his parents. Her name is Beth Mackie. She's the daughter of the man who runs the engineering company that employs Richard. I've found this out by myself. I've asked questions and checked the facts, making absolutely sure I've not missed a single thing. It's all about joining up the dots, isn't it? That's how a police investigation works, and Beth Mackie is the line connecting the dots.

Most of the information I got from Miriam, who is one of the few people who still comes to visit me. I asked Miriam about the *likeness, but she professed not to see it herself. When I pressed her about it, she admitted there was a vague similarity, nothing more than that. Not that Miriam's opinion counts for much. I only tolerate her because any companion is better than none at all.*

The chief constable is a clever man. He'll understand when I point it out to him. I may be forbidden from following Richard, or going anywhere near him, but there's no law in the land that can stop me speaking to the police about him if I uncover evidence that he's a cold-blooded murderer.

I was in the living room, standing in my usual spot by the window, watching the street outside. Nicola was in the kitchen and she was shouting, asking why there was no bread in the house. When I told her to wait, she grew angry and stormed upstairs to her bedroom. She used to be such a good girl, but recently she's been nothing but trouble. They were strolling down the street arm in arm, her head turned up to his, hanging on his every word, so I couldn't see her face at first. But I saw her hair, long and wavy and auburn. Copper and gold highlights captured in the bright sunshine, creating a halo effect. They paused outside our house and Richard said something. I couldn't hear the words but I didn't need to. When she turned away from him to stare into my home, she was frowning, her pretty little mouth shaped into a circle of shock.

I stepped away from the window, but my movements were clumsy. I stumbled against the side of the armchair and almost fell over. I'm sure they saw me, but I didn't care. My head was spinning, thoughts coming too fast and colliding with each other as I tried to make sense of it.

He'd made a mistake. He'd chosen a fiancée who looked like the woman he killed. They say all men have a 'type', and Richard is proof of this theory. His 'type' is a woman with copper-coloured hair and pale skin. A woman like Mary Palmer or Beth Mackie.

I've thought of nothing else since. I've sat here, three nights in a row, going over and over it in my head, writing and rewriting it until I am absolutely certain. Richard killed Mary because she rejected him. Afterwards, he waged a campaign of gossip and rumour against my son, goading thugs into killing him.

He knows I know. He saw it in my face that morning outside the church, and he's been playing with me ever since. Calling the police, claiming I'm harassing him, when we both know which one of us is the real criminal.

Twenty

Dee stepped inside the hotel foyer. She hadn't heard from Ed today, and was starting to think maybe that was for the best. She needed time to reassess their relationship and work out what she wanted to do. She'd spent the morning finishing the first of her articles for the *Guardian*. When that was done, she'd decided to pay Derek French another visit.

Jaime was at the reception desk, looking a lot perkier than the last time Dee had seen her.

'Hi.' Jaime smiled. 'How are you today?'

'Good,' Dee said. 'You?'

'Good days and bad days,' Jaime said. 'You know.'

'Hang in there,' Dee said. 'You won't always feel the way you do now. It will pass, I promise.'

'I assume you're not here just to check I'm okay?'

'Not just that,' Dee said. 'I'm hoping for a chat with your boss. And I wanted to see how you're getting on with Joana's photo.'

A red blush spread up Jaime's neck and face. 'I'm not sure, to be honest.'

'What do you mean?'

'Derek wasn't too happy about the photo being passed around. He's told us not to get involved.'

'I'm trying to find a young woman who's gone missing,' Dee said. 'What's wrong with that?'

Jaime wouldn't look at her when she answered.

'He says that's a job for the police, not a journalist.'

Dee rolled her eyes.

'And you, Jaime? What do you think?'

Jaime glanced up. 'You've got to understand this is a really stressful time. Derek's just trying to do what's best.'

'I know that,' Dee said, not believing it for one second. Derek couldn't stand the fact that something had happened in his hotel that he didn't know about. And now he was trying to make sure that Dee didn't find out either. 'Listen, Jaime. If I gave you another copy of the photo, do you think you could show it to a few people without Derek finding out you're asking?'

'I don't see what good it would do,' Jaime said. 'Lots of people have already seen it and no one's recognised her. I think Derek's probably right and whatever happened to that girl, it didn't happen here in the hotel.'

'So what harm will it do to show the photo to a few more people? That way, I can be absolutely sure Joana was never here. And once I'm sure, I'll stop coming here asking questions, and Derek won't need to worry about me any more.'

Jaime frowned, and Dee had to resist the urge to lean across the desk and shake her.

'I don't want to risk losing my job.'

'Joana has a little boy.' Dee took her phone out of her bag. 'Look, here's a photo. His name is Jakub. He's four years old and he's missing his mother so much right now.'

She shoved the phone under Jaime's face so she had no choice but to look.

Jaime looked at the photo, then up at Dee. 'Okay. Leave me another photo and I'll ask around. But don't keep hassling me about it. If anyone recognises her, I'll call you.'

'Brilliant.' Dee beamed at her as she pulled the folder from her bag, extracted a copy of Joana's photo and slid it across the desk to Jaime. 'You're a star. Thank you so much.'

She was just trying to work out how she could ask Jaime where Derek was when she heard him, behind her, calling her name.

Checking Jaime had hidden the photo, Dee turned and gave him her best smile.

'To what do we owe the pleasure today?' Derek asked. He was puffing slightly, no doubt from the effort of walking fast enough so he caught her before she left.

'I was just passing,' Dee said. 'And I remembered how upset Jaime had been the last time I saw her. I wanted to check she was okay.'

'Very kind of you. As you can see, she's doing just fine. I take care of my staff, Dee. They'll all tell you that.'

'I'm sure you do,' Dee said. 'Actually, I'm glad you caught me. I wanted to speak to you about something.'

'If it's about your Romanian friend, I've already told you, she wasn't here the night she disappeared.'

'Polish,' Dee said, pointlessly, because he was still talking, and didn't seem to have noticed she'd spoken.

'She's done a bunk. They get restless, these foreigners. Can't stick at one thing for too long. It's why I don't employ them.'

'I saw Kyle yesterday,' Dee said, taking a step back from the smell of his cologne and the stink of his racism. 'He's still pretty upset, isn't he?'

'He'll be okay,' Derek said. 'The truth is, Lauren was far too ambitious for him. She would have got sick of him sooner or later. Don't get me wrong, he's a lovely kid. But if he had his way, he'd spend all his time surfing and hanging out with his surfing mates. I mean, it's fine for a hobby, but no one's going to make a living out of being a surfer these days, right?'

'You think he minded that she was more ambitious than he was?' Dee said.

'I think she minded. She had big dreams – money, fame, that sort of thing. She was never going to achieve all that with our Kyle. She needed a different sort of man and she knew it.'

'Someone like you?'

'Are you serious?' Derek's face darkened. 'She was my son's girlfriend. I would never have touched her. You're worse than she was, do you know that? Digging, digging, digging. Looking for a story even when there isn't one. You can't keep coming in here sniffing about, implying all sorts of shit and acting like you're someone important. You're not a detective. I've had enough. I want you to leave and I don't want to see you inside this hotel again. You got that?'

The sudden shift from smarmy to threatening was unexpected.

'Hit a nerve, have I?'

Derek leaned forward, pressing his face so close to hers their noses were practically touching.

'Get the fuck out of my hotel. And keep away from my family too. If you go anywhere near my Kyle again, I'll report you to the police.'

'Thanks for your time.'

Dee turned on her heel and left before he could say anything else. She'd got to him. But not for the reason she'd come here. His disgusted reaction to her questions about Lauren made her fairly sure he hadn't been sleeping with his son's girlfriend. Which meant there was something else Derek French didn't want her to find out.

–

Back home, she finally cracked and called Ed. Her spirits, already low, sank further when she got his voicemail. She hung up without leaving a message, and poured herself a glass of wine. It was seven o'clock. The rest of the evening stretched out in front of her, an empty space that she'd have to fill somehow. She had a choice. She could either sit here drinking and feeling sorry for herself, or do something productive. After several sips of wine, she decided getting pissed wasn't going to help her mood.

So she opened her laptop and went onto Facebook. Earlier, she had requested to join the true crime group Kyle had told her about. Now, scrolling through her list of notifications, she saw that her request had been approved.

Lauren's murder was one of the major topics of conversation. Reading through the comments was an eye-opening, if sometimes painful, experience. Several of the group members were convinced Kyle was the killer. There were also a few comments about Ed, following the latest revelations in the press. Dee read the different comments, sickened by the way some people's minds worked. One thread was devoted to the theory that Lauren had been having an affair with someone – possibly Ed – who was helping her with her investigation into Graham's murder. When Kyle had found out about the affair, he'd killed her.

Dee was about to leave the group when she noticed another thread, this one with the topic heading 'What about Annabelle?' The content here was far more interesting. The general gist of the conversations was that Mary Palmer's aunt, Annabelle, had been the person with most to gain from her niece's death. Annabelle and Mary's father were brother and sister. There were no other siblings. George was a widow and Mary was his only child. With Mary out of the way, Annabelle was set to inherit George's vast fortune. Which is exactly what happened, according to someone called Mike Dixon, who seemed to be an expert on every murder that had taken place in the UK over the last hundred years.

Quickly, Dee ran back over what she already knew about Annabelle: George's sister, who became Annabelle Shaw after her marriage. Nigel's mother and Lauren's grandmother. Dee took the bottle of wine from the fridge, poured herself another glass and called Philip Flint.

'The second time in two days,' he said. 'How can I help you?'

'I was wondering if you're free to meet for a coffee tomorrow?' Dee said. 'My treat. I'd like to ask you a few more questions.'

'I'm not free tomorrow,' he said. 'But I could meet you the following day. Would the Hydro be a suitable meeting place? It's around the corner from my apartment, you see, and I don't like entertaining visitors at home.'

'The Hydro would be lovely,' Dee said. 'Three o'clock? We can have afternoon tea.'

She'd just hung up when her phone started to ring.

'Ed?'

'Sorry it's taken me so long to call back,' he said. 'I've been busy. I'm working tomorrow as well, but I wondered if you'd like to meet for a morning walk first? If we head out early enough, I'll be able to buy you breakfast in Nelson's afterwards.'

Nelson's was Dee's favourite place to have breakfast, and Ed knew it.

'I'm not sure,' she said.

'Please, Dee. I'd really like to see you.'

'Okay,' she said. 'But make sure you do pick me up early. I'm not missing a free breakfast at Nelson's.'

'Great.' She heard the relief in his voice and something inside her relaxed as well.

Damn and blast you, Ed Mitchell, she thought as she hung up. She should have said no, told him she didn't want to see him until he'd sorted himself out. But the truth was, she did want to see him. She owed it to herself to make one last attempt at getting their relationship back on track. And if that didn't work, well, then she'd just have to deal with it.

Twenty-one

At the top of the hill, Dee paused to get her breath back. A morning haze hung over the downs, shot through with shades of pink and pale grey as night turned to day. The green hills of the South Downs National Park rolled out before her, ending abruptly as land became white cliff at the start of the English Channel. Teetering at the top of the cliffs, Belle Tout lighthouse was a black silhouette against the brightening sky. When she turned the other way, Dee had a perfect view of Eastbourne town, laid out along the coast on the flat stretch of land at the bottom of the downs. The sun was rising over the sea, light moving across the town, pushing away the last traces of a long night.

'Beautiful, isn't it?' Ed said.

'It really is,' Dee agreed. 'I'm glad you suggested this. It's such a lovely way to start the day.'

She hadn't felt that way at five thirty this morning when her alarm went off. Then, all she'd wanted to do was roll over in bed and go back to sleep. Now, with her heart pumping fast and steady, and her body full of the good feelings you only get from physical exercise and being close to nature, she promised herself she'd do this more often.

They turned right and walked along the ridge. The geography of this corner of England meant they had sea views on either side of them. With the sea and the rolling hills and the air full of birdsong, Dee couldn't imagine there was anywhere lovelier in the entire world.

'I'm sorry,' Ed said.

Dee stopped walking. 'What have you done now?'

The corners of his lips twitched and she felt a tug of her old feelings for him.

'Nothing else,' he said. 'I mean I'm sorry for being so crap recently.'

'And?'

This time she got a proper smile.

'And for not telling you about Lauren coming to see me, or what happened with Graham. All of it.'

'I can understand why you didn't say anything,' Dee said. 'It's just… I thought I knew you better than I do. That's a weird feeling.'

'I'm still me,' Ed said.

'Unfortunately.'

'Hey.' He punched her arm. 'Watch it or you'll be buying your own breakfast.'

They started walking again. Half an hour later, they reached Jevington, a tiny village nestled in the bottom of the valley. They walked through the village, past the row of cottages that were once the Hungry Monk restaurant, where the banoffee pie was created.

'Which way?' Ed asked. 'Continue through the village or turn here and walk up to Butt's Brow?'

'This way.' Dee pointed to the path that led across the fields and over several more hills to Butt's Brow. Her body would regret this later, but the views from the top of Butt's

Brow were some of her favourite. It seemed a shame not to take advantage of them on a clear, sunny day like this.

'I got a call from a journalist at the *Mirror* last night,' Ed said. 'Wanted to ask me about Graham. Apparently they're running their own story today.'

'God, I'm sorry you have to go through all that,' Dee said. 'Don't speak to any of them. No matter how much they make you think it would be a good idea. What exactly are they going to say in their story, do you know?'

'Nothing new, as far as I know. The journalist wanted to know if I had any comment so, of course, I said no. I called Ness, but so far no one's contacted her. Although I'm sure it's only a matter of time.'

Dee wished there was something she could do to make this go away. He didn't deserve to have to deal with tabloid intrusion on top of everything else he'd already been through. Her journalism career sat like a wedge between them at times.

'This could turn into a bit of a shit storm,' she said. 'Why don't you let me handle the journalists? The next time someone calls you, give them my number and tell them to speak to me instead.'

'You don't need to do that,' Ed said. 'Besides, it'll pass soon enough. Before we know it, they'll have moved on to the next big story and I'll be yesterday's news.'

His easy dismissal of her offer to help hurt, but she let it go. He had enough to deal with without worrying about her feelings on top of everything else.

'You think Nessa will be okay?' she asked, as they continued up the hill.

'She'll be fine,' Ed said. 'She's in such a good place now. And Javi's a very steadying influence. I offered to drive up to see them this weekend, but she said there's no point.'

Dee had only met Ed's sister a handful of times, but she'd liked her instantly. Unlike her older brother, Nessa was scatty and bohemian and a total hippie. She was also vegan and didn't drink alcohol or caffeine. Despite these vices, she was great fun and Dee had enjoyed her company enormously.

They didn't speak much for the next twenty minutes, saving their breath for the hills. As they neared the brow, Ed told Dee about his visit to Nigel the previous day.

'Doesn't sound like the most sensible thing you've ever done,' Dee said, when he'd finished. Which was mild considering what she could have said. What the hell had he been thinking? Sharon Spalding, Ed's boss, would go ballistic if she found out, and Dee couldn't see how Sharon *wouldn't* find out.

'I thought he'd want to know the truth,' Ed said. 'But he doesn't care about the truth. The only thing he cares about is protecting his family's precious reputation.'

'You don't know that,' Dee said. 'He might have all sorts of reasons for not wanting to speak to you. You told me yourself the two of you have never got on. You're probably the last person he wants to see right now.'

'I'm not going to sit back and do nothing,' Ed said. 'Especially now, when my own family's private business is about to be raked over by the tabloid press.'

'I understand that,' Dee said. 'But you can't around upsetting people like Nigel Shaw. You know the right thing to do is leave Rachel to get on with her job.'

'Even if Lauren's death is directly linked to what happened to Mary?' Ed said, sounding irritated.

If he'd been less grumpy, she might have let it go. But his irritation was obviously rubbing off on her. 'For all you know, whoever killed Lauren put her body in the church and cut off her hair as a distraction.'

'A distraction from what?'

'From the real reason she was killed. Think about it. If the killer knew about Lauren's connection with Mary, it would be the perfect way to take attention away from himself.'

'Lauren was writing a story about Mary's murder,' Ed said. 'She found something that proved Graham – my uncle – was innocent. That's why she was killed. There's no point anyone wasting their time thinking there's any other reason she was killed.'

'So who killed her then?'

'Well clearly I don't know that,' Ed said. 'Not yet.'

Dee could see there was no point continuing this conversation. His mind was made up and nothing she did or said was going to change what he thought. Ed normally had such a cool head and took his profession seriously. But on this, he was unwilling to listen to reason. And that irritated the hell out of her.

They'd reached the car park and, as she waited for Ed to unlock his car, she wished she'd driven across by herself. She didn't want to get into the car with him, and she certainly didn't want to have breakfast with him at Nelson's. She couldn't bear to be with him when he was like this – obsessed and irrational and nothing like the man she'd started to fall in love with.

'Ed?'

When he turned and smiled, waiting to hear what she had to say, she wanted to beg him to let it go – Lauren and Graham and Mary, all of it. Just put it behind him and focus on this relationship. Because she was scared of what would happen if he didn't find the answers he wanted.

'I've got a deadline this morning,' she said instead. 'I'm not going to have time for breakfast.'

'You okay?' he said.

'Fine,' she lied. 'I've just realised how much I've got left to do, that's all.'

'Okay,' he said. 'Probably better, anyway. I was planning to go and speak to Kyle after work today. But if I'm not having breakfast with you, I can try to catch him this morning instead. Come on, don't stand there looking at me like that. Jump in. We've both got work to do.'

Twenty-two

Today, the red Mazda was the only car in the driveway. Two minutes earlier, Ed had watched Nigel Shaw get into the silver Lexus and drive away from the house. He waited until Nigel's car turned left at the end of the road and disappeared before he approached the house. He shouldn't be here. If Sharon found out he was visiting Lauren's family, she'd slap a misconduct charge on him.

He hadn't planned this. After dropping Dee back home, he'd driven to the Frenches' house, but despite the early hour, no one seemed to be at home. By then, he was too wired to focus on work. So he'd come here instead.

He lifted his hand to ring the doorbell. Then paused. Dee's voice, as clear as if she was standing here beside him. *You can't go around upsetting people like Nigel Shaw.* Except Nigel wasn't here, so what harm could it do? Dee wasn't here either, come to that. And what she didn't know wouldn't hurt her.

Bollocks.

Again, he hesitated. She was right. Not telling her something was another form of lying.

'Ed?'

The front door had opened while he stood here, trying to make his mind up. Flashes of memory, moments suspended in time. People he hadn't thought about in years. Bonfires on the beach, a bottle of warm beer being passed around, the air thick with the bitter smell of weed. Her face when she smiled, and the soft touch of her lips on his. All rushing back with just one word.

'What are you doing here?'

'Can we talk?' he said. 'Please, Maxine.'

After a moment, she nodded her head.

'You'd better come inside.'

In the kitchen, she gestured for him to sit at the table.

'What are you doing here?' she asked, sitting opposite him.

'I just wanted to see you,' he said. 'I'm so sorry, Max.'

'It doesn't feel real,' she said. 'Nothing in life prepares you for this. It's like being in a nightmare that you can't wake up from.'

'Is there anything I can do?'

'Find who killed her.' She used her sleeve to wipe her face. 'I'm glad you came, actually. Nigel said she'd been to see you. Is that true?'

'It's why I'm not part of the investigation,' Ed said. 'Well, that and my family history. Obviously.'

'What did she want to talk to you about?' Maxine asked.

'I don't know. She first approached me a few months back. Said she was writing about Mary's murder and wanted to ask me some questions. I wasn't interested, and I told her that. Then, a week before she was killed, she sent me an email. Said she needed to see me. I never replied.'

'Oh God.' Maxine put a hand over her mouth. 'What the hell was she up to?'

Grief had aged her. She had none of the bouncy energy that he'd once found so exhilarating. And no sign of that big, wide smile that used to beam pure joy out to the world and made you want to find ways to keep her smiling all the time. Her face had caved in on itself. She'd lost a lot of weight, and looked hollowed out, empty. Her eyes, usually so bright and curious, were dull.

'You're lucky Nigel isn't home,' she said. 'You really wound him up the last time you were here. It took a lot of persuasion to stop him calling your boss and making a complaint.'

'I didn't mean to upset him,' Ed said. 'I swear, Max. I just wanted him to know – wanted you both to know – that Lauren had contacted me.'

'He's not coping. Neither of us are coping, of course. But he's… I'm worried about him, Ed. At least, I would be worried if I was able to. Mostly I can't think or care about how he's feeling. It's all I can do to keep myself going without trying to keep him going as well. It's too much.'

'I was hoping you might know why she emailed me,' Ed said.

'She wanted to be a journalist.' Tears started running down Maxine's face, but she continued speaking as if she hadn't noticed. 'I'm sure she would have succeeded. She was very determined. Very like Nigel, in fact. Although not as messed up, because… well, because his mother was a horrible woman who probably should never have had children of her own.' She frowned. 'Sorry. I've forgotten what I was saying. What were we talking about?'

'Lauren,' Ed said. 'You were telling me that she wanted to be a journalist.'

'That's right. But then something happened. I don't know what, exactly. She had a big row with Nigel, and the next thing I knew she was packing her bags and moving in with Kyle.'

'What did they row about?'

'Some letter she found.' Maxine frowned. 'I wish I could tell you more than that, but I can't. Because neither of them would talk to me. All I know is, one day Lauren was writing a story about Mary's murder. The next, she refused to talk to me about it. She moved out and now I can't forgive him for that, because if he hadn't been such a pig-headed idiot, she wouldn't have spent the last few weeks of her life living somewhere else.

'Karen loved it, of course. Kept calling around, pretending she wanted to help when all she really wanted to do was rub my nose in it. Sorry. That probably sounds cruel, but I don't care. That's the thing, I don't care about anything any more. I don't care that Nigel's cracking up, or Kyle is heartbroken. I don't care about any of it. All I care about, the only thing I think about every single minute of every day, is finding out who killed my daughter and making sure they pay for what they've done.'

She was speaking too fast, her words tumbling over each other, voice rising until she was shouting. Ed guessed this was the first time she'd said a lot of this out loud.

She paused to take a breath and wipe her face.

'I've never believed in capital punishment,' she continued. 'Now, I wish we still had it. I want to see him die. The person who did that to Lauren. I want to stick a knife into his heart and stand over him as the life drains from his body. I want him to suffer, and understand what it's like to experience pain like you couldn't even imagine.'

'I'd feel the same.' Ed thought of his nephews, Cielo and River. He couldn't imagine how he'd feel if something like this happened to one of them.

'Nigel still won't tell me what they rowed about. Even now, when our daughter is dead, he refuses to speak about it. There have been times these last few days when I've hated him.' Maxine shook her head. 'Sorry. I don't know why I'm telling you all of this.'

'It's fine.' Ed wanted to stand up and wrap his arms around her, but he wasn't sure how she'd take it so he stayed where he was.

'Have you spoken to Kyle?' she said.

'Not yet. Why?'

Maxine started to reply but she was interrupted by the sound of the front doorbell ringing. Ed offered to go and see who was there but Maxine shook her head.

'I'll go. You stay here.'

He listened as she opened the front door and spoke to whoever was outside. A moment later, he heard the slam of the door being shut, footsteps in the hall and a familiar voice speaking to Maxine.

Ed groaned. He looked around the kitchen, searching for a way out. He tried the back door, but it was locked and he couldn't see a key. Before he could find one, Maxine was coming back into the room with Rachel Lewis right behind her.

Rachel stopped in the doorway.

'Maxine,' she said, looking at Ed. 'Is there anywhere we can speak in private?'

'Oh.' Maxine frowned. 'Sorry. I didn't realise… yes, of course. We can go into the living room.'

'There's no need.' Ed grabbed his jacket off the back of the chair where he'd put it earlier. He felt Rachel's eyes on him the whole time. 'I was just leaving. Thanks for the chat, Maxine.'

At the door, he paused to speak to Rachel but she looked away. Ed pushed past her into the corridor and walked towards the front door. He didn't look back, but he knew Rachel had turned around and was watching him as he opened the front door and walked outside into the chill wind and grey light of the early spring morning.

Twenty-three

Dee was working on her second article for the *Guardian* when she had an unexpected visitor in the form of Karen French. One look at Karen's face told Dee this wasn't a friendly visit.

'What do you think you're playing at?' Karen demanded as soon as Dee opened the front door.

'What can I do for you, Karen?'

'I thought you were meant to be helping my son. Instead, you're going around the place making all sorts of wild accusations about my husband.'

'What sort of accusations?'

'Implying there was something going on between him and Lauren. Which is ridiculous. Derek would never do something like that. And why are you accusing him of being involved in the disappearance of some girl who should never have even been in this country in the first place?'

'Excuse me?'

'She's an illegal immigrant, isn't she?'

'She's a young woman who's disappeared,' Dee said. 'She was meant to have been meeting someone in your hotel the night she went missing. I'm trying to find out what happened to her. I don't know what Derek's told you, but I've never accused him of anything. If he's got a problem with my questions, why doesn't he speak to me himself?'

Karen's shoulders slumped.

'He's upset. We're all upset. This terrible business with Lauren, it's broken my poor boy. It's a nightmare with no end in sight. I really hoped you'd be able to help. Instead, all you're doing is… I don't know. What are you doing exactly?'

She was right. This was a terrible time for Karen and her family. Dee should have handled things with a bit more tact.

'Do you want to come in for a coffee?' she said.

'I don't suppose you've got any wine?'

'I'm sure I've got a bottle of white in the fridge.'

She was surprised. Karen didn't strike her as the sort of woman to drink in the afternoon. She led Karen into the sitting room, took a bottle of Pinot from the fridge and poured them both a glass.

'What a wonderful house,' Karen said. 'I had no idea you lived somewhere so beautiful.'

'It was my parents' house,' Dee said. 'My dad was an architect. He designed the place.'

'And you inherited all of it? Lucky you.'

Lucky wasn't the word Dee would have chosen to describe the death of both her parents, but she let it pass.

'I'm really sorry if I've upset you,' she said, handing one of the glasses to Karen and gesturing for her to sit down.

'You can't help it, I'm sure. You know Lauren had moved in with us? Everyone thought they were a perfect family, but they had all sorts of problems. Nigel is very difficult, and Maxine lets him walk all over her. Lauren had a bit more spirit so he couldn't do the same with her.

He didn't like that, I can tell you. I've told all of this to the police, but they're useless. Which is why I was counting on you.'

'I can't exactly go over to their house and start questioning him,' Dee said. 'The man's just lost his daughter. And, as your husband pointed out yesterday, I'm not a detective. I've got no right to ask Nigel anything. Joana and Lauren knew each other, so it makes sense to see if Lauren's murder has anything to do with Joana's disappearance.'

'Like what?'

'That's what I'm trying to find out.'

'Derek said you have a photo of her,' Karen said. 'Can I take a look?'

Dee got her bag, took out one of the copies of Joana's photo and handed it to Karen.

'She's very attractive,' Karen said, after a moment. 'Isn't she?'

'Do you recognise her?'

Karen shook her head. 'Never seen her before. You've really got no idea where she could have gone?'

'She left her flat one Saturday night in February,' Dee said. 'And she hasn't been seen since. She told her flatmate she was meeting a man at the Aldrington. That's all I know.'

'Yet none of the hotel staff remember seeing her,' Karen said. 'Which means she was lying, surely?'

'Or maybe something happened to her before she got to the hotel.'

'Well.' Karen handed the photo back. 'I hope you manage to find her. It's sad to think she could just disappear without a trace. But I really don't think her disappearance could have anything to do with Lauren. Nigel's relationship with Lauren, it wasn't normal. Most of the time, he acted as if he hated her. Over the years, I've tried to understand why he was like that.'

'And?'

'I shouldn't really say,' Karen said, although it was clear she was going to. 'I mean, it's not as if I can prove it. But I've often wondered if Nigel really was her biological father.'

Dee opened her mouth to speak, then changed her mind, deciding it was better to let Karen finish.

'I know how that sounds,' Karen said. 'And I hate to say anything, especially now. But if Nigel knew he wasn't her father, it would explain the way he behaved.'

'Have you told the police?'

'Of course,' Karen said. 'But you know how things work in this town. Nigel's a very influential man. He's friends with the chief constable. The police aren't going to treat him as a serious suspect, no matter what I tell them.'

'You can't really believe that,' Dee said. 'If he killed his daughter, it doesn't matter who he's friends with. I know the detective leading the investigation. She's not going to let anything like that influence her.'

'You can think what you want.' Karen stood up. 'But I'm telling you the truth. Nigel Shaw hated his daughter, and when he found out she was writing a story about his aunt's death it tipped him over the edge. That's why Lauren was killed, not because of some non-existent link with some Polish girl she hardly knew.'

'How did you know she's Polish?' Dee asked.

'Derek told me, of course. What a strange question.'

Karen thanked Dee for the wine and said she'd see herself out. As Dee listened to her leave, she ran back over the last conversation she'd had with Derek. He hadn't remembered then that Joana was from Poland, and Dee doubted very much he'd remembered it later. Which meant Karen had lied to her.

From the diary of Emma Reed

3 October 1961

I'm confused and disorientated. The single belief that has anchored me and kept me going has gone. After today, I don't know what to think. I've tried to make sense of it, but each time I think I've found an answer, it disappears again. It's like trying to hold on to sand.

Richard and Beth were in Eastbourne again this weekend. She comes with him almost every time he visits. I wonder if he thinks that showing off his fiancée will stop people wondering why he no longer hangs around with his brother? If that's the case, his plan hasn't worked. It's clear there's a rift between Richard and David, and I can guess what's caused it. I've tried speaking to David, but he told me he has nothing to say. I want to try again, but he's not going to be around much after he starts university later this month. Miriam tells me he's training to be a doctor, although neither of us can understand where his family have found the money for that.

I saw them this morning, as they passed my house. I assumed they were going to the station to catch the train to London. Nicola was in the kitchen having her breakfast. James had already left for work. I was doing my best to deal with Nicola's bad mood, a messy kitchen and a thumping headache. Unable to bear Nicola's sullen attitude any longer, I went into the living room and sat down on the sofa. I'd only been there a few minutes when they passed the window, walking arm in arm as if they didn't have a care in the world.

Something snapped inside me. I ran out of the house and followed them down the street. I took care to stay well back so they didn't see me, mindful of the chief constable's warning the last time we spoke. Although he's a silly fool if he thinks 'consequences' are going to stop me seeking justice for my son.

Despite the chill in the air, I'd worked up quite a sweat by the time we reached the station. My skin was clammy and my headache had intensified as I'd hurried along the streets after them. I'd promised myself I'd take it a little easier on the gin this evening, but the truth is I need something to help with the shock.

At the station, I expected them both to get on the London train. If that had happened, I would have come straight home again. Instead, only Beth boarded the train, while Richard waited on the platform, waving goodbye to his beloved (ha! He doesn't love her! He's not capable of loving anyone other than himself!).

Imagine my shock, dear diary, when I watched him skip away to the other platform a few minutes later, and board the train to Brighton. I had no choice, did I? I had to see what he was up to.

I had a mountain of washing to do, and a shepherd's pie to make for supper, but all of that would have to wait. James wouldn't like it, but there's not much that makes James happy these days. His barbed comments about a messy house and irregular meal times are starting to bore me. Besides, it wasn't going to kill him if his supper was served a little later for once.

I climbed onto the train and moved through the carriages until I saw him. He was sitting with his back to me, staring out the window. I slipped into a seat a few rows behind him and didn't take my eyes off him as the train moved away from the platform.

We were almost at Lewes when I remembered doing the same journey soon after the war. The details of that day escape me now, but I remember – as if it was yesterday – Graham's childish excitement at being on a train for the first time. The memory caused a spasm of pain so bad I had to lean over in my seat until it passed.

People say time is a great healer, but it's been a year now and the pain hasn't eased. I cannot imagine a time I won't feel like this. The grief has become part of me. If I lost it now it would be every bit as real as losing a limb or an organ. It's who I have become.

We stayed on the train all the way to Brighton. The train was pulling into the station when I saw Annabelle standing on the platform. I thought it was a coincidence. It never occurred to me it could be anything else. But then she saw him and she waved. And as he stepped down from the carriage, she ran forward and threw herself into his arms.

My memories immediately after that are a blur, like trying to see inside a house through a dirty window. I know I got off the train and left the station, although I have no memory of doing either. I remember being on the beach, walking as if I was in a dream, with no clue where I was going. Later, I remember getting off the train at Eastbourne and walking home. But none of it felt real. I felt separate from the world around me, as if I were a ghost, not a real person.

James was home before me. He was angry and he shouted at me but I ignored him. Nicola was crying, I think, although again I barely noticed her tears. I feel bad about that now, but at the time I was incapable of feeling anything. While I was preparing supper, I stuck the tip of the chopping knife into the palm of my hand and watched the blood run out of me and still I felt nothing.

It was better like that. Sitting down tonight and writing about it brings it all back. Now I've started to feel, it won't stop. Pain and anger and red raw grief that scrapes away at me until soon there'll be nothing left.

Richard and Annabelle. I've given it a lot of thought, and I think I know what's going on. He's using her, whispering his poison into her ear, filling her foolish head with lies. That's why she spread those rumours about Graham. Richard doesn't love her. How could he? She's older than him by several years, and she simply isn't the sort of woman to drive a man so crazy with love he would kill for her. I wonder how she feels now he's engaged to be married to someone else. I wonder if she hoped it would be her.

Twenty-four

Stepping inside the Hydro Hotel was like stepping into the set of a Poirot film. The elegant interior oozed art deco charm. Dee walked through the foyer into the large conservatory with stunning views over the hotel's private gardens and the sea beyond. Philip Flint was already there, seated at a table by the window. Dee recognised him from the author photo at the back of his book, although he looked at least ten years older than he did in the photo. When she walked over and introduced herself, he pushed himself up and shook her hand.

'A pleasure to finally meet you,' he said. 'I've taken the liberty of ordering afternoon tea, as you suggested. I do hope that's all right?'

'Perfect.' Dee had skipped lunch in anticipation of this. She was looking forward to tucking into cake and sand-wiches.

'When we spoke the last time,' Philip said, once they were both sitting down, 'you didn't actually tell me what your interest is in this story? Is there something specific you're looking for, or is your interest more general than that?'

'I'm not sure,' Dee said. 'I've been trying to find a young woman who's gone missing. She was a friend of

Lauren's and I thought maybe that had something to do with why Lauren was killed.'

'And now?'

'Now I really don't know. The more I find out, the more confused I get. I know Lauren was writing a story about Mary Palmer's murder. Which is what led me to your book. And then, when I'd read it, I suppose my journalist's instinct kicked in. Like you, I want to know who killed Mary and why.'

'Fascinating,' Philip murmured. 'Ah look, here's our order.'

Dee waited until the food and tea had been laid out in front of them before she continued speaking.

'I know you don't think Graham killed Mary,' she said. 'So I wanted to ask you who you think did kill her. And why you didn't address this directly in your book.'

'I imagine you've already worked that out.' Philip smiled.

Dee took a cucumber sandwich from the cake tray and bit into it before replying.

'Delicious,' she said. 'Why can I never make them like this at home?'

'You need to peel your cucumber,' Philip said. 'And add white pepper. Never black.'

'Thanks.' Dee smiled.

'So, tell me,' Philip said. 'Why didn't I name the person I think killed Mary?'

'Because you had no proof,' Dee said. 'And the person you think killed her was still alive when you wrote the book? If you named someone without any evidence to back up your claim, you risked being sued for libel.'

'Marvellous.' He clapped his hands, his blue eyes twinkling with a mischievous delight. Dee guessed he'd been a handsome man in his day.

'You think Annabelle killed her,' Dee said. 'Why?'

'It's very simple. She was the person who had the most to benefit from Mary's death. With Mary out of the way, Annabelle inherited everything.'

'But that doesn't make her a killer,' Dee said.

'I know.' Philip frowned. 'I spoke to a lot of people when I was writing this book. I couldn't find anyone who had a good thing to say about her. By all accounts, she was a nasty, vindictive woman. Of course, being nasty and vindictive doesn't make her a killer, either. But Graham Reed was neither of those things. And if Graham didn't kill Mary, then someone else did. But I never found anything to prove it was Annabelle, so it's possible I'm wrong. She was a tiny woman, you know. If she killed Mary, I doubt she'd have been able to do it without help. You know her son tried to stop the book being published?'

'Really?'

'Oh yes,' Philip said. 'He threatened me with legal action if I went ahead with it.'

'But you didn't let that stop you?'

'Of course not. Although, as you'll have observed, I was very careful not to name his mother as a potential suspect.'

'Any regrets?'

'Not really. The book was hardly a best-seller. I self-published and, quite frankly, I don't know the first thing about how the publishing industry works. I only sold a handful of copies and they were mainly to friends and family. It's likely sales will have increased over the last few weeks, but I can hardly celebrate the fact. A young woman has been murdered, after all.'

'You said Annabelle would have needed help,' Dee said. 'Who would have helped her do something like that? And why?'

As she waited for him to answer, Dee took a slice of Victoria sponge and added it to the little pile of sandwiches and cake already on her plate. She was being greedy, but she'd always been a sucker for a proper afternoon tea.

'Not her husband. She didn't meet him until several years after Mary had died.' Philip refilled his cup and helped himself to a sandwich. 'There was a rumour that Annabelle had been seeing another young man around the time Mary was killed. But I looked into that and I don't think there was any truth to it. The gentleman in question was several years her junior and, by all accounts, had a reputation as quite a ladies' man. He was a flamboyant character and I doubt he'd have dated someone like Annabelle. By all accounts, she was a rather unattractive woman.'

'What can you tell me about Nigel?' Dee asked.

'Not much, I'm afraid. The only dealings I had with him were when he was trying to stop me publishing my book. Based on that experience, I'd describe him as something of a bully. But I'm sure he's capable of being quite charming when he wants to be.'

'And his wife?'

'Maxine?' Philip's face cleared. 'A lovely woman. She contacted me, you know. After the book was published. Told me she thought I'd done a very good job and she'd make sure her husband didn't overreact.'

Dee took a bite out of the Victoria sponge to avoid thinking of Ed's ex-girlfriend.

'I heard a rumour that Nigel might not be Lauren's biological father.'

'Utter nonsense,' Philip said. 'All you've got to do is look at the photos of Lauren and Mary to see they're related.'

Of course. She should have asked Karen how she could explain that if she thought Nigel wasn't Lauren's real father.

When their tea was finished and they'd run out of things to talk about, Dee thanked Philip for his time and promised she'd keep in touch with him. As they stood up to go, he handed her a brown leather satchel.

'My notes,' he said. 'All handwritten, so apologies if you struggle with my writing. But I thought they might be helpful. If you promise you'll take care of them and return them when you're finished.'

Outside, the sun was starting to set. Over the course of their time together, the sky had changed from deep blue to pale pink. Philip's face was pale in the evening light. He looked, Dee realised, like a man who didn't have much time left.

'Thank you so much,' she said, moved by his generosity.

'I hope it helps,' he said. 'Who knows, Dee Doran? Maybe one day when all of this is over, we might write a book together on what really happened to Mary Palmer.'

Dee offered to drive him home but he insisted on walking. Deciding not to get into her car straight away, she crossed the road and walked down to the beach. The tide was out and the water was still and quiet. A row of cormorants stood on the rocks that appeared at low tide, their backs to the shore, guarding the coastline.

As the sun disappeared behind the downs, the temperature dropped. When she couldn't stand the cold any longer, Dee walked back to her car. She'd been dreading this evening, having to spend it by herself instead of having pizza with Tom, Ella and Jake. But now she had Philip's notes to go through, she was quite looking forward to driving home and getting stuck into work for the evening. It had been a while since Dee had wanted to spend an evening alone without a bottle of wine for company. Another sign she'd moved on from the dark depression that had been her constant companion for too long after her mother died.

Each day, she was moving forward with her life, putting the past behind her and learning to be grateful for what she had now, not what she'd lost. It wasn't always easy, but she was doing okay. Things with Ed were difficult right now, but – one way or another – she'd get through this. She would be okay.

Twenty-five

When Ed's doorbell rang that evening, he knew before opening his front door who it was. He'd spent the day keeping out of her way, but it was inevitable she'd track him down sooner or later.

'Rachel,' he said. 'What a surprise.'

'Can I come inside?' Rachel said. 'I'm freezing to death out here.'

'You want a cup of tea?' Ed asked. 'Or something stronger? I've got some beers in the fridge.'

'This isn't a social call,' Rachel said. 'You know exactly why I'm here.'

He led her into the kitchen and put the kettle on.

'You put me in an impossible situation earlier,' Rachel said. 'What the hell were you playing at? I mean, I understand this case is personal. And I sympathise with that. But I've asked you more than once to keep clear of this. How do you think it's going to look when I tell Sharon you've been speaking to Lauren's mother?'

'Maxine's an old friend,' Ed said. 'What was I meant to do, Rachel? Not go and offer my condolences?'

'You were meant to tell me about it before you went to see her,' Rachel said. 'What the hell were you thinking? Can't you see that you are jeopardising this whole investigation? Let's say we charge someone with Lauren's murder. The first thing a defence solicitor will do is to try to prove it's a set-up. Why? Because one of our detectives has been going around harassing the victim's family.'

'I'd hardly call it harassing.'

'That's not how Nigel sees it,' Rachel said. 'He came home while I was there, you know. Told me you'd been around to the house yesterday as well. Is that right, Ed?'

When Ed didn't say anything, she shook her head. 'Can't you see how crazy this is? And how much you're undermining me? This is my first time as senior. You know how long I've waited to be SIO, Ed. I want to find Lauren's killer. I'm doing everything I can to do that as quickly as possible. But everywhere I turn, you're already there. It's like you're waiting for me to mess up.'

'That's not true. You're doing a brilliant job, Rach. Heck, if I'm ever killed I'd want you leading the investigation,' he said, trying to lighten the mood. 'This has got nothing to do with you.'

'You say that,' Rachel said. 'But you don't mean it. If you really believed in me, you'd leave me to carry out this investigation in whatever way I choose. What do you think it's like for me? Working with a tosspot like Barry who's watching my every move, waiting for me to mess up? And then there's you. Someone I thought was my friend, doing exactly the same thing.'

'I'm sorry,' Ed said.

'You mean that?' Rachel said.

'Yes,' Ed said. 'You're completely right. I've been bang out of order, but it won't happen any more. I swear.'

'No more nasty surprises like finding you sitting in the kitchen of the victim's family?'

'No.'

'No more sneaky coffees in the canteen where you try to pump me for information?'

'Cross my heart.'

'Good.' Rachel nodded. 'Okay then.' She pulled out a chair and sat across the table from him. 'I'll have that beer now, thanks very much.'

They drank a bottle of beer each and bitched about their colleagues for a bit, before moving on to their personal lives. Rachel and her partner, Grace, were getting married in October and the wedding plans were well underway. Even though, as Ed pointed out, October was seven months away.

'Seven months is nothing,' Rachel said. 'I never realised there was so much organising to do. Thankfully, Grace seems to be doing most of it and doesn't expect me to do much more than turn up on the day and say "I do". You'll be there, won't you? And Dee, of course. We haven't done invites yet but you'll definitely be invited.'

'Wouldn't miss it for the world,' Ed said. 'And neither would Dee, I'm sure.'

'Things going well with you guys?' Rachel asked.

'I think so,' Ed said.

The truth was, he didn't know. She'd definitely been in a mood after their walk. On the drive back, he'd tried to ask her what was wrong but she'd shut him down. Since then, he'd called her a couple of times and left messages but she hadn't called him back yet.

'We haven't seen much of each other lately,' he told Rachel. 'My fault. I've been so caught up in other stuff.'

'Is that why you've been such a pain in the arse?' Rachel asked.

'Probably.' Ed smiled. 'Although I'm pretty sure you've been telling me I'm a pain in the arse ever since we started working together.'

'Is there anything I can do?'

Ed raised his eyebrows and Rachel held her hands up.

'Apart from being part of the investigation,' she said. 'Obviously.'

'I know that's not an option,' Ed said. 'And I know I've been a liability. Everything about this case, it's too personal. I can't see it objectively.'

'You need to stop trying to see it at all,' Rachel said.

'You're right.' Ed drained his beer and stood up. 'One for the road?'

'I'd better be getting off,' Rachel said. 'I've got another few hours of work to do before I can stop for the night. It was good to chat, though. Thanks, Ed.'

'Thank you,' Ed said. 'Not many people would have been as understanding as you've been, Rachel. And I promise, no more interfering.'

'I'll hold you to that.' Rachel leaned in and kissed his cheek. 'Enjoy your beer, buddy. I'll see myself out.'

He opened another beer and listened as Rachel left. When he was sure she was gone, he got his phone and checked his text messages. He still had Kyle's mobile number from when he used to be his rugby coach. He'd sent him a message earlier, asking if they could meet up. So far, Kyle hadn't got back to him.

Ed's thumb hovered over his screen as he tried to decide whether or not to send another text. He thought of the promise he'd just made to Rachel. A promise he had no intention of keeping. He felt bad lying to her. Of course he did. But this was more important than worrying about someone's feelings. Besides, he'd already sent one text. Which meant he really couldn't see what difference it would make if he sent another one now. And if Kyle still hadn't replied by tomorrow, Ed would drive across to the house and make Kyle speak to him, even if he didn't want to.

–

Dee's eyes shot open. Something had woken her. The sound of glass smashing. A burglary. Not the first time it had happened. Foolishly, she'd let herself believe it wouldn't happen again. She sat up, eyes adjusting to the darkness, heart pounding in her chest. She strained her ears, listening, but all she could hear was her own breathing – too fast, too loud – and the steady sound of the sea, crunching in and out over the shingle.

Gradually, her heartbeat slowed down and her body started to relax. It was nothing. Her imagination, or a bad dream or a crash of thunder. Or any of the hundreds of sounds that we don't notice during the day but seem amplified during the silent hours of night-time. Whatever it had been, there was no one else in her house.

She went into the kitchen to get a glass of water. There was enough light from the moon for her to see. She got a glass and was midway through filling it when, out of the corner of her eye, she saw a movement outside the window.

She turned slowly and looked through the glass. A pair of eyes stared back at her. Screaming, she jumped back. The glass fell from her hand and smashed onto the tiled floor. Water splashed onto her bare feet and ankles. Another flash of movement and the eyes were gone. Replaced by a sound she recognised. Footsteps. Someone was on the wooden deck that ran along the back of the house.

Her mind ran back over the last few days. The phone calls. The silence punctuated with the sick sound of someone breathing into her ear. A stalker. Maybe not. But she knew now, as clearly as she knew her own name, that those phone calls hadn't been made by some random stranger. They were a message.

She knew she needed to act, do something – anything – to protect herself. But she couldn't stop thinking about the last time there'd been a stranger outside her house. She'd been attacked and beaten, and now her mind refused to move past that night. It was like she was back there again, lying face down on the beach, fighting for her life.

She was frozen. Unable to move.

A shrill sound cut through the silence, and suddenly she was running, shards of broken glass slicing through the bottoms of her feet. She'd reacted before her brain had time to register the noise. Her phone, ringing from the bedroom.

She already knew who it was. No one else called her in the middle of the night.

'Hello?'

Nothing. And then, there it was – the heavy sound of someone breathing.

'Who the fuck is this?' she shouted.

Throwing the phone down on her bed, she ran into the living room and pulled open the doors leading onto the deck. Gusts of freezing wind whipped into her. She stood at the top of the steps that led to the beach, peering into the darkness.

'Who's out here?' she shouted.

Inside the house, her phone started ringing again. At the same time, she heard something running along the shingle, footsteps crunching over stones. She couldn't work out where the sound had come from. She peered into the darkness, scanning the beach, trying to see who was there.

Then two things happened at the same time. A hand shoved into her back, pushing her so she fell forward, into the empty space beyond the steps. And the world exploded in a burst of sound and light and colour.

She landed on the stones, unable to get up as the ground reverberated beneath her and the sky above her burned bright and white, obliterating the moon and the stars and everything else.

Twenty-six

'Someone's trying to scare me.'

'Scare you about what?'

'I'm not sure,' Dee said.

A fire had started in her car. The explosion she'd heard had been caused by the fire reaching the petrol tank. The sound had woken Ella and her friends, who had called the emergency services. By the time Dee had staggered to her feet, Ella was already there. Ed arrived twenty minutes later and had been here since.

'We won't know for sure what happened to your car until it's been examined by forensics,' Ed said. 'There could be all sorts of reasons for the fire. Oil leaks can cause parked cars to go on fire.'

'It wasn't an oil leak,' Dee said. 'First I get a series of creepy phone calls, and now this? Plus, an oil leak doesn't explain why I heard someone running around outside. Or why someone pushed me off the deck.'

'I wish you'd told me about the phone calls.'

'I didn't think they were anything serious,' Dee said.

She wanted to add that they'd seen so little of each other recently, it was hardly a surprise she hadn't told him.

'And now?'

'Now I think they were a warning. Someone wants me to stop trying to find out what happened to Joana.'

Ed started to say something, then stopped.

'What?'

'It doesn't matter,' he said. 'I can't bear thinking someone would want to hurt you. I'll make sure this is fast-tracked, Dee. I'll get someone onto your phone records, see if there's any way of tracing those phone calls. Getting anything back on your car's going to take a while, I'm afraid. All of that work is outsourced now. There's quite a backlog.'

'How long?'

'A few weeks, at least. But let me see what I can do, okay?'

'Thanks, Ed.'

'You're lucky the car wasn't closer to the house,' he said. 'You could have lost a lot more than just the car.'

Dee didn't feel lucky. The car, a battered old Volvo, had belonged to her mother. Now it was gone and, with it, Dee had lost another precious reminder of her mother's life.

'Sorry,' he said. 'I know how much that car meant to you.'

'It's fine.' Dee wiped her face and stood up. 'I need to get going, actually. I'm meeting Eliza, remember?'

Eliza had called yesterday evening and told Dee she needed to see her. They'd arranged to meet this morning at a cafe on the seafront.

'You're not going ahead with that, surely? You've had a nasty shock, Dee. You need to stay indoors and give yourself time to recuperate. I've taken the day off work so I can look after you.'

'I don't need looking after,' Dee said. 'But thank you, anyway. And there is no way I'm going to let something like this scare me away. If anything, it's made me more determined than ever. If someone's trying to frighten me off, it means I must be getting close.'

'It also means you could get hurt.'

Dee closed her eyes and took several slow breaths. The last thing she wanted now was another argument.

'I'll need a lift.'

She opened her eyes, then wished she hadn't. The disapproval on his face was hard to stomach.

'Fine,' he said, sounding as if it was anything but. 'I'll give you a lift. But only if you tell Eliza you won't be able to help her after today. I'm not going to let you get hurt over this, Dee. It's not worth it.'

'Joana's not worth it?'

'That's not what I meant,' Ed said. 'You need to let the police take this over now. I'll speak with Brian Douglas. He's the detective who was looking into Joana's disappearance when she was first reported missing. He's a good detective.'

'You can speak to Brian if you want to,' Dee said. 'But I am not going to let Eliza down now. I'm going to keep trying to find Joana, whether you like it or not.'

She braced herself for his counter-argument, but it didn't come. Instead, he shook his head, called her a stubborn bloody woman and told her to hurry up and get ready.

'Thanks, Ed.' She leaned down and planted a kiss on the top of his head. 'You're the best.'

–

Half an hour later, Dee and Eliza were walking along the seafront, their hands wrapped around the cups of hot chocolate Dee had insisted on buying for them.

'I'm glad you called, actually,' Dee said. 'There's something you should know. Last night, someone set fire to my car.'

'Oh Dee, I'm so sorry. You've reported it to the police? Have they found the person who did it?'

'Not yet,' Dee said. 'But I think it might be someone who doesn't want me asking questions about Joana.'

'Shit.' Eliza stopped walking. 'This means you're getting closer, yes? Ah. But it also means this could be dangerous for you. Maybe you should stop what you're doing. I don't want you to feel unsafe.'

'I don't feel unsafe.' Dee linked her arm with Eliza's. 'I just thought you should know, that's all. Maybe we both need to be a little more careful when we're asking questions from now on.'

'I wish there was more I could do,' Eliza said. 'I'm working so many hours. It's the only way I can make enough money. This is a shit life, Dee. I plan to do one more year only before returning to my country. It's too difficult for me here.'

'I keep my ear out for any better-paying jobs,' Dee said. 'But there's not much around at the moment.'

'It's not your fault,' Eliza said. 'All I want now is to find out what has happened to Joana before I go home. I don't know how I'll bear it if we still haven't found her by then.'

'We'll do everything we can to make sure that doesn't happen,' Dee said. 'I promise.'

'Thank you, Dee.'

'So, do you want to tell me why you wanted to meet?'

'My boyfriend Marcel has a friend,' Eliza said. 'His name is Charlie. Have you spoken to him?'

'No.' Dee shook her head. 'Why?'

'Hang on.'

Eliza took her phone from her jacket pocket. 'Let me show you a photo. Ah. No internet. Can we walk back the other way? There's a signal nearer to the restaurant.'

They had walked west from the pier towards Holywell, where the mobile phone signal was poor to non-existent.

'What do you want to show me?' Dee asked as they turned back. It was the first sunny Sunday in a while and the seafront was busy, although Dee didn't pass one person she recognised. So different to when she'd lived here as a teenager. Back then, she'd felt as if she knew every single person living in the town. At the time, she'd hated that. Now, she missed that feeling of belonging.

'Charlie's photo.'

Eliza scrolled through her phone and handed it to Dee, who took the phone and studied the Instagram profile photo of someone called @ChefCharlie.

'Never seen him before,' Dee said, handing the phone back.

'But you said you'd spoken with the people working at the hotel.'

'I said I'd spoken to a few people,' Dee said. 'And left a copy of Joana's photo and asked for it to be circulated to the rest of the staff. Why, Eliza? Who is this guy?'

'He's one of the chefs at the hotel,' Eliza said. 'And also a friend of Marcel's. Marcel was in the Anchor on Friday night and Charlie was there too. And he started to tell Marcel about a journalist who had been visiting the hotel causing problems for his boss. He said the lady journalist is crazy, but Marcel told him no, you're not crazy, you are helping us to find Joana. And I don't know how, but Charlie didn't know about Joana, so Marcel told him what had happened and about Joana going to the hotel to meet someone the night she disappeared. And then Marcel asked Charlie if he'd seen the photo and Charlie said no. So Marcel showed him a photo of Joana he has on his phone, and he said Charlie went really quiet and Marcel asked him what was the problem, but Charlie said there's no problem. But he left soon after that, and Marcel hasn't been able to contact him because Charlie isn't answering Marcel's messages.'

'Slow down,' Dee said, knowing that when Eliza started on a topic she would talk and talk until you forced her to stop and listen. 'Are you saying Marcel thinks Charlie might have seen Joana at the hotel the night she disappeared?'

'Of course.'

'Okay,' Dee said. 'Well if he works at the hotel, why don't we go there now and see if he'll talk to us?'

'He's not working today,' Eliza said. 'I've already called and asked to speak to him. They said he is off work sick. But I have his phone number. I was hoping you would try calling him, Dee? Or maybe you could find out where he lives and go and speak to him.'

'Is there any chance Charlie was the person Joana was going to meet?' Dee asked.

'No. I mean, he's a cute guy but he's a chef. Joana was more interested in the men who stayed there, the ones with money. Unless Charlie was helping her get the job she told me about? That is a possibility all right. Do you think the police will listen to me if I tell them this?'

'Let me try and speak to him first,' Dee said. 'If you go around shouting that Charlie has something to do with Joana's disappearance, that's the surest way of making sure he doesn't tell me or anyone else what he knows.'

'Promise you'll speak to him?'

'I promise,' Dee said. 'But only if you do something for me first.'

'Of course,' Eliza said. 'Anything.'

'I have this old coat I don't wear any more.' Dee opened her rucksack and pulled out the coat. It was black cashmere. She'd picked it up online in the M&S sale.

'This is not old,' Eliza said, examining the coat. 'And if it was ever your coat, Dee, it was a long time ago when you were a lot thinner than you are now.'

'I used to be very slender, I'll have you know,' Dee said.

'I can't take this,' Eliza said. 'It's too much.'

'It's too small for me,' Dee said. 'You said as much yourself. If you don't take it, I'll give it to a charity shop. Come on, Eliza. Try it on, at least.'

Reluctantly, the girl slipped one arm inside the coat, and then the other. She buttoned it up, and when she was finished she was beaming like a little girl on Christmas morning.

'It's perfect,' she said.

'Good.' Dee smiled. 'So you'll take it?'

'You haven't given me much choice,' Eliza said. And then, in a gesture that Dee suspected surprised both of them, Eliza grabbed Dee in a hug and planted a big, slopping kiss on her cheek.

—

Louise switched off the engine but didn't make any move to get out of her car. Through the windscreen, she could see the downstairs lights in her house were still on. Which meant Martin was still up. Waiting for her, no doubt. She couldn't face seeing him yet. If she went in now, she wouldn't be able to hide it from him. He would guess immediately where she'd been and what she'd been doing. Until a few months ago, Louise would have said she was an accomplished liar. Apart from Dee, other people seemed to believe the white lies she sometimes told to get what she wanted. And getting what she wanted was something Louise was exceptionally good at. Except now, she was starting to realise that always getting what you wanted had its drawbacks. Most significantly, it meant you had to lie over and over to people you should never lie to. Her husband, her children, her best friend.

She looked at her reflection in the rear-view mirror, searching her face for the person she knew was in there. The faithful wife, the loving mother and the loyal friend. But all she could see was this new person she'd become: a deceitful, lying bitch. An old Eagles song started up inside her head. 'Lyin' Eyes'. She looked away from the mirror, sickened. She imagined she could still smell him, even though she'd showered afterwards. Spicy cologne and smoke from the single cigarette he allowed himself after sex.

It had been exciting when he first started pursuing her. Exciting and dangerous. Two things she hadn't much experience of. A naturally disciplined child, she'd grown up to have exactly the sort of life she'd planned for herself: a career, a husband, two beautiful children, and a big house in the most desirable part of town.

She'd had everything she'd ever wanted. Then he'd come along and blown every smug conviction about her tidy little life to smithereens. For the first time, she'd realised just how conventional, provincial and plain boring her life really was. It had started as a bit of fun that rapidly turned into something deeper and more intoxicating than she could ever have imagined. She'd been reckless, impulsive, besotted.

She couldn't remember now how things had got so out of hand. A drunken mistake that had, somehow, turned into this out-of-control mess. He was a drug. A dangerous addiction. Louise didn't know how she was going to break the addiction, but she knew she had to. If she didn't, she risked losing everything.

From the diary of Emma Reed

4 October 1961

Perhaps it was a mistake, but what else was I meant to do? Sit in my house like a good little wife and do nothing? If James had his way, that's all I'd do each day. But James is out of touch with the modern world and doesn't seem to grasp that women are capable of so much more than being mere housewives, waiting on their husbands as if they're servants rather than life partners.

I didn't go to cause trouble. I simply wanted to tell her a few home truths. But some women are foolish when their heads have been turned by a man's attention and Annabelle is clearly one of them.

I lay in bed all night, tossing and turning and waiting for morning to come. Time dragged by as I prepared breakfast for James and Nicola and waved them out the door, one after the other. Nicola doesn't want to go to school these mornings. I had to practically push her out of the house, and when she left, she walked so slowly it was all I could do not to run after her and take her in my arms and bring her here into the warm, safe home where no one can tease her or taunt her.

It started raining when I was less than halfway there, which meant I was dripping like a drowned rat by the time I reached the house and rang the doorbell. I assume the woman who opened the door was the housekeeper. She was very efficient and businesslike, and not at all friendly or welcoming. She knew who I was. I could see it in the way her lips curled when she looked at me, and the ice in her voice as she informed me that Miss Palmer was out and she didn't know when she'd be back.

I knew she was lying. I told her I wasn't going anywhere and could she at least let me inside out of the pouring rain? We argued back and forth, neither of us giving ground. At one point, I tried to push past her but she grabbed me by the arms and shoved me back outside into the rain. We must have made a bit of a racket, because suddenly Annabelle appeared in the hallway behind the harridan, demanding to know what in heaven's name all the noise was about.

'I thought you were out,' I said, glaring at the housekeeper. 'I need to speak to you.'

'So speak,' she said. She told the housekeeper to leave and motioned for me to step into the hallway, out of the rain.

'Richard Partridge is using you,' I blurted out. It wasn't the way I'd planned to tell her, but all that nonsense with the other woman had left me flustered. 'He's not in love with you, no matter what he tells you. He was in love with Mary, and he killed her because she didn't love him back. He told you it was Graham, but he knows Graham wasn't capable of something like that. Please, Annabelle. You've got to believe me. He's evil and he's using you.'

I'm not sure if those were my exact words, but they're close enough. I was speaking too fast, the words falling over each other, and when I ran out of breath, I had to stop altogether. I expected her to get angry. Instead, she threw her head back and laughed.

'Look at you,' she said breathlessly, between bouts of laughter. 'Turning up here at this time, drunk already. You've lost your mind. You'd better leave now, before I call the police.'

'I need to see George,' I said. 'He'll believe me, even if you won't.'

She took a step towards me, and I felt a shiver of fear. She's a small woman, but I got the sense she could hurt me if she put her mind to it.

'George won't see you,' she said. 'He won't see anyone, especially not the mother of the man who killed his daughter. You raised a monster, Emma Reed. I'm glad he's dead, and I'm not the only one. This town is better off without him.'

I screamed that my son wasn't a monster, but it was no good. She had already turned her back on me and was walking away from me. I started to charge after her, and I swear to God if I'd got hold of her I would have thrown her to the ground and punched her and kicked her until she cried and apologised for the things she'd said about Graham. But the housekeeper was back, and she had someone with her. A man as big and wide as a carthorse. He grabbed me and wrapped his arms around me and shoved me outside.

I stumbled down the steps, weeping with rage and helplessness. The door slammed shut behind me. I banged on it with my fists, screaming at her to come back and talk to me, but it was pointless. The door stayed closed and after a while, I turned around and walked home, deflated and defeated.

Twenty-seven

Dee strode across the foyer of the Aldrington. There was a different girl at the reception desk this afternoon, someone she hadn't seen before.

'I'm here to see Derek French,' she informed the girl.

'Is he expecting you?'

'Tell him Dee Doran's here. And tell him I'm not leaving until he sees me. I'll be in the bar.'

She walked away without another word. In the bar, she ordered a sparkling water, took a seat and waited. She'd only been there a few minutes when Derek joined her, settling himself into the chair opposite.

'Scotch on the rocks, Jim,' he said to the waiter hovering nearby. 'And this lady's drink is on the house, okay?'

'I'm happy to pay for my own drinks,' Dee told him as Jim slipped away to get Derek's drink.

'I'm glad you dropped by,' Derek said. 'I've been meaning to apologise for the other day. I was bang out of order, and I'm sorry.'

'Why did your wife come around to my house yesterday?' Dee asked.

'Karen?' He shook his head. 'I didn't know she had.'

'She tried to convince me Nigel wasn't Lauren's real father.'

Jim had reappeared with their drinks. Derek waited for him to set them on the table in front of them before he spoke.

'Karen gets some funny ideas, sometimes. That business about Nigel not being Lauren's dad, she's been banging on about that for years. She claims Maxine said something to her one night after she'd had a few too many. Maybe she did, who knows? The thing is, Karen's convinced Nigel killed Lauren and she's frustrated because no one's taking her seriously.'

'Why is she so certain it was Nigel?'

'You ever met the bloke?' Derek said.

Dee shook her head.

'Well, if you had then you'd understand,' Derek said. 'He looks down his nose at people like us. Hard-working, honest to goodness folk who've had to work hard to make something of themselves. Thinks because his wealth was handed to him on a silver platter it makes him better than the rest of us.'

He took a sip of his drink.

'Macallan single malt. Heaven in a glass. Would you like me to order you one?'

Dee shook her head.

'My car was set on fire last night.'

'I'm very sorry to hear that,' Derek said. 'Hope you were insured?'

'Insurance won't cover arson,' Dee said.

'You're sure that's what it was?'

'Police found evidence at the scene.' A lie, but he didn't need to know that.

'Well, let's hope they catch whoever did it. Crime is a growing problem in this town. It's all those gangs moving out of London, apparently.'

'I'm pretty sure this had nothing to do with any London gangs.'

'Whoever they are,' Derek said, 'I'm sorry it's happened. It must have been a terrible shock.'

He sounded sincere, but good liars always did, Dee thought.

She stood up.

'I'll leave you to enjoy the rest of your whisky in peace.'

She turned to go, but he called her back.

'Was that it?' he said. 'Hardly seems worth coming all the way into town simply to tell me Karen went to see you. Especially now you haven't got a car.'

'I didn't come here to tell you about Karen,' Dee said. 'I came here to watch your reaction when I told you what had happened to my car. Goodbye, Derek.'

She left before he could say anything else. Outside, she stood for a minute, waiting for the rush of adrenaline to die down. She hadn't been able to tell if he'd had anything to do with her car being set on fire. But by God, it had felt good to rattle his cage a little.

She was walking towards the taxi rank when Philip Flint called.

'I got your email,' he said. 'You said you had some further questions for me.'

With everything else that had happened, Dee had forgotten about the email she'd sent him last night. She'd spent the previous evening reading through the notes Philip had given her. There was one person in particular Dee was interested in – the man rumoured to have been seeing Annabelle Palmer at the time of Mary's murder. His name was Richard Partridge.

Using Philip's notes, and information she'd found on the internet, Dee had learned as much as she could about him. Richard Partridge had grown up in Eastbourne but spent most of his adult life in London. He had died three years ago, leaving a wife and three children. His family were wealthy. Richard had made his money as the head of a successful engineering firm called Mackie & Partridge Electrics, based in north-west London. The firm was now run by Richard's son, Conor. Dee tried to find out who the Mackie was in the company name, but that information wasn't available on the company website or anywhere else.

'I wanted to ask you about Richard Partridge,' she said.

'Ah yes. The young man who may, or may not, have been in a relationship with Annabelle. What do you want to know about him?'

'Did you try to interview him for your book?' Dee asked.

'For all the good it did. The man denied there'd ever been anything between them. He claimed he barely knew Annabelle. And he was adamant Graham Reed was guilty.'

'What was he like?' Dee asked.

'Arrogant, bordering on rude. The sort of man with more money than manners. He had a younger brother, David, who died eight or ten years after Mary's murder. Richard's widow is still alive, but I doubt she'd be willing to speak with you.'

'I can be very persuasive when I want to be,' Dee said.

'I believe that,' Philip said. 'But there's someone else you may want to speak to as well. Miriam Anderson.'

The name was familiar and, after a moment, Dee remembered reading about Miriam in Philip's notes.

'Emma's friend,' she said. 'You interviewed her several times, I think.'

'That's right,' Philip said. 'A lovely woman. Miriam knew more about the family than anyone else I spoke to. I still see her from time to time. Unfortunately, she hasn't been very well. Her family moved her into a nursing home at the end of last summer.'

'Do you think she'd talk to me?'

'I'm sure she would,' Philip said. 'Assuming she's well enough, of course. Would it help if I give her your name and telephone number and ask her to contact you?'

'That would be wonderful,' Dee said. 'Thank you so much.'

She said goodbye to Philip and hung up. Then, before she could change her mind, she called Ed.

'It's me,' she said. 'Do you fancy coming over this evening? I'll make some dinner and we can have a proper catch-up?'

Twenty-eight

As Ed hung up, he caught a glimpse of his face in the rear-view mirror. Grinning like an idiot, just because things with Dee seemed to be back on track. Luckily, she hadn't asked him where he was, or he'd have been forced to tell her another white lie.

He was in his car, parked outside the Frenches' big, ugly house in the Harbour. Kyle hadn't returned any of his texts or phone messages and Ed was running out of patience. So he'd driven over here earlier, determined to make Kyle speak to him.

Putting his phone back, he got out of the car, approached the front door, rang the bell and waited. And waited. He rang it twice more, and still nothing. Yet when he stood back and looked through the downstairs windows, he was sure he could see the shadow of someone moving around in there.

He pressed his finger down on the doorbell again, and this time he got a response.

'What do you want, Ed?' Karen had opened the door a fraction, her face peering out at Ed through the gap.

'I want to see Kyle.'

'Well he doesn't want to see you. He doesn't want to see anyone. Don't you think you and your girlfriend have caused enough trouble?'

'Sorry?'

'Don't pretend you don't know,' Karen said. 'She's practically accused Derek of having an affair with Lauren. As if he'd do that to Kyle.'

'I didn't know anything about that,' Ed said.

He ran back over everything he and Dee had talked about recently. She hadn't mentioned anything about Derek and Lauren.

'I knew it was a bad idea the first time she turned up here,' Karen continued. 'But when she said you'd sent her, I thought maybe she could help us. But all she's done is cause us trouble. Why did you send her, Ed?'

For a moment, he didn't trust himself to speak. How could Dee do that? Didn't she realise how much was at stake here? But that was the problem with Dee – she went headlong into things without thinking through the consequences. In this instance, she'd seen the potential for a story and that had blinded her to everything else. He'd seen her like this before. He hadn't liked it then, and he didn't like it now either.

'I'm really sorry if Dee's upset you,' he said. 'But you can hardly blame me for that.'

'She's your girlfriend, isn't she?'

'Yes, but that doesn't mean I control what she does.'

Under different circumstances, the idea that he had any sort of control over Dee's actions was laughable. Except right now he was too angry with her to find anything funny about this situation. She'd used his name – and their relationship – to her own advantage. Following up some cock and bull idea she had that Lauren was killed because she knew something about Joana Helinski's disappearance.

'Maybe you should choose your girlfriends a bit more carefully,' Karen said.

He should have told her that who he dated was none of her business. Instead, he got to the real reason he was here.

'I need to see Kyle.'

'He's not here. And even if he was, I don't think he'd want to see you. Dee really upset him, you know. As if he hasn't got enough to deal with right now.'

'I've already apologised for that,' Ed said. 'And I'm happy to apologise to Kyle too, if you'll just let me see him. Please, Karen, this is really important.'

'You shouldn't even be here,' Karen said. 'We all know about your uncle and what he did.' She narrowed her eyes. 'Did you know that's what Lauren was writing about? Is that why you're not part of the investigation?'

'Of course not.' But something in his face must have given him away.

'No, you knew,' Karen said. 'That's why you want to see Kyle, isn't it? Because you want him to tell you what Lauren told him about your uncle. Well, I'm afraid that's not going to happen. My son isn't here, and when he comes back I'll make sure he keeps well away from you and your busybody girlfriend.'

She started to close the door and Ed pushed his body against it, preventing her from shutting it.

'Lauren found a letter at her grandmother's house,' he said. 'I want to ask Kyle about it. That's the only reason I want to speak to him.'

'You'd better let me shut this door right away,' Karen said. 'If you don't I'm going to dial 999 and report you.'

'Just tell him I need to see him,' he said, stepping back. 'Please?'

But he was too late. She'd already slammed the door shut.

On the way back to his car, Dee called again. This time, when he saw her name on the screen he switched his phone off. He needed to calm down before he spoke to her. Because the way he felt now, he would say things that he might regret later. Part of him knew that his anger was irrational, that Dee had only been doing her job. But a bigger part of him didn't care how irrational he was being.

Early on in their relationship, they'd spoken about the challenges of a detective and a journalist being in a relationship together. They'd agreed that, where possible, they would do everything they could to keep work separate from their relationship. Except the moment it had suited her, Dee had ignored that and used Ed's name to get what she wanted. Right now, Ed didn't see how he could forgive her for that.

From the diary of Emma Reed

6 April 1966

Annabelle Palmer got married yesterday. The wedding took place in St Michael and All Angels in Berwick. Before Mary's murder, Annabelle's wedding would have taken place in St Mary's in Old Town, or St John's in Meads. It would be inconceivable, of course, to do that now. Her niece was murdered in the former, and buried in the latter. I've never been to the little church in Berwick, although I've read about the murals. Miriam's brother got married there. She says the murals are beautiful, but the way she describes them, I think they sound rather ugly. They were painted by Vanessa Bell and her lover, Duncan Grant.

Annabelle's new husband is the Right Honourable Andrew Shaw. He's a Member of Parliament for the Conservative Party. According to Miriam, he's a man with a lot of ambition but not enough money to take him to where he wants to go. Which is where Annabelle comes in. She's a rich woman now her brother has passed away. It doesn't take a genius to work out why Andrew Shaw would find her an attractive prospect.

Miriam and Stuart were invited to the wedding. She was giddy with the excitement of it all when she came to visit this morning. It wasn't easy, sitting across the table from her and listening to her jabbering on about the bride and groom, and what a fine day it had been and how lucky they'd been with the weather

228

and did I know the Prime Minister's nephew was a friend of the groom's? On and on she went, her voice like a woodpecker's beak peck-peck-pecking at the side of my head until it ached.

When she told me the bride looked beautiful, I almost laughed. Because we both know that couldn't have been true. I'd decided I couldn't take any more and was about to tell her to put a sock in it when she told me Richard Partridge had been there with his new bride by his side.

I asked if she was sure about that, and she said oh yes, and his wife looked so beautiful in her pale pink silk shift dress, and didn't I think it was strange David wasn't there too and blah, blah, blah. It's strange to think I used to admire Miriam. She's one of the few women I know who's managed to have her own career, alongside a family. Now, there are times I think she's one of the silliest women I've ever known. But beggars can't be choosers and she's the only friend I've got left.

I let her blabber on, while my mind wandered back to that morning when I'd seen them together in Brighton. I'd been so sure then. Yet five years later, I'm no closer to proving what I know – that Richard killed Mary and used Annabelle to spread rumours about my son.

Since then, Richard has married and had two children, and now Annabelle is married too. I'd assumed their affair – or whatever it was – had ended. But if he attended her wedding, does that mean they are still seeing each other behind their spouses' backs? No. I've given it a lot of thought, and I think it's something else. Something darker, and stronger, has kept these two people close to each other all this time.

Richard killed Mary. Annabelle told everyone Graham did it. And then Graham was killed, because of the things Annabelle said about him. Why was she so ready to lie for him? Annabelle may not be the prettiest of women, but there's no doubting how *clever she is. Her sharp mind and her quick wit are the two things people always mention when talking about her.*

If she's as clever as everyone says she is, wouldn't she have worked it out? But if she knew, why would she lie to protect him? The answer's here somewhere, but no matter how hard I look for it, I can't see it.

Twenty-nine

On Monday morning, Dee woke to a blue sky and a silver sea as still as glass. She lay in bed, watching the wind whisper across the surface of the ocean and thinking about Ed. Something was wrong, but she didn't know what or how to fix it. He'd been due to come over Saturday evening, but he'd called at the last minute and cancelled. Told her he had to work late, but she could tell from his voice that he was lying. Since then, she hadn't heard from him. She'd called him a few times and left messages, but he hadn't got back to her.

At least she had a busy morning ahead to take her mind off Ed. True to his word, Philip had put Dee in touch with Miriam Anderson – Emma Reed's friend. The two women had spoken on the phone yesterday evening and arranged to meet later this morning at Sunshine Nursing Home, where Miriam had lived since last year.

Dee was familiar with the nursing home – a large, elegant, three-storey Victorian building on Darley Road in Meads. A friend of her mother's had lived out the last few years of her life there. As Dee got a taxi across this morning, she remembered the times she'd driven her mother to the same place so she could catch up with her old friend. It felt strange coming back this morning without her mother. Stranger still to be doing this journey by taxi instead of her mother's Volvo. Yesterday evening, she'd gone online and booked a hire car. She was due to pick it up later today. Until then, she'd have to keep using taxis to get around.

At the reception, Dee signed in and was directed to Miriam's room on the first floor. She knocked on the open door and stepped into a light and airy space with beautiful views across the landscaped garden and the South Downs. A small, frail-looking woman with short white hair and a lined face was sitting in an armchair by the window.

'Mrs Anderson?' Dee said.

'Miriam, dear. And you must be Dee. Oh, what beautiful flowers. Are they for me?'

'Of course.' Dee had picked up a bouquet of twelve roses on her way over. She looked around the room for a vase and, when she couldn't see one, she put the flowers in the sink and filled it with water.

'One of the nurses will bring a vase if I ask for one,' Miriam said. 'Would you like a hot drink?'

'I'm fine,' Dee said. 'Thank you.'

'Do you mind if we go outside?' Miriam took a packet of cigarettes from her cardigan pocket and winked at Dee. 'Ciggies are strictly off-limits in this place, but there's a little corner of the garden where you can smoke without anyone seeing you. Shall we?'

Feeling like she was back at school, Dee followed Miriam back down the stairs and outside to a covered patio area in one corner of the extensive grounds.

'You smoke?' Miriam offered the pack to Dee, who shook her head.

'Very sensible.' Miriam put a cigarette in her mouth, lit it with a gold Zippo lighter and inhaled deeply.

'I have no idea why we're not allowed to smoke in this place. We're all dying anyway.'

'I'm sure they'd like to delay that for as long as possible,' Dee said.

Miriam chuckled.

'I rarely get visitors, you know. My son lives in Australia and I don't have any other relatives nearby. This is quite a novelty. I didn't want to talk to you at first, you know. Not when I heard you were a journalist. They were terrible to Emma and her family first time round. But Philip has promised me you're nothing like that.'

'I'm not going to write anything nasty about the family,' Dee said. 'In fact, Graham's nephew is a close friend of mine. I wouldn't do anything to upset him.'

'A close friend?' Miriam's watery blue eyes twinkled. 'What sort of close friend, exactly?'

'Close enough,' Dee said, smiling.

'That would be Nicola's boy. Edward, isn't it? He had a sister too, although I can't for the life of me remember her name. Don't grow old, Dee. I really don't recommend it. Your body stops working properly and your mind is incapable of remembering anything important. You spend your days wondering how your life has passed by so fast you barely noticed it happening.'

'The alternative's worse,' Dee said. 'Or so I've heard.'

'No doubt.' Miriam threw her cigarette to the ground and stubbed it out. 'Would you disapprove if I smoke one more before we go back inside?'

'I wouldn't disapprove,' Dee said. 'But I might point out it's freezing out here and you're shivering like a leaf.'

'Spoilsport.' Miriam smiled. 'Very well then. Let's go back inside.'

On their way back to her room, Miriam gave Dee a running commentary on the other residents, the staff and what it was like moving from the house she'd lived in all her life into this nursing home.

'I hated it at first,' she said, sitting down and gesturing for Dee to do the same. 'But I've got used to it now. I suppose you get used to anything after a while. Vanessa! That's the girl's name, isn't it?'

'Ed's sister?'

'That's right. She was a pretty little thing. Those children had a difficult time too, you know. Mary's murder didn't just hurt her own family. So many people were affected by what happened. Nicola, Edward's mother, had a terrible time growing up. Poor Emma was never the same after Graham's death. I always felt her obsession with proving Graham's innocence meant she neglected the child she had left.'

'Why were people so quick to assume Graham was the killer?' Dee asked.

'He was an easy target,' Miriam said. 'I never believed he'd killed her. But I was in the minority back then, I can tell you. That family were shunned after Mary's murder. Within a few days, that Partridge boy had convinced the whole town of Graham's guilt. The truth is, Graham wasn't capable of something like that. I'm not saying he was perfect, because he was far from that. But he was a soft lad.'

'When you say that Partridge boy, you mean Richard?'

'The very one.' Miriam frowned. 'A horrible child who grew up to be a horrible man.'

'Philip told me there was a rumour Annabelle and Richard were seeing each other. Did you ever hear about anything like that?'

Miriam shook her head.

'That's nonsense. Richard had a real eye for the girls, but he liked them young and pretty. I'm afraid Annabelle was neither of those things. Emma thought Annabelle was in love with Richard, and she might have been right. But it was never reciprocated, I'm sure of it.'

'You said Emma was obsessed,' Dee said. 'Did she ever talk to you about it?'

'It was all she ever talked about. Poor Emma, she was such a complicated woman. Even before all that happened. She was very clever, you know. I liked her enormously when I first got to know her. She used to make me laugh. Although not everyone warmed to her as easily as I did. She thought she was better than everyone else, you see. It's one of the reasons that whole business hit her so hard. She didn't like people feeling sorry for her. As time went by, she cut herself off from everyone. It didn't have to be like that. There were plenty of people who would have been there for her, but she wouldn't have it. I was the only person she saw. And that wasn't because she particularly liked me. It was because I was happy to let her pretend she was cleverer than I was.'

'Why would you do that?'

'She'd lost so much,' Miriam said. 'I felt sorry for her. Although I have to admit, as her obsession with Annabelle grew worse, she became very difficult. It was Myra Hindley's fault, you know.'

'Sorry?'

Whatever Dee had been expecting, it wasn't that.

'It doesn't matter now,' Miriam said. 'She was always changing her mind about who the killer could have been. Although towards the end, she did rather fixate on Annabelle. But no matter how hard she tried, she was never able to prove anything. In the end, I think it simply became too much for her.'

'Did she ever confront Annabelle about her suspicions?'

'Probably,' Miriam said, 'towards the end of her life, Emma was drinking too much. She could be a bit impulsive after a few drinks. I've always thought that's what happened the night she died.'

'What do you mean?'

'Annabelle was there,' Miriam said.

'The night Emma killed herself?'

Miriam's eyes filled with tears.

'Those two women hated each other. I'm convinced Annabelle said something that tipped Emma over the edge. I really can't see any other reason Emma would have done what she did. She wasn't remotely suicidal. I know people say things like that after someone takes their own life, but in Emma's case it's true. She was driven by her determination to clear Graham's name. I've never understood why she took her own life before she was able to do that.'

An idea flickered at the back of Dee's mind, but when she tried to focus on it, it faded away.

'What about you?' she asked. 'You must have had your own ideas about who killed Mary.'

'Annabelle had the most to gain by Mary's death,' Miriam said. 'And I admit, for a while, Emma's arguments were quite persuasive. But Emma never found anything to back up her theory. I think she realised, at the end, that her fixation on Annabelle had been a mistake.'

'Did she tell you that?'

Miriam shook her head.

'I barely saw her towards the end. She was drinking a lot, and she'd become rather difficult to be around. I regretted it later, of course. Always wondered if I'd been a better friend, if she'd had someone to talk to, maybe she wouldn't have gone up to Beachy Head that night and done what she did. Or maybe she'd have done it anyway. We'll never know, will we?'

Dee wanted to ask more questions, but she could see Miriam was getting tired. When she asked if Miriam would like her to go, the old woman nodded.

'I'm not used to talking for such a long time,' she said. 'It's been lovely to see you though. I do hope you'll come again sometime.'

Promising she would, Dee thanked her for her time and said goodbye. On her way back to the entrance, she thought over the conversation, trying to work out what – if anything – she'd learned. She hadn't come any closer to finding out what Lauren had discovered. But she'd found someone else who believed Graham Reed was innocent. Which was good news for Ed, at least.

–

Louise was running late. She'd been due to pick the children up from Sadie, the childminder, twenty minutes ago. Sadie was normally pretty laid-back, but she was going out this evening and Louise had promised she'd be on time. A promise she wouldn't be able to keep unless, by some miracle, there was no traffic between her office and Sadie's house in Old Town.

She'd spent the afternoon visiting a bereaved family. The father, a man in his early fifties, had been killed the previous week in a road accident. This aspect of the job was the one Louise liked the least – having to visit the family of someone who'd died, asking if they wanted the paper to do a write-up on the deceased. 'The death knock', Louise and her colleagues called it. Today, the dead man's family had been falling over themselves to tell Louise all the wonderful things about him that she needed to include in her obituary. Which meant she'd stayed longer than she'd planned. By the time she'd got back to the office, she had a mountain of emails to get through, as well as the dead man's obituary to write, before she could finish for the day.

She'd planned to call Dee as well, but that would have to wait. They'd barely spoken since Dee had called Louise the other day to tell her what had happened to her car. Dee had sounded fine, but Louise knew shock could hit people in different ways. As she ran towards her car, rummaging in her bag for the key fob, she made a mental note to phone Dee as soon as she got home. She normally kept the key in the same part of her bag, but it wasn't there when her fingers scrabbled around for it. She was so intent on finding it that she didn't see the man standing in front of her and she ran straight into him.

'Sorry.' She stepped out of his way to let him pass. 'I wasn't paying attention.' She would have said more but her brain caught up with her eyes and she realised the man she'd bumped into was Nigel Shaw. Louise didn't have time to stop and talk, but she could hardly hurry past without at least asking how he was doing. Even if she already knew the answer. He looked dreadful. Wild-eyed and red-faced and... something else as well. There was a desperation about him that made her uneasy.

'Are you okay, Nigel?'

He grabbed her arm and held it tight. She yelped, a combination of shock and pain, as his fingers dug into the soft flesh of her upper arm.

'I need your help,' he said. He pulled her close, too close, the smell of sweat and alcohol invading the air she breathed in. He looked like a man on the edge, a man capable of anything.

'Okay,' Louise said. 'But let me go first. You're hurting me.'

He looked down, frowning, and took his hand off her arm. Louise started to ask again if he was all right but he held his hand up.

'Shut up,' he said. 'Just shut up and listen. I know about you and Derek.'

Ice ran through her veins. This couldn't be happening. Nigel was a friend of Martin's. They played golf together. Nigel's wife, Maxine, and Louise did Zumba classes together. Oh Jesus, Louise thought, you stupid, stupid cow.

'I don't know what you're talking about.' She brushed her hair back from her face and looked him straight in the eye.

Nigel shook his head, the disgust in his face mirroring the disgust Louise felt at herself for being such a bloody idiot.

'The Sussex Ox,' he said.

She could have tried denying it, but there was no point. Derek had taken her there for dinner last month. It was midweek and they'd checked the place carefully first, making sure there was no one they recognised. They'd drunk two bottles of wine and by the time the meal was finished, they were drunk and more than a little amorous.

'I was meeting a colleague from Brighton,' Nigel said. 'You were already drunk when I got there. I doubt you even noticed I was there, did you?'

Louise shook her head.

'I thought maybe it was a one-off,' Nigel said. 'But then Maxine bumped into you a few weeks later, remember?'

Louise remembered all right. She'd been coming out of the lift in the Aldrington after being with Derek. She was alone. They were clever enough not to be seen together in the hotel, but, clearly, not nearly as clever as they'd thought. Maxine had been having coffee with a friend in the lobby. She'd spotted Louise coming out of the lift and had waved her over, asking where on earth Louise had been coming from.

'I didn't think there were any public areas upstairs,' Maxine had said, her voice booming around the lobby.

'You told her you'd been interviewing one of the guests for a special piece you were writing,' Nigel said. 'She believed you, of course. But when she told me about bumping into you, I knew right away why you were really there.'

'Oh God.' She couldn't believe her own selfishness and stupidity. If only she'd stopped for a single second and thought about the consequences of what she was doing; but she hadn't done that. For the first time in her life, she'd given in to temptation. And look where it had landed her. In a whole load of trouble.

'What do you want?'

'After my mother died, Lauren found a letter in her belongings. I'm sure she meant to give it to me, but she didn't get a chance. I need you to help me find it.'

'I can't do that. I didn't even know Lauren.'

'You know Derek,' Nigel said. 'Which means you have access to Kyle. He was her boyfriend. If anyone knows where Lauren put that letter, he does.'

'So ask Kyle about it,' Louise said. 'Not me.'

'He won't tell me,' Nigel said. 'Pretends he doesn't know, but of course he does. He thinks he's being loyal to Lauren by not telling me, but she wanted me to have it. She told me that before she died.'

'Have you told all this to the police?'

'The contents of that letter are private. I don't want anyone else reading what's in there.'

'Not even if it helps the police find out who killed your daughter?'

'The letter's got nothing to do with what happened to Lauren.'

'How can you be so sure?' Louise asked.

'Because that's impossible. For Christ's sake, Louise. Just help me find the bloody thing, would you? Get Derek to speak to Kyle and tell him where the letter is. Kyle is scared of his parents. He'll tell his father, even if he won't tell me or the police. Do this for me, and I'll keep quiet about your affair. If you don't, I'll tell Martin what you've been up to behind his back.'

Louise was quiet for a moment, pretending to think about it.

'Give me a few days,' she said eventually. 'I'll see what I can do.'

She already knew she wasn't going to do what he wanted. She'd behaved appallingly and didn't deserve to get away with what she'd done. Besides, no matter how stupid she'd been, even she had the sense not to interfere with a murder investigation. But she owed it to Martin to sort this out. It was inevitable he would find out what she'd been up to – she could see that now. If he had to find out, she would make sure he heard it from her. Not anyone else.

From the diary of Emma Reed

30 April 1966

It turns out Miriam is more intelligent than I've given her credit for. She called over this morning, full of opinions on the only topic anyone is talking about these days: Ian Brady and Myra Hindley. The horror of their crimes has shocked the nation. And when people are shocked, there's nothing they like better than endless conversation about the thing that's shocked them.

Unsurprisingly, all of Miriam's conversation was focused on Hindley. Hatred for the woman has reached near-fever pitch. Despite all the talk of women being equal to men, when it comes to committing murder — especially the murder of children — none of us are willing to view men and women in the same way. The simple truth is, we cannot bear to think of a woman carrying out those heinous acts. So Hindley is vilified, in the press and down the pub and anywhere people are talking about it, in a way that Brady is not.

I haven't got a problem with people hating Hindley. It's hard not to, especially when you see that photo of her face. I have gazed at it daily ever since the story came to light, and I am unable to see anything but pure evil in those eyes. But now, Miriam has challenged my thinking on this matter.

'Why should we be so surprised?' she asked, as she sipped her third cup of tea and finished off the last of the biscuits I'd put out for her.

'Because it's not natural,' I told her. 'It goes against a woman's natural instinct to kill.'

Miriam told me she disagreed, that women are every bit as capable of evil as men and she was surprised a forward-thinking woman like myself could hold such outdated views. At the time, I dismissed this in the same way I tend to dismiss most things she says. It was only later this evening, after James and Nicola were in bed and I was sitting here preparing to write, that her words came back to me. She's right, of course. If we believe – as I do – that women are men's equal in every way, then why shouldn't we believe they can be equally bad, as well as equally good?

I've been searching for the answer to who killed Mary, and all the time it was right there in front of me. I'd assumed it was Richard, and Annabelle had covered up for him because she was in love with him. Just as I'd assumed, when I first read about the Moors murders, that Hindley had killed because she was in love with Brady. But turn those misconceptions around and you get a very different picture.

What if it's Annabelle, not Richard, who is the killer?

It makes sense. Annabelle was jealous of Mary and the fortune she would inherit. With Mary out of the way, Annabelle got all her brother's money. I'd believed she was nothing more than a silly woman, in love with a man who didn't care for her.

I was wrong.

Annabelle Palmer (now Shaw) killed her niece.

Seeing the words written down like this turns the idea from a mere thought into something else. It becomes closer to fact.

It makes perfect sense.

I spent so long focusing on Richard. Stupid, stupid, stupid. I tried to convince myself that Richard was in love with Mary. But Richard isn't capable of love. I've spoken to everyone I can possibly think of and not once has anyone confirmed my theory that he loved Mary. Yet I persisted, despite the lack of evidence. I saw his fiancée and I made too many assumptions.

Richard never loved Mary. The only person Richard has ever loved, or ever will love, is himself.

Annabelle is the same, and I suspect that money is the basis to their 'friendship'. I doubt she could have killed Mary by herself. So she paid Richard to help her. Soon after Mary's death, Richard moved to London and started a new life for himself. His brother enrolled in a university. They were only able to afford this with Annabelle's money. I still don't understand what David's role has been in all of this, or what is the basis of the rift between the two brothers. But I know David is somehow involved. He's working as a doctor in east London. It won't be difficult to find out where he is and pay him a visit.

I should go to bed, but I won't sleep. There are too many emotions racing through my body; too many thoughts raging through my mind.

I'm getting closer. I can feel it.

Thirty

It had started raining mid-afternoon, and hadn't stopped since. Dee was at the mobile home, babysitting. She'd offered to have Jake at hers for the night, but Ella was taking him to a playgroup early the next morning and asked if Dee would come to the mobile home instead. The rain thundered off the flat roof in a deafening downpour that, somehow, Jake was managing to sleep through. Dee checked him regularly, listening to the steady in-out sound of his breathing, marvelling at the simple fact of his presence in her life.

Seven months earlier, she'd come close to losing him. Most of the time, she tried not to think about that terrible period in her life. But nights like tonight, when it was just the two of them, it was impossible not to remember the fear and dread that had increased with each day that passed without him.

Ella had gone to the cinema with some of 'the girls'. Dee and Jake had eaten dinner together – fish fingers, peas and mashed potatoes – and spent an hour building a railway track that wound all around the sitting room and down the hall. At bedtime, Dee sat on the floor beside Jake's bed and read stories from the row of books on his bookcase. There were some new books that she didn't recognise, but Jake had wanted her to read from the ones she already knew – *Courtney*, *The Very Hungry Caterpillar* and some old Dr Seuss stories that had belonged to Ella when she was a child.

She read until Jake's eyes started drooping shut. Then she'd sat beside his bed, holding his hand until he drifted off to sleep. Now here she was, alone in this little mobile home that she'd once lived in with her parents.

In the forty-something years that had passed since Dee had lived here, the mobile home had barely changed. Like most mobile homes, it didn't wear the signs of age well. Jake's bedroom was the exception. When Ella had first moved in, she'd earned a living as a piano teacher. Since coming out of prison, she'd given up the lessons. Tom had decorated the second bedroom and Jake had moved in there.

There was a shabbiness to the rest of the place that no amount of fresh paint could disguise. Damp was spreading from one corner of the ceiling, the windowpanes needed replacing, and the carpet that ran throughout the house that was so faded it was impossible to tell what colour it had been originally. It was no wonder that Tom and Ella were keen to move out of here into a place of their own.

There was no TV, but at least Tom and Ella had a decent Wi-Fi signal. With the sound of the rain drumming overhead, Dee curled up on the sofa with her laptop. She checked the latest comments in the true crime group. Nothing further on Annabelle Shaw, but a whole load of opinions about Ed's relationship with the dead women. One thread was dedicated to different theories on the different reasons Ed might have killed Lauren.

Disgusted, Dee shut down Facebook and was thinking about what she could watch on Netflix when her phone started ringing. She didn't recognise the number, but she answered anyway, welcoming the distraction.

'Um, could I speak to Dee please?'

'Speaking.'

'Oh, hi. This is Charlie Steadman. You left a message asking me to call you?'

Charlie Steadman. The guy Marcel had spoken to about Joana's disappearance.

'Thanks so much for calling,' Dee said. 'I'd started to think you were avoiding me.'

She'd called him several times, leaving a message each time. She'd almost given up hope of hearing from him.

'I wasn't sure about speaking to you,' he said. 'But my girlfriend said I should call you.'

Thank the Lord for sensible girlfriends, Dee thought.

'I wanted to ask you some questions about Joana Helinski,' Dee said. 'Is now a good time?'

'I can't,' he said. 'I'm at work. I was thinking tomorrow morning, maybe?'

'At the hotel?'

'I don't want to talk there,' he said. 'Do you know the Boardwalk?'

'The place on the seafront? Yes, I know it.'

'I'll meet you there. Nine o'clock tomorrow morning.'

'Nine's perfect,' Dee said. 'See you then.'

She'd barely hung up when someone started banging on the front door. The sound made her jump. She ran to see who was there, her heart pounding as different scenarios played through her head. None of them good. No one came out to this stretch of beach late at night. Especially not in rain like this. Whoever was banging on the door hadn't come to deliver good news.

When she opened the door and saw Louise standing there, her wet hair stuck to her head and her eyes red, Dee's insides contracted. Her first thought was that something had happened to one of the children.

'What is it?' she said, grabbing Louise by the arm and dragging her inside. 'What's the matter, Lou?'

'I've done something terrible,' Louise said. Her voice was barely above a whisper, the words muffled beneath the rain that was louder since Dee had opened the door.

'What did you say?'

She shut the door and, this time, there was no mistaking what Louise was telling her.

'I've messed up, Dee. Really badly messed up. I can't go home. I'm sorry. I didn't know where else to go.'

–

'You've been what?'

'Don't make me say it again,' Louise said. 'Please.'

They were sitting side by side on the sofa in the small sitting room. Dee had made mugs of tea while Louise dried herself with a towel from Ella's bathroom. The rain was still drumming down outside, Jake was still sound asleep, and Dee's world view was being ripped apart and rebuilt into a different, unfamiliar narrative.

Louise was having an affair. Louise, her perfect cousin with her perfect family and her perfect life. Only it turned out she wasn't perfect, after all. It turned out everything Dee had believed about her cousin was a lie.

'How long?' Dee said. 'Come on, Lou, it's not a difficult question.'

'Three months.'

Dee opened her mouth to speak, then changed her mind because she had so many things she wanted to say, she didn't know where to start. Three months. Louise had been lying to her for three months. During that time, they'd gone for walks together, met for coffee and glasses of wine and shared happy times with Louise's kids. And all the time, Louise had been having an affair.

'I wanted to tell you,' Louise said. 'I nearly did a few times. But I always stopped because I knew how upset you were when Billy did it to you. The last thing I wanted to do was remind you of all that. Especially now when you're so happy with Ed. And I kept telling myself I'd end it. Only, somehow, I never did.'

Dee put her mug of tea on the floor and stood up.

'I don't know about you,' she said. 'But I need something stronger than tea if I'm going to have to listen to this.'

She'd seen a bottle of Sauvignon Blanc in the fridge earlier. She took it out and poured some wine into two glasses that she carried back to the sofa. She handed one glass to Louise, took a long swig from the other and sat back down.

'Is it serious?' she asked.

'No.' Louise sighed. 'I know that makes it worse. I mean, if I thought I was in love that might be an excuse. But I'm not.' She took a sip of wine, then another. 'I'm nothing more than a boring cliché, Dee. Middle-aged, middle-class, middle-of-the-bloody-road. I was feeling old and bored and like I'd lost my edge. And he was right there. Flirty and charming and full on and I fell for it.'

Dee thought of all the things Louise had in her life. A husband who, despite his faults, clearly adored her. A job she loved and was brilliant at. A big house in a beautiful part of town. Two happy, healthy children. A life. A lovely, big life full of love and friends and family.

'You'd risk your marriage and your children's happiness for a fling?' she said. 'I can't believe you've been so stupid.'

'I didn't expect you to understand. The thing is, Dee, I'm not like you. I'm shallow. I've always relied on my face and my body to get me the things I want in life. And that worked great for me for a long time, but it's changing. You know when women say they become invisible when they hit a certain age? I used to think that was self-indulgent nonsense, but it's not, is it? Over the last few years, I've become one of those invisible women. And I hate it. I know it's wrong and shallow and I should... I don't know, I should be thankful I've still got all my faculties and I haven't had a stroke or a heart attack or early-onset dementia. And I *am* grateful for all of that, of course I am. But it's not enough. I miss being me. This affair made me feel like myself again. I know how pathetic that sounds, Dee. But if you want to understand why I did it, that's why.'

Unexpectedly, Dee started to laugh. She couldn't help it. The idea of Louise – so gorgeous she literally turned heads wherever she went – feeling like she'd become invisible just because she'd turned fifty was preposterous.

'It's not funny,' Louise muttered when Dee's laughter finally subsided.

'It is,' Dee insisted. 'Dear God, Lou. Haven't you looked in a mirror recently? If you're invisible what the hell does that make me?'

'But you're nothing like me,' Louise said. 'You've got bags of confidence and you don't care what anyone thinks of you. I'd love to be more like you, but I'm not. I have tried, you know. One day last week, I even went to work without wearing any make-up. Just to prove to myself I could do it. But I hated it, Dee. I hated it so much I had to drive home mid-morning and sort myself out.'

'You hardly ever wear make-up,' Dee said.

Louise gave her a pitying look.

'Of course I wear make-up. I just apply it carefully so it looks as if I'm not wearing any. Invisible make-up. Takes twice as long to apply and costs three times as much. But it's worth it.'

'If you say so.' Dee wondered how it was possible to know someone as well as she knew Louise, and yet know so little about them.

'What about Martin?' she asked. 'Does he know you've been seeing someone else?'

'He knows something's wrong,' Louise said. 'But I don't think he's worked it out yet. He keeps trying to get me to talk, but how am I meant to tell him something like this? He'll be devastated.'

'You don't have to tell him,' Dee said. 'I mean, normally I'd say you shouldn't lie, but if you're planning to finish the affair anyway, then maybe it's best to do that and keep quiet about it to Martin. Mark it down as a stupid mistake and move on.'

'I can't do that,' Louise said.

'Why not?'

'Nigel Shaw knows about the affair and he's trying to blackmail me. He said he'll tell Martin unless I help him.'

Dee drained her glass and went to retrieve the bottle from the fridge. She'd replace it tomorrow, but right now she needed more wine.

'Okay,' she said, refilling both their glasses. 'Rewind. Start at the beginning, and don't leave anything out.'

'He thinks Kyle is hiding something,' Louise said. 'And he wants me to find it for him.'

'Hiding what?'

'Apparently Lauren found a letter.' Louise frowned. 'It must have been written to Nigel's mother. Lauren found it after she died. According to Nigel, the letter has private information about his family. He's desperate to get his hands on it.'

'Why did he ask you? Isn't it up to the police to find it?'

'He doesn't want them knowing about it.'

'It still doesn't explain why he thinks you can find it.'

'He knows I'm a journalist,' Louise said. 'Or maybe he's so desperate he doesn't know what he's doing. Either way, it doesn't matter, because I'm not going to do what he's asked me to. It's blackmail, pure and simple. Don't get me wrong, I feel sorry for Nigel. He's suffered a terrible loss. But he's asking me to interfere in a murder investigation. I can't do that.'

'There's something else,' Dee said. 'What is it you're not telling me, Lou?'

'I don't know what you mean.' Louise did her best to look confused, but Dee knew her better than that.

'Nigel knows the man you've been seeing, doesn't he?'

'Of course not,' Louise said. 'Honestly, Dee. He's just a guy I met a while ago at a local networking event. He's not local to Eastbourne. He lives in Lewes, I think. Although I've never actually been to his house. We meet in hotels, normally. He's got his own business and he does a lot of work across East Sussex. He's nothing to do with any of this, if that's what you're thinking.'

It was funny, Dee thought, how some people never learned. Ever since she was a child, Louise had always tried to cover a lie by speaking too much. She'd lie, and then embellish the lie with a whole lot of useless information. The first time Dee had observed this, both girls were eight years old and Louise was trying to persuade Dee that she hadn't taken Dee's Barbie doll. Forty-two years later, she was still at it.

'What are you going to do?' Dee asked, knowing better than to challenge Louise on the lie. That was another thing she'd learned that summer afternoon all those years ago: if you called Louise out on a lie, she wouldn't admit it. Not ever. Dee was pretty sure Louise would still deny stealing the doll if she asked her about it today.

'Tell Martin I've been seeing someone else, I suppose. And once I've done that, I'll tell Nigel he can go to hell.'

'What about the police?'

'I need to tell them,' Louise said. 'Don't I? They need to know he's desperate to get his hands on this letter. I mean, it could be relevant to the investigation, couldn't it?'

Dee thought back over everything she'd learned about Mary Palmer's murder. Different pieces of information, starting to fit together. She still didn't know everything, but she could see now where the gaps were. All she needed to do was fill them in.

'We need to find out what was in that letter,' she said.

Thirty-one

The Boardwalk was one of several cafes and bars dotted along the seafront. Like the others, it had a decking area on the beach where customers could sit outside in warm weather and enjoy the breathtaking views. But this morning, the views were muted by the blanket of grey clouds hanging over the town.

Dee arrived half an hour early. There was no sign yet of Charlie Steadman. The only other people in the cafe were three older men drinking coffees and arguing about Brexit

She ordered a coffee, sat at the window and called Miriam Anderson.

'When we spoke yesterday?' Dee said, once they'd got the pleasantries out of the way. 'You told me Emma believed that Annabelle was behind Mary's murder.'

'That's right,' Miriam said. 'Although she was never able to prove it.'

'Is it possible she might have written to Annabelle about her suspicions?'

'I think that's quite likely, actually. Why are you asking?'

'Lauren found a letter when she was clearing out Annabelle's belongings. I'm trying to find out who sent it.'

'I told you Emma could be quite impulsive after a few drinks,' Miriam said. 'I wonder if that's why Annabelle came to see her the night she died?'

'Possibly.'

The idea that had started yesterday was back. Clearer now. Refusing to be ignored. While Miriam continued to talk, Dee zoned in on the idea, trying to see whether it made sense or not.

'What if Emma found proof?' she said.

'Proof of Annabelle's guilt? Then why would she kill herself?'

Unless she didn't, Dee thought.

A young man and woman came into the cafe and looked around. Saying a hurried goodbye to Miriam, Dee ended the call.

'Charlie?'

He nodded and walked over to her table.

'This is Marnie,' he said, introducing his companion. Dee presumed she was the girlfriend he had mentioned on the phone. 'We don't have long. I start work at nine thirty.'

'That's fine.' Dee smiled. 'Thanks for agreeing to see me. Can I get either of you a drink?'

'I'll have an espresso, please,' Marnie said, pulling out a chair and sitting down. 'Charlie will have a cappuccino. You like a cappuccino, don't you mate?' She had a strong Australian accent and gave Dee a cheeky grin as she issued her request.

Dee went to get the drinks. When she came back, Charlie and Marnie were huddled and Marnie was saying something Dee couldn't catch.

'Thanks for this,' Marnie said. 'So, Dee. Before Charlie speaks to you, we need to know why you're asking about Joana.'

'She's been missing for almost seven weeks,' Dee said. 'Her friend has asked me to see if I can help find her. The police have looked into it, but they can't find any evidence something bad has happened. They think she's simply packed her bags and moved on.'

'Cops don't give a shit about folk like Joana,' Marnie said. 'Same where I come from. I'm part Aboriginal. Guess you worked that out? On my mum's side. People like us, we're invisible to the police unless someone commits a crime. Then the police are all over us like a bad case of crabs. Know what I mean, Dee?'

'I know exactly what you mean,' Dee said. She was starting to like Charlie's girlfriend.

'Go on then.' Marnie nudged Charlie. 'Tell her. I reckon you'll feel better if you get it off your chest.'

'You know Joana?' Dee asked him.

'We both do,' Charlie said. 'Sort of. There's a group of us who are into surfing. She joins us sometimes when the waves are good. She's only been a few times, so we don't know her well. But she seems cool.'

'Did you see her at the hotel the night she disappeared?'

Charlie looked down at his coffee and didn't reply.

'He doesn't want to get the boss into trouble,' Marnie said. 'That's Charlie all over, always thinking about other people.' She smiled at Dee, a big, happy smile that brightened up the whole room. 'I'm a sucker for a nice guy, Dee. Can't help myself.'

'Why would you be getting Derek in trouble?' Dee asked.

'I'm not saying he's done anything,' Charlie said. 'You understand that, right? Derek's been good to me. He gave me a job when I came out of prison. Helped me get back on my feet again. He's a good man.'

'If he hasn't done anything wrong,' Dee said, 'you've got nothing to worry about, have you?'

'She was in the hotel,' Charlie said. 'I only saw her for a second. She didn't know I'd seen her. No one did. There's a suite on the top floor. We had a private dinner there. I was doing the catering. Some rich dude's birthday. I'd never heard of him, but him and his mates were okay.'

'You're saying Joana was at this party?'

'No.' Charlie shook his head. 'It was later. I'd just come out of the suite and I was waiting for the lift. There's a row of four lifts, you know? Two of them arrived at the same time. I had a trolley and I was pushing it into one of the lifts when she came out of the other one. I only saw her out of the corner of my eye. I thought it was some mistake, because no one except guests goes up to that floor. You need a special room key to get the lift to take you there. Which is why I assumed it was just someone who looked like her, you know? Because I know Jo doesn't have much money. She's always scrabbling around for any work she can get. I did a sort of double-take. I turned to get a better look, and she was standing outside one of the rooms. I saw her face in profile and I realised it wasn't someone who looked like her. It *was* her. Joana.'

'And?' Dee said when Charlie stopped speaking.

'She knocked on the door and a man opened it. He whispered something in her ear and then he took her hand and they went into the room together. The man was Derek. Joana was there to see him.'

'When was this?' Dee's mind was racing, going back over all the encounters she'd had with Derek French, trying to work out exactly how many times he'd lied to her.

'I checked the work calendar yesterday,' Charlie said. 'The private dinner was Saturday the eighth of February.'

Bile rose at the back of Dee's throat. On the eighth of February, Joana had told Eliza she was going to meet someone at the Aldrington Hotel. She'd said goodbye to her flatmate, left the house at seven fifteen, and she hadn't been seen since.

From the diary of Emma Reed

7 May 1966

James and I had a terrible row tonight. He thinks I've lost my mind. I was late home and I made the mistake of telling him where I'd been. I should have kept quiet, but my head was so full of it all that I had to tell someone, and who else should I talk to if not my husband?

He was already upset when I came in. He'd been 'home for hours' apparently, with 'not a scrap of food to eat', because I hadn't prepared anything. As if, just because he's a man, he's incapable of boiling a few potatoes and frying up some mince and onions.

It didn't help that Nicola was out with Henry, so James had come home to an empty house. He doesn't approve of Henry, although he's too much of a coward to tell Nicola to her face. Instead he grumbles about it to me, and drops heavy hints that I should be the one to tell her she could do better for herself. The problem is, I'm not sure she could. She's a surly, difficult young woman. If you ask me, she's lucky to have found any man interested in dating her. But no one ever does ask me, do they?

I hadn't planned to arrive home so late, but the journey across London took longer than I'd expected. I'd only been on the Underground a handful of times before. I'd forgotten what

260

distances it covers. I travelled on the District Line all the way to Mile End, where David Partridge has his doctor's surgery.

When I heard he had his own practice, I expected something quite glamorous. The truth, I'm afraid, is rather different. His 'surgery' occupies the ground floor of a terraced building on a grimy backstreet five minutes' walk from Mile End station. The neighbourhood is like nowhere else I've ever visited. Immediately outside the station is a wide road and the first thing you notice is the noise. From the buses and the black cabs and the cars. So many cars, it's difficult to imagine where all these people can be going to.

Then there's the people. I don't know how many different nationalities live in Mile End, but I imagine it's a lot. Many of them, judging by their appearance, from India or Pakistan. Women in black robes that cover their faces, and men with turbans on their heads. The air stank with cooking smells and I had to cover my face as I pushed my way through the bustling street market, men and women shouting things in their Cockney accents that were so strong I had no hope of making out their words.

I had an address, but no idea how to find the place I was looking for. I'd imagined it would be easy to stop a stranger and ask for directions, but I was too scared to speak to anyone. I must have looked very lost because an older woman approached and asked me if I needed help. Her name was Angie, and she gave me very precise directions, which led me to David Partridge's surgery less than five minutes later.

I thought at first that Angie had misled me. But then I saw the brass plaque, almost invisible beneath a thick layer of grime, with David's name on it. I gave my name to the receptionist (an overweight woman wearing too much make-up) and told her I was a family friend. She instructed me to take a seat while I waited.

It was a deeply unpleasant experience, sitting alongside all the sick people. They were mostly elderly, and the majority looked as if they might keel over at any moment. There was an air of poverty and desperation about the place that made me want to run out of there. But I'd come this far and I was determined to stick it out.

I waited for over an hour and a half. Several times, I asked the receptionist if she'd told him I was here. Each time, she assured me 'the doctor' knew I was waiting, but I had to understand he was a very busy man.

I'd almost given up when he finally came out of wherever he'd been hiding. By this time, I was the only person left in the waiting room. He didn't look as I'd expected, and I realised it was several years since I'd last set eyes on him. He'd aged and lost weight. In truth, he looked haggard. As he walked towards me, I saw his features more clearly and I recognised the little boy who used to come knocking at my back door asking if Graham could come out to play.

I stood up.

'Mrs Reed.' He took my hand and held it for a moment. 'It's lovely to see you. Although I'm a little confused. Was I meant to know you'd be visiting me this morning?'

I asked if there was somewhere we could go and talk. He hesitated, as if he was trying to think of an excuse.

'I've still got my home visits to do,' he said. 'I'm afraid you've caught me at a very inconvenient time. If I'd known you were coming, I could have made arrangements.'

I had no idea what arrangements he might have made, and I didn't care. I told him I wanted to talk to him about Annabelle Palmer. He frowned and said he didn't understand.

'I know what she did,' I said. 'And I know your brother helped her.'

Several expressions passed across his face – shock, embarrass-ment and fear.

'You knew Graham couldn't have killed that girl,' I said. 'All this time, you've known, yet you kept quiet. And for what, David? To end up working here in this horrible, dirty place? Is that all my son's life was worth to you? And what about Mary? Don't you think she deserves to see justice done too?'

He stood there, in the empty waiting room, saying nothing at all. Not even trying to defend himself.

'You could have stopped it.' I was angry and my voice was too loud for the small room. 'Those savages killed my son and you could have stopped it all by telling the truth. But you didn't, because she promised you money if you kept your mouth shut. How much, David? How much did she pay you to stand back and do nothing while my son was beaten to death?'

He started moving away from me and I grabbed his arm, shouting that it wasn't too late. All he had to do was tell the truth now and Annabelle would pay for what she'd done. But he shook me off and shoved me away from him, so hard I almost fell.

I ran after him but he was fast and by the time I was outside on the street, there was no sign of him. I tried to go back inside to ask the receptionist where he'd gone but she had locked the door behind me. My heart was beating too fast and I was finding it difficult to catch my breath.

David knew what they'd done and he'd kept quiet about it. In return for his silence, Annabelle gave him the money he needed to train as a doctor. Which means there are three people who know the truth: Richard, Annabelle and David. Two of them killed Mary, and the other one kept quiet about it.

Thirty-two

Louise had an umbrella, but the wind kept blowing it inside out. Eventually, she gave up and hurried along the pier, battling her way through the pounding rain and the howling wind.

Nigel was already there, sitting under the cover of one of the benches. His hair was lank and greasy. He was wearing the same clothes he'd been wearing yesterday. He looked like an old man. She remembered a party he and Maxine had hosted in their house last summer. A blazing hot day. Their garden full of Eastbourne's great and good. Liveried waiters and waitresses moving smoothly through the crowd carrying trays of champagne and bite-sized canapés. And in the middle of it all, the golden Shaw family: Nigel, Maxine and Lauren.

Louise had been envious that afternoon, she remembered. Jealous of their wealth and beauty and the easy way they seemed to accept their privileged lifestyle. At the time, it had seemed to contrast sharply with her own life. All the effort and hard work it took to keep everything going – the private-school fees, the mortgage repayments and two parents working full-time. She'd been an idiot, of course. No one's life was that perfect; it only seemed that way to people stupid enough not to look beyond the surface.

She dipped beneath the shelter, out of the rain, and sat on the bench beside Nigel. His lit cigarette dangled from his hand, thin trails of smoke disappearing into the rain.

'You're late.'

He took a drag from the cigarette, and started coughing. When the coughing stopped, he sucked on the cigarette again before flicking it to the ground. The burning end sizzled once before it was extinguished by the water all around it.

'I got here as quickly as I could,' she said.

There used to be a disco on the pier. In the pavilion at the end. Louise and her friends used to come here all the time when they were teenagers. She'd had a crush on Ed in those days, although he'd never given any indication he knew she even existed. Some of her friends liked Ed, too. The rest of them liked Nigel. Quite simply, Ed Mitchell and Nigel Shaw were the two boys everyone wanted to date.

Ed switched between girls like he was running out of time, but Nigel was different. All through their school years, he'd only ever had eyes for one girl: Maxine Pearson, as she was then. Except, Louise remembered now, they hadn't gone out with each other back then. The summer after they all left school, Maxine became Ed's first serious girlfriend. Louise had been gutted. Although that, too, had passed. When Ed and Maxine split up two years later, Louise barely gave them a second thought.

'You said you had something to tell me,' Nigel said. 'Is it about the letter? Have you found it?'

'I haven't tried to find it,' Louise said. 'And I'm not going to either.'

'I wasn't kidding around yesterday, Louise. I swear to God I will call Martin right now and tell him what you've been playing at. Maybe I should call him, anyway. Poor fucker deserves to know.'

'I've already told him,' Louise said. A lie, but Nigel didn't need to know that. She had tried to tell Martin this morning, but she couldn't do it. Which meant she'd have to tell him tonight. Or tomorrow. As soon as she found the courage to look him in the eye and rip his world apart.

'No.' Nigel shook his head. 'No, no, no, no, no. You don't understand. I need you to do this for me. I don't care if you've told Martin. I'll tell everyone else. I'll make sure the whole town knows the sort of person you really are. How do you think that would work with the paper? You think people will want to read your stupid fucking opinion pieces if they know what a two-faced, devious person you really are? And what about your kids? What's it going to do to them when they learn their mother's nothing but a common or garden slag?'

'Shut up!' Louise stood up, her whole body shaking. 'How dare you?' She had to shout to make herself heard above the roaring of the waves beneath her and the pounding of the rain as it hit the pier and bounced off the surface.

'You think it's acceptable to blackmail me?' She reached into her bag and took out her phone. 'I'm not some little woman you can push around and manipulate. I'm calling the police. I should have done it already but I didn't because, stupidly, I felt sorry for you.'

She scrolled through her list of contacts, searching for Rachel's number. But before she could find it, Nigel leapt up and knocked the phone out of her hand. Louise bent down to pick it up, but he grabbed both her arms and shoved her back, away from her phone and towards the edge of the pier.

She screamed, but the sound was lost in the whirling wind and pounding waves. She tried to fight him off, but he was too strong. He held her tight, his fingers digging into her arms, as he leaned his face close to hers. She could see the tiny black pores on his nose and when he spoke again, drops of his spit splashed onto her face, mixing with the rain but feeling different because the rain was cold and his spit was warm.

'It's not my fault,' he shouted. 'None of this is my fault. All I'm trying to do is what's right. But you don't care. No one cares.'

He stopped speaking. For one terrible moment, she thought he was going to lift her up and push her over the iron railing that ran along the sides of the pier, protecting people from falling off it into the swirling grey sea. She screamed again, and this time she kept screaming, louder and louder until her throat was raw.

He pushed her away from him. She crashed down, landing hard on the wet, wooden boards. Her elbow struck the ground first, and it was only as the pain shot up her arm that she realised she was okay. He hadn't thrown her over. She wasn't drowning in the icy sea.

As she scrambled to her feet, she saw her phone lying face down in a puddle of water. She picked it up. Her heart was beating too fast, and she was struggling to breathe. Shock or fear or some combination of both. She had to get away. Holding her sore elbow, she scanned the length of the pier. She couldn't see Nigel, but there was no one else here either. The rain had driven people indoors. Waves roared beneath her as she hurried back towards the exit, rain splashing against her face, dripping down the back of her neck and soaking through the soles of her shoes.

On the pavement outside the pier, she stopped. She couldn't remember where she'd parked her car. She'd driven here earlier, but the memory of parking, getting out of her car and walking to the pier was gone. She looked up and down the road, helplessly. There were lots of parked cars, but none of them looked like hers. The rain made it impossible to see more than a few feet ahead of her.

She held her phone up, thinking she would call a taxi, but the screen was cracked and when she tried to dial the number for her local taxi firm, nothing happened. Tears pricked her eyes. She wiped them away, angry at herself for being so weak. But it was no good. Shock and cold and an aching elbow got the better of her and the tears started falling.

She might have stayed there for ever, crying in the rain, except right then a car pulled up alongside her. The driver's window rolled down and Derek was there, asking if she was okay and telling her to get in beside him, quickly, before she got any wetter than she already was. She didn't want to see him again. She was going to end it. But he was here and maybe it would be okay if she said yes and got into his car and let him take her somewhere warm and safe and far away from here.

Thirty-three

Using the hands-free unit in her hire car, Dee called Ed.

'Dee. I'm in the middle of something now. Can I call you back in a few minutes?'

'This can't wait. I know you're annoyed with me about something, but can we put that to one side for a moment? I really need your help.'

As quickly as she could, she recounted everything Charlie had just told her.

'And you're sure it was the same night?' Ed asked.

'Positive. Charlie checked the dates on his work calendar.'

'Okay. Let me speak with Brian.'

'Brian?'

'Brian Douglas. The detective who first looked into Joana's disappearance. I told you about him before.'

'You'll tell him Derek lied?' Dee said. 'He knew her, Ed. Yet he looked me in the eye and told me he'd never seen her before.'

'I'll make sure. Brian's a good detective. He'll do the right thing. But remember, just because Derek lied about knowing her doesn't mean he had anything to do with her disappearance.'

'Like hell it doesn't.'

'I'll call Brian now,' Ed said. 'Promise you won't do anything stupid in the meantime?'

'Like what?'

'Like try to speak to Derek yourself?'

Dee was approaching the Martello roundabout. She indicated right so she could take the third exit into the Harbour.

'I wouldn't dream of it. Ed, there's something else too.'

'Go on.'

'The thing that Lauren found – it was a letter.'

'How do you know that?'

'I spoke to a friend of your grandmother's.'

'What?'

'I'll explain later,' Dee said. 'The thing is, I think the letter Lauren found might have been written by your grandmother.'

'Of course. Maxine said something about a letter. But she didn't say anything about it being written by my grandmother. Are you sure about that?'

'I didn't realise you'd spoken to Maxine. When did that happen?'

'A few days ago,' Ed said. 'Sorry, I thought I'd told you.'

'How could you have told me when you haven't spoken to me since Friday?'

'I'm sorry,' Ed said, after a moment. 'Listen, we need to talk. Could I see you after work this evening?'

'I'm not sure.' She'd been planning to suggest the same thing. Until he'd let slip that he'd been to visit his ex-girlfriend and hadn't bothered telling her.

'Please? The longer we go without talking, the harder it's going to be to sort this out.'

He was right. But he was also the one who'd ignored her all weekend.

'Let me think about it,' she said. 'I'll call you later.'

She hung up before he could say anything else. She'd told him what she'd found out. Now, it was up to him to do whatever the hell he wanted with the information.

A few minutes later, she was parking outside Derek and Karen's monstrous house on the waterfront. She probably should have told Ed where she was going. But if she'd done that, he'd have told her not to, and the next thing you knew they'd be having another row. And right now, that was the last thing she wanted.

After her chat with Charlie, Dee had gone straight to the Aldrington looking for Derek, but she was told he hadn't come into work yet. So she'd driven across to his house. Part of her knew she should leave this up to the police. But the anger at being lied to, repeatedly, and knowing he'd done everything he could to prevent her from finding Joana, meant she couldn't simply sit back and do nothing.

But Derek wasn't at home, either.

'He's in Brighton today,' Karen told Dee. 'Although I'm surprised you don't know that. You've been spending almost as much time with him as I have these days.'

'What's that supposed to mean?'

'You're always at the hotel, harassing him with your questions and insinuations. And now you've turned up here, at his house. Don't you think you're taking things too far?'

'It's called doing my job,' Dee said. 'That's all.'

'If you say so.' Karen folded her arms across her ample chest. 'What's so important you need to come here to speak to Derek about?'

'He lied to me,' Dee said. 'And I want to know why.'

A woman appeared in the hallway before Karen had a chance to respond.

'All finished, Mrs French.' The woman tried to leave but Karen put a hand out, stopping her.

'Not so fast,' she said. 'I need to check you've cleaned the bathroom properly. You didn't do a very good job last week.'

The woman pulled a face but stepped back inside as she was told.

Karen turned her attention back to Dee.

'I want you to leave my property. If you come back here, or turn up at the hotel, I'll call the police and report you for harassment.'

'Why do you stay with a man like that?' Dee asked.

But Karen had already slammed the door shut and Dee doubted she'd heard her. She contemplated banging on the door until Karen opened it. But then she had a better idea. She walked back to her car, got inside and waited.

Ten minutes later, she saw the cleaner coming out of the house. As she approached the road, Dee jumped out of her car and waved her over.

'Can I speak to you for a few minutes?' she said.

The woman shrugged. 'I guess.' She was small and very thin, with pale skin and light brown hair tied back in a scraggly ponytail. She didn't look strong enough to have a job cleaning houses.

'How long have you worked for Karen?' Dee asked.

'Mrs French?' The woman smirked. 'She doesn't let me call her by her first name. Thinks she needs to keep *the staff* in their place.'

'That can't be very pleasant for you.' Dee held a hand out. 'I'm Dee, by the way.'

'Paula.' The woman briefly touched Dee's hand before letting it go again. 'Why are you asking about Mrs F?'

'I'm a journalist and I'm writing a piece about how people are being exploited by employers who pay cash in hand to get around paying national insurance or any other benefits.'

It was the right thing to say. She spent the next fifteen minutes listening to Paula tell her how difficult it was to keep her head above water, the number of hours she had to work to make ends meet, the nastiness of some of her employers and the all-round crappiness of trying to earn a decent wage in the gig economy. Unsurprisingly, Paula blamed the influx of cheap migrant labour on her circumstances and Dee didn't think this was the time to point out that Brexit had made this problem worse, not better.

'I couldn't believe my luck when Mrs F got in touch,' Paula said. 'She doesn't want foreigners working for her. The last cleaner was an Eastern European and she left one day without any warning. Mrs F said she wasn't going to risk something like that happening again.'

'How long ago was this?' Dee asked.

'Maybe a month, month and a half?' Paula said.

'Do you happen to know which part of Eastern Europe she was from?' Dee said.

'Sorry,' Paula said. 'I don't think Mrs F ever mentioned the country.'

Dee asked about Derek and Kyle, but Paula claimed she'd never met Derek and only ever saw Kyle in passing.

'The husband's always at work as far as I can tell,' she said. 'All my dealings have been with Mrs F.'

Dee thanked Paula for her time, and said goodbye. She was getting into her car when the cleaner called her back.

'There's one thing,' Paula said. 'Don't know if it will help or not. Mrs F was always bitching about her.'

'Who?'

'The other cleaner,' Paula said. 'Her name was Joana. Would that help you work out what country she came from?'

'Joana,' Dee repeated. 'You sure about that?'

'A hundred and ten per cent,' Paula said. 'Her name is branded onto my brain, the number of times I've heard Mrs F going on about her.'

From the diary of Emma Reed

10 October 1978

It's like unpeeling an onion. The truth is hidden beneath layers of lies. I have spent the last eighteen years trying to unpeel each and every lie so I can find out what really happened. Around me, people continue to get on with their lives. There are days I think I'm the only person who still remembers Graham, or cares about discovering the truth. James has become an utter golf bore since his retirement. It's all he talks about, and I suspect all he thinks about too. Materially, we want for nothing. But spiritually and emotionally, our lives are empty and barren.

I called to see Nicola and the children this afternoon, but she made it clear she didn't want me there. She said she had work to do, but it was a lie. The truth is, I wasn't the best mother when she was growing up and she's punishing me for it now. Recently, she's stopped asking me to babysit too. She says I was drunk the last time. Which is a lie, but there's no point trying to tell her that. She won't listen. Edward, at least, still loves his gran and comes to see me whenever he can. He'll be eleven on his next birthday, and Nessa turned eight last month. They are growing up too fast. I want to hold them and keep them safe for ever.

I wanted to ask Edward today if there'd been any more trouble between him and little Nigel Shaw, but I didn't get a chance. Nicola didn't give us any time alone together, and I know from

275

experience she won't tolerate any criticism of Annabelle or her family. It sickens me to think of that woman ingratiating herself in my daughter's life, but that's exactly what she's done. Nicola is too lonely to see Annabelle for what she really is. I'll invite Edward over for his tea next week, and I'll speak to him then.

None of us speak of Graham any longer. I've told my grandchildren all about him, but everyone else seems to think it's easier to pretend he never existed. The single photograph I have of him still stands in pride of place above our fireplace, but the conversations we have within our family are never about the son and brother we had and lost.

James thinks I've finally let it go, but he's wrong. You can never speak of something and still think about it all the time. Over the years, I've spoken with so many people and recorded every conversation here, in my diaries. Eighteen years of trying to discover the truth.

Until today, I was starting to despair. I am getting older and my determination to clear my son's name is the only thing that keeps me going. But determination alone isn't enough, as I've learned the hard way.

The envelope was tucked among the other envelopes when I gathered the post from the floor this morning. My name and address on the front, written in a hand I didn't recognise. I've read the contents so many times that I know them by heart. Each word branded onto my brain.

Dear Mrs Reed,

I apologise for writing to you out of the blue after all this time. I've thought many times of the day you came to visit me in London. There is so much I should have told you, information I've kept to myself for far too long.

Earlier this year, I was diagnosed with lung cancer. I am dying. Before I go, I would like very much to see you and tell you what I should have told you a long time ago. If you would like to meet me, please call me on the number at the top of this page, and we can arrange a date and a meeting place that's convenient for you.

Yours sincerely,
David Partridge

Thirty-four

'No.'

Louise pulled away from Derek, not trusting herself to be this close to him.

'I've already told you,' she said. 'I can't do this any more.'

'I don't get it,' he said. 'If you're going to tell Martin anyway, what's the problem?'

'What's the problem? The problem is that what we've been doing is wrong. What about Karen? Don't you ever worry that she'll find out you've been seeing someone else?'

'Karen doesn't give a damn,' he said. 'You know that.'

They were sitting in the bar of the Grand Hotel in Brighton. After Derek had picked her up, Louise had tried to end things with him. He'd got upset, and begged her to take the morning off so they could talk properly. Reluctantly, she'd agreed, thinking she owed him that at least. She'd called work and told them she had food poisoning.

'I could kill Nigel for this,' Derek said. 'I don't know why the police haven't charged him yet. We've never got on, you know. We made a bit of an effort for the kids' sake, but it was hard work. At least we won't have to do that any more. I'll be glad if I never have to spend another minute of my life in that man's company.

'He resents me. I'm self-made and he can't stand that. I'm a threat. Because if someone like me can pull myself out of my working–class roots and make something of myself, then what's to stop anyone else doing it? And the more of us that do it, the less power is left in the hands of people like him.'

'His daughter's just died,' Louise said. 'In the most unimaginable way possible. He's grieving, that's all. He doesn't know what he's doing.'

She shivered, remembering again that moment on the pier when she'd thought he was going to kill her. Now, she wondered if she'd got it wrong and the person most in danger from Nigel was Nigel himself.

'I didn't want to believe he could have killed her,' Derek said. 'Not at first. But after what you've told me today, I think he's capable of anything. Promise me you'll tell the police what he tried to do?'

'Will it make any difference?'

He reached across the table and took her hand in his.

'I know you feel sorry for him,' he said. 'But you've got to listen to me. Apart from what he did to you, which in my mind is reason enough to get him arrested, the man is trying to interfere in a police investigation. You have a responsibility to tell the police. You don't have to mention me, or us. But you need to tell them he tried to blackmail you.'

Suddenly, she didn't want to be here. She wanted to be at home, with Martin and the children. She wanted to feel safe again. Because ever since she'd started this affair with Derek, she'd been living in a state of anxiety. It had been fine for a while – the edge was what she'd been looking for – but now she'd had enough. She wished she could wind the clock back to three months earlier, before she'd started this affair. Before Lauren's murder. Before any of this had happened.

'I need to go.' She pulled her hand away and stood up. Then, realising they hadn't paid for the meal yet, she opened her bag, looking inside for her purse.

'Can we pay up?' she said, and looked around, caught the eye of one of the waitresses and gestured for the bill.

'Stop, Louise.' Derek stood up too, but she shook her head.

'Please. Can't you just let me go?'

Tears blurred her vision and she rubbed them away angrily. She'd done enough crying for one day.

'I'll sort the bill,' Derek said. 'Let me do that, at least. Afterwards, I'll drive you back to Eastbourne and then, I swear to you, if you don't want to see me again, that's what we'll do. We'll finish it. Today.'

'Okay.' She nodded. She didn't want to have to go back in the car with him. But it seemed churlish to get the train when he was being so good about everything. When he'd cancelled his work meeting and spent all this time making sure she was okay.

Outside, the rain had stopped and when he suggested a walk along the seafront before getting into the car, Louise agreed. The fresh air felt good after the artificial warmth of the hotel. And the anxiety that had been like a tight band across her chest started to ease.

Brighton seafront was bigger and bolder than East-bourne. Louise remembered coming here as a child and teenager, wanting to live in this place that seemed so much more exciting and vibrant than her own home town. She experienced that same giddy feeling this afternoon. Even on a blustery day like today, Brighton was buzzing. People of all ages out and about, rollerblading and dog-walking and couples holding hands. Children too young to be at school running along the promenade, zigzagging around the adults.

'My mum used to bring me and Pete here when we were kids,' Derek said. 'The first time we came, I was seven years old. Pete was three. I'd never seen the sea before. I remember it like it was yesterday. That sense of wonder that something like this could exist in the world and I'd never been close to it before. That's why I decided I'd live by the coast when I grew up.'

'That's sweet,' Louise said. She tried to picture him as a young boy but the image wouldn't work. He was too streetwise, too much of a schmoozer and fixer.

'That sense of purpose is what's made me who I am today,' he continued. 'I always knew I didn't want to live the sort of life my mother had. Two kids to look after with no money and no one to help her. Trying to hold down a job while keeping the two of us out of trouble. It's a wonder only one of us went off the rails.'

'You've done so well,' Louise said. 'I bet your mum would have been so proud of you.'

'At least she had one son she could be proud of,' Derek said.

'Maybe Pete will sort himself out,' Louise said. 'There's still time, you know.'

'Not a chance.' Derek snorted. 'You know he called me last night? Drunk out of his head, of course. Going on about some bloody business idea he has. Just another excuse to pump me for money. I tried putting him off but he wouldn't have it. So like a bloody fool I've agreed to meet him tomorrow and listen to this latest hare-brained idea of his. As if I haven't got enough problems of my own, I have to deal with all his shit as well. The only good thing is if I meet him tomorrow that's me done for another six months.'

The wind kept blowing Louise's hair across her eyes, which made it difficult to see his face. She brushed her hair back, holding it in place.

'You only see him every six months?' she asked.

'Never more than that,' Derek said. 'I'm not able for it. It's over six months this time so I suppose he's due a visit from his big brother. You know, if you wanted to, you could give me the perfect excuse for standing him up tomorrow?'

Her hand dropped down, hair whipping across her face again as soon as she let go.

'I'd love to,' she said, dipping her head down so he couldn't see her face. 'But you know I can't.'

He didn't say anything, but she could feel his eyes on her, boring into her. She forced herself to smile and looked up at him.

'It's freezing,' she said. 'Would you mind if we headed back?'

'Good idea,' Derek said. 'Car's parked just up here.'

He took her elbow, steering her across the road. As soon as they'd crossed, she pulled her arm free, grateful they were in a public place and he wouldn't be able to force her to go with him.

'I've just remembered some shopping I need to do,' she said. 'I promised Daisy I'd pick something up for her the next time I was here. I may as well go and get it now.'

'That's okay,' Derek said. 'I'm not in any rush.'

'No.' Louise shook her head. 'I'd rather go by myself. Being with you like this is too painful. I need some time by myself. I'll get what I need for Daisy and I'll take the train.'

She leaned forward and kissed his cheek, the smell of his aftershave clogging her nose and coating the inside of her mouth.

'I'll see you around,' she said. 'Bye.'

She turned and walked away before he could stop her. She walked fast, but not too fast, knowing she couldn't make it look like that was what she was doing. She walked all the way to the end of the street, and when she turned the corner and knew he couldn't see her any longer, she started running.

Thirty-five

By mid-afternoon, Dee had written the first draft of her story on Joana Helinski's disappearance. There were still gaps – gaps that couldn't be filled in until the police had found Derek French – but what she had was a good start. It was also a grimly depressing read. The story of a young girl coming to this country to make life better for herself and her young child. But the dream of a better life never materialises. Instead, the girl ends up working a series of low-paid, dead-end jobs and is forced to find another way to earn money. Then, one night, she meets a man for sex and something bad happens. The girl disappears without a trace.

He'd killed her. Dee couldn't prove it yet, but she knew. Derek French had killed Joana Helinski that night and, somehow, he'd managed to get her body out of the hotel without being seen and he'd dumped it somewhere. Worse, the man was so arrogant he thought he could get away with it.

Several times during the day, she'd taken her phone out to call Eliza before changing her mind. It was better to wait until she had as much information as she could get. Which shouldn't be taking this long. She'd called Ed earlier and told him what she'd found out about Joana working for the Frenches. He told Dee he'd pass the information on to Brian Douglas, and promised to call her as soon as he had any news. So far, he hadn't called her back. Sick of waiting, Dee decided to take matters into her own hands and called him instead.

'I was about to call you,' he said. 'Brian's spent the afternoon trying to track down Derek – no luck so far, but he's spoken with Karen. She claims she didn't lie to you about Joana. She acknowledges that you showed her Joana's photo, but said you never asked if she recognised her.'

'What utter bullshit.'

'I know,' Ed said. 'But that's her story, and she's sticking to it. She confirmed Joana was her cleaner, and said the girl simply didn't show up for work one day and Karen hasn't seen her since.'

'Did Brian tell her that Joana was with her husband the night she disappeared?'

'She says that's not possible. Claims Derek was at home that night. Unfortunately for Karen, Brian's also spoken with Charlie, who's agreed to give a statement saying he definitely saw Derek with Joana the same night.'

'What about Kyle?' Dee said. 'When I asked him about Joana, he never said a word about her working as their cleaner.'

'I'll make sure Brian speaks to him as well,' Ed said. 'Our priority now is finding Derek. He has to come home sooner or later. As soon as that happens, we'll arrest him. If he's got anything to do with Joana's disappearance, we'll find out, Dee. I promise.'

'Thanks, Ed.'

'Anything I can do,' he said. 'You know that, right? I've missed you, Dee. I'd really like to see you.'

'Me too,' she said.

'You would? Good. That's really good. I should be finished here by six thirty at the latest. How about I come straight over after that?'

'I'd like that,' Dee said.

As she hung up, she realised she was smiling. She was glad they were speaking again. For the first time since their falling-out, she felt hopeful they would find a way through this difficult patch.

–

Louise pulled up outside her house. She switched the engine off, but didn't get out of the car. She'd got the train back from Brighton and walked from the station. She had a tonne of work to get through but she couldn't face it. Instead, she'd found her car on the seafront and driven straight home. It was later than she'd imagined. She should have called Martin and told him she was running late. But her mind had been so caught up with Derek, she hadn't given a thought to anything else.

Inside the house, the curtains were drawn and the lights were on. In the sitting room, she could just make out the blue glare of the TV screen. She pictured Daisy and Ben in there, cuddled up together on the sofa watching something on CBeebies. All she wanted to do was go in there and cuddle up beside them both, holding them close. But she couldn't go in yet. First, she had to decide what she was going to do.

At Brighton station, there'd been an Eastbourne train ready to depart. She'd jumped into the last carriage, just as the doors were about to close. It was only as the train pulled away from the platform, and she realised there was no way Derek could catch her now, that her body caught up with the thoughts churning inside her head. She started shaking, so badly she could hear her teeth rattling inside her mouth. She closed her eyes, breathing deeply – in and out, in and out – waiting for the worst of it to pass. She'd suffered panic attacks in her early twenties, and knew the best thing to do was to breathe slowly until her mind realised there was no danger and she could relax.

Except this time, she couldn't relax. The danger was real and present. Or was it? She tried to tell herself there was some mistake. That she'd misheard him, or he'd simply forgotten. But she knew Derek, and she knew he wasn't the sort of person to forget meeting his own brother. Especially a meeting that was meant to have taken place the night Lauren was killed.

Louise's face burned when she remembered her angry defence of Derek the night Dee had asked her about him. It had never occurred to her – not for a second – that he might have lied. But that was what he'd done. He'd told her, the police and everyone else that the night Lauren was murdered he was in London visiting his brother, Pete.

A shadow moved behind the curtains. Martin. A wave of sadness washed over her. Martin was the opposite of men like Derek. Louise knew some people – Dee, for example – thought Martin was boring. But boring wasn't the worst thing a person could be. Boring also meant predictable, dependable, reliable. And Martin loved her. Really, properly loved her. She didn't deserve him.

She knew what she had to do. She was going to go inside, feed her children and get them ready for bed. And then she was going to call Rachel Lewis and tell her Derek had lied about his alibi the night Lauren was murdered. She opened the door and got out of the car.

A wave of cold air hit her. To her left, a sudden movement as something ran towards her. A dark shadow. Instinctively she turned away, trying to block it, but she wasn't fast enough. Something smashed into the side of her head. Pain and a burst of white light. She was falling, the ground rising to meet her and her own voice screaming as she fell. And then there was nothing, except darkness and pain.

Thirty-six

Dee was in the shower when she heard her phone ringing. She ran to get it, but it had stopped by the time she got to it. When she checked her call history, she saw the call was from Ed. She tried to call him back, but got his voicemail. Hanging up, she saw he'd sent her a text as well.

> Running late – something's come up last minute. I'll call when I'm done x

She was about to send a text back, telling him not to worry, when her phone started ringing again. Expecting it to be Ed, she answered without checking the caller ID.

'Are you okay?' she asked.

'Dee?' Not Ed. Martin. His voice sounded strained and immediately Dee knew something was wrong.

'What is it?' she said. 'What's happened?'

Because something had happened. In the whole time she'd known him, Martin had never once phoned her. She closed her eyes, bracing herself for whatever she was about to hear. Images she didn't want to see raced through her head – Louise's car, crashing head-on with another car down the quiet road where they lived; Ben or Daisy running out of the house into the road, their little faces caught in the glare of headlights from a car driving too fast to stop.

'I need to see you,' Martin said.

'What do you mean?'

'I'm at the house. Can you come over? The kids are in bed. I can't leave them alone.'

He sounded empty. As if someone had hollowed out the little bit of personality he had and there was nothing left.

'What's happened, Martin?'

But he'd already hung up. And the only person who could hear Dee speaking was herself.

Traffic was light and Dee made it across town in ten minutes. She pulled up outside Louise's house and ran to the front door. Martin must have heard her, because he'd already opened the door and was standing waiting for her. She'd been running, but she stopped when she saw his face.

'It's Louise.' His voice cracked and Dee put a hand over her mouth to stop the sob she could feel at the back of her throat. 'What's going on?'

'How would I know?' Dee asked. And then she realised. He hadn't called because Louise had been in an accident. He'd called because he knew about the affair.

'I can't stand it,' he said. 'The lies and the knowing, but not knowing. How stupid does she think I am? You can't hide something like that. Well, maybe other people can, but not Louise. She's a terrible liar. I thought it would pass. I told myself the worst thing I could do was to confront her without any proof. I know I haven't always been the best husband. It's not easy for her. I'm away so often and she gets lonely. It's why I've been home so much lately. I've cut my hours right back. I thought if I was around more the affair would stop. Only it hasn't made any difference. Now she's gone and I don't think she's coming back.'

Dee took a tentative step forward. Then another. Close enough now to smell the booze on his breath and see the fear in his eyes.

'Martin,' she said. 'Can we go inside? I'm freezing out here.'

He moved away from the door and wandered into the sitting room. Dee followed him, shutting the front door behind her and glancing upstairs. The landing light was on and both children's bedroom doors were open, lights off inside.

'They're asleep,' Martin said. 'I put them to bed about an hour ago and I've checked them a few times since. I'm not quite the rubbish father you think I am.'

'I don't think you're a rubbish dad,' Dee said.

She sat down on one of the sofas and suggested he might like to sit down too.

'Tell me what's happened.'

'It's simple enough. My wife is having an affair. I didn't want to believe it. I've done everything I could to tell myself it's not true. But then I saw her this morning. I was driving home after dropping the kids to school. I thought it was a mistake, that it was just someone who looked like her. But it wasn't.'

'Where was she?'

'On the seafront. She was getting into someone's car. I couldn't see the driver, not properly, but enough to see it was a man. When I realised what was going on, I turned the car around to follow them, but I was too late. They'd already gone.'

Nigel. Louise had arranged to meet him on the pier, but they must have changed their plans because of the bad weather. Although no amount of rain explained why Louise was still with Nigel. If that's where she was.

'She must meet all sorts of people for work,' she told Martin. 'How can you be sure it wasn't a work appointment?'

'Because I've spoken with the people she works with, and she didn't go in today. She called in sick. And now she's somewhere in the middle of the South Downs National Park with some other man, instead of at home with her husband and children.'

His voice rose as he spoke. Worried the children would wake, Dee stood up and closed the sitting room door.

'Sorry,' Martin said, in a more regular voice. 'Can't you just tell me, Dee? She's my wife, for Christ's sake. I need to know. Is this it? Is she leaving me? What did she think? That she could just run off and not come home and somehow that would be okay?'

'If I knew where she was,' Dee said, 'or who she was with, I swear on the children's lives that I would tell you, Martin. But I don't.'

She tried to work out where Louise and Nigel could be. And why Louise would have called in sick to spend the day with a man who'd tried to blackmail her.

'What sort of car was it?'

'White Merc. A-class, I think. Although I didn't get a proper look.'

A-class didn't mean a thing to Dee. She didn't know what sort of car Nigel Shaw drove, but she imagined it would be something expensive – like a Mercedes.

'I'm going to get her.' Martin stood up. 'Will you stay here and keep an eye on the children? You can stay the night if you want. The bed in the guest room is made up.'

Dee opened her mouth to speak but he shook his head.

'No. Don't try to talk me out of this. I've stood by and done nothing for too long. I'm going to find her and make her tell me what the hell she's playing at.'

'Hang on.' Dee took her phone out of her bag. 'Let me call her. Maybe she'll speak to me, even if she doesn't want to talk to you.'

She dialled Louise's number but got her voicemail. Dee left a message, asking Louise to call her back, and hung up.

'We need to call the police.'

'What are you talking about?' Martin said. 'She hasn't been gone long enough, they won't be interested.'

But Dee held a hand up, stopping him from saying anything else. She dialled the police emergency line and waited for her call to be answered. But instead of a real person, she got a recorded message, thanking her for calling and telling her she was in a queue and her call would be answered as quickly as possible.

She ended the call. They didn't have time to wait.

'Right,' she told Martin. 'Before we do anything, you're going to sit back down and tell me how the hell you know where Louise is if you haven't spoken to her?'

Thirty-seven

Ed walked into the bar of the Aldrington Hotel and looked around. He saw Kyle almost immediately, sitting on his own at a table near the window. He'd called Kyle several times this afternoon. An hour ago, when he'd almost given up hope, Kyle had called him back and asked if Ed was free to meet.

'Sorry I've been ignoring you,' Kyle said, when Ed sat down opposite him.

'How have you been doing?' Ed asked.

'About as bad as you'd expect. She was my life.' He looked miserable. His face was pale and he had deep, dark rings beneath both bloodshot eyes. 'I know everyone says she was too good for me and we'd never have lasted, but those people don't know shit. She loved me, and I loved her, and now she's gone. My parents don't care. They pretend they do, but really all they care about is trying to prove Nigel killed her. And I've gone along with that because I'm scared. I'm bloody terrified the police will think I killed her. But I didn't. I wouldn't ever have hurt her.'

'I know.' Ed put his hand on Kyle's arm.

'Nigel didn't do it, either,' Kyle said. 'I feel sick because I've told the police that I think he could have done it. But it's not true. He can be an idiot sometimes but he did love

294

her, you know. He didn't think I was good enough for her, and I hated him for that. But I can't carry on saying he could have killed her when he didn't.'

'If that's what you believe,' Ed said, 'then you need to be honest, Kyle. You need to tell Rachel what you really think.'

'I know.' Kyle nodded. 'I'm sick of all the lies and bullshit.'

'I'm glad you got in touch,' Ed said. 'You're not an easy man to track down, you know that?'

'Sorry.'

'Some of my colleagues are trying to find your parents. Do you have any idea where they are?'

'Not a clue. Why?'

'We're trying to find out what's happened to Joana Helinski. She used to clean your house, is that right?'

Kyle nodded, looking more miserable by the second.

'Mum asked me not to tell anyone. She said it was no one else's business. And she was right. Joana's done a bunk, that's all. Mum was rightly pissed off when she didn't turn up for work.' Kyle frowned. 'Is that why you've been trying to get hold of me?'

'I need your help with something.' Ed leaned forward. 'It's important. I wouldn't ask otherwise. I know Lauren found a letter when she was going through Annabelle's things.'

'And?'

'I think the letter was from my grandmother.'

'Nigel said it was a letter too,' Kyle asked. 'How come both of you know what she found, but she wouldn't tell me? When she first decided to write about Mary's murder, she spoke to me all the time about it. She was so determined. She thought this story could be her big break. Then she had that row with Nigel and everything changed after that. I knew it was to do with what she'd found in Annabelle's house, but whenever I asked her about it she just clammed up.'

The flicker of hope he'd had since Kyle got in touch fizzled and died.

'She didn't tell you what she found?'

'Sorry, Ed. I can't help you. Whatever Lauren found, she didn't want anyone else finding it. The police have already searched my house. It's not there. And it can't be at her parents' house because Nigel keeps hassling me about it. I get the impression he'd like to find it before the police do. But I can't help him, or you, because I don't know where it is. I'm starting to think she destroyed it.'

'Shit.' It was unbearable, knowing he'd got so close to finding the truth only to discover the letter was gone.

'Unless…'

'What?'

'There's one other place,' Kyle said. 'I can't be sure, but if you want I can let you have a look?'

'If I want?' Ed stood up. 'What are we waiting for? My car's outside. Where are we going?'

'You don't need your car.' Kyle stood up as well. 'Come with me.'

As he followed Kyle through the bar and across the ornate lobby of the five-star hotel, flashes of Ed's childhood ran through his mind. Memory after memory, all of them tinged with the guilt and sadness that had travelled down through his family ever since Mary Palmer's body had been found on a church altar sixty years ago.

'If she wanted to hide something,' Kyle said, ten minutes later. 'I think she might have chosen this place.'

They were on a mezzanine floor of the Aldrington. A narrow, dark space accessed by a set of stairs at the back of the building, hidden from the public areas.

'My mum makes Dad keep a close eye on me,' Kyle said. 'She's a total control freak. And because he's scared of her, he does what she tells him to. When Lauren and I started going out, this is where we'd come. It was the only place we could be by ourselves without him looking over our shoulders every few seconds. It looks a bit grim but it's not too bad really.'

Ed followed him along the corridor to a space at the end that had been set up as a sort of living area. There was a sofa and two mismatched armchairs, a coffee table and a small fridge that had clearly served as a minibar at some point.

'I was a teenager when I first discovered the mezzanine,' Kyle said. 'I think it was used for storage, years ago. But no one ever comes here now. I swear, it felt like the best secret ever. Even now, I love it. Sometimes, I think this is the only place I can really be myself.' He glanced at Ed. 'Sorry. I'm a bit emo at the moment. Can't stop sharing everything I'm feeling.'

'I have no idea what being emo means,' Ed said. 'But telling people how you're feeling sounds pretty healthy to me.'

'Lauren was always on at me to be more open about stuff like that. Normally, it's not something I find very easy to do. But recently... well, maybe she's, I don't know, maybe I'm finally being the person she wanted me to be.'

'I'm sure you were already that,' Ed said gently. 'She wouldn't have gone out with you otherwise.'

He looked around the room, trying to find something else to talk about.

'Where did all this furniture come from?'

'Some of it was already here,' Kyle said. 'Other bits, like the fridge, I brought myself. We're always replacing furniture in the rooms. When something is damaged or there's a stain you can't get off, it has to go. I've brought lots of stuff here over the years. Look at this.'

He opened the mini-fridge, and a glow of blue light escaped. Inside were two bottles of beer and two small cans of gin and tonic.

'Lauren didn't drink beer.' Kyle slammed the door shut, moved past Ed and switched on a floor lamp Ed hadn't noticed before. Light flooded the space and Ed saw that it was bigger than he'd first thought.

'We used to come here all the time,' Kyle said. 'Until Lauren said she didn't like it any more. She said it was dingy and why spend time here when we could hang out at mine? That's why I hadn't thought of it before.'

Ed's chest ached with pity. He could picture them here – Lauren and Kyle, holed up in their secret hideaway, full of youth and life and plans for the future. It was heartbreaking to see how brief that future had been for them.

'My mum was so strict back then,' Kyle said. 'But over the last year, she finally accepted that Lauren was my girlfriend and it was okay for us to share a room when she stayed over. She never really approved, though. She thinks girls should save themselves for marriage. It's bullshit, but what can you do? You can't make someone believe something else if they don't want to.'

'But you're... what? Twenty-three? Why haven't you moved out?'

Ed thought back to when he was Kyle's age. There was no way he'd have let anyone tell him how to live his life. Yet Kyle seemed oddly dependent on his parents. Ed knew if he'd been brought up in that claustrophobic family environment, he'd have been gone long ago.

'We were saving up to buy a place,' Kyle said. 'Lauren wanted us to rent in the meantime, but I was against it. I didn't see any point throwing money away on rent. We'd almost got enough. Next month we were going to start looking at apartments together.'

'I'm sorry.'

'Everyone's sorry,' Kyle said. 'It doesn't change anything though, does it? She's still dead.'

'I know. But from everything you've told me, Kyle, she was very lucky to have found you.'

'You think?'

The longing in the boy's eyes made Ed want to look away, but he forced himself not to.

'I really do.'

'Thanks. That means a lot. You've always been good to me, Ed. I used to love playing rugby. I know I was never any good, but you never made me feel rubbish.'

'You weren't rubbish,' Ed said.

Kyle grinned. 'I hope you don't tell lies like that to your girlfriend.'

'I'm too scared to lie to her,' Ed said.

'I like her, you know.'

'Yeah.' Ed smiled. 'Me too.'

'I suppose we'd better start looking,' Kyle said. 'You sure it's a letter we're looking for?'

'Pretty sure.' Ed looked around the room, but couldn't see any obvious hiding place. 'Any idea where it could be?'

Kyle shook his head. 'I guess we try everywhere.'

They spent an hour searching, without any luck. By the end of it, Ed was hot, covered in dust and despondent. He'd been foolish to believe it could have been this easy.

'I'm sorry.' Kyle slumped down on the sofa, looking as bad as Ed felt.

'At least we tried,' Ed said. 'What about the rest of the hotel? Could she have hidden it somewhere else?'

'I guess,' Kyle said. 'But the hotel is huge. There must be hundreds of places you could hide a letter where no one would ever find it.'

He said something else, but Ed had stopped listening. His mind was racing ahead, trying to work out how he could persuade Rachel to get a search warrant.

'Kyle, I need you to do something for me.'

But Kyle had got off the sofa and was crouching down on the uncarpeted floor, pulling up one of the plain, wooden floorboards that creaked each time Ed and Kyle walked on them.

'I used to hide my dope in here,' Kyle said. 'Sorry, probably shouldn't tell you that. I don't do that any more. Lauren didn't approve. Hang on.' He reached down into the space beneath. 'What's this?'

A moment later, he pulled his hand out and Ed saw he was holding something.

'It's not a letter,' Kyle said. 'But this definitely wasn't here when I used to store my dope in there.'

It was a leather-bound notepad, the leather faded and aged so it was impossible to know what colour it had once been.

'Looks like a diary.' Kyle held his hand out, but Ed couldn't move.

The air in the room seemed to thicken and he struggled to breathe. Another rush of memories, more vivid now. Her sharp humour, her inability to suffer fools, the bottle of gin under the kitchen sink that got her through the days. Her single-minded determination to prove that her only son wasn't a killer. And her diaries. The collection of leather-bound notebooks she kept in a box in the cupboard underneath the stairs. The box his grandfather had thrown out after she died.

'Ed? Are you okay?'

Ed leaned forward. He put his hand out. And he took the diary.

Thirty-eight

'Find my iPhone.' Martin's eyes slid away from Dee as he spoke. Not before she saw shame there.

'Find my what?'

'I set it up on her new iPad,' he said. 'When I first suspected she was seeing someone.'

'Hang on,' Dee said. 'The iPad you bought for her. It was a birthday present, right?'

Martin nodded.

'And you got it so you'd be able to spy on her?'

'No. I haven't used it before this evening. Not even this morning when I saw her getting into that car and driving away. Even then, I was going to wait and talk to her when she came home this evening. But she hasn't come home, so what was I meant to do? Just sit back and do nothing?'

'How does it work?'

'It's simple.' Martin took out his own phone and tapped something on the screen. 'This is a map of the area where she is right now. This blue dot here? That's her iPad. Charlton village, in West Sussex. And I'm going to get her. Right now.'

'You can't.' Dee grabbed the car keys off the table in the hall. 'You've been drinking. I smelled it on your breath when I arrived.'

'So what?' He lunged for the keys, but Dee was too fast for him. She held them out of his reach.

'We'll go together,' she said. 'I'll drive. But first we need to get someone to sit with the kids while we're gone. Let me call Ella.'

While they were waiting for Ella to arrive, Dee went into the garden – so Martin couldn't hear her – and called Ed.

'Where the hell are you?' she said when she got his voicemail, not bothering to hide the irritation in her voice. 'Call me as soon as you get this message. It's important.'

She hung up, annoyed. He was the one who'd pushed to meet up this evening. And now he'd disappeared without any proper explanation. Well sod you, Ed Mitchell, she thought.

She called Rachel, who, unlike Ed, answered right away.

'Dee? Is everything okay?'

'I'm not sure,' Dee said. 'Sorry to phone, but I can't get through to Ed. I wasn't sure what else to do.'

'You can call me any time,' Rachel said. 'You know that. What can I do for you?'

'Louise is missing,' Dee said.

'How long has she been gone?'

'Since this morning. Her husband doesn't know where she is, and neither do I. I know it's not long enough for you to treat this as a missing person case, but I'm worried.'

'I can understand that,' Rachel said. 'But there's probably nothing to worry about. She does a lot of evening work, doesn't she? Chances are she's got caught up in something and has forgotten to tell her husband.'

'I don't think so,' Dee said. 'Martin's tracked her location with Find my iPhone. She's in Charlton in West Sussex. It's a tiny village. She wouldn't be doing anything work-related there at this time.'

'If you know where she is then she's not missing, is she?'

'Nigel Shaw was trying to blackmail her. Louise went to meet him this morning to tell him she wasn't going to do what he wanted. No one has seen her since. She didn't go to work, and she hasn't come home.'

'Okay,' Rachel said. 'Can we step back a bit? What exactly did Nigel ask her to do?'

As quickly as she could, Dee gave Rachel a summary of what Louise had told her last night, concluding with Martin's account of seeing his wife getting into a white Mercedes.

'He couldn't see the driver,' Dee said. 'But he's pretty sure it was a man.'

'All right. I'll send someone around to Nigel's to have a word. There's not much else I can do for now, Dee.'

'You'll let me know how you get on?'

'Of course.'

As Dee hung up, a taxi pulled into the driveway and Ella climbed out.

'Sorry,' Dee said. 'I forgot you didn't drive. I'll pay you back for the taxi.'

'Don't be stupid.' Ella pulled Dee into her arms and hugged her tight. 'After all you do for me, I'm only too happy to be able to do something for you. Is everything okay?'

'I hope so,' Dee said.

But she couldn't shake the feeling that Louise was in trouble. Because she knew her cousin, and she knew that whatever turmoil was going on in her personal life, she'd never disappear without making sure Martin and her children knew where she was and that she was okay.

–

Something was wrong. Louise opened her eyes but couldn't see anything. She was blind. Or dead. She tried to sit up but her head smashed into something hard and she fell back down. Panic rose inside her. A huge wave of fear that she couldn't control. She started banging on the roof that was too close to her body. She screamed, her voice bouncing off the walls of this tiny, confined space. Flashes of colour, red and black and purple and then black again. Her body jerked and rolled and banged against the sides. Pain shot up her arms and shoulders. Her hands were trapped behind her back, but when she tried to move them something cut into her wrists.

And then she remembered.

She thrashed her body against the hard metal walls, screaming louder. She was inside the boot of a car. Her car. She could feel her iPad, pressed against the side of her face. She'd put it in the boot a lifetime ago. When she'd gone to meet Nigel on the pier.

The car was moving. Driving fast and screeching around corners, throwing her body against the hard edges of the boot. Her mind travelled back to earlier in the day, and she knew who had hit her and put her in the car.

She forced herself to breathe slowly, focusing on each breath – inhaling, exhaling, over and over. Not allowing her mind to travel anywhere else, concentrating on this one thing: the gradual rise and fall of her chest as she breathed in, slowly, and then released the breath, slowly.

It worked. To a point. The panic gradually subsided, but as her mind and body lowered their defences, she was unable to stop the sadness that rushed in to replace the panic. Tears rolled down her cheeks, sobs shook her body. She curled over on her side, keeping her mouth shut to muffle the sound because she would not let that bastard hear her crying. The first wave passed, and she forced down any further sobs. There would be time for crying later, when she got herself out of here. Because she was going to get out.

And after she did that, she was going to make Derek French pay. He had already killed Lauren. Louise didn't know why he'd done it, but she knew – absolutely – that he had. How could she have been attracted to a killer? She pushed the thought away. He thought he'd got away with it. He almost had. If it hadn't been for one, stupid throwaway comment this afternoon in Brighton. But now Louise knew. He knew she knew. And he was going to try to kill her. But she wouldn't let him. One way or another, Louise was going to find a way out of this.

She was going to survive.

From the diary of Emma Reed

12 October 1978

David died early this morning. His housekeeper, a large Jamaican woman called Claudette, told me she'd phoned my house first thing but I'd already left for London by then. I could barely take it in. It seemed impossible to have got this close to the truth, and then for it to be taken from me at the very last moment. At least, that's what I thought. Until Claudette handed me the letter he'd left for me. She didn't know what was in it, she said, but he'd made her promise she would give it to me.

It's a relief to finally know the truth. But the anger and the need to take action are making it impossible for me to focus on anything. I went directly to the police station when I arrived back at Eastbourne but no one was available to see me. I informed the officer on reception that I wanted to report a murder. He seemed interested until I told him the murder had happened eighteen years earlier and if the police had done their job first time around, the murderer would have been caught a long time ago. He took my name and phone number and made an appointment for me to come into the station the day after tomorrow to give a statement.

But I can't wait until then. I want to look her in the eye and tell her that I know everything. I want her to know the damage she has done to my family. She is an evil, despicable woman and I want her punished.

If James was here, he'd tell me not to do anything foolish. But there's three more days before the golf trip finishes. I tried calling the hotel earlier but the person who answered the phone wasn't able to track him down. At least without him, there is no need to hide the bottle I bought on my way back from London. He thinks I have a 'problem'. He's right, but the problem isn't gin. The problem is Annabelle Palmer and Richard Partridge.

Perhaps I've drunk too much tonight, but who wouldn't in my situation? I'd hoped it would calm me, but it's having the opposite effect. It's sharpening my resolve, giving me the strength and clarity I need. I've waited too long and I won't wait a minute longer. I'm going to walk across to her big, fancy house and ring the doorbell until she answers. And when she's standing in front of me, I'll her that I know what she did. I want to watch her crumble before me, broken and sobbing as she realises she's lost. I will destroy her. Just as she destroyed my family.

To whom it may concern,

This is a true statement of the events surrounding the murder of Mary Elisabeth Palmer in East-bourne in 1960. Mary's body was found in the church of St Mary the Virgin in Old Town on Saturday 5 March 1960. It was widely assumed that her killer was a local man called Graham Reed, but Graham never harmed her. The people who killed Mary were my brother, Richard, and Mary's aunt, Annabelle Shaw (née Palmer).

Richard and Annabelle met at a garden party hosted by Annabelle and her brother, George. Despite the difference in their ages, they soon became close friends. They were similar in their characters and this is what formed the basis of their unusual friendship. Like my brother, Annabelle is sharp-witted, greedy and used to getting her own way.

Unlike Annabelle, our family were not wealthy. My father was a drinker who could never hold down a job. He was also a violent man who used to beat his wife and children. He liked to tell his sons that we would never amount to anything. In our different ways, Richard and I were both determined to prove him wrong.

Richard, in particular, had an insatiable desire for status and wealth. His new friend Annabelle was the same. They both felt angry at the hand life had dealt them. In Annabelle's case, she was jealous of her niece. George was a hugely successful businessman, as well as a devoted father. He provided well for his only sibling, but he'd always made it clear that Mary would inherit his fortune one day. This wasn't good enough for Annabelle. When George was diagnosed with heart disease, Annabelle must have known she was almost out of time.

I don't know who first came up with the idea. All I know is that they both saw it as the solution to their problems. With Mary out of the way, Annabelle would inherit everything. All she needed was someone willing to do her dirty work. In return, she would make sure that person was well-rewarded for this one, abominable act. I say 'this person', but of course I mean Richard.

There were so many ways they could have done it, but they chose something dramatic and spectacular. Something no one who'd ever met Mary would forget in a hurry. They wanted to make it look like crime of passion, and they succeeded.

I didn't know what they were planning. Richard and I normally went out together on Friday nights, but that night he told me he already had plans. I was relieved, truth be told. I'd started to find his company difficult. He was becoming like my father, embittered and using alcohol as a means of drowning whatever darkness lay inside him.

We shared a bedroom, so I always knew when he came home after a night out. I woke with a start just after five in the morning and his bed was empty. I knew the time because there was enough light in the room for me to see the hands on my watch.

I was wide awake, and worried. Richard never stayed out this late. He had girls, plenty of girls, but he didn't spend the night with any of them. Once they'd given him what he wanted he didn't care for them, or want to be anywhere near them.

I got dressed and went outside. Part of me just wanted to walk in the early morning light and watch the sun rising over the town. Another part of me hoped I'd find him and he'd tell me all about the night he'd had and we'd walk home together, the way we'd done so many nights before.

I hadn't known, until that morning, that his relationship with Annabelle was more than just friendship. They were huddled together on one of the benches in Manor Gardens. I almost walked past them, but I recognised my brother. I smiled to myself, thinking I'd been right. He'd picked up some girl and was, no doubt, in the process of trying to extricate himself.

'Hey!'

At the sound of my voice, he looked up, and it was only then that I got a proper look at his companion. I didn't know what to think. I knew the sort of girls Richard went for, and Annabelle was nothing like that. She was from a respectable family, and whatever people say about the Swinging Sixties, girls from respectable families didn't stay out until five o'clock in the morning with men like my brother.

I walked away, feeling oddly embarrassed by what I'd witnessed. I didn't want to talk to him about it, but he gave me no choice. He came running after me and told me it was nothing. He said they were friends who sometimes had sex and where was the harm in that? I knew there was more to it. He's my brother and I can always tell when he's lying.

I didn't challenge him, though. I didn't care enough. By then, I'd already grown bored of listening to the lies he told and the made-up stories he recounted as if they were facts. I'd long ago learned it was easier to go along with it all and pretend I believed him.

His shirt was streaked with rust-coloured stains that I recognised as blood. When I asked him about this, he said he'd been in a fight. I believed that, all right. Richard liked to fight when he'd had a

*few drinks. I remember feeling sorry for Annabelle,
having to embrace a man who stank of another
man's blood.*

*I didn't give it another thought, and probably
would have forgotten about it altogether. But then
the news started trickling through. My first reaction, like everyone else's, was shock. Mary Palmer,
beautiful Mary, had been killed. That was all the
information we had in those first few hours. But
then our mother came home from the shops and
told us, with breathless excitement, that Mary's
body had been found on the altar of St Mary the
Virgin. The vicar had discovered her when he'd
gone into the church that morning.*

*I knew immediately. The convergence of too
many things at the same time was more than coincidence. The blood on Richard's shirt. His unlikely
dalliance with Annabelle. Their presence in the
park, directly across the road from the church where
Mary's body was discovered.*

*Richard tried to deny it, but not for long. In
fact, once he started telling me what they'd done
and how they'd planned it and why, he couldn't
stop speaking. He was eager to share his good news
and he promised me, if I kept my mouth shut, they
would make it worth my while.*

*God forgive me, but I let my greed get in the
way of doing what was right. I promised to keep
quiet in return for the money that Annabelle was
only too happy to give me. I used the money to
pay for my university education, something I would
never otherwise have been able to afford. If I'd been*

less hasty, if I'd waited just a few more years, I'd never have had to make such a choice. But by the time university grants became available, I'd already taken the money and there was no turning back.

I've tried to make up for it in the years since. But the truth is, there's no way to do that. I know now how impossible it is to live a life that's rich and meaningful when you carry a dark secret around with you. Ever since my illness was diagnosed, I've wondered if this is my punishment for not doing what was right and proper. For putting my own greed before that of a grieving father and an innocent young man.

It was Annabelle's idea to start the rumours about Graham. And it was Richard who stirred up a group of drunks in the Prince Albert that night and helped them chase Graham through the streets of Old Town on 11 April 1960 and beat him to his death.

I am ashamed and sorry for my part in these terrible events, and my subsequent silence. I know my apology is too little, too late, but it's all I have left.

I will leave this statement with Mrs Emma Reed and she can do whatever she feels is right. More than anyone, she deserves to know the truth.

David Partridge, 11 October 1978

Thirty-nine

Graham was innocent. And now, after all this time, Ed was able to prove it. There were things he needed to do, so many things. But he couldn't do anything until he'd processed what this meant. He was at home, on the sofa in his sitting room. The letter in one hand, a glass of whisky in the other. Each time he finished what was in the glass, he topped it up from the bottle on the table beside him. But the whisky wasn't doing its job. It wasn't helping him manage the rush of emotions coursing through his body – relief, regret, anguish, joy. And anger. A rage that was threatening to overwhelm him if he couldn't find a way to keep it in check. Because he knew there was only one reason why Annabelle Palmer would have had his grandmother's diary.

He'd found the letter tucked into the back of the diary. The diary entries covered the last year of her life. He'd read all of them. There were references to the other diaries – things she'd written earlier, events and encounters she'd chronicled. But those earlier diaries were long gone. If his grandfather had bothered to read them – which Ed doubted – the diaries would have merely confirmed his grandmother's deteriorating state of mind as her obsession with clearing her son's name increased over the years.

Helping to explain why, eventually, the stress became too much and she took her own life.

Except that's not what happened.

Ed drained the rest of the whisky and refilled the glass. The whisky burned his throat and warmed his stomach, fuelling the red–hot rage.

Emma had done exactly what she'd written in her diary. She'd gone across to Annabelle's house that night, and told her about David's letter. So Annabelle killed her, and made her death look like suicide. Adding further pain to a family that had already endured so much.

Ed didn't know how she'd done it. Maybe he would never learn the exact details of what happened. But he had enough evidence to cast doubt over the suicide verdict. More importantly, he had cast iron proof that Graham was innocent. Finally, he was able to finish what Emma had started and make sure the world knew the truth.

He drank more whisky, holding the glass so tight his hand hurt. When he realised what he was doing, he put the glass down beside the bottle. He needed to calm down. He closed his eyes, breathing slowly and counting his breaths the way he'd been taught on some stress management course he'd been forced to attend a few years ago. But the breathing and the counting didn't work.

Little granny's boy has lost his granny.

'Bastard.'

Nigel knew. Maybe not back then, but he knew now. It explained the row he'd had with Lauren. He knew, and he'd decided that protecting his family's reputation was more important than the truth coming out. Even after his own daughter's murder.

And suddenly it hit him. The reason why she'd been killed.

He fumbled around on the sofa until he found his phone. The screen was blurred and when he tried to navigate the menu, his thumb kept hitting the wrong icons. But eventually he got the number he needed and called it.

'Rachel, it's me.' He could hear his voice slurring. He tried to speak slowly but it didn't seem to make any difference. 'I need to tell you something.'

'It'll have to wait,' she said. 'I'm up to my eyes at the moment. Can we speak tomorrow?'

'Tomorrow's too late. I know who killed Lauren. I have proof.'

He was vaguely aware the letter wasn't proof exactly, but it was a bloody good lead.

Rachel said something, but he missed it. He asked her to repeat it.

'I asked you if you'd been drinking,' she said.

'Not really. Maybe a drop, but I'm fine. Swear to God, Rach. This is important. Nigel did it. He killed her because she was going to tell people what happened. I'm coming over to the station now. You need to see what I've found.'

'Don't you dare,' she said. 'You're pissed, Ed. You're slurring your words and I can barely understand what you're saying. Do yourself a favour, go to bed and sleep it off. We'll speak in the morning.'

She hung up before he could say anything else.

'Pissed,' he muttered, pushing himself off the sofa. The room swayed, and he swayed with it. The whisky roiled, rising up his throat in a sudden gush. He put his hand over his mouth and ran towards the downstairs loo. But he wasn't fast enough. Vomit sprayed through his fingers.

He bent over, heaving, as the whisky-fumed puke splashed onto the stripped wooden floorboards. He puked until there was nothing left. When it was finally over, his body was shaking and his cheeks were wet with sweat and tears.

In the background he could hear his phone ringing, but he didn't have the strength to go and answer it. He collapsed onto the floor, landing in the puddle of vomit. He rolled over onto his back, staring up at the ornate cornice moulding that ran along the edge of the ceiling. He felt his eyes starting to close. He tried hard to keep them open but the weight of exhaustion forced them shut. The moulding disappeared and, soon, everything else did too.

Forty

Time had lost all meaning. She could have been in here days, weeks or months. Her shoulders and neck screamed with pain. She couldn't feel her hands any longer. The tight plastic had cut into her wrists until they bled. At some point she'd wet herself, and the boot stank of urine. Her wet trousers had hardened as they dried. She was cold. So cold. Shivering uncontrollably. Her teeth chattering, her jaw aching.

She'd managed to shift the iPad, trying to move it closer to her hands. Convinced if she could just touch it with her fingers, she'd be able to send an email. But that had proved impossible. When she'd eventually managed to get it into a position where her hands could touch it, she hadn't even been able to find the power button. It didn't stop her trying, though. Even when she realised her movement was causing the plastic cable ties to tighten, she kept going. Until her wrists were rubbed raw and her hands were sticky with blood. It was only when the car swerved around a tight corner and the iPad slid away from her that she realised it was hopeless.

She couldn't tell if her eyes were open or closed. The dark was intense and all-consuming. Her mind kept drifting to Martin and the children. The idea that she might never see them again was unbearable. Each time her mind travelled to that possibility, she dragged it back. She couldn't think like that. She was going to get out of here, somehow.

She tried to picture what would happen when he stopped the car. What would he do? She wondered if he had a weapon – something heavy, like a hammer or a shovel. She hated him. He'd killed Lauren. He was a killer. She repeated it over and over, making herself believe it.

She'd known his reputation before anything happened between them. A ladies' man. A wandering eye. Can't keep it inside his trousers. She'd heard all the things people had said about him. When they first got together, it was part of the attraction. Because she'd never been looking for someone to save her. She didn't need saving. She hadn't wanted some easy excuse to end her marriage. She loved Martin. Loved the life they'd built together, loved her home and her kids and her job. All of it. Except...

Martin was away so much. And when he wasn't away, he was still barely present. Louise knew he hadn't always been like that, but when she cast her mind back over their years together, she couldn't pinpoint the exact moment he'd changed. All she knew, with increasing certainty as each month passed, was that something had gone wrong between them, and she didn't know how to fix it. Derek had been the perfect way of taking her mind off everything that was wrong with her marriage. But all the time, she'd been having sex with a murderer. The thought chilled her even more than the frigid air.

Suddenly, the car slowed and then stopped. Her ears hummed in the silence that came as the engine was switched off. She'd longed for this moment, but now that it had finally happened, she was terrified. She held her breath, her ears straining to hear any sound through the silence. Nothing at first. And then the low rumble of a man's voice. She thought, at first, he was speaking to her. Then she realised. There was someone else with him.

The car creaked as doors opened and they got out. The doors slammed shut, followed by the heavy crunch of footsteps. She cowered back into the furthest corner of the boot, but there was nowhere to hide. The bright glare of a torch, too bright after the darkness, blinding her.

'No, no, no, no.' She pressed her body tighter against the back of the boot. A dark shadow appeared behind the light. Darker and wider and more terrifying than she'd imagined. She started screaming, her legs kicking out, but there was nothing she could do as his hand reached in, grabbed her arm and dragged her up and out.

She fell hard onto the stony ground. More pain shot through her shoulder and elbow. But she didn't care about the pain. All she cared about was getting away. She tried to stand, but with her hands still tied behind her back, she couldn't do it.

The bright light was shining down on her. She could just make out his shape, behind the light. Only one person. She looked around, but couldn't see anyone else. The torch went out and she was plunged once again into darkness.

He grabbed her arms and pulled her off the ground. He held on to her, his body pressed into her back.

'I'm sorry,' he whispered, his breath warm against the side of her face.

'Bastard.'

She let her head drop forward and then, dredging up every last bit of strength, she threw it back as fast and hard as she could.

He screamed and staggered back, letting her go. She ran, stumbling into the darkness, not caring where she went. The only thing that mattered was staying alive. And that meant getting as far away as possible, as quickly as she could. Before he killed her just like he'd killed Lauren.

She ran towards the trees. No time to look around and think about where else she could go. Dark shapes of trees crowded into her, rough ground beneath her feet. Stones and the thick roots of ancient woodland that she tripped and stumbled over as she ran. Branches cut across her face. She could hear him behind her, getting closer. She tried to focus, but her mind was skittering and slipping, and all she could do was keep running. Up ahead, a shade of pale grey, moonlight trickling along a narrow path. She swerved left, onto the path, narrowly avoiding a tree trunk that had fallen across the path. She jumped over it and kept running.

And suddenly something changed. There were no footsteps following her. She stopped running, held her breath so she could hear properly. Listening out for the crunch of feet on dead branches and the crashing sound as he pushed through the overgrown woodland. But there was nothing.

She lifted her head, looking at the grey sky through the pattern of leaves and branches. Her breath was coming in short, sharp bursts that were too loud in the silence of the dark night. She looked around, trying to work out which way she could go. But the choice was limited to carrying on down this narrow path and hoping it led to a way out, or going back the way she'd come. She gave herself a moment for her breathing to slow down and her legs to stop shaking. And then she ran forward, deeper into the heart of the forest.

She knew she had to keep quiet, but she couldn't manage it. Each time a branch whipped across her face unexpectedly, each time she stumbled over the twisted root of a tree, she cried out. But she ran on regardless, knowing the only thing that mattered was getting out of here.

Her foot caught in something and she fell before she could stop herself. With her hands tied behind her back, she had no way of protecting herself as she flew forward and landed face first on the wet, rocky ground. She must have twisted her head sideways at the last minute, because it was the right side of her face that got the worst of it. A blinding pain across her cheekbone, a burst of liquid in her mouth that she knew was blood. She lay, winded, knowing she had to get up but not knowing how she would manage it.

And then, out of nowhere, the shuffle of feet through the dead foliage, the noise too loud and too close. No. No, no, no. She tried to scrabble forward but her body wouldn't do what it was meant to. Hands on her shoulders, pulling her, dragging her, rolling her over until she was lying on her back.

Too many things happening for her mind to process. The blood streaming down her face. The agonising pain in her left ankle. The plastic cable ties cutting into her wrists. The shadow of the person standing over her.

As her eyes adjusted to the dark, the shadow became clearer. She blinked, but it didn't make any difference.

When she looked again, her eyes saw the same thing. Except it didn't make any sense. Because the person who'd chased her through the woods and was standing over her now: it wasn't Derek.

Forty-one

As they drove to Charlton, Dee told Martin about Louise's encounter with Nigel the previous day.

'She'd planned to meet him this morning. She was going to tell him she couldn't help him.'

'And you think that's who she was with when I saw her?'

'It seems likely,' Dee said. 'She'd arranged to meet him on the pier, but if it was raining maybe they changed their plans.'

'Shit.' Martin banged his fist against the dashboard. 'Shit, shit, shit.'

'Try to stay calm,' Dee said. 'Losing it now isn't going to help anyone.'

'You don't understand.' Martin was practically shouting. Dee reached across and put her hand on his arm, but he shook it off.

'It's him,' Martin said. 'Nigel's taken her.'

'We don't know that,' Dee said sharply.

'Yes we do!' Martin held up his phone. 'She's in Charlton, right? Nigel has a house there. Used to belong to his father and now the family use it as a second home. He bored me senseless one evening at the golf club telling me all about it. Drive faster. We need to get there as quickly as possible. And we need to call the police. Now.'

'I've already done that.'

Dee told him about her earlier conversation with Rachel.

'That was over an hour ago,' Martin said. 'Can you call her back and see if she's spoken to him? And tell her about the house. If she knows about the house, she might take this a bit more seriously.'

'You do it,' Dee said. 'Use my phone if you want. It's in my bag. You'll find Rachel's number in my call list.'

She gave Martin the code for her phone and listened as he called Rachel and spoke to her. She couldn't hear Rachel's side of the conversation, but heard enough to know the police had already learned about the house in Charlton.

'Hang on,' Nigel said. 'She's driving. I'll put you on speakerphone.'

'Driving where?' Rachel asked, her voice tinny through the phone speaker.

'Where do you think?' Dee said. 'She's his wife, Rachel. He can't sit at home doing nothing.'

'You need to stay away,' Rachel said.

'Why?'

'Because I've spoken with Nigel's wife and she doesn't know where he is. But she thinks he might be at Charlton because that's where he likes to go when he wants to be by himself.'

'Except he's not by himself,' Dee said. 'Louise is with him.'

'I've spoken to my colleagues at Chichester,' Rachel said. 'They're sending someone to check out the house. As soon as they've done that, I'll call you back and let you know what's going on. In the meantime Dee, I need you to stay away. Okay?'

'Okay.'

Dee motioned at Martin to end the call.

'You're not serious?' he said.

'Of course not.' Dee smacked his arm. 'What do you think I am?'

'Who is he?'

She'd been waiting for the question ever since getting in the car.

'She told me it wasn't anyone I knew.'

'But you didn't believe her.'

'No,' Dee said. 'I didn't. Look. We're almost at Charlton. Maybe you should wait and ask her yourself.'

'Or maybe you could tell me who you think it is, and that way I can at least prepare myself.'

'Derek French.'

'You cannot be serious,' Martin said after a moment.

'It's just a hunch. I don't know for sure.'

'You really think she'd have an affair with someone that fucking plastic?'

Dee smiled. Plastic was the perfect word to describe Derek. The sort of shiny, slightly slippery cheap plastic that would be illegal in a few years because it was so bad for the environment.

'What am I going to do?' Martin said.

'You're going to find her,' Dee said. 'And worry about everything else after you've done that.'

Following his directions, Dee turned left down a narrow road that was more of a track than a proper road. The track ended abruptly in a dead end. When Dee parked the car, the lights switched off and the world outside was plunged into darkness. It felt as if they'd arrived in the middle of nowhere.

'There's nothing,' Martin said. 'We've come to the wrong place. Shit. Where is she if she's not here?'

'It's too dark to tell what's here,' Dee said. 'Come on, let's get out of the car and see what we can find. Quietly. We don't want to anyone to know we're here.'

The cold air hit her as she got out, shutting the door gently and waiting for Martin to do the same.

'What now?' he whispered.

Gradually, Dee was able to make out shapes in the darkness as her eyes adjusted. She took a step forward, her hands out in front of her, then another step. Touched something cold and hard. Metal. She felt the shape with her fingers, identified it as a gate. Feeling her way along the structure, she found the handle, pushed down on it and the gate opened. Creaking loudly.

'What was that?'

Martin was beside her, breathing too loudly in the silence of the night.

'Come on,' Dee whispered.

She took his arm and, still holding the gate so it couldn't move, shoved Martin through the gap before following him. She could see that the gate led onto a path that, in turn, led to a single-storey structure of some sort.

They stood for a moment, side by side on the narrow path, waiting to see if anyone had heard the gate creaking. After what felt like an hour but was probably closer to five minutes, Dee took her phone out of her pocket and switched on the torch. Now, she could see they were standing in the garden of a squat stone cottage with a thatched roof and a red front door. They crept closer, walking around the cottage, peering through the windows, trying to see inside. But there was nothing to see. The house was in complete darkness and there was no sign anyone was in there.

'Look.' Martin grabbed Dee's arm.

The garden backed onto some woods. A line of trees, long branches swaying in the breeze. And parked in front of the trees, Louise's red SUV. A series of images played through Dee's mind, none of them good.

'Let's try in there,' she said, pointing at the trees. 'I think we should split up. It's our best chance of finding her. You've got a torch on your phone? Good. Turn that on and switch your phone to silent.'

When he'd done this, Dee dialled his number and waited for him to answer.

'Put me on speakerphone,' she said. 'I'll do the same. This way, we'll know if either of us gets into trouble.'

'No,' Martin said. 'I can't let you go by yourself. It's too dangerous.'

'It's no more dangerous for me than it is for you.'

'Ed would kill me if I didn't stay with you.'

'No he wouldn't.' Dee was pretty sure Ed actually would want to kill Martin if he found out, but she wouldn't tell if Martin didn't. 'All Ed would care about is finding Louise as quickly as possible.'

'I am not letting you go into those woods by yourself.'

'You don't have a choice. I'm going this way. You follow that path on the left.'

She walked away before he could protest. She couldn't stop him following her if he absolutely insisted, but she hoped he'd be sensible enough to realise that wasn't the most effective way of finding his wife.

'Dee?' Martin's voice, whispering out of the phone she was using to navigate her way through the thick, overgrown path.

'What is it?' she asked. 'Have you found something?'

'I wanted to make sure you're okay.'

'I'm fine,' Dee said. 'Now shush and let me focus on not tripping over anything.'

She would never have admitted it, but the further she went into the woods, the more grateful she was for Martin's presence on the other end of the phone.

'What if we don't find her?' Martin said, after a few minutes.

'We will.'

Any other scenario wasn't worth thinking about. Louise was her cousin and oldest friend. Their lives were inextricably bound up in each other's.

Branches hung across the path and she had to push them out of her way as she walked deeper into the forest. She'd expected silence, but the forest seemed alive. At first, the constant noise kept making her jump. Animals squealing, creatures shuffling in the undergrowth, the creak of trees and branches swaying in the wind. But after a while, she became used to it and thought that, if all the noises suddenly stopped, it wouldn't feel right somehow.

When she reached a fork in the path, she used her torch to peer down both alternatives, trying to work out the best way to go. The path on her right was narrow and looked less used, while the one on her left was wider and less overgrown. Dee chose the right path. If Nigel had taken Louise out here to harm her, he was going to do that somewhere no one would find them.

But getting through the path wasn't easy. Despite the cold, Dee was soon sweating from the effort of pushing heavy branches out of her way. After fifteen minutes, and with no sign of the path becoming more accessible, she started to wonder if she'd made a mistake.

'How are you getting on?' she asked Martin.

And right then, before he could answer, someone screamed.

'Martin!'

But Martin didn't answer. Using the torch to guide her through the brambles and leaves and branches and all the living, breathing parts of the forest, Dee ran faster than she'd ever run before.

Forty-two

'Karen?' Louise's head was swimming and she couldn't think straight.

'What?' Karen said. 'You think Derek would have been capable of all this?'

'All what?'

'You know what.' Karen leaned down, pushed her face close to Louise's, 'You thought you were being so clever. Pretty little Louise with your skinny body and your blond hair. You think I didn't know? I know everything, you stupid little bitch.'

She grabbed Louise's arm, fingers digging into the soft flesh of her upper arm as she made her stand up.

'This way.'

Still holding Louise's arm, Karen shoved her forward, pushing her through the woods to some unknown destination. She was strong. With her hands tied behind her back, Louise didn't stand a chance against her.

'I could turn a blind eye when it was just sex. I didn't approve, of course. But men are weak creatures and women like you don't make it easy for them. Flaunting yourselves like prostitutes, opening your legs for any man that gives you a bit of attention. It's up to us to keep control. But instead of doing what's right, you go around telling yourselves you can have everything a man can have

– a family and a career and sex whenever you want it with whoever you want it, regardless of who gets hurt. When I think of you with him, letting him do whatever he wants to you, even though you're married to another man… it's disgusting.

'And sleeping with my husband wasn't enough, was it? You wanted to destroy everything else too.'

'No.'

'Don't lie to me!'

Karen shook her, hard.

'He told me. You'd worked it out and you were going to tell everyone. Because you can't keep your legs shut and you can't keep your mouth shut, either. Even though it's none of your business.'

She was practically screaming by now, her voice loud and angry.

Louise forced herself to breathe, trying to manage her rising panic. Because it was clear to her that Karen was deranged. And dangerous. She scanned the gaps in the trees, searching for Derek, wondering what his role was in all of this. She knew he was here because she'd heard two voices earlier.

'Why did he do it?' Louise said. 'Why kill Kyle's girl-friend?'

'She didn't give us any choice.'

'What do you mean?'

The longer she kept Karen talking, the more chance she had of staying alive and finding a way to escape.

'She was like you,' Karen said. 'An interfering little bitch who couldn't keep her nose out of other people's business.'

They had come to a clearing. Louise could make out some sort of building – a cottage, maybe – the other side of a low stone wall.

'I don't understand.'

'It was an accident.' Karen pulled Louise towards the stone wall and through an open gate into what looked like a garden. 'And nobody would have cared, because she wasn't anybody important. But then your stupid cousin started asking questions and Lauren got involved and we had no choice. We had to control it. She knew, you see. Sneaky little Lauren worked it out.'

'Worked what out?'

Louise was stalling for time, but Karen didn't seem to notice. Too busy boasting about what they'd done and how clever they'd been.

'That foreign tart. It was all her fault. She was drunk and she fell. Hit her head on the corner of the fireplace. Marble fireplaces in all the rooms. Did you know that? That was all it took. One bang to the head and she was dead.'

'Lauren?'

Karen laughed.

'Not Lauren. Joana. Derek panicked so, of course, I had to sort the whole mess out. It was quite a task, I can tell you. Do you know how hard it is to remove a body from a hotel without being seen? But we managed it.'

'Where is he?' Louise said, when she was able to speak.

'You broke his nose, you vicious cow. He's gone to try to clean himself up because of the damage you caused and all the blood. Leaving me to clear up his mess, like he always does.'

'Why do you stay with him?'

'He's my husband,' Karen said. 'I made a vow to love, honour and obey him. Unlike you, I take my wedding vows seriously. If more women did the same the world would be a far better place than it is today.'

Karen pushed her forward, too hard. Louise stumbled, lost her balance and fell. She landed hard on her shoulder, crying out with pain as she rolled onto her back.

It was a clear night. Thousands of tiny white stars sprinkled across the black sky. She swung her head left, then right, looking for a way to escape. But all she could see was Karen, towering over her. Something in her hand, a stick or a rifle. Louise couldn't tell.

'Tell me,' Louise said. 'You're going to kill me, anyway. Where did you put Joana's body?'

As slowly as she could, Louise slid her foot along the ground, closer to Karen's legs.

'Here. My idea, of course. Derek was useless. Kept crying, if you can believe that. What sort of man cries like a baby when things go a bit wrong?

'This house belongs to Nigel's family. They brought us here last year. Showing off their second home. Nigel lording it over us, boasting about the history of the building, and how much land his family own and blah, blah, blah. I didn't take in most of what he told me. But I remembered what he said about the well. Eight hundred feet deep. A body could stay down there a long time without anyone ever finding it. There's a heavy stone slab covering it so no one can fall down by accident. But they keep this to lever off the slab if they need to.' She lifted her arm and now Louise could see she was holding a thick metal bar, flattened at one end.

Louise's mouth was so dry it was difficult to speak, but she had to understand everything.

'And Lauren?'

'Lauren got what she deserved. When she heard Dee was trying to find Joana, Lauren decided to contact her. She told Derek all about it one evening. Bragging to him about how she was going to help solve the mystery of the missing girl. They were alone in the house. I was at church and Kyle hadn't come home from work. I think Derek was enjoying having her to himself. Until she told him she'd seen Joana at the hotel that night.

'Luckily, he had the sense to act quickly. He managed to push her into the basement and lock her in. There's no mobile signal down there, so she wasn't able to call anyone. After that, it was easy enough. There were two of us and only one of her.

'Of course, we couldn't just dump her body and pretend she'd disappeared. That was fine for Joana, but Lauren's from a powerful family. We had to do something different. The church was my idea. I arrange the flowers there, which means I have my own key. We thought that making her killing look like a copycat murder, it would distract the police. And it worked like a dream.'

'She was your son's girlfriend,' Louise said. 'How could you do that to him?'

'He's better off without her. He was such a good boy until she came along, offering herself up to him on a plate. You want to know the truth? I'm glad she's dead. I hated her being in my house. Hated what she'd turned him into. I used to lie in bed listening to them. Having sex.'

She spat out the final word like it had a bad taste.

'Groaning and moaning like a pair of animals. She turned my son into a disgusting pig who went around doing those things with her and making those noises when he should have been saving himself for his wedding night.'

'You won't get away with it.' Louise was so angry she could barely breathe. The arrogance of this woman. The absolute lack of remorse. She was a psychopath. A dangerous psychopath. 'My husband and family won't believe I've just run off and left them.'

'Derek's brother is willing to admit he's been having an affair with you,' Karen said. 'It's not ideal – he's not the most reliable of people – but he'll do it for the money. When your husband finds out you've been seeing someone else, he won't try too hard to find you.'

Vomit rose up Louise's throat and she had to turn her head to spit the sick onto the ground. She was repulsed. At Karen and Derek, but also at herself. She'd had sex with that animal. She'd betrayed her husband and her family with him. She was beyond forgiveness. She deserved everything that was coming to her.

Except when Karen moved closer and lifted the iron bar, instinct kicked in. Louise's right foot lashed out and caught itself around Karen's ankle and she pulled as hard as she could. Karen's large shape wobbled precariously. For a moment, Louise thought she hadn't done enough. Then the wobbling got worse and suddenly Karen was tumbling forward and Louise had to roll sideways to avoid Karen landing on top of her.

On the ground beside her, Karen grunted once. Then, too fast, she was already starting to get up. But she didn't have the iron bar. It had fallen from her hand and now

Louise rolled over again so she was lying on top of it, the metal pressing into her stomach and ribs.

A hand grabbed her hair, Karen's screams in her ear, deafening. Karen's weight on top of her, too heavy. Louise couldn't breathe. Mud in her mouth and down her throat. Punches battering the side of her face, her back, her kidneys. And there was nothing she could do to get away from it.

–

Dee ran. Tripping and stumbling over branches and the roots of trees, until she was out of the forest. She looked around, trying to get her bearings. She could see the house, and the driveway leading up to it. But Louise's car was gone. Panicked, she thought she was too late. But then she heard more screams, coming from the other side of the stone wall. She ran through the open gate. They were on the ground. Fighting. One person was on top, punching and hitting whoever was beneath them. Someone cried out. Dee recognised her cousin's voice and realised Louise was the person being hit.

She threw herself forward, pushing him off Louise. He fell sideways and Dee fell with him, landing beside him on the ground. As he rolled away, she saw his face. It wasn't Derek. The realisation wasn't quick enough. Karen was already up and moving away from her. Dee pushed herself off the ground just as Karen swung back around to face her. She had picked something up off the ground and was running towards Dee, her arm raised above her head.

Dee tried to duck out of the way, but Karen was too fast. Something solid smashed into the side of her head. Flashes of white light exploded before her, pain obliterating everything else as she fell into the darkness.

Epilogue

Ed listened to Dee's voice, asking him to leave his name and number. He hung up without speaking. He'd already left messages. Twice, he'd driven out to her house. Both times, her hire car had been parked outside, but when he'd rung the doorbell – repeatedly – she hadn't come to the door.

He put his phone down, and was wondering whether or not to drive over there again when his front doorbell rang. Dee, he thought. Finally. But when he opened his front door, it wasn't Dee he saw.

'Nigel? What are you doing here?'

'Can I come in?' Nigel said. 'I'd really like to talk.'

Ed hesitated. He'd had time to get used to knowing what Nigel's mother had done, but he was still angry. At work, he'd started the painfully slow process to get the investigation into Mary's murder reopened. He'd handed Emma's diary, along with the letter from David Partridge, in as evidence. Plus, there was the not insignificant fact that Nigel had known the truth and chosen not to tell anyone.

'Please,' Nigel said. 'I owe you an explanation. And an apology.'

In the kitchen, Ed made coffee and gestured for Nigel to sit down.

'I was there,' Nigel said. 'The night your grandmother was killed. She came to our house. I heard them arguing. Emma and my mother. After that, everything gets confused. Over the years I've tried to remember it properly but it's one big blur in my mind. What I remember more than anything is being terrified. I was so young. Sorry. That sounds like self-pity, doesn't it? I didn't come here to get you to feel sorry for me.'

'Milk or sugar?' Ed asked, putting a mug of coffee on the table in front of Nigel.

'Black's fine,' Nigel said. 'Thanks.'

Ed pulled out a chair and sat down opposite Nigel, waiting for him to continue.

'She screamed,' he said. 'I don't think I'll ever forget the sound of it. This long, terrible scream. And then nothing. I was upstairs in bed, too scared to go down and see what had happened. I thought at first it was Mother, you see. I thought Emma had come to the house to kill her.

'I don't know how long I lay there. At some point, Father must have come home.' Nigel frowned. 'He'd been working late. Well, I assume that's where he was. He wasn't at home very often. It wasn't a happy marriage. How could it have been? She was a monster.'

He stopped speaking.

'Are you okay?' Ed asked.

'Not really.' Nigel sighed. 'But you need to know the truth. I didn't realise, until that night, that Father was every bit as bad as she was. Because when I eventually worked up the courage to go and see what had happened, he was there. Helping her.'

'Helping her do what?'

340

'They were dragging her out the front door.' Nigel's voice wobbled, but he managed to keep going. 'Father on one side of her body, Mother on the other.'

A tremor ran through Ed's body. He put his hand out, wanting Nigel to stop.

'Sorry,' Nigel said. 'I thought you'd want to know.'

Ed nodded. He'd wanted to know so badly. But now he knew, it didn't make things better the way he'd assumed it would. If anything, knowing what had been done to her made him feel worse.

'They must have driven her to Beachy Head,' Nigel said. 'Although I didn't work that out until much later. At the time, I didn't know what was happening. It was only later, after I read the diary, that I understood.'

'How did you get it?'

'Her handbag,' Nigel said. 'She must have dropped it when... you know. My parents would have been panicking. I think they simply missed it. After they left, I stayed where I was, standing at the top of the stairs, and I saw it. I still don't know why I went and got it, but that's what I did.

'I didn't look inside until weeks later. I was too scared. I kept it hidden in the back of my wardrobe, but eventually I couldn't bear knowing it was there. So one night, after I'd gone to bed, I took it out and looked through it. That's when I learned the truth.'

'And you never told a soul.'

Ed knew he should be angry. Yet, somehow, the rage that had driven him through the last week seemed to have disappeared. Now, all he felt was an unbearable sadness.

'I was scared,' Nigel said. 'I knew if the truth got out, my mother would be sent to prison. I couldn't bear the

341

thought of that happening. So I hid the diary in the attic of our house and did my best to forget all about it.'

'Emma's neighbour saw your mother at Emma's house that night,' Ed said. 'Do you know why she would have gone there?'

'I assume she wanted to find the letter,' Nigel said. 'She must have spent her entire life worrying about it, wondering where Emma had hidden it and when the truth might come out.'

'Good.'

'If it's any consolation,' Nigel said, 'the whole incident left me terribly messed up. I've done a good job, over the years, pretending I'm okay. If Lauren hadn't died, maybe I'd have been able to carry on pretending. But that's not an option any longer.

'I did my best with Lauren. My single objective as a parent was to try to be the opposite, in every way, to how my own parents had been with me. But in the end, I messed everything up with Lauren as well.'

'I'm sure that's not true,' Ed said. Pointlessly, because didn't every parent believe that after the death of a child? No matter what sort of parent you'd been, the guilt at letting your child die before you – even when it wasn't your fault – would be almost impossible to bear.

'When she first started to write about Mary's murder, I tried to discourage her, but she wouldn't listen.' He smiled. 'She could be very stubborn when she set her mind on something. But I wasn't too worried. By then, I'd done an excellent job of putting the diary to the very back of my mind. It never occurred to me Lauren's research would extend to going through Mother's belongings. The house had been locked up since her death at the end of last year. Clearing it out was one of the things I was going to do at some point, but hadn't yet got around to.

'Lauren only went there to see if she could find something that had belonged to Mary. She'd assumed – wrongly, of course – that Mother might have kept some keepsakes to remind her of her niece. Instead, she found proof that her grandmother was a psychopath.'

'I'm so sorry, Nigel.'

'You have nothing to be sorry about,' Nigel said. 'Your family suffered unnecessarily because of my mother, and I have to take the blame too. I should have agreed with Lauren we'd go to the police. But I'd spent so long trying to hide the truth, I wasn't able to do the right thing. I owe it to her to do that now.'

'Why did you wait until now to tell me this?'

'I was scared,' Nigel said. 'I didn't want anyone to find the letter. I thought it would be a distraction. I knew Lauren's death had nothing to do with the story she was writing. How could it? The only person who had anything to lose if the truth came out was me. I knew I hadn't killed her, which meant she'd been killed for some other reason. I had to make sure the police focused on that.'

'The police are going to reopen the investigation into Mary's murder,' Ed said.

'Good.' Nigel nodded. 'Lauren would have liked that.'

After Nigel left, Ed put on his coat and went out. He needed to walk while he processed everything Nigel had told him. More than anything, he needed to find Dee. Speaking to Nigel had made him realise the importance of telling the people closest to you how much they meant to you while you still had time. Over the last few weeks, he'd lost sight of what was important – focusing on the past instead of the present. Taking Dee for granted when he should have been spending every moment with her.

He'd told himself he wasn't going to call her again. That he'd wait until she was ready to speak to him. But anything could happen between now and then. If he wanted to fix things with Dee, he had to do it now. Before it was too late.

—

The tide was high, waves crashing in and out over the shingle shore. Loud, but not loud enough to block the thoughts raging through Dee's head. She walked fast, head pushed forward into the wind. By the time she reached Cooden Bay, she was out of breath and ready to stop. She went into the hotel, directly to the bar. Her spirits lifted when she saw the four people she'd come to meet, already seated at a table by the window.

'Dee! You're late. We'd started to think you weren't coming.'

Martin stood up, grabbing Dee and hugging her tight before letting her go, so she could turn her attention to Daisy and Ben.

'My turn,' Louise said, when Dee had finally finished greeting her niece and nephew.

The cousins embraced, holding each other longer than normal.

'Your face looks a little better,' Louise said, tentatively touching the fading bruises on Dee's cheek. 'Is it still hurting?'

'Not really,' Dee lied. She sat down and picked up a menu. 'I'm starving. Have you ordered yet?'

After lunch, Martin took the children out to play on the beach so Dee and Louise could catch up properly. It was their first time alone together since the night in Charlton Forest. Dee had woken up in the back of an ambulance. None of the paramedics treating her had been able to tell her anything about Louise. She didn't find out anything until later that night at the hospital. She would never forget those long hours not knowing if her cousin was alive or dead.

It was Martin, in the end, who'd saved them. He'd arrived just as Karen was about to hit Dee a second time. He'd managed to overpower Karen and keep her restrained until a team of police arrived from nearby Chichester station. Since then, he hadn't left Louise's side.

'You guys okay?' Dee asked, nodding at Martin and the kids on the beach outside.

'We've got a lot of work to do,' Louise said. 'But yeah, I think we'll be fine. We've been talking a lot. Proper talking, like we haven't done for years. It's helping. How about you? Have you spoken to Ed yet?'

Dee shook her head. She didn't want to think about Ed. He'd called – repeatedly – asking to see her. So far, she hadn't returned any of his calls.

'Why not?'

'It's complicated,' she said. 'There are so many things he hid from me. And that night, when I needed him most, he wasn't there for me. Turns out Ed's not the person I thought he was.'

'None of us are perfect,' Louise said. 'You do know that? You could waste the rest of your life waiting for a man who fits every single one of your ideas of what makes a perfect partner.'

'Or I could choose not to waste any more of my life hooking up with men who let me down.'

'They've found Derek,' Louise said, after a moment. 'Have you heard?'

'Yes. Rachel called earlier to let me know.'

Derek had been there when Martin and Dee arrived. As soon as they went into the woods, he'd got into Louise's car and driven away. Leaving his wife to take the blame for everything. It had taken a nationwide manhunt to track him down. He'd finally been arrested yesterday evening at a rural hotel in West Yorkshire, and charged this morning for his role in the killings of Joana Helinski and Lauren Shaw, and the abduction of Louise.

'According to Rachel,' Dee said. 'Derek's blaming Karen for all of it. Including those dodgy phone calls I was getting, and setting fire to my car. The only problem is, Karen's already given a statement saying it was all Derek's work, and she didn't know anything about it.'

'It was both of them,' Louise said. 'Unfortunately for them, Karen told me far more than she should have done.'

'And I'm pretty sure there were two people there the night my car was set on fire,' Dee said. 'And that's what I've told the police. But now they've been caught, Karen and Derek will do all they can to blame each other.'

'I still can't believe I let myself get involved with that man,' Louise said. 'I feel sick every time I think of him. You know, if Martin can forgive me for that, surely you can find a way to forgive Ed?'

'Can we talk about something else?' Dee said. 'Please, Lou?'

She couldn't explain how she felt, because she didn't understand it herself. She'd never expected Ed to be perfect, and she knew people made mistakes. But his lack of trust, his inability to talk to her, felt like a betrayal. After the break-up of her marriage, Dee had sworn to herself she would never let herself be betrayed by a man again.

'Tell me about Joana's family,' Louise said. 'When are they getting here?'

'Her mother and son are flying into Gatwick tomorrow.'

They both fell silent. Dee imagined that like her, Louise was picturing poor Joana's body lying at the bottom of the well. And thinking how close Louise had come to ending up with her.

'You were right all along,' Louise said. 'Lauren's murder had nothing to do with what happened to Mary Palmer.'

'Poor Kyle.' Louise shuddered. 'Imagine having parents like that.'

'How's he doing?' Dee asked. 'Do you know?'

'Not great,' Louise said. 'But he'll be okay. He's moved in with Nigel and Maxine for now. They'll take care of him until he works out what he wants to do with the rest of his life. In a way, Nigel must understand better than anyone what Kyle's going through at the moment.'

'Of course,' Dee said. 'His mother was a killer too. Just like Karen. All those deaths. It's so sad.'

Louise pointed out the window at Martin and the children.

'When I think how close I came to losing them... I'll never, ever be that stupid again.'

'We all mess up.' Dee reached across the table and squeezed Louise's hand.

Right then, her phone started to ring. When she took it out of her bag, she saw Ed's name on the screen. She was about to divert the call when Louise grabbed the phone.

'Speak to him.' She answered the call, handed the phone back to Dee and stood up. 'I'm going outside to Martin and the kids.'

Dee could hear Ed's voice on the phone, saying her name. Outside, she watched as Louise joined her family. Martin leaning down to kiss the top of her head; Ben and Daisy playing tag. A perfect picture of an imperfect family. Because Louise was right, no one was perfect.

'Dee? Are you there?'

She didn't want a perfect relationship. Just an honest one.

She ended the call and switched her phone off.

It was over.

Acknowledgements

Special thanks to my agent, Laura Longrigg; my fellow crime writers (especially Chris Curran and Lorraine Mace); and all my friends and family who have been so kind and supportive. I am so grateful for the generosity and support I've received from the lovely people at the *Eastbourne Herald* (especially Annemarie Field and Laura Sonier – two of the best women I know!). Thank you Miriam Anderson for lending your name to one of the characters through an auction for the Salvation Army – I hope you like what I've done! Thanks also to Henry Young, Rachel Sweeney and Tamsyn Sutton from East Sussex libraries who have been amazing! As always, thanks to the wonderful team at Canelo – Louise Cullen, Francesca Riccardi, Siân Heap and Sophie Eminson. A big thank you to the wonderful blogging community who support authors in so many ways. Finally, a very special shout out for Chris Simmons who runs Crimesquad.com – a lovely, funny man who has become a very special friend over the last few years.

⊙ CANELO CRIME

Lost Cause
Rachel Lynch

DI Kelly Porter has solved some of the Lake District's most gruesome murders but nothing has prepared her for the monster she's about to meet. The answers may lie with a local oddball – is he a victim, or a killer?

Lies to Tell
Marion Todd

Since she joined the St Andrews force, DI Clare Mackay has uncovered many secrets lurking in the picturesque Scottish town. When there is a critical security breach inside Police Scotland, she realises she may have put her faith in the wrong person – will it be a deadly mistake?

The Body Under the Bridge
Nick Louth

DCI Craig Gillard has spent his career hunting criminals. When a missing person case reveals itself to be far more than a routine disappearance, it isn't long before the perpetrator has another target: DCI Gillard himself. Suddenly the detective isn't just running the case – he's part of it.

A Front Page Affair
Radha Vastal

Capability 'Kitty' Weeks is determined to prove her worth as a journalist. Headlines about the Great War are splashed across the front pages, but Kitty is stuck writing about society gossip – until a man is murdered on her beat and she is plunged into a story that threatens the life she has always known.

When the Past Kills
M J Lee

The Beast of Manchester was the case that defined DI Thomas Ridpath's career, but the wrong person was convicted and only later was the true culprit put away. Now, those connected to the case are being targeted. Someone is desperate for revenge, and Ridpath risks losing more than he can stand.

Small Mercies
Alex Walters

DI Annie Delamere is off duty and enjoying a walk in the Peak District when she comes across a mutilated corpse. As the body count increases, Annie is under intense pressure to solve the case. But are the crimes the work of a deranged mind – or a cover for something even more chilling?

Home Fires Burn
Lisa Hartley

DS Catherine Bishop is dealing with the aftermath of the most brutal case of her career. Her small team is overwhelmed by an arsonist, and a new murder case provides far more questions than answers. The pieces finally fall into place, but have Catherine's demons already won?

When the Dead Speak
Sheila Bugler

Eastbourne journalist Dee Doran is investigating a woman's disappearance when the body of another is found. There are startling similarities between the dead woman and one who was killed sixty years previously. Dee is determined to uncover the connection, but sometimes the only thing more dangerous than secrets is the truth...

them in a shrine, and set them over the altar. That
was on Lucy's day [December 13] before Yule; and
then there had passed twenty years since the
slaying of Earl Magnus. The day of his death is
celebrated in spring, the sixteenth of the calends
of May [April 16]. Bishop William directed the
festival to be held on either of the two days over
all his bishopric; and he was afterwards in great
devotion towards the holy Earl Magnus. William
was the first bishop in Orkney, and ruled sixty-six
years.★

Then the lord Bishop enshrined the holy relics
of the blessed Earl Magnus with honour and
reverence and the hymns of all the people, and
there were healed all who were lacking health,
and in need of pity, who sought his sacred relics.

*Of the countless miracles performed through the merits
of the holy Magnus.*
From that time were spread abroad and celebrated
the miracles of the holy Earl Magnus over all the
western and northern parts of the world, and men
fared from neighbouring lands, burghs and towns,
castles and districts, with great hearts and offering

★ The narrative of the Greater Saga is resumed here.

hands, to seek his holy relics, and some sent
presents to his sacred shrine, to his honour but for
their own healing and salvation, both in this
world and in the next. Therefore shall here be told
some miracles, though but a few, from the countless number which God granted because of his
merits:

When Bergfinn, the franklin north in Shetland,
who was named before in this history, heard the
joyful tidings of the translation of the holy Earl
Magnus, he fared a second time south from Shetland with his leprous son, named Halfdan, to
Kirkwall; and watched, both father and son, at the
sacred relics of Earl Magnus. And the holy man
of God appeared to Halfdan and passed his hands
over his body and at once all his leprosy fell from
him and he rose up healed.

Earl Magnus also appeared to the franklin
Bergfinn in a dream and said to him: "Now you
shall receive clear sight, for you have come hither
with a true faith and did not distrust my sanctity,
and offered to me fair vows, both in prayers and
offerings."

Then he made the sign of the Cross over
Bergfinn's eyes; and he awoke seeing as well as

when he had been sharpest sighted. And father and son both went home healed, praising God and the holy Earl Magnus.

A man, named Thorkell, who dwelt in Orkney, fell off his barley-rick and was maimed all over one side when he landed on the ground. He was carried to the holy Earl Magnus and received there the speedy healing of his hurt, so that his broken bones grew together again and his body was made strong. He thanked God and the holy Earl Magnus for his healing gift.

A man named Sigurd Tandrisson dwelt in Shetland at the farm called Dale. He became mad, so that he was sewn up in hide. This man was carried to the holy Earl Magnus and got there his senses and complete health, and left there sound and whole, praising God and the holy Earl Magnus.

Another man, also called Sigurd, north in Shetland, had his hands so twisted that all the fingers lay in the palm. He sought the sacred relics of the holy Earl Magnus and received there healing, with straightness and suppleness of his fingers for all his needs. He thanked God for the mercy

which He had granted him for the merits of Earl
Magnus.

Thord, who was surnamed Dreka-Skolptr
(Dragon-Snout), was hireling to the aforenamed
franklin Bergfinn. He was threshing corn in the
barley barn on the day before the Mass-day of the
holy Earl Magnus. But about three o'clock in the
afternoon Bergfinn bade him leave off work.

"It is very seldom," said Thord, "that it seems
to you that too much has been done."

Bergfinn said: "The festival which falls tomorrow ought to be kept with all the honour we may
and can."

Bergfinn then went away, but Thord worked
on as before. When a little while was past, Bergfinn went out again and said to Thord in great
anger: "It is the greatest offence to me that you
work at holy times. Leave off at once."

The franklin went away very angry, but Thord
went on working as before. But when the men
had nearly done eating, in came Thord in his
working clothes and began at once to drink
greedily. When he had drunk one horn of ale, he
became mad, so that the men had to bind him at
once and that continued for six days. Then the
franklin Bergfinn promised for him to give half a

mark of silver at the shrine of the holy Earl
Magnus, and to let Thord watch there three nights
if he might be made whole. Thord was at once
healed the next night after the promise had been
made for him. And all praised the Highest King
of Heaven and his beloved friend the holy Earl
Magnus.

There was a woman called Sigrid; she was the
daughter of Sigurd of Sand north in Shetland. She
was blind from tender babyhood until she was
twenty. Her father took her south to Orkney and
let her watch at the shrine of Earl Magnus where
he made a great offering. Sigrid received then
clear sight in both eyes, and they departed, father
and daughter, rejoicing and praising God and the
holy Earl Magnus.

There was a woman named Ragnhild; she became a cripple when she was four winters old and
this lasted till she was twenty, then she watched
three nights at the holy relics of the Earl St
Magnus. On the third night there appeared to her
in her sleep a man bright and glorious, and
splendidly clad, who said to her: "Long and often
have you lain here, great is your need, rise up now

and be made whole and take this staff in your hand."

After that he vanished from her. But she woke up; she was holding on to the lock that was on the ambry on the other side of the Magnus choir. She then rose up at once completely healed, as if she had never been crippled, with sound bones and sinews, praising God and the holy Earl Magnus. She stayed with the bishop many winters.

It happened in Norway, in the days of Harold Gilli, that some rich and powerful men gave out that two brothers intended to seduce their kinswomen. But the accusation was not true. All the same, the two rich men attacked them and took them away captive into a wood, and slew the one whom they suspected more. Afterwards they tortured the other with much cruelty, breaking both his legs and arms. Then those cruel men put out both his eyes and cut out his tongue, and in this inhuman way they left him there half dead. As soon as they had departed, there leaped out from the woods a pack of wolves, riving and tearing the flesh from the bones of the dead man, then running back among the trees. But the wounded man, though he could no more pray aloud for pity, thought continually that Almighty God would grant him help. And his mind turned especially towards the holy Earl Magnus, for at that time much was going abroad of all his miracle-working. And when he had made a vow, he became aware that a man came to him and was stroking his broken arms and legs. The stranger took the short part of his tongue and replaced it; he then laid his hand on the sockets of his eyes. And with this handling came a wonderful change; the wounded man's eyes were restored with clear vision, the tongue immediately became ready for speech, the broken limbs were healed, and all his former health restored. He saw standing by him a man of fair countenance, with whom he spoke, saying: "What is your name, noble lord?"

The resplendent man answered: "Here is Earl Magnus, but take good heed to perform that which you have promised to the Lord."

At this he became joyful, and spoke to him again: "Since, exalted friend of God, you have granted to me a great gift of healing, I beseech also of your clemency to intercede with God for my brother's life."

After he had spoken, the holy Magnus vanished away from his sight without answering to his prayer. But he fell down and thanked God for the mercy vouchsafed to himself, intending to bide in that place two nights in steadfast prayer for the help of his brother. And as the time wore on he looked round, and saw a great pack of wolves run from the wood to where the corpse lay, and spew up there all they had eaten of his flesh and bones, and turn back again to the wood. And when a little time was passed, he saw St Magnus come, and bless with his right hand all the wolves' vomit and the bones; then after this the body became all sound.

St Magnus blessed again his lifeless body, wherefore he rose up whole and living and went to his brother. Then each of them greeted the other, giving thanks to God and the holy Magnus for so marvellous a mercy as had been granted them.

*How Earl Rognvald caused a cathedral to be built in honour of the saint; and of the curing of Eldjarn in the church.**

There was a trusty franklin in Westray, called Gunni. He dreamt that the holy Earl Magnus came to him and said: "This shall you say to

* This and the following chapters are from the Lesser Saga.

Bishop William, that I would fare out of Birsay east to Kirkwall, and I trust that God will there grant me of His mercy that those who seek me there with a true faith may be healed of their pains. You shall tell your dream boldly."

But when he awoke, he did not dare to tell the dream, because he feared the wrath of Earl Paul. The following night Earl Magnus appeared to him and bade him tell the dream for many to hear: "But if you do not do so, you shall suffer punishment in this world and more in the next."

And when he awoke he was filled with fear and journeyed to Hrossey to see the bishop, and told the dream at the bishop's Mass in a great crowd of men. Earl Paul was there, and all the people prayed the bishop to bear the sacred relics to Kirkwall as Earl Magnus had shown. But Earl Paul stood by silent, and turned blood red. After that Bishop William went east to Kirkwall with a noble retinue and bore there the sacred relics of Earl Magnus. The shrine was set over the altar in the Church which is there. Kirkwall was then but a trading village with few houses, but it has since greatly increased. Many men have since travelled thither and watched there in the Church at the

holy relics and have been healed if they vowed to
Earl Magnus with true faith.

When Earl Rognvald Kali, the son of Earl
Magnus' sister, had come to rule in Orkney, and
was quietly established, he caused the ground-
plan of the Magnus Church in Kirkwall to be
marked out, and obtained workmen for it, and
the work went on well and swiftly; and it is a
noble work and well finished. Afterwards the
sacred relics of Earl Magnus were removed there,
and many signs were wrought there at his holy
relics. There is now also a bishop's see which was
before at Christ's Kirk in Birsay.

A man, called Eldjarn, the son of Vardi, had a wife
and many children, and lived north in Kelduhverf.
But during a bad season he became poor and sick,
so that he could not help himself, and so little
strength had he that he was unable to walk and
was driven about among the homesteads. It happened one spring after Easter that he had been
driven about on Thursday, Friday, and Saturday,
and had had no food. He came at Nones on
Saturday to where the priest lived and stayed there
through the night. In the morning when men

went to Matins, he prayed that he might be taken to the Church; and it was done.

After the Matins men went indoors between the services. But he lay out of doors there where his bed was made; he was so weak that he thought he was about to die. It came into his mind how he had been before his poverty when he still had all his property intact, and his prayer which he prayed, touched him so much that he was greatly moved. Then he promised a six days' fast, if God would give him some relief: this fast he vowed both before St Olaf's and St Magnus' day.

When he had uttered his vow, men came to the service and the priest sang Mass. When the Epistle was read he fell asleep, but those who were beside him thought he was about to die. In his sleep a vision passed before him, in which he thought he saw a great light within the choir, and that it shone out to him. He saw with the light a beautiful man, who said to him: "Eldjarn! have you little strength now?"

He thought he answered: "So I think, though perhaps it may not be so. But who are you?"

He answered: "I am Earl Magnus Erlendsson. Would you be made whole?"

He answered: "I would."

He replied: "King St Olaf also has heard your prayer and the vow which you made to us two for your healing. But he sent me hither to give you healing: for a woman made a vow to him west in the Firths, and he has fared there to make her whole."

Then Earl Magnus began to pass his hands over him, but he woke up when the Gospel was begun. He asked the men who stood nearest him to lift him up. But they answered: "Why should we lift you up, when you have no strength?"

He replied: "I think I am now cured."

They took him and raised him to his feet, and he stood all through the Gospel and so on to the end of the Mass. After Mass he went in to the priest and told the miracle, how God had given him healing. And all praised God for the mercy which He had granted for the merit of Earl St Magnus. May he obtain for us mercy and pardon for our sins from our Lord Jesus Christ who, with the Father and the Holy Spirit, lives and reigns God for ever and ever. Amen.